This was it, she realized, the moment to prove to Travis that she was the woman for him. And when she succeeded, he'd pull her close and touch her with those magic hands that were capable of soothing the most skittish of horses, and make her his. Finally she'd belong.

"You know what I want, Travis. I was hoping you might give it to me." Despite her best effort at a sultry whisper, her voice shook. Rising on her tiptoes, she brought her mouth to his in a feather-light kiss. His lips were warm and she caught the tantalizing taste of the butterscotch Life Savers he always carried in his pocket. Opening her mouth, she let the tip of her tongue trace the curve of his lips. The rush of pleasure she felt at learning the contour of Travis's mouth made her dizzy. She pressed closer, seeking the hard, thrilling length of his body. And when Travis's hands locked about her upper arms, holding her, Margot's excitement was like a hot liquid melting her insides. *It was happening. Travis wanted her.* Her knees buckled and she moaned helplessly against his lips. But her moan became a gasp as she was abruptly pushed away.

Books published by The Random House Publishing Group
are available at quantity discounts on bulk purchases for
premium, educational, fund-raising, and special sales use. For
details, please call 1-800-733-3000.

Remember Me

Book One of The Rosewood Trilogy

LAURA MOORE

BALLANTINE BOOKS • NEW YORK

A Ballantine Books Mass Market Original

Published in the United States by Ballantine Books, an imprint of The Random House Publishing Group, a division of Random House, Inc., New York.

BALLANTINE and colophon are registered trademarks of Random House, Inc.

ISBN 978-0-345-48276-1

Cover art: Tom Hallman
Title lettering: Iskra Johnson

Printed in the United States of America

www.ballantinebooks.com

9 8 7 6 5 4 3 2 1

To Julia

Prologue ❧

EIGHTEEN and no cleavage to speak of: life was so grossly unfair.

Clad in matching panties and bra, Margot inspected her image in the cheval mirror. Her boobs did seem a bit bigger with the help of the push-up bra, didn't they? At least her legs were okay, and the high-heeled mules she had bought to go with her dress would make them look even longer. For reassurance, she stepped into the new shoes. Beneath the soft light of her bedroom chandelier, her tanned skin glowed. She'd made sure to slather moisturizer all over. She'd even remembered perfume, spritzing a cloud into the air before walking through it, a trick she'd read in a magazine. As nervous as she was, she needed all the help she could get.

Margot gave herself a last hard look and imagined Travis standing close enough to breathe in the sultry scent she'd chosen. She pictured desire flaring bright in his flint-gray eyes, felt the heat of his passion as his dark head lowered. His breath, warm and butterscotchy from his favorite flavor of Life Savers, would mingle with hers. Then the long-awaited touch of his lips, firm and commanding, as his strong, calloused hands reached for her. . . . A thrill coursed through her.

Yes, she thought, dizzy with excitement. Tonight, after so many nights lying in her bed and dreaming of Travis Maher, those dreams were going to become reality.

She spun around and scooped up the dress lying neatly on

her double bed. A vibrant peony-pink wraparound, it was deliciously simple, held together with a single large rabbit-eared bow. She tugged it on. Once she'd gotten the bow just so, Margot pivoted this way and that in front of the mirror, pleased with how the soft fabric hugged her body. If only she were curvier. Still, the dress was a far cry from her usual attire of breeches and polo shirts. He wouldn't be able to ignore the way she looked in it.

Grabbing a brush from the mahogany dresser, she gave her hair several vigorous strokes and debated whether to leave it down so that Travis might see how glossy and shiny it was. No, a loose knot was more sophisticated. Her hand trembled slightly as she applied mascara, and she grimaced when a black clump stuck to her lashes. Plucking it off, she abandoned the task. Her lashes were dark enough. After coating her lips with a raspberry-tinted gloss, she gave the mirror an inviting smile. Yes. This was definitely a new Margot Radcliffe. She looked worldly and mature. . . . She looked hot.

Surely Travis would think so.

Tonight she was going to make Travis forget she was the boss's daughter. When he looked at her, he wasn't going to be thinking of the skinny kid who for years now had been trailing after him from one horse barn to the next, peppering him with questions every step of the way, thrilled when he answered, because getting Travis to talk was like pulling teeth. And when he spoke to her this evening, he certainly wouldn't be calling her by that odious nickname he'd invented: Princess Margot. He'd have no reason to, because she wouldn't have to resort to ordering him about, demanding he fetch her hoof pick or her longe tape just so she could get his attention and have him acknowledge her existence. Tonight she'd be gracious and charming and witty, and he'd be dazzled. Everything would be different between them.

The Radcliffe Roast—as her family's annual party was known throughout the county—was the absolutely perfect setting to show off her new self to Travis. The roast was a shindig her family threw every summer without fail—except the year Mama died, Margot corrected quickly. Remembering her mother's drawn-out battle with cancer made her heart squeeze painfully. Then Dad had married Nicole and everything changed for the worse, including the Radcliffe Roast. Once an event to celebrate a successful foaling and breeding season with friends, neighbors, and Rosewood Farm's hands, now the party was as large and splashy an affair as Nicole could make it. At least Dad still insisted on inviting all of Rosewood's staff, otherwise Nicole would have figured out a way to bar Travis and everyone else who worked with Rosewood's horses. The corners of her mouth curved in a soft smile as she imagined walking up to Travis on the lawn. It would only take one glance. Finally he'd recognize that she was no longer a spoiled kid but a woman. A desirable woman.

The party was at six o'clock. Margot checked her bedside clock. Only a quarter to. Still loads of time, but that was okay. She wanted to talk to Jordan before heading downstairs.

Margot opened her bedroom door, slipped out, and hurried down the hall toward her older sister's room. As she rounded the corner, though, she heard her dad and Nicole talking and Jade's pip-squeak voice chiming in. Instinctively she did a one-eighty, intending to sprint back to the safety of her room rather than deal with her stepmother. But the soles of her new shoes offered no traction on the floral-patterned runner. She was caught with her arms pumping ineffectually, going nowhere fast.

"Margot, whatever are you doing?" The acoustics of the hall amplified Nicole's grating voice. "The guests will be arriving any second. You should be downstairs, not practicing cheerleading routines in the hallway, for God's sake." There was a moment's silence, then, "What in the world are you wearing?"

Trapped, Margot turned. Her father and Nicole stood arm in arm, Jade at her dad's side. She felt the familiar spurt of jealousy at the sight of them together, a portrait of a happy family. A family that, as Nicole devoted much energy to making Margot and Jordan understand perfectly, didn't include stepchildren. Nicole had been beyond ecstatic when Jordan had married Richard Stevens earlier in June. Not because Jordan had found a man to love and cherish her, but because Richard's job as a lobbyist meant that he and Jordan would be moving to Washington, D.C. One unwanted stepdaughter down and one to go was doubtless the way Nicole saw it. For Margot, though, her sister's imminent departure was too awful to contemplate.

Nicole's green eyes were narrowed on her. "Where did you get that dress?"

"Annabelle's." It was a new boutique in Warburg, positively daring in that it didn't sell only madras, taffeta, and cashmere sweater sets.

"Well, it's totally inappropriate and far too revealing. Do I have to remind you that Byrdie Shaw's been an utter angel and has contacted someone she knows who's top brass at Condé Nast? They're sending a photographer to take pictures of the party. Our roast has become *the* party in Warburg and you've decided to dress like a—" She paused.

Margot knew her stepmother was just dying to say "slut." But she couldn't; not unless she was willing to destroy her image as a genteel Southern belle in front of Dad.

Pivoting on her spiked heels, Nicole plucked at an invisible speck of lint on the lapel of his jacket. "RJ, honey, will you *please* inform that daughter of yours that her outfit is unacceptable? Whatever will our guests think?" Nicole's voice had gone all breathy and sugar-spun, as it did whenever she wanted something from him. It made Margot sick.

Her dad inspected her in silence. Tilting her chin, she met his gaze defiantly. It didn't matter that she was wearing heels, he always loomed larger than life. Dressed in his dark jacket and pristine white pants, he exuded the confidence that came with being Robert James Radcliffe V, the last male in the long, illustrious line of Virginia Radcliffes. Though her dad was fifty-six, his hair, the same shade of blond as hers, was only just beginning to gray at the temples. "Margot, you heard your mother." His tone was hard and brooked no dissent.

Her first instinct was to remind him that Nicole was *not* her mother, but she knew better. "Dad, the dress is fine—"

Nicole's trill of laughter cut her off. "Oh, please, I think I know a bit more about fashion than you."

Oh, sure, turquoise satin halter dresses were the definition of *chic*. With her boobs practically falling out of the plunging V-neck, it was Nicole who looked like a streetwalker, but, then again, when didn't she?

Margot opened her mouth to argue, but her father spoke. "Go change now, Margot. Do it, or don't come down to the party," he commanded, already moving past her.

"Now, there's a good idea," Nicole murmured with a triumphant smile as she passed. Then, more loudly, "Come along, Jade sweetie. I want the photographer to take a portrait of you and me together for Daddy." She tugged her daughter's hand.

Towed in her mother's wake, Jade trotted awkwardly, half-turned as she was to stare back at Margot with eyes as wide as two green saucers.

Swept by a wave of resentment, Margot curled her lip at the little brat, refusing to feel sorry when Jade's face crumpled with hurt.

Why did it always have to be like this, she wondered. Blinking back sudden tears, she rushed down the hall to Jordan's room and pushed open the door.

"Jor—" she began, only to gasp in surprise at finding Richard and Jordan locking lips. As they jumped apart, she exclaimed, "Oh! Sorry, guys. Didn't mean to interrupt." The apology felt as awkward as it sounded. It was hard to get used to the fact that this wasn't Jordan's room anymore; it was Jordan's *and* Richard's.

"That's all right, Margot, we should be heading downstairs anyway." Jordan's cheeks were bright pink with a becoming blush.

"Do we, babe?" Richard grinned. "Here I was hoping I'd convinced you there were infinitely more pleasurable ways to spend the evening."

Jordan's blush deepened. "You know I'd much rather explore some of the, uh—alternatives you suggested, but there are so many people coming who want to talk to you who didn't get a chance at the wedding. This is my last opportunity to show you off before we move. . . ."

"Okay, I get the picture. Well, at least I have the pleasure of escorting the two most beautiful girls in Loudon County downstairs to the storied Radcliffe Roast." He crooked his elbows wide.

"How gallant." Her sister's smile glowed with happiness and she made to link her arm through her husband's. But when Margot gave an infinitesimal shake of her head, she paused. "Um, I should check my makeup first and reapply my lipstick. It's probably completely worn off. Would you mind going on ahead, darling? Margot and I will be right down."

Richard's smile faltered. "As you wish." With a cool glance at Margot, he stepped forward and kissed Jordan lingeringly. "Come down soon, sweetheart. Five minutes is as long as I can stand being without you," he whispered.

Dreamy-eyed, Jordan watched him leave. She looked so happy, so very much in love. Margot was thrilled for her. Jordan was probably the sweetest and kindest person in the world and she was going to make Richard a wonderful wife. But a small selfish part of Margot wanted her sister back.

"Isn't he wonderful?" Jordan asked with a contented sigh.

"Yeah, and what I most like about Richard is that he's totally nuts about you. If I were you, I'd have taken him up on his suggestion and held a very private, intimate party up here. That would be loads more fun than grappling with the Viper, who's at her most poisonous tonight."

"Oh, no. What's Nicole done now?"

"She said my dress was inappropriate. It was on the tip of her forked tongue to add that I look like a whore." Pierced with sudden doubt, she asked, "Do I, Jordan?"

"Of course not," she replied stoutly. "That's ridiculous. You look gorgeous. Nicole's jealous at the thought of you stealing the limelight."

"She got Dad to order me to change my dress. He said if I don't, I can't go downstairs." The insult of being treated like a five-year-old still stung. "No way am I going to change. The dress is perfect and I don't care what Nicole says."

A worried look crossed her sister's face. "No, of course you don't, but Dad, well, that's a different matter. He's been awfully angry with you lately, hasn't he?" She chewed her lower lip. "You know, I may have something in my closet you might consider borrowing."

Margot shook her head. "No, thanks. I love this dress and I'm going to wear it. Oh, don't worry so, sis, it'll give you lines," she said, teasing her into a little smile. "You know Dad. He'll be so busy talking horses and passing around his cigars, he won't even see me." Especially as she intended to be out of sight of everyone—except for Travis. But she decided against sharing her plan. Jordan would only worry more. Realizing that Travis might already be out on the lawn with the rest of Rosewood's staff, cradling the first Rolling Rock of the evening in his tanned hand, a thrill of excitement shot through her. "Come on, sweetie, let's go be the belles of the ball."

Together they hurried down the wide circular staircase. When Margot was a kid, she used to terrify Ellie, the house-keeper, and send her running for Dad by swinging a leg over the polished banister and flying down its shiny length. That was long ago, though, back when Dad was so preoccupied with Mama's illness and consulting with every kind of specialist to try to save her that he never yelled or rebuked Margot. Sometimes he even timed her as she raced down the banister so he could tell Mama what a daredevil their younger daughter was.

At the bottom of the stairs, Jordan gave a small cry of pleasure. Richard was waiting for them in the center hall.

"I was just coming to fetch you. From the looks of it, all of Virginia's converged on Rosewood. No way am I braving this kind of crowd without you on my arm." The corner of his mouth lifted in a crooked grin.

"You know perfectly well you'll have everyone eating from the palm of your hand in three minutes flat," she said and laughed, kissing Richard on the cheek and entwining her arm through his.

They walked through the double parlor toward the French doors that opened onto the garden. Like the rest of the house, the double parlor was brightly lit and the silk-upholstered sofas and armchairs gleamed jewel-like. The sound of animated conversation grew louder as they approached the French doors. Over the noise, a sudden boom of laughter erupted, and Margot saw her father, his head thrown back, his broad shoulders shaking with mirth. Nicole, smiling adoringly, stood next to him.

"Margot?" Jordan asked, glancing over her shoulder when she hung back.

"You and Richard go on ahead. I'm not quite ready to go another round yet with Dad and Nicole," she confessed.

Her sister frowned. "But—"

"Don't worry about me. Go make all the women jealous with that handsome husband of yours. I'll be fine."

She watched them join Dad and Nicole, watched her father's face light up at the sight of his eldest daughter, and felt a piercing sadness when he enveloped Jordan in a hug. It wasn't that she was jealous. Her sister was like Mama—

sweet and thoughtful and kind to everyone. But why, Margot wondered, couldn't her father accept *her,* imperfect though she was?

"You by any chance debating whether this bash is worth your time? 'Cause if you feel like blowing this joint, I'm your man."

Margot whirled around and came face-to-face with a total stranger. She guessed him to be in his late twenties, with a deep golden tan and shaggy sun-streaked hair. Definitely not from around here, she decided. "Who are you?"

The guy grinned, the skin crinkling around his bright blue eyes. He looked like he smiled a lot. She immediately thought of Travis, who smiled so rarely that when he did her heart swelled to bursting with happiness.

"I'm the talent," he answered, buffing his nails against his button-down shirt.

She raised an eyebrow skeptically. "Really?"

"You betcha, beautiful." He raised his hands in front of his face. One he cupped in a wide C, while with the index finger of his right hand he pressed down, making a clicking noise as he did.

Nicole's photographer, Margot thought with disgust. "The party's out on the lawn, in case you hadn't noticed."

"Sure did. I've been dutifully snapping away. Quite a crowd out there. Had to take a leak, though, and then I got lost trying to find my way back. This pile certainly has a lot of rooms."

She shrugged, secretly shocked at hearing her home referred to as a "pile." She could have replied that Rosewood had been built and designed in 1840 by her ancestor Francis Radcliffe, and was one of the finest examples of Greek Revival architecture in the South, but she doubted he was remotely interested in a history lesson. With his shaggy hair and casual attitude, he seemed more likely to be interested in discussing great surfing locales.

"But you know, this place and you kind of go together," he said, surprising her.

"How so?"

"You've both got exceptionally fine lines. Elegant." He cocked his head, studying her. "Wow. You really do have a killer face." He brought his hands together to make a frame. "Mind smiling for me, gorgeous?"

She scowled. What a pathetic pickup line.

He laughed. "Even better. I love that 'go to hell' look. You ever thought of modeling?"

"You've got to be kidding me."

"Dead serious. Here," he said as he dug his wallet out of the back pocket of his khakis. Fishing a pen from the inside of his jacket, he pulled a business card out of the wallet and scribbled on its back before passing it to her. "You ever want to give modeling a shot, go and see Damien Barnes in New York. He's one of the few honest agents in the business. I put his address on there. Damien'll treat you right. And if you ever want a date, my number's on the front." He gave her a quick wink. "Gotta go earn my rent check. See you around, hot stuff."

Bemused, she looked at the card in her hand. "Charlie Ayer, Photographer," it read.

Me, a model? As if, she thought, carelessly tossing Charlie Ayer's business card onto the marble mantelpiece. It landed beside a blue Chinese vase filled with enormous purple hydrangeas. Still, it was nice to hear a photographer tell her that she had model looks. After her last run-in with Nicole, she needed an ego boost.

She glanced through the open door. Her dad and Nicole had moved off to mingle with the guests on the sweeping lawn that ran all the way to the front pastures. She straightened her shoulders and walked out into the summer evening, determined to find Travis Maher and convince him that she was the woman for him.

A short while later Margot wondered if her months of

dreaming of Travis making passionate love to her would remain just that. She'd searched among the guests clustered on the lawn without once spying him. He was so handsome and sexy, she sometimes felt she'd be able to single him out of a packed football stadium.

That the dress she'd bought looked good on her was confirmed by the men she passed. In the midst of raising their drinks to their lips, they would pause to gaze at her with approval, but she brushed past them and their hails of "Margot! You're looking great! Come and tell us what you've been up to!" with a polite wave and continued her hunt for the one and only man whose eyes she wanted to see light up.

Near the barbecue pit, where the aroma of succulent roasting pig was enough to make one's knees go weak, Margot saw Rosewood's stable hands standing in a loose circle, joking and taking long pulls of their beer. Disappointment flooded her when she realized Travis wasn't among them, but then her gaze landed on Ned Connelly, Rosewood's manager. Ned would know where Travis was.

Ned, who'd worked at Rosewood Farm forever, was all spiffed up in his pressed checked shirt and khakis and carefully combed silver hair. His neat appearance was unfortunately marred by the navy blue sling supporting a thick white plaster cast on his right arm. Last week, he'd taken a nasty spill off Stoneleigh, one of their Thoroughbred stallions. The break was bad enough that he would be out of commission for a couple of months, a crummy situation for Ned but a stroke of luck for Margot. While Ned was recuperating Dad would really need the extra help with the horses. There'd be no way he could shoot her down this time.

She approached the circle with a friendly smile. "Hey, Ned. Hi, guys."

"Hi there, Miss Margot. You're looking pretty as a picture," Ned said as the men standing beside him offered her greetings and shy smiles of their own.

Her cheeks warmed at the compliment. "How's the arm feeling?" she asked.

"The arm's okay, it's the cast that's driving me nuts. The dang thing itches like crazy. I don't know how I'll stand being stuck in it for another eight weeks."

"You know the willow tree in the west pasture? Its branches are just thin enough to slip inside a cast. That's what I used after I fell off Suzy Q and broke my wrist. I remember the itching got so bad, it felt like an army of ants was crawling around in there."

Ned chuckled. "At last someone who understands what I'm going through. Thanks for the tip, Miss Margot. I'll snap off a branch tomorrow and give myself some therapeutic relief. I'd clean forgotten about your break. You were just a tiny mite back then but braver than most grown men. You didn't shed a tear when you tumbled off old Suzy Q."

"Catapulted, Ned," she corrected wryly. It wasn't that she'd been particularly brave about getting hurt. It was that her tears had been reserved exclusively for Mama, who'd become so weak from the cancer invading her body that she couldn't leave her bed.

"Taking a spill now and again is an occupational hazard when you work with horses. But the way I figure it, the joy of riding is worth every aching bruise and broken bone. Ain't that right, Miss Margot?"

"Absolutely, Ned." She glanced around at the other men. They were all as neatly turned out as Ned. Why wasn't Travis with them? Where could he be? "Are you getting enough to eat and drink?"

"We're doing mighty fine," Ned replied for the group. "Your family sure knows how to throw a party. Seems like the Radcliffe Roast gets bigger every year."

"That it does. By the way, Ned, have you seen Travis? I, uh, have to tell him something."

If he was surprised by her need to talk to Travis when the lawn was crawling with Dad's and Nicole's guests, he didn't show it. "Travis? I think he's still down at the main barn. Told me he had some work to do. I'm sure he'll be coming along real soon, though. When I see him I'll make sure he knows you're looking for him."

"Thanks." Happiness bubbled inside her. He was in the barn. She should have guessed that's where Travis would be and that he'd be working as usual. But she needn't wait for him to finish whatever he was doing. She couldn't. She had to see him now. And really, when she thought about it, the barn was the perfect place. They'd be alone, far away from prying eyes.

"The pigs must be nearly ready," she said, gesturing toward the smoking pit. "Hope you brought your appetites, gentlemen."

"We sure did. Travis better show up soon or there won't be any left for him," Felix, one of the grooms, joked.

Margot smiled. She didn't think Travis would be too concerned about missing any roast pig. Not when he tasted what she was offering.

She found Travis in the tack room, in the midst of cleaning a bridle with a damp sponge and an amber cake of glycerin soap, worn to a sliver from use. The dusty old boom box sitting on the worktable was playing Springsteen's "Born to Run." Travis's booted foot tapped the cement floor in rhythm.

For a moment she hovered near the threshold looking at him. Just looking. His dark brown hair was in its customary stubby ponytail. Sometimes, when he was currying a horse, for instance, a thick lock would come loose of the rubber band and it would hang, an inky J against his cheek, until he tucked it absently behind his ear. Lord, he was so handsome. With his high, slanting cheekbones, deep-set gray eyes, and leanly muscled body, he was all thrilling, sexy, dangerous male. A real bad boy. Give him a Harley to straddle and he'd be Springsteen's song incarnate . . . except that, strangely enough, this bad boy had been born to ride horses. Stranger still and infinitely more frustrating, he seemed completely blind to the come-hither glances she'd recently been sending his way. But that was about to change.

She spoke, partly because she didn't want to be caught staring at him, but also because she wanted to gauge his reaction when he saw her. Had he ever seen her dressed like this?

"Hey, Travis." Margot was sure she detected a silver flash of surprise in his eyes. But any sense of triumph was fleeting. Travis looked away, fixing his attention on the throat latch he was cleaning. She told herself that he was just being his usual self, cool and distant, like Clint Eastwood in those old Westerns, and that he wasn't truly more interested in a dirty strip of leather than in her.

She mustered an air of nonchalance. "Everyone's up at the house drinking beer. The caterers are going to start serving dinner any minute. You haven't even changed yet." Privately she thought Travis in his dusty work boots, jeans, and faded Pearl Jam T-shirt was a million times better-looking than any other man. "So what are you still doing here in the barn?"

He paused in the middle of soaping the sponge. "Funny you should ask, Princess. Recognize this bridle?" His left brow rose, a dark mocking line that underscored his question. "It's Killarney's. The one you couldn't be bothered to clean. I already did your saddle."

Her gaze flew to the row of saddles on the wall. There on the rack with the small brass plate engraved with her initials was her saddle. Its leather gleamed softly. She flushed remembering how she hadn't even bothered to put away her tack after she'd cooled Killarney down, but merely propped the saddle and bridle outside the gelding's box stall. She'd been in a hurry, afraid she was going to miss her appointment at Serenity, the local beauty salon. She slipped her hands behind her back, hiding her brand-new manicure. "You didn't have to do that. I'd have cleaned them tomorrow."

"Sure, you would," he agreed in a tone so bland Margot knew he didn't believe her. Once more she wished she hadn't played the role of Miss Fancy-Pants-Princess-of-the-Barn quite so often, except that those were the only times when she had Travis's full attention. He was so good at ignoring her.

Right now was a perfect example. He'd already gone back to cleaning the bridle, as if he considered their conversation over. He was running the sponge over the braided reins, and she knew that when she rode Killarney tomorrow the leather would feel soft and supple between her fingers.

Seconds ticked as he continued to ignore her, Margot left to stand there, watching his long fingers deftly reattach the full cheek snaffle to the cheek straps and reins.

What was wrong with her? Here she was, dressed, primped, and perfumed, and still Travis acted as though she were invisible. Did he truly find her so unappealing that he couldn't be bothered to check out her legs or her breasts?

Perhaps she was standing too far away. Yes, that must be it, she decided. Travis was hardly about to sweep her into his arms if she were on the other side of the tack room.

At the click of her heels on the concrete floor, Travis went still, his hands curved around the metal mouth of the snaffle, his dark head lowered. She stared at his angled head in frustration. Why wouldn't he look up so he could see how her heart was pounding against the fabric of her dress? Why couldn't he see how much she cared?

"Travis?"

"Christ." The muttered curse sounded rough in the quiet of the tack room and she realized distantly that the CD must have ended. Travis rose from the wooden stool and grabbed the bridle. "Go back to the party, Margot. Go back to where you belong. I've got work to do," he said flatly before turning away.

She stared in dismay at his broad back. She simply couldn't let him brush her off as though she were an

annoying gnat. If she did, then she'd never have the courage
to show him how much she wanted him. And there'd be no
better opportunity than now, when they were alone and she
was looking her best.

Bolstered by the thought, she quickly crossed the tack
room to where he was hanging Killarney's bridle on its hook
alongside the other bridles, walking on the balls of her feet
so the sound of her heels hitting the floor wouldn't alert him.
When he turned around, he was so close she could see the
storm brewing in his gray eyes.

"Damn it, Margot." His lips were pressed in a grim line.
"What is it you want?"

Love. The word entered her head unbidden.

No, not love, she quickly amended. She couldn't, mustn't,
let the L-word slip past her lips. It'd be fatal. Guys hated too
much emotion, and Travis was a guy through and through.
She could never admit how much she longed to know she was
special in his eyes. At least not yet. For now, all she wanted
was to know that he desired her, that the storm in his eyes was
born from passion and desire rather than anger. She wanted
him to ache for her, as a man does for a woman he can't resist.
She'd wanted that for so long, she was going crazy with it. . . .

And this was it, the moment to prove to Travis just how
irresistible she was. Then he would pull her close, touching
her with those magic hands that were capable of soothing
the most skittish of horses, and make her his. Finally, she
wouldn't be so terribly alone.

She had the line from *Cosmo* memorized. The article
promised it was one that would drive a guy wild. She swallowed the nervous lump in her throat and remembered to
curve her lips in a smile.

"You know what I want, Travis. I was hoping you might
give it to me." Despite her best effort at a sultry whisper, her
voice shook. Not trusting it to fail her altogether and realizing that actions spoke louder and more convincingly than
any words, she rose on tiptoe and leaned in to him, brush-

ing his lips in a feather-light kiss. The hint of butterscotch on his breath triggered quivers of excitement inside her. She opened her mouth, letting her tongue trace the firm curve of his lips, and the rush of pleasure made her weak. Hadn't she known kissing him would be like this? So different from the wet, sloppy kisses the boys at school practiced.

She pressed closer, moving her arms up and entwining them about his neck. She was vaguely aware of Travis's still-ness, but even that, the hard strength of his body held in check, was unbearably thrilling. Any second now he'd begin kissing her back, she was sure of it.

She felt Travis's hands lock about her upper arms, hold-ing her. Excitement flooded her. It was happening. Travis did want her. Her knees buckled. She swayed against him with a soft moan, a moan that became a gasp as she was abruptly thrust away.

"What in hell kind of game are you playing at, Margot?"

For once she had no trouble reading him. The anger stamped on his features was forbidding. But she could also see the wild hammering of his pulse at the base of his throat. Its beat matched the pounding of her own heart.

Knowing that she affected him and reveling in her nascent power, she boldly met his gaze. "I'm not playing at any-thing." Travis was twenty-four years old. He wouldn't be satisfied with mere kisses. She had to prove that she was seri-ous about giving herself to him. "I want you—the way you want me, Travis."

She didn't let herself hesitate. Grabbing hold of the bow at the front of her dress, she gave a single tug and the dress fell open. A slow, sensual shimmy of her shoulders sent it sliding to the floor. She stood before the man she'd been dreaming of night and day for months wearing her lacy bra and panties, trying not to tremble from head to toe, and telling herself she was shaking from elation and not from fear. So what if she'd never done anything this outrageous in her life? It was worth it. Travis did look stunned, kind of like he'd been poleaxed.

Conquering her fear, she gave him a tremulous smile. "Show me what it's like to be a woman, Travis."

His head dropped as if in defeat. Her heart hammering against her breast, she took a step forward and made to take another. Travis's soft laughter stopped her in her tracks, the unexpected mirth like a slap in the face.

Shaking his dark head as if enjoying a good joke, he said, "Sorry, but no dice, Margot. Not that putting on a strip show in a tack room isn't a real attention grabber. But the truth is, screwing a spoiled princess just isn't my idea of a turn-on. You want to get down and dirty, go corner one of those pretty boys out there posing on your daddy's lawn. You see, I'm only interested in real women. I don't do pity—"

She didn't hear the rest. Didn't have to. With a broken sob, she grabbed the dress and, clutching it, ran outside. His voice called after her, but that only made her run faster.

She fled into the night, not stopping until she reached the far side of the carriage barn, now used to store the tractors. Leaning against the clapboard for support, she pulled on the dress and retied it with trembling hands.

Oh, God, she had to get back to the party. She would die of embarrassment if she accidentally ran into Travis alone out here—not that he really would come looking for her. She knew better now. Travis didn't care about her.

She'd been such a fool. How could she ever look him in the eye after what she'd done? She'd offered herself to him and he'd laughed. But, then, why shouldn't he? She was nothing but a spoiled princess. And he was interested only in *real* women.

His words cut like a whip, flaying her heart and her pride. She'd never imagined that he thought so very little of her, that he truly disliked her. Was she really that awful? She wished she could go find a place to hide and bawl her heart out until it was emptied of Travis Maher.

But that wasn't the Radcliffe way. Besides, if she crept off to her room and Travis showed up at the party, he'd assume he was the reason for her absence; she refused to give him the satisfaction of knowing how much he'd hurt her.

As she neared the flickering lights of the party, the sounds of boisterous laughter and the clinking of glass grew, making her feel more alone and unwanted than ever. Spotting her father standing beneath one of the hanging paper lanterns, she was seized by an urgent need for reassurance.

She smoothed her dress and plastered a confident smile on her lips before walking up to him.

"Hi, Dad. Hello, Mr. Harvey, Mr. Williamson, Mr. Swift," she said to the cluster of men.

"Oh, Margot, there you are. Eleanor and George McCallister were just asking for you. They brought Topher with them." Her father's easy tone indicated that he'd forgotten his earlier irritation with her.

"Topher's had a great year riding for Farleigh University. High Point champion," John Harvey chimed in. A friend of her father's from the Warburg Hunt Club, John paid attention to collegiate riders the way other men followed college football.

"How nice." She remembered Topher McCallister. Handsome, arrogant, and totally conceited, he was convinced he was God's gift to women. Once again Travis's voice mocked her: "*You want to get down and dirty, go corner one of those pretty boys out there posing on your daddy's lawn. . . .*"

Impulsively she plucked the sleeve of her father's jacket. "Dad, could I speak to you in private?"

He gave her an astonished look. "Now?"

"Please, Dad. It's important."

"All right. Come with me to my study. I was going inside anyway to get my box of Montecristos."

"Three cheers for Margot," Roger Swift said with a grin as he raised his glass, toasting her. "Honey, your dad's been bragging about this new shipment of cigars for the past half hour but so far he has yet to deliver the promised goods. Now, is that any way to treat his old friends?"

"Roger, you greedy bastard, didn't your mama teach you, all good things come to those who wait?"

"That's rich, coming from you of all people, RJ!" Craig Williamson said, laughing.

"Yeah, maybe," he conceded with a wide smile. "Well, the wait is over. You all are in for a rare treat. Back in a few, gentlemen."

Her father's study was a male sanctum, its walls made of dark oak paneling and covered with framed prints of hunters galloping over fields and soaring over fences. His desk was massive, as was the overstuffed Moroccan leather sofa with matching chairs at either end. The room smelled of furniture polish and her father's favorite cigars. Even the thick Persian rug beneath her feet was masculine, with its deep blues and maroons.

He closed the door with a click and turned around. "All right, Margot, what is it? What do you have to discuss that's so important it can't wait until tomorrow, when we don't have a house full of guests to entertain?" Now that they were alone, his voice was tinged with impatience.

"It's—it's about Ned."

"Ned Connelly?" His eyebrows came together in a severe line. "You dragged me away from our party to talk about Ned?"

"No, yes—not exactly," she stammered. "It's just that now you're really going to need the extra help while he's laid up with his broken arm. I'd like to take over his responsibilities while he recovers."

"Ned is my manager," he said, as if she hadn't been living at Rosewood for the past eighteen years. "You're saying you want to take on the job of Rosewood Farm's manager?"

She nodded. "Yes, though I'd be more like a substitute manager until Ned's fully healed. Then afterward I could be his assistant." She didn't let herself consider what it would be like working with Travis. She'd deal with that later. The only thing that mattered was to hear Dad say yes and have him give her the job. She could do the work, she was sure of it. She just needed to be given a chance. Nevertheless she felt compelled to add, "Of course Ned will be around to make sure I don't screw up or anything. It'll be great, Dad. Hands-on training, the best way to learn all—"

"Aren't you forgetting a minor detail? You're starting college in a few weeks."

Oh, Lord, not the "You must go to college talk" again. They'd been having it for months. Why couldn't he understand that college was unnecessary when all she wanted was to work at Rosewood, raising and training their horses? It was all she would ever want. She drew a deep breath and tried again. "Come on, Dad, what could I learn sitting in a stuffy lecture hall that could equal actually working with our broodmares and stallions or listening to you and Ned analyze a yearling's potential? Don't you want me to have the best training to help you run Rosewood? My taking over for Ned would be a perfect opport—"

Her father cut her off with an emphatic shake of his head. "No. I've already picked Travis for the job. Spoke to him about it yesterday. He's the man—"

"But—"

"Don't interrupt, Margot," her father said automatically. "I admit Travis is a little rough around the edges, but when it comes to horses—"

Her father's voice receded. *He was giving Travis the job, without even considering her as a possibility.* In all these weeks, nothing she'd said had made an impression. The news that he'd chosen Travis over his own child was yet another lash to her heart. Not only had Travis rejected and humiliated her, her dad was giving him what Margot considered her birthright—the opportunity to help run Rosewood Farm, to learn all the facets of their business, and above all to know her father trusted and relied on her. Travis wasn't the only one who was good with horses. She could handle the job of manager—if only her father would give her the chance. "Please, Dad. Just let me try—"

"You'll go to Farleigh as planned. Topher McCallister is enrolled there. He's entering his junior year. The boy comes from good stock. He'd be a fine catch for you, Margot." His blue eyes skimmed over her. "You're pretty enough."

And what did that have to do with anything? She nearly laughed, but then she looked at his expression. He was serious. *Oh, my God.* It had taken the words *good stock* and *pretty enough* for understanding to finally dawn. Dad didn't want her to work beside him at Rosewood Farm . . . not now, not ever. His goal was for her to snare some man, become his wife, and bear his children.

And she'd bet he'd be praying for male grandkids. His insisting on her enrolling in college wasn't because he cared about her education but because at Farleigh there'd be a nice pool of eligible young men for her to attract. Like Topher McCallister, who just so happened to know the difference between a horse's fetlock and forelock. He'd be just the candidate Dad would pick to take the reins at Rosewood Farm.

Wasn't it ironic that Topher also happened to be the exact sort of "pretty boy" Travis had mockingly suggested she try her luck with? Until tonight, she'd never realized how similar her father and Travis were—both considered her good enough only for the likes of Topher.

So where did that leave her? She could be a dutiful daughter, go off to Farleigh, and marry some conceited drip . . . and maybe, just maybe, she'd finally please her father. If she chose that path her future would be predictable: she'd spend her days doing lunch with other wives and volunteering for the Warburg Hunt Club's social committee, and producing babies every two years. There was nothing wrong with that life, except that she had always assumed she'd get to be a part of Rosewood Farm and help breed and train their horses. But clearly her father had no intention of having her work alongside him, and all those excuses that she was too young or inexperienced were just a load of bull. It was a question of chromosomes.

Wasn't life just too funny? Travis didn't want her, either, because he didn't believe she was *enough* of a woman. She'd offered herself to him and he'd laughed. He was probably still laughing.

The pain of the dual rejection was unbearable. How could she stay at Rosewood knowing that the two most important men in her life cared so little? She couldn't. She would have to leave. There was no other choice.

Her father had gone over to the side table to retrieve his precious cigars from the humidor. Closing its lid he turned back to her. "Come, Margot. Let's go back to the party. You can find Topher and talk to him about college and the riding team. I bet the two of you get along like a house on fire," he said, an indulgent smile on his face.

She shook off the hand he'd placed under her elbow. "No."

"No, what? This is really too much. What's the problem now?"

"I am not going to college this fall," she said. "If you don't want me to work with you, I'll leave home and—" The rest was cut short as the study door opened.

Nicole's head appeared around the edge of the door. "RJ? What are you doing in here?"

Margot's stomach clenched as her stepmother's gaze landed on her.

"What's going on? What's she done now?" Nicole demanded, stepping into the room.

"Margot's just announced that she's not going to college."

Nicole rolled her eyes. "Oh, Lord, again? Honestly, RJ, why do you put up with this nonsense?"

"Damned if I know." Any warmth or patience toward her had vanished the second Nicole appeared. "Margot was about to tell me what she plans to do instead."

"This should be good. Do tell, Margot. What do you think you're actually qualified to do?" Nicole's smile was openly mocking, perfected by constant practice.

The sight of it made Margot remember the guy she'd met earlier, the photographer. He'd said she had the looks to be a model. He'd gone to the trouble of giving her the name of some agent, so he must have been serious. Modeling. Why not? If she was going to sell herself, at least she'd be doing it on her own terms rather than as a two-legged broodmare for her father.

"I'll go to New York," she said to him, studiously ignoring Nicole.

"New York? New York?" he repeated incredulously. "What in the world would you do in New York?"

"I'll get a job as a model." The party was going strong. Maybe that guy, Charlie something, was still around. She could find him, ask him if he'd been straight with her about her chances.

"Are you joking?"

She lifted her chin. "No. If I can't work at Rosewood, why shouldn't I take a shot at modeling? After all, as you yourself said, Dad, I'm pretty enough."

Having his words thrown back at him pushed her father over the edge. A deep red flush flooded his face. "Damn it, Margot! You are beyond belief. What is wrong with you?"

Maybe I just need to know that you love me. But her answer went unvoiced. Nicole was pointing an accusing finger at her. "RJ, do you realize she still has that dress on, the one you explicitly told her to change out of? My God, I simply cannot believe how selfish she is. Prattling on about being a model when there's a party going on and I've worked so hard to make everything perfect. But why should I be surprised when at every turn, your daughter deliberately tries to spoil what I do."

"I do not!"

"Enough!" her father bellowed. "Nicole's right. She's

worked incredibly hard to make the Radcliffe Roast a success and here you are doing your level best to ruin the
evening!"

Margot stared, stricken that he would side with Nicole on
this issue, too. Nicole hadn't done a thing to organize the
party. For the past five years she'd hired a party planner who
was in charge of everything, from writing out the invitations
to overseeing the caterer and choosing the table decorations.
Nicole had spent most of today at a spa with one of her
friends.

"Even if what you just said were true, Dad, aren't I as
important to you as a party?" she implored, her voice thick
with tears. "Aren't I as important as Nicole? Don't I matter
to you at all?"

"Christ Almighty!" He made a chopping motion with his
hand. "That's it. Enough. I've had it with your theatrics.
This discussion is over. I've made my decision. Travis will
take over as Rosewood's manager. It's too damned big a job
for a woman to handle. And you," he roared, his blue eyes
ablaze with anger, "will enroll in college as planned. And let
me tell you another thing. If you choose to defy me and
carry out this harebrained modeling scheme, I promise you,
Margot, the only way you'll ever come back to Rosewood
is over my dead body. Now, get out of here and don't let me
see you again tonight or you won't like the consequences."

She looked at her father, so angry and unyielding, then at
Nicole standing by his side, reveling in her stepdaughter's
defeat, and she knew that nothing would ever change
between them.

"Good-bye, Daddy."

Chapter ONE

Eight Years Later . . .

SOUNDS REVERBERATED all around. Horses whickered and kicked out at their wooden stalls, impatient for their morning flakes of hay and rations of grain. Wheelbarrows landed with a heavy thud as they were set down upon the concrete flooring. The voices of the grooms talking while they worked their way down the rows of spacious box stalls accompanied the rhythmical scrape and clatter of grain being scooped out of the barrows and poured into rubber feed buckets. The noises of the barn at this hour—or at any time—were as familiar to Travis as the sound of his own breathing. This morning, however, they might as well have been miles away, for inside the barn's office a tense silence reigned.

Travis stared in disbelief at the man sitting behind the scarred oak desk. For the past fourteen years, RJ Radcliffe had been mentor, friend, and father figure all rolled into one. Also his boss . . . only now his *ex*-boss if he'd heard correctly.

"What the hell are you saying, RJ? Have you lost your friggin' mind?"

RJ's tanned face grew mottled. "I think I made myself damned clear. And no, I haven't lost my mind—I've only been a damned fool. But no longer. I've wised up. Here." With short, angry tugs he ripped a check from the checkbook reserved for Rosewood Farm's payroll and thrust it at Travis with a shaking hand. "Here's this month's salary, plus two weeks' severance. I want you gone from Rosewood by five o'clock today."

Travis made no move to take the money. Instead he looked at RJ's hand gripping the check and thought of how much this man had given him. Knowledge. The kind of knowledge a teenage punk growing up on the wrong side of town could never have gained on his own. A sense of belonging. Rosewood Farm meant more to Travis than any other place on earth. Hope. Learning to ride and train Rosewood's horses, some of the finest in Virginia, had allowed him to escape his sordid, sorry origins. RJ had offered him the chance to be known as something other than the good-for-nothing son of the town drunk.

In exchange, Travis had given RJ his unswerving loyalty and gratitude. Even when he'd hungered for the forbidden, he had forced himself to remember how much he owed RJ.

"Go on, take it." The rough command broke into his thoughts. "Take this and get the hell out of here." RJ was shaking with anger, and the paper check rattled in his grip.

Travis's jaw clamped tightly in frustration. "I don't want your damned money," he ground out. "What I want is to know why you're firing me."

"'Cause I know everything, you son of a bitch. You're lucky I haven't come after you with a shotgun."

For an awful second Travis wondered if RJ had somehow learned about that long ago night. But no, that was impossible. He'd never breathed a word of it to anyone, and she—hell, she was gone, caught up in her glitzy world of parties and millionaire playboys. He'd seen the glossy magazine photos of her with a different guy in every shot. She looked as maddeningly beautiful as ever. Beautiful and distant.

Ruthlessly pushing aside thoughts of her, he laid his palms flat on the desk. "What are you talking about, RJ?" he growled. "You could be speaking Chinese and making more sense."

"I'm talking about my *wife*, you shifty whoreson. I've had

my suspicions for months. But I kept telling myself that I could trust you. That you wouldn't stoop so low. Instead you played me for a fool." He tossed the check so it landed by Travis's hand and then grabbed a bright pink leather journal and shook it accusingly. "See this? It's Nicole's diary. I found it last night. It's all here, all her secret meetings with TM. TM," he spat, "as in Travis Maher—took me three seconds to figure who the son of a bitch was who was cuckolding me."

Travis felt like he'd been sucker-punched. Outraged, he exploded, "Jesus, RJ, you don't really believe I'd—"

"Go on, deny it, damn you! Look me in the face and deny that you've been sleeping with her! Go on! It'll give me an excuse to tear you apart limb from limb." Surging to his feet, he stood, chest heaving, his blue eyes lit with fury and pain.

Damn Nicole. It didn't matter that there were probably a couple of dozen men in Loudon County besides him who had the initials TM, more than half of them happy to take whatever she offered. It didn't matter that the idea of making love to Nicole Radcliffe was about as appealing as making love to a snake—and probably comparable. The damage was done. RJ ruled Rosewood like a feudal lord, meting out justice as he saw fit and brooking no opposition.

Travis straightened to his full height. His voice was flat and hard when he spoke. "You're wrong, RJ. Maybe someday you'll find out just how wrong." Without another word he turned, strode to the door, and yanked it open.

The slamming of the door startled the hands that were mucking out the stalls. Felix, who was nearest to him, hurriedly set his pitchfork against the stall door. "Everything okay with you and the boss?"

Travis's gaze swept up the row of stalls, where the horses he trained were munching their hay contentedly. He looked at the faces of the men who'd stopped their morning's work out of concern for him. Damn it, these were his friends. This was his life. . . .

"No kidding, man, what went down with RJ?" Tito asked.

Too choked with emotion to answer, Travis gave a quick shake of his head and made for the tack room. Bypassing the bridles and leather girths hanging neatly from their hooks, he grabbed his suede chaps off the wooden peg and slung them over his shoulder. Then he crossed the room that carried the unique scent of leather and saddle soap and the undimmed memory of a beautiful, reckless young girl standing nearly naked before him and grabbed his saddle off the rack with a vicious curse. From behind came the scratchy sound of footsteps. He glanced over his shoulder and shame churned in his gut. Would Ned believe RJ's accusation?

"Hey, Travis," he said by way of greeting. Pushing the brim of his battered straw fedora up his forehead, he fixed Travis with his canny eyes. Ned had practically grown up on Rosewood Farm. A horseman of the old school, he possessed the kind of deep knowledge that comes from a lifetime of looking at and listening to horses. He knew a thing or two about the man they both worked for, too. "So what was all that hollerin' about?" he asked. "I could hear RJ practically all the way from the south pasture."

"He found Nicole's diary," Travis answered. "Read it, too. According to him, I'm her lover."

Ned let loose a string of curses before lifting the paper cup in his hand and spitting a brown jet of tobacco juice into it. "That woman is pure, one-hundred-proof trouble. And RJ's a dang idiot where she's concerned. Did you set him straight?"

"No point." Travis flipped open the lid of his tack box and grabbed his saddlebag. With the saddle propped against his hip, he slipped the cover over the well-oiled leather and zipped it shut. Setting the saddle down beside the tack box, he straightened. "RJ's fired me. Looks like you got your old job back."

Ned's weathered face went slack with shock. For a second

Travis thought the wad of chaw wedged against his lower lip might splat on the floor, but then his friend's mouth began working—double time.

"What the hell! I don't *want* my old job back! I'm so damned long in the tooth, I should be put out to pasture. Problem is, I ain't got no use for TV and I can't abide bingo. What in blue blazes is he thinking? Has he forgotten we're showing at Culpeper—tell me who's going to ride Harvest Moon if you're not around?"

"Afraid that's not my problem, Ned. I've got a few of my own—like finding a new job."

"Now, wait just a minute, son. I'm going to go in there and give RJ a piece of my mind—"

"Don't bother. You know RJ. No point in us both getting sacked." Dropping his folded chaps into the tack box, Travis shut the lid and glanced around the tack room. The ache in his gut intensified. Beside him Ned was shaking his head in disgust and muttering into his cup of tobacco spit about blind fools. Abruptly he raised his head. "You should call Hugh Hartmann."

"Hugh Hartmann? Down in Richmond?"

"Yeah. He's got a nice place with at least thirty boarders. A lot of money walks into his barn looking to buy hunter or jumper prospects."

Travis considered for a moment. Richmond. That was far enough away for him to forget the name Radcliffe. Perhaps even far enough away to stop thinking of her. Maybe.

He gave a short nod. "Thanks, Ned."

A half hour later, the back of Travis's SUV was loaded with all his worldly possessions: his tack box, saddle, two duffel bags of clothes, and a toaster oven. He slid behind the steering wheel and turned the key in the ignition. The SUV's engine roared to life. But his foot remained heavy on the brake while his gaze swept over the barns and the seemingly endless line of fenced pastures.

Rosewood's broodmares were already out and grazing

in the late-summer sun. In an adjacent pasture, yearlings cavorted, racing one another, bucking, nipping, and squealing their high spirits. God, they were beautiful. He had helped foal a number of them, had worked with all of them.

Bitter regret added to the ache inside him.

Damn it all, just a few months back he and RJ had been talking about buying a new stud for Rosewood. There'd been so many things he'd wanted to do, so many plans for improving the stock, and now it was over. He slammed the heel of his hand against the steering wheel. Christ, hadn't he always known deep down that he would lose his job at Rosewood, that he would lose everything he'd worked for, because of a Radcliffe woman?

Only trouble was, RJ had guessed wrong.

The corner of Travis's mouth lifted as he imagined what RJ would have done if he'd leaned over the desk and told him just how far off the mark he was. It had never been RJ's wife that Travis lusted after, but his daughter.

MARGOT'S HEART POUNDED in sync to the driving beat of techno music as she led the parade of models down the runway. Her skin, spray-painted a shimmery bronze, prickled beneath the hot glare of the lights and the weight of hundreds of eyes tracking her every step. She hid her discomfort and fatigue behind a haughty mask—her expression, the angle of her head, as remote as a goddess's.

It was the show's finale, and though the platform felt like a never-ending highway and her feet ached inside her stiletto heels, Margot's steps remained light and confident, her hips maintaining their I'm-too-sexy-for-you swing. As she neared the end of the catwalk, she lowered the feather-fringed silk wrap from her shoulders and revealed the dark gold appliqué of her vibrant pink evening gown. She paused, sent her smile into the dark sea of shadowed faces illuminated by brief flashes of camera strobes, and then twirled. The gauzy layers of the dress and wrap swirled about her in a cloud of color.

Over the music she heard the bursts of applause and her smile widened; the grueling past hour of frantic wardrobe changes and makeup adjustments, the near-manic frenzy of the assistants, forgotten. The knowledge that she'd helped win the critics over chased away her fatigue. The applause continued. Buoyed by the audience's enthusiasm, she headed back up the runway toward the silver-threaded curtain that hid the barely controlled chaos reigning backstage.

Slipping behind the curtain she was swept into the ecstatic embrace of Carlo de Calvi, whose genius had inspired the collection. In the Italian designer's excitement, English abandoned him completely, and though Margot had been flying the golden triangle of the fashion world between New York, Milan, and Paris for seven years and had learned enough of both languages to order a café au lait on the Boulevard Saint-Germain or an espresso on the Via Montenapoleone like a pro, she caught only about one-tenth of Carlo's full throttle speech.

But she'd been on the runway; his words needed no translation. From the buzz in the air, it was obvious the critics loved the show, and the retailers were hungry to place their orders. In the past two weeks, the period during which Milan held its ready-to-wear fashion shows, Margot had modeled nearly twenty-five different collections. Of all of them, Carlo de Calvi's cunning use of fabrics and colors, the drama of his ensembles, combined with his fine, craftsman-like attention to details, had generated the most red-hot response. The spring collection was a hit and Carlo's designs would be the must-haves for next season.

Carlo was still gushing and Margot still nodding and interjecting a laughing "*Sì, sì,*" when the other models, having finished their trip down the runway, joined them. Each arrival upped the level of bubbly euphoria. Everyone was kissing and laughing, the whole motley crew that comprised the backstage world—models, makeup artists, hairstylists, assistants, VIPs, even security guards. Pumped on the adrenaline of the past madhouse hour, they shared the fleeting moment of sweet success.

Then Carlo clapped his hands. "Come, girls, we show them how beautiful I make women one more time," he said in heavily accented English.

His remark elicited groans of "Oh, God, Carlo!" and "Someone please explain why we're always surrounded by men only a mother could love?" "Or another guy," someone else chimed in.

"We mustn't mind Carlo," Margot said. "He hasn't finished all his Berlitz tapes yet." She gave his chin a playful chuck. "Carlo, sweetie, the thing to do is to *thank* us all for making your clothes look so darned good."

"Ahh, yes! *Mille grazie, belle,*" he said, and his goateed face split into a wide boyish grin of apology. "You all were *perfette.*" He brought his fingers to his mouth and kissed them.

The girls laughed, their good humor restored. With a flourish, Carlo held out his arm to Margot. As the show's featured model she had the privilege of walking down the runway beside him as he took his bows. Margot slipped her arm through his and as one they turned toward the curtain, only to come up short as Carlo's assistant, Paolo, called out, *"Scusi, Carlo. C'è per Margot—è urgente!"* He broke through the throng, waving a cell phone.

Urgent. The word sent a chill through her. Not once in her eight years of modeling had she ever been interrupted by a phone call. She stared at Paolo's leopard-print cell with an impending sense of dread. Reluctantly she took it, with Carlo and the other models looking on with rapt fascination. But then Anika, her apartment-mate and closest friend, stepped forward.

"We'll give you some privacy, Margot," she said, her kohl-lined eyes filled with concern. "Come on, Carlo. Come on, girls."

Carlo nodded vigorously. "*Sì,* we go. Come, my beautiful girls, we go out and take our bows together, like one big *famiglia.*"

The other girls trailed after Anika and Carlo, casting curious glances Margot's way. She barely noticed. Lifting the cell, she pressed it to her ear.

"Hello?"

"Margot? Oh, thank God! I called your agent in New York. He gave me this number. I was so worried I wouldn't—"

"Jordan?" The spurt of happiness she felt at hearing her

sister's voice—proof that she was okay—was short-lived. Even with the lousy connection she could hear the strain in it. Her mind raced as she tried to calculate the hour in D.C. It must be the middle of the night. "What's the matter? What's happened? Are you all right? Is it the baby?"

"No, no, I'm fine, *we're* fine," Jordan quickly reassured her. "Listen, Margot, it's Dad and Nicole. There's been an accident—"

"Oh, God! No!" she whispered. "What happened? Are they all right?"

"The Piper went down in the Chesapeake. Something must have gone wrong. Dad gave a Mayday signal just before it crashed." There was a pause, then, "Margot, Nicole didn't survive. She's—she's dead."

Her stepmother dead. It couldn't be. Dazed, Margot wondered if perhaps she wasn't caught in the middle of some horrific nightmare. But the plastic contour of the phone biting into her hand and the sudden, salty sting of tears in her eyes were all too real.

"Margot? Are you there?" came her sister's crackly voice.

She jerked her head and then remembered to speak. "Yes. It's just—so terrible." How appallingly inadequate the word sounded.

"I know."

"And Dad?" The question was met with silence. She clutched the phone even more tightly. "Jordan, tell me. Is he—" She swallowed. "Is it bad?"

"Yes, but we don't know how bad. A navy boat was in the area. They were able to reach Dad and airlift him to the hospital. The nurse I spoke with couldn't tell me much, except that they'd rushed him from the ER into the operating room."

Oh, Daddy! The mute cry tore through her, sending her reeling back in time. She was once again a helpless girl, grasping for the first time that her beautiful mother was never going to get better, that she might die. An uncontrollable trembling seized her. "I'll be on the first flight to D.C.—"

"No, Margot, wait. There's Jade."

Jade. How could she have forgotten her half-sister? She must be what now, sixteen? Older than when she and Jordan had lost their mother, but still, how awful. Margot remembered Jordan telling her that RJ and Nicole had decided to send Jade to some prestigious boarding school in New England because none of the Virginia schools, not even Foxcroft, were good enough for Nicole's daughter. . . . Nothing had ever been good enough for Nicole's little darling. Margot winced, ashamed of herself. Jade had just lost her mother; this wasn't the time to dwell on past wrongs or to think ill of the dead.

"Where's Jade at school again?" she asked.

"Malden Academy. It's outside of Boston."

"All right. I'll go there and bring Jade home as quickly as I can." Home. Rosewood. Despite all her years of exile, the stately old mansion was still the only place Margot considered home.

"Thanks, Margot. I'm leaving for the hospital right now. I'll be able to get updates on his condition more easily if I'm on the premises. Once you've got your flight, call Richard here. He'll have the school's address and telephone number."

"Isn't he driving you to the hospital?" Margot asked.

"No, it's better if he stays with Kate and Max. I don't want the children more upset than they have to be. And Richard was stuck in the office until two o'clock this morning. He's exhausted."

Maybe, but you're four months pregnant and most likely in shock, Margot was tempted to reply. But she bit back the words. She supposed her sister had a point. Kate and Max were only four and two and a half. Still, she didn't like the idea of Jordan, pregnant and upset, driving alone at this hour.

"You'll be careful?"

"Of course. Don't worry about me. You know I hold the Miss Cautious title."

She hated the note of self-deprecation in her sister's voice, but before she could speak, Jordan continued, "I better get going. Thanks again, Margot. I knew I could count on you. Love you."

Her throat tight, she whispered, "Love you back, sweetie."

The line went dead. For a moment Margot stood with her shoulders trembling, her eyes fixed on the scaffolding from which the tech crew had hung the massive speakers.

But she saw only her father.

Since the night she left Rosewood, huddled in the passenger seat of Charlie Ayer's car and trying not to bawl from misery and fear, her father had refused all contact with her, never answering her letters, never accepting her calls. He was stubborn, inflexible, a titan, too; a larger-than-life, vibrant man who habitually went for prebreakfast cross-country gallops, a fearless, indomitable man who piloted his own plane. Her mind revolted at the idea of him lying injured, perhaps critically, on a hospital operating table.

Margot's lips moved in a silent prayer. *Please, please, Lord, don't let Dad die. Don't let his last words to me become prophecy.* "*If you choose to defy me and carry out this harebrained modeling scheme, I promise you, Margot, the only way you'll ever come back to Rosewood is over my dead body.*"

At the Milan airport, Margot and Anika waited beside the limo while the driver unloaded her two suitcases and placed them onto the luggage cart. At the slam of the trunk, Anika gave her a final hug, squeezing tightly.

"You take care now." Her eyes searched Margot's face. "You sure you don't want me to come in with you?"

Margot shook her head. "No, you've done so much for me already. Thanks, though. Thanks for everything. When you see the others, will you tell them how grateful I am for their help?"

Never had Margot so appreciated the bonds she'd forged with the nomadic band that constituted the world of international modeling. Her friends had been amazing. Without wasting an extra second to pose for the photographers or preen before the fashion groupies and VIPs, they'd rushed backstage.

Margot only had to whisper disjointedly "Plane," "accident," "father," "hospital," for them to spring into action. Leading her to the metal rack where all the ensembles she'd worn during the show were hanging, Christy and Fiona had made quick work of stripping off the chiffon evening gown, removing her makeup and jewelry, and brushing out the outrageous crown of curls resting atop her head. From the jumble of discarded outfits, shoes, and accessories, Sasha had unearthed Margot's own clothes while Zoe diligently checked that Margot had all her personal items—wallet, passport, portfolio, Filofax, iPod, cell phone, and cosmetics—tucked inside her black messenger bag.

While her friends bustled about, Carlo, who'd cut his press conference short, arranged for his driver to take her to the hotel and then on to the airport. His assistant, Paolo, called the airlines to find which one could get Margot stateside the quickest. After a hurried round of hugs and a dozen whispered "It'll be okay's," they'd all escorted her from the fashion show tent to where Carlo's limo idled by the side entrance. Then Anika, bless her soul, had slipped into the seat beside her and accompanied her to the hotel. After helping Margot pack her things in record time, she had chosen to skip Carlo's sumptuous après-show party and come to the airport, holding Margot's chilled hand in hers the entire way. This last in a string of kindnesses was the most needed;

the simple human contact had kept Margot from falling apart.

Once again she tried to express her thanks, but Anika brushed them aside. "You know you'd have done the same for me, Margot. We girls have got to stick together."

Margot nodded tightly. "You're the best."

"Oh, I know that. You call me as soon as you can, all right?"

"I will."

"Okay, then," she said with a lopsided smile. "You'd better get going. You've got a long trip before you reach home."

Home. The word rang in Margot's head like a chime as she navigated the crowded airport, retrieved her ticket at the airline counter, checked her luggage, passed through security, and finally boarded the plane to Boston's Logan Airport.

Home. The word sounded again over the thrust of engines as the jet prepared for takeoff. How many times had she imagined her homecoming? The number was countless. Always triumphant returns, where her father would be standing on Rosewood's front porch, his arms stretched wide in welcome, pride shining in his eyes. And there, standing off to the side, like the loner he was, would be Travis. But when he saw her, his mouth would curve in that rare smile.

As months and then years passed, Margot was forced to stop her fanciful dreaming and face reality. Her father would never bend, would never forgive. She abandoned the hope she'd nurtured that he would ever see her as someone with the strength and determination to run Rosewood Farm. These eight years had changed her. She'd learned a lot about responsibility and self-discipline, but her father simply didn't care enough to discover that for himself. As for Travis Maher, the man to whom her father had entrusted the breeding, training, and selling of his prized horses, well, unfortunately the old adage that time heals all wounds didn't apply here, either.

Even after all these years, his harsh rejection was still etched on her heart.

Chapter
THREE

IT WAS EARLY afternoon when the driver Margot had hired rolled through the iron-gated entrance, from which hung a discreet white wooden shingle with the name MALDEN ACADEMY written in black script. A serpentine asphalt drive bordered by majestic pines led to the heart of the campus. Designed to evoke a colonial village, the ivy-covered buildings were set around a large open green. In the center of the manicured expanse rose a flag that waved gently in the autumn breeze. The school's campus quietly screamed class and money and the promise of a glorious future for the students who passed through its wrought-iron gates. Nicole's green eyes must have gleamed with satisfaction at the prospect of her daughter enrolled in a place like this.

Poor Nicole. Margot hadn't been able to stop thinking about her. She could only imagine her stepmother's terror at being a helpless passenger, unable to fight for her life as the plane lost altitude and hurtled into the choppy waters of the Chesapeake.

Her death was too awful to contemplate. It didn't matter that there'd been no love lost between them—only buckets of rank bitterness and jealousy. Margot wouldn't have wished such a horrible and premature end on anyone.

The driver pulled up in front of a large brick building. For a second, Margot gazed at the wide bluestone steps leading up to the entrance, the limestone lintel with EDWARDS HALL engraved in block letters, and then the smaller bronze plaque on which read the single word *Admissions*. When she'd last telephoned Richard, her brother-in-law had said Jade would be waiting here in the headmaster's office.

She drew a deep breath. She wasn't looking forward to this particular reunion. Any normal sibling affection Margot might have felt for her half-sister had been poisoned by Nicole's relentless campaign to drive a wedge between Margot and Jordan and their father. From the day Nicole gazed into RJ's eyes and pronounced the words "I do" in front of God, the minister, and the whole of Warburg, Virginia, she quickly shed all pretense of having any interest in her two young stepdaughters. When Jade came along barely nine months to the wedding day, Nicole, possessed by an us-versus-them mentality, hadn't hesitated to conscript her own child into the battle of wills being waged at Rosewood.

Eight years of distance and perspective allowed Margot to see that Jade was blameless. To hold a grudge against a mere kid was too petty for words. But the knowledge did little to ease Margot's tension.

"I'll only be a few minutes," she told the driver before opening the car door and stepping out into the crisp autumn air. She mounted the shallow steps determined to put aside the deep-seated resentment she felt toward her cosseted younger half-sister, who'd never had to beg, scream, or yell for her father's affection.

A secretary with a buttercup-yellow headband that matched her cardigan showed her into the headmaster's office. The office was large and decorated in the spirit of Norman-Rockwell-meets-John-Harvard: framed portraits, papered walls, and a solid mahogany desk in front of a large bay window. There was a fireplace and a pair of burgundy-upholstered wingback chairs.

Jade was sitting in one of them.

At Margot's entrance, she sprang to her feet. Margot saw tears shimmering in her green eyes, eyes so huge they all but swallowed up her pale face. The shock of seeing those eyes—Nicole's eyes—was almost as disorienting as the fact that Jade had grown so tall.

Get a grip. Of course Jade's grown. And she always had Nicole's green eyes, she reminded herself impatiently as she crossed the room and embraced her half-sister. That Jade's body felt as stiff as her own came as no surprise. After all, they were practically strangers.

She stepped back and tried to smile. "Hi. You okay?"

Jade nodded jerkily, but then had to blot the tears that spilled down her cheeks with a crumpled Kleenex.

Margot's heart welled with pity. "I'm really sorry about your mother."

"Thanks," she said in a voice thick with tears.

Margot was searching for what to say next when the door opened and a middle-aged man dressed in crisply pressed khakis and a navy blazer entered. He approached with his hand thrust out.

"Ms. Radcliffe? I'm Thomas Selby, the head of Malden Academy."

She shook his hand. "Hello."

"On behalf of our school, please allow me to extend our condolences to your family."

With a polite smile, she extricated her hand from his. He seemed to have forgotten he was holding it. "Thank you, that's very kind."

"A terrible tragedy. I only had the pleasure of meeting Jade's parents a few times, but even from those brief encounters I could tell they were devoted to her. Absolutely devoted." He cleared his throat. "When I spoke with your brother-in-law earlier this morning, he informed me that your father was taken to Jefferson Hospital. An excellent place. One of our alumni, Andrew Marston, was chief of staff there. Although he's retired now, I'm sure your father will receive the finest medical attention."

"We hope so." Dad was strong. If anyone could survive this kind of accident, it was he. Please, God.

"It's fortunate your brother-in-law was able to reach me and inform me that you were coming for Jade, Ms. Radcliffe," he continued. "You see, at Malden, we're very concerned about our students' security and your parents didn't include you on the emergency contact form. Indeed, we had no idea Jade had such a famous relative." He smiled over his bow tie, his eyes bright with curiosity behind his tortoiseshell glasses.

Thomas Selby was sorely mistaken if he thought he was going to discover a juicy tidbit of gossip to share at the next faculty meeting, such as the reason why she wasn't on any family contact list. Hearing that her father hadn't spoken to her in eight years would certainly enliven the meeting. But after evading paparazzi who hunted with telephoto lenses and media journalists who spied and probed relentlessly in an attempt to uncover her "real life" story, Margot found his bumbling attempt almost laughable. Almost.

She gave a careless shrug. "With the amount of traveling I do as a model, it hardly makes sense to list me as an emergency contact."

"Of course, I understand completely."

She glanced at Jade, who hadn't uttered a word since Selby entered the room, and was surprised by the faint sneer on her half-sister's pale face. What was that about?

"Are you ready, Jade? Have you got all your things?"

"Yes," she said and pointed to a small mountain of black nylon in the corner. Margot counted three bulging duffel bags, an equally overstuffed backpack, and a laptop computer case.

"I see Jade's packed her computer. That's good. While she's gone she can e-mail her teachers about her assignments. But I do hope that she'll be returning as soon as possible. Sophomore year is quite challenging. We'd hate to see her fall behind."

"I'm not coming back to Malden. My dad will want me at home," Jade said.

God, what must it be like to be so assured of a father's love? Margot thought.

Thomas Selby had stiffened visibly at Jade's pronouncement. "I hardly believe a decision of this magnitude is yours to make."

The sneer on Jade's face grew marked. "Yeah, it is. And you can—"

Worried that Jade might say something she'd later regret, Margot quickly intervened. "As I'm sure you understand, Mr. Selby, Jade is quite distraught. My sister Jordan or I will contact you as soon as we have more information about our father's condition and a better idea of when Jade will be returning to school." She glanced at her wristwatch, ignoring the fact that it was still set to Milan time. "I have a car waiting to take us to the airport. Perhaps someone can help us carry these things outside."

The forty-five-minute ride to the airport was completed in virtual silence, with Margot and Jade, like the near strangers they were, staring out the opposite windows at the other cars speeding down the highway. Margot honestly didn't know if under normal circumstances she would have found much to say to her half-sister, but exhaustion, shock, and stress were taking their toll. Pre–fashion show nerves had made it so she managed to eat only a slice of toast for breakfast. After Jordan's call, she'd been too overwhelmed with grief and worry even to consider food. She'd traveled thousands of miles and still had several hundred to go. Margot only hoped she had enough energy left to get her and Jade to their father's side at the hospital as fast as possible. For now that was as far as she could plan.

Logan Airport wasn't especially jam-packed with travelers. But that didn't make the airline agent any more patient or sympathetic when it was Margot and Jade's turn to check in and one of the overstuffed bags Jade heaved onto the metal scale split along its strained seam. Books, DVDs, perfume bottles, various lotion jars, an ancient-looking teddy bear, and a dog-eared album tumbled onto the terminal floor.

The agent glanced with contempt at the ripped bag and muttered something about people who traveled with every single one of their possessions.

Jade, beet-red with embarrassment, immediately dropped to her knees and began gathering up her scattered belongings.

"Could you please give us some tape so that we can patch the bag?" Margot asked the agent.

"A rip that big, the bag's pretty much a lost cause."

A sudden headache pounded Margot's left temple. "Please, could you just find some," she enunciated through gritted teeth.

The agent wandered away, ostensibly in search of tape, and Margot knelt beside Jade.

"Here, let me help," she offered. She stretched out a hand toward one of the bottles, wishing that instead of Marc Jacob's Blush it was a bottle of aspirin, so that she could down three of them.

With a cry, Jade snatched the perfume bottle from her and shoved it back through the bag's gaping hole. "Leave it. I'll do it myself."

Startled, Margot looked at her, but Jade's dark blond hair hung like a curtain, hiding her expression. "Hey, it'll be all right," she said softly.

"No, it won't be all right. Nothing will *ever* be right. Just leave it!" she repeated when Margot reached for the bulky album.

Margot stilled. "Fine."

She didn't know why the rebuff should sting so. Jade had just lost her mother and her father was lying in a hospital. Of course she was an emotional wreck. What kid wouldn't be?

Rising to her feet, she smoothed her skirt in place, and

then stood at the counter waiting for the ticket agent to return. She did her best to ignore both the sight of Jade manically cramming her things back into the bag and the pain hammering away inside her head.

But, like the headache, the problems with Jade's luggage persisted even after the agent returned with a roll of duct tape and Jade had grudgingly accepted her help in patching the duffel bag.

"I'm sorry, but I'm going to have to charge you extra. Your luggage exceeds the weight limit," he said, pointing to the bags.

"What? This is so lame! What kind of bogus airline is this?" Jade demanded loudly enough for the other passengers as well as airline personnel to look at them curiously.

Jade clearly had no clue how obnoxious she sounded. Margot drew a breath and glanced at the name tag pinned to the agent's white shirt. "Look, Mr. Ellis, couldn't you give us a break? We've had a death in the family and we're trying to get home. My sister wasn't aware of the airline's restrictions."

The agent gave her a smile of sympathy about as real as the carved Halloween pumpkin sitting on the counter inches from her elbow. "I'm sorry, Ms. Radcliffe. I have to abide by the company's regulations. No exceptions, I'm afraid."

Jade gave a loud snort of disgust, earning a nasty glare from the agent. "That will be two hundred dollars," he informed them.

"I can't believe how unfair this is!"

"It's all right, Jade, don't worry about it," she said as she withdrew her credit card from her wallet.

Alerted perhaps by Jade's protest, another airline agent came over to the check-in counter. A good twenty years Ellis's junior, he eyed the two of them with interest. "Is something the matter here?"

"Their bags are over the weight limit," Ellis informed him testily. "Thank you, Ms. Radcliffe," he said, handing Margot back her credit card and the printed receipt to sign.

"Radcliffe? As in Margot Radcliffe? Holy Toledo, I was sure your face looked familiar!" The younger agent's face split in a wide smile. "Wait till I tell my fiancée. She owns a salon in Newton—Susie's Style. Susie says that each time you appear in a new ad or shoot, her customers come streaming in. Every last one of them wants to have your look. I'm Greg. Greg Perelli." He thrust his hand over the counter.

"Hello." Although Margot had grown used to being recognized, it still amazed her when she heard stories like this. She couldn't pinpoint the exact date, but sometime in the last year she'd ceased being an anonymous flesh-and-blood mannequin and become a "personality," someone worthy of being copied. She tried not to let it bother her that the reason she was emulated wasn't because of her opinions, talents, or accomplishments but rather because some stylist had dressed and made her up just so. *Quit being so serious,* she chided herself. *No woman honestly dreams of looking or dressing like Mother Teresa.*

"If you think your fiancée would like it, Greg, I have a headshot in my portfolio. I'd be happy to autograph it."

"Would she? Oh, man, Susie will flip!" he answered with a grin. Turning to his coworker, he asked, "Frank, what flight is Ms. Radcliffe on?"

"Flight 327 to Dulles."

"And where are they assigned?"

"Five A and five B," Ellis said grudgingly.

"Mind if I take a look at the screen?"

For a few seconds both men stood, heads bowed, staring at the computer. Margot heard the quick tap of fingers on a keyboard and then he looked up. "Yup, like I thought," he said happily. "The flight's only half-full, so there's really no need to impose the extra weight penalty for your luggage, especially as you're VIP first-class passengers. If you'd just give me your credit card again, Ms. Radcliffe, I'll cancel that charge."

Margot gave him what felt like her first real smile of the day. "Thank you."

Jade rooted through her backpack and pulled out her iPod before shoving the bag into the overhead compartment. Plopping down into the wide leather seat, she jammed her earphones as close to her eardrums as she could, scrolled down to Pink, and pressed the play button. She sat listening broodingly. To make sure Margot got the message that she was totally uninterested in her company, she reached forward and retrieved the airline magazine from the leather pouch and began flipping through its pages. But through the veil of her lashes she watched the other passengers board, noted how every one of them paused in midshuffle down the aisle the instant their gazes landed on her beautiful and glamorous half-sister.

Jade had never felt so ugly before. Or so very lonely and afraid. Mom was dead. She'd never see her again, and would never be able to say how sorry she was for all the fights they'd had last summer, or for walking away without a good-bye hug when Mom left her at that stink-hole of a school.

It was only that she'd been so angry with her for having turned into some kind of Gestapo-type for no good reason. For years, Jade hadn't been able to do anything wrong. She'd loved being "Mommy's darling." Then one day, out of the blue, Mom began accusing her of all sorts of totally ridiculous stuff, and calling her a liar when she denied it. At first she'd been too hurt and confused to do more than retreat to her bedroom and cry. But after a while, she got fed up. She began sticking up for herself and yelling right back.

That clinched it. Mom freaked and started bitching to Dad, telling him that she was the worst teenager in the whole world. The only solution was to send her away to school before she got completely out of control. And Dad really, really hated having to deal with anything—unless it

involved some horse he was planning to buy, breed, or sell—
so Mom wore him down real quick. He caved and the next
thing she knew, they were dumping her at Malden Academy.

She'd hated her parents for that, her mom especially, for
having turned into the psycho of the century. But that didn't
mean Jade had wanted her to *die*. A sick, crampy feeling
settled in the pit of her stomach. God, she was so scared.
Her skin felt clammy and cold with fear.

And what if Dad died, too? No, no, she wouldn't let herself go there. Dad wouldn't. He simply wouldn't die. He
wouldn't leave her.

Her gaze slid sideways. Margot had slipped on a pair of
oversized Chanel dark glasses, but Jade could see her eyes
were closed. Napping. That showed how upset *she* was that
her stepmother was dead and that their father was probably
hooked up to a hundred different machines while the doctors operated. She didn't care what happened to their family.
It was like Mom always said: Margot thought she was better
than everybody else and that the universe revolved around
her. According to Mom, she'd never given Dad anything but
heartache. That's why she wouldn't let Margot talk to him
on the phone after she'd run off to New York, why she
checked the mail for any letters or cards with Margot's
handwriting and buried them deep in the garbage. Mom
wasn't about to let Margot's manipulations upset him again.

There'd been times when Jade wondered if her mother
might not be exaggerating how selfish and conceited Margot was. But now she believed every word. It had been
beyond gross watching Thomas Selby drool over her. And
she had acted as if it were only natural for Selby to treat her
like visiting royalty. And then that other guy—the agent at
the airport, the one she'd thought was kind of cute at first—
had made it sound as if his fiancée were going to set up a
holy shrine to Margot at her beauty salon. All because she'd
offered him a lousy signed photograph.

Thank God her scrapbook hadn't fallen open when that

stupid bag ripped apart in front of a couple of hundred people. It would have been beyond mortifying if Margot had seen the pictures of herself neatly taped to its pages. She'd started the album a few years back because what kid wouldn't think it cool that her older sister was a fashion model? But she knew better now and the thought of Margot knowing about the album freaked her out. That's why she hadn't let Margot help pick up her stuff. Not that Margot had really wanted to; she'd probably been delighted to get back to that bald-headed loser of a ticket agent so she could complain that everything was Jade's fault . . . "My sister wasn't aware of the airline's restrictions." God, Margot had made it sound as if she were an utter dweeb.

The first thing she'd do when she got home to Rosewood would be to toss the scrapbook in the garbage. She didn't need Margot, or Jordan, either, who was way too wrapped up in her own kids' lives to care about her. The only person she needed was Dad.

Chapter ❧
FOUR

BY THE TIME Margot pulled the rental car into the hospital's parking lot, the sky was deep lavender and the trees lining the lot looked like black cutouts. The hospital's windows glowed fluorescent bright as she and Jade ran toward the entrance.

"Could you tell us the room number of Robert J. Radcliffe?" Margot asked the attendant at the information desk.

"Radcliffe?"

"Yes, Robert J. Radcliffe," Margot repeated.

The woman lowered her gaze to the screen. "He must still be in surgery or post-op because there's no room assigned here."

Margot tried not to panic at the news that her father might still be undergoing surgery after so many hours. "Then can you tell us where the waiting room is? Our sister should be there."

"Take the elevator to the seventh floor. Turn right and follow the signs."

Jordan was standing by the bank of windows in the waiting lounge, her auburn head lowered. At the sound of their footsteps hurrying over the linoleum floor, she turned, and a smile of relief lit her face.

"I'm so glad to see you!" she said, embracing Margot and Jade in turn. After giving Jade a second, even fiercer hug, she said, "I'm really sorry about Nicole. Your mom loved you so much."

Jade managed a whispered, "Thanks," before pressing her trembling lips together tightly.

"How's Dad doing?" Margot asked.

"Yeah, how's my dad?"

The worry lines on Jordan's brow deepened. "I haven't heard anything yet. But it seems like he was in surgery forever."

"How—how bad is he hurt?" Jade whispered.

"The first nurse I spoke to told me he had a collapsed lung and was bleeding internally. There was more, too, something about a contusion to the heart, and at that point I kind of went blank with fear so I didn't catch everything she said. Another nurse came by about forty-five minutes ago to let me know they'd finished operating and that the surgeon would talk to me soon. I tried to ask about Dad's other injuries but she couldn't spare any more time. Apparently there was an accident on the highway this afternoon involving a motorcycle and three cars. Some of the families and friends have been here in the lounge. It's terrible to see their fear." She shook her head sadly. "Anyway, that's all the information I have so far. At least he's out of surgery." She reached for both Margot's and Jade's hands and squeezed them. "I'm so glad you're here," she repeated. "Time really crawls when you have no one to talk to."

"You haven't been here alone the entire time, have you?" Margot asked.

"Oh, no. Richard came at lunch to keep me company." A small smile lifted the corners of Jordan's mouth. "He brought my knitting and my green tea—the vending machines only stock sugar or aspartame. He stayed for as long as he could, but he's swamped with work just now. And our sitter has to leave at five, so . . ." She shrugged. "It hasn't been that bad. I've almost finished the baby's blanket."

Resting beside one of the brown upholstered chairs, Margot spied a clear plastic shopping bag. Inside it were folds of knitted yarn the color of sweet butter. Margot knew that if she touched it, it would be incredibly soft and that each stitch would be neat and uniform—beautiful, like everything her sister did.

Jordan had let go of their hands and was kneading the small of her back.

"How are you feeling?" Margot asked.

"Oh, I'm fine, but all this sitting and waiting has me feeling like a beached whale."

"You're joking, right? You look wonderful. And way too young to have a third kid on the way."

Jordan flushed at Margot's compliment. "You're the one who looks fantastic. I can't believe you were in Italy when I called. After traveling halfway around the world, I'd be as wrung out as a washcloth. It's so good to see—"

"You were in Italy before you came to get me?" Jade interrupted.

Margot's eyebrows rose in surprise. This was the first sentence Jade had addressed to her since boarding the plane in Boston, and her answers had been strictly limited to "yes," "no," or "dunno."

"I was in Milan modeling the spring collection. Jordan called right at the end of Carlo de Calvi's show. We didn't want you to have to travel here on your own so I got on the first available flight to Boston. Why?"

An odd expression crossed Jade's face. She shrugged and dropped her gaze. "No reason," she muttered to the floor.

Jordan aimed a quick, questioning glance at Margot. She answered with a shrug of her own. What could she say, except that if the past few hours were anything to go by, Jade disliked her as much as Nicole had. Thank goodness Jordan was here. She'd know how to deal with their half-sister. She was a mom, after all.

The three of them had just sat down when the blue metal swinging doors opened. A nurse with a clipboard and a doctor wearing green scrubs beneath a white coat entered.

Everyone in the lounge turned to look at them expectantly, hopefully.

"That's one of the nurses I spoke to earlier," Jordan said in an undertone. They watched as the nurse said something to the doctor and then pointed to Jordan. The doctor gave a quick nod and walked toward them. In unison they rose as he approached. Up close, Margot noted violet smudges of fatigue beneath his eyes and the heavy stubble darkening his cheeks.

"Mrs. Stevens?" he said to Jordan. "I'm Kurt Lyons, head of surgery."

Jordan extended her hand. "Hello." The lines bracketing the doctor's mouth deepened as he smiled and shook her hand. "Dr. Lyons, these are my sisters, Margot and Jade Radcliffe. They've just arrived."

After exchanging a quick greeting, Dr. Lyons cleared his throat. "First, please accept my condolences on the death of your mother. While this may provide small consolation, I spoke with the hospital's coroner who examined her. Your mother died on impact. There was no pain."

"Thank you, Doctor. It does help knowing she didn't suffer." Jordan slipped her arm around Jade, who'd begun crying, and pulled her close. "And our father? How is he doing?"

"Your father was lucky that the navy was performing exercises in the area and that they were able to extricate him from the aircraft and transport him here via helicopter. Otherwise it's doubtful he would have survived given the extent of his internal injuries."

"But the surgery, it was a success?" Margot asked.

"Our immediate goal was to stop the internal bleeding and reinflate the left lung, which had been pierced by one of his ribs. We were successful there. But you should be aware that your father's heart suffered considerable trauma. We'll be monitoring his vitals very closely. Once he's stronger and out of danger, we'll address the other injuries."

"You mentioned a broken rib. Is he hurt elsewhere?" she asked.

"Actually he sustained four broken ribs. He also broke both his right leg and right wrist. Our orthopedic surgeon was able to set the wrist, but I'm afraid the break in his leg isn't clean and will require extensive reconstruction. That will have to wait until we're confident he can survive the surgery."

The description of her father's injuries, recited in such a straightforward and steady manner, made Margot even more frightened. She almost wished he'd thrown a lot of obscure medical terms at them so she wouldn't have understood how dire Dad's condition was. At the thought of the pain his broken body was suffering, a wave of dizziness swept through her.

"Would it be possible for us to see him?" she asked.

Jade, wiping tears from her face with the back of her hand, nodded vigorously. "Yeah, I want to see my dad."

"I'm going to the intensive care unit to check on him now. If he's holding his own I can let you visit him—but only for a few minutes."

"Thank you, Dr. Lyons," Jordan said. "My sisters and I are so very grateful for all you've done."

"I only wish I could tell you that your father's in the clear. But the fact is that these next seventy-two hours are critical. If he can make it through them, his overall chances of surviving will be greatly improved."

"Dad'll make it. I know he will." Jade's voice was fierce.

"I'm sure your father will fight as hard as he can," he replied, sympathy evident on his tired face. Turning to Jordan, he said, "Mrs. Stevens, Nurse Wilcox informed me that you're expecting."

Color bloomed over Jordan's cheeks. "Yes. But I'm as healthy as an ox."

A smile lit his eyes. "You may not believe this but that's what we doctors really like to hear. Do you live nearby?"

"No, we live in Georgetown, but our parents' home is in Warburg. I've talked with my husband and he thinks it's best if I spend the night there with my sisters."

Dr. Lyons nodded approvingly. "Good. It's best to avoid the added stress of a long commute. Now, if I may, I'd like to recommend that after you've seen your father, you and your sisters go home and rest. This is going to be a long and difficult period for your family. You, especially, Mrs. Stevens, cannot afford to wear yourself out. Consider that sound medical advice," he said, and the lopsided smile he gave Jordan erased the fatigue and care from his face. "I know you're anxious to see your father. A nurse will come notify you when you can visit him."

They watched him disappear behind the blue metal doors. "What a nice man. I'm sure Dad is in excellent hands," Jordan said with a forced cheer Margot knew was for Jade's benefit. Jordan wouldn't have missed how he'd repeatedly emphasized the fact that their father's condition remained critical. She wished she understood more about the procedures they'd performed, wished she knew the right questions to ask next time they talked with Dr. Lyons. Did Jordan know anything about the heart and how much trauma it could stand?

But Margot didn't dare ask, not in front of Jade. A frank discussion would only terrify the teen.

She settled for a weak nod of her head. "Yes, I'm sure he'll do everything he can for Dad." Then, in an attempt to lighten their collective anxiety, she added, "And I liked how concerned he was about you, too. I think Dr. Lyons may be smitten with you, sweetie."

"Oh, please! You saw how tired the poor man looked, positively cross-eyed with exhaustion. Dr. Lyons was simply saying all that to avoid admitting another Radcliffe into the hospital. But he's absolutely right—we have to take care of ourselves." Without skipping a beat, Jordan turned to Jade. "Have you eaten anything? I noticed the vending machine was stocked with chips, pretzels, and granola bars. Let me grab my purse."

After another forty-five minutes a nurse appeared in the lounge and called out, "Radcliffe." Jumping to their feet, they followed her through the swinging doors and down a peach-colored corridor. She stopped at an open door opposite the nurses' station and motioned for them to go inside. Margot's heart pounded as she entered the half-lit room.

Their father lay in the bed with a thin white thermal blanket drawn up to his waist. Underneath, a bulky protrusion ran the length of his right leg. They must have put a splint on his broken leg, she thought, as her eyes moved over the rest of his body, taking in the heart-rending changes: the plastic tubes sticking into his left arm, the snow-white plaster cast encasing his right arm from hand to elbow, and the wires attached to his chest connecting him to a wall of softly beeping machines, their screens monitoring his battered body.

His eyes were closed. The strong, commanding face Margot remembered looked sunken, his perennially tanned skin tinged with gray. He lay motionless. And despite the two plastic tubes snaking into his nostrils and the hum of the machines, Margot worried he might not be breathing. A painful lump lodged in her throat as she stared at her father's inert form. *Dear Lord, he was so badly hurt. If he looks like this on the outside, how do his lungs and heart look? Can a body recover from so many injuries?*

"Dr. Lyons wanted me to remind you that you must keep your visit brief," the nurse told them as she turned to go. "I'll be back in a few minutes."

"Thank you," Jordan said.

At the sound of Jordan's voice, Margot saw her father's eyelids flutter. "Dad?" she whispered.

A muscle in his cheek twitched.

She rushed to the side of the bed. The guardrail pressed

against her stomach as she leaned forward. Jade and Jordan brushed her shoulders as they, too, huddled around him.

"I'm here, too, Dad," Jade offered.

His lips moved.

"We're all here. Everything's going to be all right." Jordan reached forward to stroke his forearm with her fingertips. "We're all here for you, Dad."

Slowly, as if making an enormous effort, their father opened eyes glazed from pain and medication. His gaze moved slowly, touching on each of his daughters, then coming back to rest on Margot. His lips moved again, this time forming a single word. "Margot."

"Yes, Dad. I'm here. I missed you so much," she whispered, tears slipping down her face. How pointless and foolish the feud-filled years seemed now with her father lying here. Her hand sought his, wanting desperately to give him her strength.

"Like your mother," he said, his voice a weak rasp. His eyes drifted shut.

"Daddy?" Jade cried.

With an excruciating slowness, his eyes opened again. "The plane." His throat worked visibly. "Nicole?"

Realizing what he was asking, Margot drew a horrified breath. Beside her, Jordan stiffened. But before either of them could offer a soothing lie until he was strong enough to bear the truth, Jade gave a gagging sob.

At the harsh sound, he fixed his gaze on Jade. A spasm of pain twisted his face. Holding his hand in hers, Margot felt a sudden shaking seize him.

"Take care of her, Margot." His whisper was a terrible imperative. Then, as if overcome by excruciating pain, his fingers clenched hers fiercely. His lids closed and were still.

"Dad!" Jordan's voice was sharp. "Dad, can you hear us?" She shook his shoulder.

At the head of the bed, the assembled machines beeped and flashed alarmingly.

"Dad?" Jade cried. "Dad, wake up!"

"Margot, something's wrong. Call the nurse!"

Margot turned and ran from the room, but in her heart she knew it was too late. She'd felt the terrible moment her father slipped away, his hand slack and lifeless in hers.

Chapter
FIVE

THE TAILLIGHTS of Jordan's car glowed like twin red beacons as Margot followed her to Rosewood. Beside her, Jade sat curled in a ball, knees raised, her head buried between them. Though her thin shoulders still shook, her sobs had grown less violent, a sign that the mild sedative Dr. Lyons had prescribed was starting to take effect. Convinced that her reaction to their father's question about Nicole had killed him, Jade had become hysterical, deaf to Dr. Lyons's assertion that an embolism had caused his cardiac arrest. With a heart already severely traumatized, the hospital team had been unable to revive him.

Dr. Lyons had counseled that the best thing to do was to let the sedative do its work and for Jade to sleep. It would be the first small step along the road to healing emotionally; Margot and Jordan had left the hospital with her as quickly as possible.

For her own part, Margot wasn't sure when she would be able to sleep; certainly not while she could still recall the feel of her father's hand in hers, then the sensation of it going limp as he passed from one world to the next. She would never forgive herself for not telling him the second their eyes met that she loved him. Now her father was dead and she'd come back too late to make things right and repair the rift between them.

They exited the highway, turning onto smaller and smaller roads, and the area, even in the dark, began to look increasingly familiar. They were soon passing houses and stores she remembered: Anderson's Foods, Warburg Hardware, the

Coach House—a restaurant with the most delicious fried chicken and corn bread Margot had ever tasted.

Just beyond the small brick post office, Jordan turned left onto Piper's Road. Margot straightened in the rental car's seat. She gripped the steering wheel tighter and her tired and gritty eyes strained to see every dip and curve of the last two miles of country road that led to Rosewood.

Then there it was: the break in the trees where the line of dark post and rail fence began that signaled the beginning of her family's property. Of course, the southern pastures were empty now, the horses safe in the barns for the night.

Ahead, Jordan signaled left and turned into the wide, graveled driveway. Margot followed slowly, feeling that familiar rush of awe when the night sky vanished, blocked out by the chestnut trees that formed a quarter-mile-long allée. The trees had been planted the year the house had been built. They towered majestically, their branches meeting in a cathedral-like arch; in the headlights, the leaves that still clung to them gleamed dark gold.

Unconsciously, Margot caught and held her breath as the car rounded the final curve and Rosewood's columned façade came into sight.

Framed by the dark night, the house appeared hauntingly romantic. The stuff of dreams. Lights shone through the sheer curtains, and suspended above the front door, the oversized iron lantern bathed the front porch in a welcoming glow. The illuminated house was a forcible reminder that the routines of daily life unfolded in spite of tragedy. Even as their father had lain in the hospital, the housekeeper—was it still Ellie Banner?—had prepared the house for their arrival before departing for the night.

As she pulled up behind Jordan's car, Margot's gaze pored over the old house, hungrily taking in the details: the graceful carved swag that decorated the frieze above the two-story-high fluted Corinthian columns; the intricately lathed railing that wrapped the length of the front porch and the

twin side porches. A sudden vivid memory sprang to mind,
of her father carrying her ailing mother downstairs to the
side porch, her frail body wrapped in wool throws needed
to keep her warm in the July heat. He'd laid her upon the
chintz-covered chaise longue near the white carved railing
so she could breathe the perfumed air of her favorite tea
roses.

A tap on the window startled her. She had no idea how
long she'd been staring at the house, lost in memories. The
passenger seat was empty. Jade had gone while she'd sat
here, her chest aching with regrets.

Margot tugged on the door handle and stepped out of
the car.

"I just wanted to make sure you were okay." The concern
in Jordan's voice was plain.

"I'm fine. Really. I guess I lost track of time." The crisp
night air stung her damp cheeks. Quickly, she turned away.
Bending inside the car, she wiped her tears with the back of
her hand before retrieving her bag off the console. She
slammed the car door shut and faced her sister. "I'd forgotten how beautiful the house was," she lied.

"Yes, it is," Jordan said as she turned to fix her gaze on
the graceful lines of the house. "It's funny, whenever I come
here now, I find myself thinking about Frank and Georgie."

The easy familiarity in Jordan's voice confused Margot
until she realized that her sister was speaking of their ancestors and not some longtime friends. "You mean Francis and
Georgiana Radcliffe, who lived a couple of hundred years
ago?"

"Yes, sorry. Frank and Georgie are the nicknames Mama
and I gave them. She knew everything about them, the history of the house, too. She used to tell me stories. I'd sit
beside her on the bed and she'd talk to me about how
Frank—*Francis*—built the house for Georgiana when she
accepted his proposal for marriage. In one of his letters to
the architect, Francis wrote that he wanted him to design a

house as graceful and lovely as his wife-to-be. Then he traveled to New York and commissioned Duncan Phyfe to build all the furniture for Rosewood, because Phyfe was the finest craftsman in America and nothing was too good for Francis's beloved. The pieces were transported here from New York by the wagonload. Can you imagine how many wagons it must have taken?"

Margot imagined the rumble and creak of the wagon wheels. Would the chestnuts in the allée have even been planted yet?

Beside her, Jordan sighed. "I loved those stories. I could never hear enough about Francis and Georgiana. Even then, when I was, what, maybe ten, I understood how rare their love was. Francis wasn't interested in building some grandiose edifice to impress the world with his wealth and social standing. He wanted a house that would symbolize his love for Georgiana, for their future children, and for their children's children. That's why Rosewood feels special, because it was built out of love." Her voice faded on a wistful note and for a moment they both stared at the graceful lines of the old house.

Then, as if waking from a reverie, Jordan shook her head and gave a soft, rueful laugh. "Lord, I am such a hopeless romantic! Richard's always teasing me about it. That reminds me, I'd better call home. I promised Richard I would as soon as we arrived."

Doubtless eager for the reassuring sound of her husband's voice, Jordan started toward the house. When she realized Margot wasn't with her, she looked back. "Margot?"

"Go ahead. I think I'll take a walk. I'm not quite ready to go inside the house yet. Too many memories."

"Oh, gosh, I am so sorry! I wasn't thinking." She turned back immediately. "This must be so hard for you. All those years and Dad wouldn't forgive you. I tried talking to him but nothing seemed to soften him. Then Nicole started up, claiming that I was upsetting him terribly by mentioning you all the time. She issued this ultimatum, telling me that if I persisted in bringing up your name when I visited Rosewood, she would arrange it so that I wasn't invited anymore. She would have, too, uncaring that it would mean depriving Kate and Max of their grandfather. So I let it go and gave up on Dad. I'm sorry. I should have been stronger and stood up to her bullying. You always did."

Margot touched her arm. "Hey, it's all right. You did what you could. I can't remember how many of my letters went unanswered, how many calls refused, before I realized he just wasn't going to forgive me. But if I hadn't left Rosewood when I did, I'd have probably been too old to break into modeling. Then where would I have been?"

"Maybe here at Rosewood?"

"No. Nicole and I were heading straight for a major blowup. Even if I'd managed to keep my temper in check for the chance to work at Rosewood Farm, Dad would still have favored"—she paused, Travis's name on the tip of her tongue—"any man over me."

"Dad always did view the world traditionally."

Margot choked back a sad laugh. "That's a fact."

"It's certainly how he chose to run the farm. Do you realize, Margot, Dad never once hired a female to work at Rosewood?"

Yeah, not even his own daughter, Margot thought. "I guess that's something we simply have to accept about him." Fighting off a chill of sorrow, she rubbed her arms. "It's all water under the bridge now in any case. I'm happy with my career. Before I left for Italy, Damien Barnes called. Dior is launching a new product line and they want me to be their face. They've offered me a two-year contract."

"Oh, Margot, congratulations! That's a huge break for your career, isn't it?"

"Yeah."

"This is so exciting. You'll be everywhere. I just loved it when you landed on the covers of *Vogue* and *Elle* last year.

I was so proud of you—and it was so darned satisfying knowing it must be driving Nicole nuts to see your face on her favorite magazines. Lord, she was unpleasant." Her voice dropped. "It's hard to believe she's gone."

"I know. I kept thinking of her on the flights to Boston and Washington. She was only forty-two, Jordan."

"And Dad only sixty-four. It's awful. They had so much left to do in life. But the person I really feel bad for is Jade. Listen, I'm going to go inside and telephone Richard and then look in on Jade. If she's still awake, I'll see what Ellie left in the refrigerator and fix her a bite to eat. Do you want anything?"

Food. Eating. The notion sounded bizarre after all that had happened. "No, thanks. I'm not sure I can keep anything down right now. Maybe later."

The moon was bright enough for Margot to wander over the grounds without fear of stumbling. Distracted by thoughts and memories, she didn't pay particular attention to her direction until she looked up and saw the main barn ahead of her, its large double doors still open so that light streamed into the courtyard.

It didn't surprise her that her feet had led her here. Rosewood's barns had always been a refuge; the warmth of a horse's sleek neck against her cheek brought solace as nothing else could. She stepped through the open doors and blinked, adjusting to the light.

It was like stepping back in time. Her heart swelled at the familiarity of the scene: the immaculately swept concrete floor, the long row of box stalls, the air redolent of hay and horse and wood shavings. Sensing her presence, the horses whickered and shifted restlessly, sending bedding scattering against the stall walls. But no human was in sight.

"Hello?" she called out.

Halfway down the aisle, a silver-haired man with a wiry build stepped out from one of the stalls. He slid the stall door shut and threw the latch in place, then hung a dark leather halter on its metal hook, taking the time to make sure it was exactly centered. The gesture triggered her memory.

"Ned?" Margot exclaimed in surprise.

Ned Connelly turned with a start. "Good Lord, is that you, Miss Margot?" he asked, already moving toward her.

"Yes, Ned, it's me." Her voice quavered. "Gosh, it's been a long time."

"Too damn long." He grasped both her hands in his. Though he must have been seventy, Ned's grip was still strong. "Let me take a look at you." His bright gaze inspected her from head to foot. He gave a pleased nod. "Like I told the boys, you're a hundred times prettier in the flesh than they make you in those glossy pictures." The teasing twinkle in his eye dimmed abruptly. "I heard about your stepmother. I'm awful sorry. How's your father? Last time I called the hospital, they said he'd been moved to intensive care. Did they let you see him? How's he doing?"

Perhaps it was because Ned had known her forever, had dusted off her behind when a horse sent her flying into the dirt before matter-of-factly giving her a leg up, boosting her right back into the saddle, that she lost it. She began trembling. "He—he didn't make it," she stammered.

Ned seemed to age ten years before her eyes. His face fell, his leathery skin crumpling into creases. His shoulders bowed under the weight of his grief, he lifted a trembling hand, and wiped his eyes.

"Oh, hell," he said thickly. "I can't believe it. I was so sure a stubborn rascal like him would pull through. Ahh, Miss Margot, I'm gonna miss RJ, hardheaded fool that he was."

The deep affection in his voice undid her. Tears welled in her eyes ready to flow down her cheeks. Futilely she tried to wipe them away, but the dam had opened. "All I can think of is that I barely saw him and then he was *gone*. If I'd just had a little more time with him. God, I'm sorry for crying like this," she said, hiccuping.

"No need to apologize. I know how you loved your dad."
He fished a bandana from the front pocket of his dickeys—
the type of work trousers he'd worn without fail for as long
as she could remember—and pressed the folded square into
her hand. It was soft with age and countless washings.
Wrapping an arm about her, he said, "Come on into the
office. There's some coffee left in the pot. And a bottle of
whiskey somewhere, too. We'll talk."

Ned waited until Margot was seated in one of the cracked
leather chairs before handing her a mug of coffee that he'd
laced liberally with whiskey. He held up his own in a toast.
"Here's to your father. He was a good friend and one of the
finest horsemen I've had the pleasure of knowing. May he
rest in peace."

"May he rest in peace," she echoed, and clinked her mug
against his before taking a sip. The heat of the alcohol-laced
coffee spread through her. Leary of drinking too much or
too quickly when she had jet lag and hadn't eaten in hours,
she balanced the mug on her thigh. "Ned, what are you
doing here so late, all by yourself?"

"One of the four-year-olds, Gulliver, has a puffy tendon.
I've been icing the leg to bring the swelling down. I'd just finished wrapping it and was saying good night to the fella."

"Shouldn't Travis be doing that?" There, she'd said his
name. Casually, too, as if this were the first time she'd even
thought of him in eight years.

But the canny light in Ned's eyes made her wonder if she
had even come close to fooling him. She thought of all the
hungry, flirty glances she'd cast at Travis, all the silly ploys
she'd stooped to in a bid for his attention. Ned had probably
witnessed every one of them and remembered exactly how
infatuated she'd been. She lifted the mug to her lips, drinking
deeply to hide the blush warming her cheeks.

Ned, too, took a long sip of his doctored coffee. "Yeah, I
guess Travis would be tending Gulliver's foreleg—if he were
around. But RJ fired him."

"What!" she exclaimed, so startled she nearly dumped the coffee in her lap. "Dad fired Travis? When?"

"A couple of months back. Although on days like these, it feels like Travis has been gone closer to a year." Ned shook his head. "I told RJ I was too old to manage the entire operation. That's why Travis took over for me in the first place. And he was doing a fine job." He shook his head sadly.

"Then why did Dad fire him?" She simply couldn't understand it. Travis had been almost a son to her father. What could have happened?

With a last swallow of his coffee, Ned leaned forward and plunked his mug onto the large oak desk, exchanging it for a round tin of chewing tobacco.

"Why did he fire Travis?" he repeated as he scooped a fingerful of chaw from the tin and packed it between his lower lip and gum. "I'll tell you why, Miss Margot. It's like they say in the movies: '*Cherchez la femme.*'"

She stared owlishly. The whiskey-laced coffee must have been stronger than she'd thought. She could have sworn Ned was speaking really bad French. "Excuse me?"

"*Cherchez la femme.* Dang it, girl, aren't you the one who's been running around Paris? It means 'look for the woman.'"

It was absurd to feel a spurt of jealousy at hearing Travis was involved with another woman. And really, wasn't eight years long enough to forget those damning words? "No dice, Margot . . . I'm only interested in real women." But that didn't stop her from asking, "What woman was this? And how could she possibly have gotten him fired?"

Ned took his time answering, first spitting a stream of brown tobacco juice into an empty paper cup. Finally he replied unhelpfully, "All that was between your dad and Travis. It doesn't matter anyhow. What's past is past. What I can tell you is that Rosewood Farm is going to rack and ruin without Travis. Gulliver probably wouldn't be injured if he'd been here to ride him."

She frowned. "How did Gulliver get hurt?"

"One day last week, I came back from my lunch break to find Nicole galloping him over a jump course like he's a seasoned Grand Prix jumper instead of a green hunter. She didn't set him up properly for a double oxer, and he stumbled badly on the landing. By the time Nicole handed over the reins to Andy to start cooling him down, I could see he was favoring his foreleg. Now, if Travis had been here, there's no way Nicole would ever have gotten on Gulliver's back. Not even Nicole would have dared go up against Travis. But none of the other guys could stop her, scared she'd have had them sacked." Ned pursed his lips as if tasting something sour.

Unfortunately the description tallied with Margot's memories of her stepmother's high-handedness.

"Well, as you can imagine, I had a few choice words for Nicole when Gulliver came up lame, but hell, the damage was done. And you know what four-year-olds are like—like teenagers in springtime, their heads lost in the clouds. If Gulliver's laid up for three or four weeks, it'll take twice that long to get him back to where he was in his training before his injury. So what are you and your sisters going to do?"

The abrupt change of topic threw her. "Do?" she repeated blankly. "Oh, you mean about Rosewood?"

He scowled impatiently. "'Course I mean Rosewood."

"I don't know. I imagine Dad and Nicole's lawyer will be contacting Jordan about the will."

"May I speak plainly?"

"Of course."

"Miss Jordan, although she's a fine rider, was never bit by the horsebug like you, Miss Margot. Right now, this farm has two studs, ten broodmares, and nine of their get, all at different stages of training. RJ had a terrible round at Culpeper last week with Harvest Moon, a six-year-old gelding who's our most promising prospect. They were eliminated after two refusals—not exactly the best advertisement for selling a hundred-thousand-dollar horse. But at least it forced RJ to accept that we needed a new rider and trainer. That's what he and Nicole were doing in New Jersey. RJ decided to fly to Hunterdon so he could watch Davie Schott compete. They were considering him for the job."

"Did Dad hire him?"

"Nope. I got a call from RJ as he was heading back to the airport. He'd seen Schott and talked to him, and decided he wasn't the man for the job—probably 'cause he didn't know a fraction of what Travis had learned working here all these years."

"So there's no one lined up for the job?"

Ned spat another jet of tobacco juice into the paper cup.

"Nope," he repeated heavily. "Now, me and RJ, we were able to handle all the work by putting in extra hours every day. But there's no dang way I can run this farm single-handedly. I need some experienced help, and I mean *experienced*." His expression softened. "I'm sorry to be burdening you with this when you and your family are grieving. But you know as well as I that it would break RJ's heart if the horses and the business aren't cared for properly."

"I understand. I promise I'll talk to Jordan about it. We'll see what can be done." She couldn't bear to point out the obvious to Ned, whose world revolved around these horses, that as her father wouldn't have included her in the will, she would have little say about what happened to Rosewood Farm. After Nicole and RJ's funerals, she'd be leaving and heading back to her own world.

TRAVIS TOOK a long pull of the beer he'd snagged from the bar. He'd come here with a bunch of the professional riders from Double H Farm, where Hugh Hartmann had hired him as a trainer. His coworkers had urged him to come along, promising that Wednesday nights at Hunters' Run was *the* happening place for horse folk in the Richmond area—Friday and Saturday nights being pretty much a bust for serious equestrians. Riders were either already on the road in a caravan of horse trailers and SUVs or they were hitting the sack early for a predawn haul to whatever weekend show, cross-country event, or hunt was on the docket.

They hadn't been exaggerating. The place was packed, bodies squeezed four deep around the bar, every table and booth taken. It was loud, too, the music cranked, with everyone shouting to be heard. Adding to the din and confusion, the volume on the oversized flat-screen TV suspended over the bar was at full blast. Perhaps as a concession to the bar's female patrons, but more likely because there wasn't a major ball game on, the TV was tuned to an entertainment channel. Right now a bee-sting-lipped starlet was being interviewed.

Lifting his beer bottle for another sip, someone jostled his arm and Travis nearly ended up with a Corona-doused shirt.

"Oops! I am so sorry!" a pretty redhead exclaimed. "Some steroid-pumped Neanderthal was bearing down on me. I had to jump out of the way to save my toes. I didn't spill your beer, did I?" she asked, her brown eyes wide with concern.

"No, not a drop," he assured her.

"Oh, good. I'm Louisa," she announced cheerfully. With a casual flick of her hand, she brushed back her hair, treating him to a very nice view of her breasts. The warmth of her dimpled smile assured him that with very little encouragement she'd be willing to offer him a more intimate inspection of her bounty.

He raised his beer in salutation, acknowledging her unspoken invitation with a grin. "Hey there, Louisa, I'm Travis."

"Travis." She said his name slowly. "I like that. Strong. Different. You new around here, Travis?"

"You could say that. I've been working at the Double H for about a month and a half."

"Hugh Hartmann's place? Very nice. What do you do there?"

"I'm a trainer."

"A trainer, huh? Do you ride, too?"

"Yep," Travis replied with an easy nod. "And what is it you do, Louisa?"

"I'm an agent with Arundel Equine Insurance. But I love to ride. I'm pretty good, but I'm always looking for tips from the experts. Maybe you could give me some pointers—"

"'Scuse me, coming through," bellowed a flushed patron.

Louisa stepped closer so the guy could get within hailing distance of the bartender, but he must have bumped her as he passed, for she gave an "Oh!" of surprise, tottered, and landed against Travis.

Her lush breasts felt pretty darn spectacular.

Instinctively he placed a steadying hand under her elbow. Instead of righting herself, however, she arched closer, looking up at him with a slow, sultry smile. For a second they stared into each other's eyes and Travis knew they'd just fast-forwarded to the "Your place or mine?" stage of the evening.

Then he heard someone call, "Yo, Travis! Over here, man!"

Reluctantly he glanced toward the bar. Jon Cahill, one of the riders at the Double H, was over by the bartender. He waved his hand and Travis saw a flash of green. "Ready for another?"

"No, thanks. I'm good."

"Damn sure looks that way," Cahill shouted with an approving nod toward Louisa. Grinning, he gave Travis the thumbs-up sign.

Directly above Jon's head, a blaze of bright colors flooded the TV. A line of models appeared, parading down a dramatically lit runway, as the TV announcer said, "While the weather may be cooling, things in Milan, Italy, have been sizzling. For all you dedicated fashionistas, here's our style correspondent, who's been attending Milan's celebrated fashion week with the inside scoop on the hottest resort wear."

A new clip flashed onto the screen. And there she was, alone on the runway, as if he'd conjured her. She was wearing a gold-patterned scarfy thing that tied about her neck and ended just below her swaying hips. Her mile-long legs shimmered under the bright lights and her streaked blond hair was teased in a tangled halo. She looked gorgeous and wild, as untamed as a lioness stalking her prey. Mesmerized, he stared as she sauntered toward him, her hands moving casually to the knot in the fabric. She stopped, her hips cocked and her shoulders squared, and let the scarf slide down her like molten gold.

A soft hiss escaped him at the fire-engine-red scraps barely covering her. Just to torment him further, a gold chain encircled her slender waist. A full-blown fantasy exploded in Travis's mind: his open mouth running over that chain, his tongue tracing the metal links and tasting the salt on her skin while his fingers slipped beneath the red-hot triangle to touch the fire inside her . . .

She was moving again, spinning in a slow circle so the world could have a 360-degree view of the bite-sized bikini.

As if anyone who saw her actually cared a flying fuck what she was wearing. Not when they could look at *her*—that face, that mouth, that body—

"*Oh, Travis!*" a husky voice purred.

As if waking from a dream, Travis slowly regained a sense of his surroundings. He was in a bar in Richmond and Margot Radcliffe was on another continent. No, he corrected. She was a world away. Like always.

He had a hard-on that was pressing against his fly and it wasn't for the woman who was plastered against him—no matter how appreciative Louisa seemed to be.

Damn it all to hell. Louisa was clinging like Scotch tape, her hands getting real familiar real fast. He tore his gaze away from the TV even though he was dying for another glimpse of Margot. He now knew for certain that God existed and that the Almighty had decided Travis should pay for his sins right here on earth. This was his personal damnation: to be forever subjected to the mind-blowing spectacle of Margot stripping without ever being able to reach out and take her in his arms. He was condemned to be left wanting her so badly he trembled.

"Oh, honey, you seem desperate," Louisa cooed, rising up on tiptoes, her warm breath teasing his ear. "Me, too. This scene is way too crowded. Let's you and I go somewhere private." She caught his earlobe between her teeth and bit lightly.

He didn't even hesitate. "Sounds like a great idea, Louisa, but I'm afraid I can't." He stepped back as far as the crush would allow. "I've got to drive to North Carolina first thing tomorrow morning. I have some clients who are looking for a hunter prospect. Another time, maybe."

She stared at him in marked disbelief. When she saw he was serious, though, she rallied enough to muster a smile. "Yeah, sure, another time. You can call me at Arundel."

"Sure thing. See you, Louisa," he lied. He wouldn't be seeing her again. Not when visions of Margot continued to torment him.

Chapter ❧
SEVEN

IT SEEMED TO MARGOT that she'd only just shut her eyes when the phone rang. Her lids heavy with sleep, she sat up, shoved her hair out of her face, and cast a bleary eye about the room. A momentary panic filled her at the strange surroundings. Where was she, Milan? she wondered.

Then, from beyond the curtained windows, she heard birds singing. Noted, too, the total absence of city noises. The events of yesterday came rushing back—Carlo de Calvi's fashion show, Jordan's call, airports, her father . . . dead. Beneath the quilted coverlet she shivered. She knew where she was now: in her childhood bedroom, which Nicole had stripped of every personal belonging, as if she might thus erase Margot's very existence.

Her cell pealed again. Margot stretched out her arm toward the bedside table and grabbed the phone. Pressing the *talk* button, she got her cotton-filled mouth working enough to mumble, "Hello?"

"Margot, that you?" Her agent's clipped British accent sounded in her ear. "Darling, your voice mail is completely full. I've been trying to reach you forever."

"Hi, Damien." She glanced at her watch. Still on Milan time. "What time is it?"

"Seven o'clock."

That meant Damien had already returned from his workout at the gym. He'd be showered and shaved, his wavy black hair perfectly combed. As this was a weekday, he'd be dressed for work: pleated flannel trousers, a custom-made English shirt, Italian loafers. His second cup of cappuccino would be half-empty and sitting near his elbow. "Sorry I didn't get a chance to call yesterday, Damien. It was—"

"I quite understand, love. Anika rang when she got back to the hotel. Have you seen your father? Is he—"

"Dad died a few minutes after I arrived." The pain was ragged and raw.

"Oh, Margot, I'm so very sorry. How devastating for you."

"Yeah."

Damien fell silent on his end of the line. Margot figured he was remembering those long-ago days when she'd first signed with his agency, back when she was still calling and writing her father. More often than not it was Damien's silk handkerchief that she wept into after her father once again ignored her attempts at reconciliation. Maybe he was remembering, too, the time she mailed her father her first shot for *Vogue,* proof that she'd succeeded where he'd believed she would fail. She'd sent an accompanying note, listing her address and numbers, sure she'd get some kind of acknowledgment. But there'd been nothing from him. Nada. Zip. That was when she'd given up trying to contact him, finally convinced that he'd never change his mind, that nothing could sway his heart.

"Listen, love, do you want me to fly down?"

Margot's mouth curled as she pictured Damien Barnes, the quintessentially hip and sophisticated cosmopolite, transplanted to Warburg, Virginia. Damien liked to order take-out food at ten P.M., and then rent an obscure 1940s Swedish movie at midnight. If he was in the mood to scope out new trends and scout for fresh faces, he'd round up a few of the girls and they'd go clubbing till dawn. Frothy cappuccinos were as essential to him as air and had to be less than a five-block walk away. Yet here he was, willing to leave New York, his beloved adopted city, so he could sit with her and lend his silk handkerchief for her to cry into once again.

She swallowed hard. "Thanks, Damien, really. But I'm okay. Jordan's here."

"Oh, good. How much longer do you need to be down there?"

"I don't know. I guess I'll have a better sense after we've dealt with the funeral arrangements."

"As luck would have it, this is a perfect time to take a brief holiday from the cameras. It'll keep everyone salivating for more Margot. Apropos of salivating, I spoke with de Calvi yesterday. He said you were *favolosa*. The *Times* thought so, too. I had Miranda run out at the crack of dawn to get a copy at the newsstand. There's a fabulous pic of you in the raw silk palazzo pants and the knitted halter top."

"Really?" Margot tried to inject the proper amount of enthusiasm in her voice.

"Your stock is sky-high, love. Oh, here's something else to cheer you up. Guess who's been hired to shoot the Dior campaign?"

"Who?"

"Charlie Ayer," Damien crowed. "Good ol' Charlie. God, I adore that man. Nobody makes you look more luscious."

"That's just because Charlie feels like he's got a personal stake in me."

"A detail he'll never let me forget. Every time he rings, it's, 'Hey, Damien, Charlie here.'" Damien's accent changed, his crisp vowels assuming a California looseness in a perfect imitation of Charlie Ayer's laid-back speech. "'Listen, I have to borrow Margot for a few days. You'll waive her fee, of course. Don't forget, I discovered her.' The cocky bastard," Damien continued affectionately in his own voice, sounding more like the fallen aristocrat than ever. "No doubt he'll be ringing to discuss the shoot. Thank heaven you're his favorite girl. He'll be flexible when it comes to scheduling—though I can't promise the same for the Dior people."

"I promise I'll call the second I have a clearer idea of how long I'll be down here. In the meantime, send Charlie my love."

"To hear Charlie tell it, your love is all he's waiting for. *Ciao, bella.*"

Shaking her head over Damien's affectionate teasing, Margot turned off the phone, slipped out of bed, and padded into the bathroom. But as she showered away her lingering grogginess, then dressed, donning a pair of pencil-leg sky-blue velvet jeans and an alabaster V-neck cashmere sweater, her thoughts kept returning to Damien's parting comment.

Ordinarily, she would have brushed off her agent's remark that Charlie was serious about her, just as she'd brushed off Charlie's repeated declarations of love.

But as of yesterday, her world had changed dramatically. And now she had to ask herself if she wasn't being foolish in not giving their relationship a real chance. After all, they had fun together and she enjoyed his happy-go-lucky charm. And she owed Charlie so much.

When he'd obligingly whisked her away from Rosewood in his vintage Mustang, she'd had no idea that she'd just been befriended by one of the hot young photographers in the business or that Charlie Ayer's work peppered the pages of *W, Vogue, Elle,* and *Harper's Bazaar.* Nor did she have any inkling of how lucky she was that Charlie insisted she go see Damien Barnes first, assuring her that Damien, of all the agents in the business, could be trusted to "treat a kid like her right."

Damien had done far more than that.

She'd gone to the agent's Park Avenue South office with no experience, no portfolio, not even a head shot—nothing but Charlie's business card, on the back of which he'd scrawled "A present for you, Damien. And, dude, I expect major thanks!"

With a weak smile, she'd handed Charlie's card to the receptionist and taken a seat in a waiting room notable for the sheer number of glossy magazines fanned out on the low, circular coffee tables. An hour passed. And then two. But she'd had nowhere else to go, so she'd sat there as girls, each one more exotic than the last, sauntered through with cheerful calls of "Hi, Miranda" to the receptionist, who waved them into the inner office, the exclusive preserve of the jaw-droppingly lovely.

What had she been thinking to believe Charlie Ayer's promise that Damien Barnes would take her on? What in the world would she do when five o'clock rolled around and Miranda politely and efficiently told her to scat?

"Mr. Barnes will see you now."

"Wha—what?" Margot had stammered. "You mean me?"

"Yes, you," came the amused reply before she went and gave a light rap on the door, pushed it open, and motioned Margot inside.

Damien Barnes sat behind a sleek glass desk. "Keep walking. I want to see you move."

With his sharp gaze riveted on her, she walked about the photograph-lined office, feeling increasingly clumsy and foolish. Just how were models supposed to walk? Should she thrust her hips forward? Wiggle them?

Then the questions began. Damien Barnes fired them off in rapid succession, asking her name, age, hometown, education, weight, height, special talents, favorite exercise, eating habits. Just when her nerves were nearly fried because she couldn't remember when the last time she'd stepped on a bathroom scale was, and had convinced herself that she didn't know how to put one foot in front of the other—which made her about the biggest dope in the world—he told her to take a seat.

Without preamble, he said, "So you want to be a fashion model? Why?"

Why? With an eighteen-year-old's stupidity she'd blurted out, "Because I can't type?"

Damien had not been amused. "Then you're wasting my time as well as your own," he'd replied, his cool tone shaming her. "You'll never make it as a model with that kind of attitude, no matter how bloody gorgeous you are."

She stared at him in astonishment. He thought she was beautiful, when any one of those girls who'd traipsed into the office was ten times more arresting?

He made an impatient gesture with his hand. "'Course you're beautiful. Charlie isn't the only one who can spot the potential of a face like yours. But I'm talking about modeling, the business. It's not a lark. To succeed you've got to have smarts and you've got to be a damned hard worker. Now, I might be able to get you a booking or two, but if you want to last longer than a couple of weeks, if you want to hit the big time and land the cover of *W* year after year, you'll need more than beauty. Reaching the top requires discipline. You know anything about that?" he asked.

"No," she said honestly. "I'm not really good at anything except riding horses. But I'm willing to learn. I'm not afraid to work."

"Good. Then here's your first homework assignment." Damien stood up, walked over to a corner bookshelf, and pulled out a thick, clothbound book. He handed it to her. "Study this carefully. It has fashion's greatest photographers in it. Educate yourself so you can adapt to the photographer's vision." Abruptly he asked, "Do you understand a bloody thing I'm saying?"

Deciding honesty was definitely the best policy with Damien, she shook her head. "No."

He smiled. "Okay. Let's take your pal Charlie Ayer. Simply put, he's brilliant, a genius with light, form, and texture. But Charlie's best pics happen when he's got a model he can really work with. What that means, darling, is that you've got to understand his work, his style, his vision. Your job as a model isn't just to be a pretty young thing but to help him create the vision he's dreaming of. Then, when he sees that perfect shot, he's going to know he was able to capture it because *you* were the one in front of his lens. It's the same story when you're on the runway. It doesn't matter whether the designer is Stella McCartney or Karl Lagerfeld. You've got to learn how to wear those bits of fabric they've stitched together so that when you walk down that runway, the audience sits up, electrified." Rounding his desk, he leaned against it and folded his arms across his chest. "So, you still want to be a model? Or shall I have Miranda look up the address of a typing school?"

She moistened her lips nervously. "I'd like to give it a shot."

"Clever girl. Now, before we sign anything, let me tell you my rules: I insist that you be honest, reliable, and drug-free. When you're not in front of the camera or strutting your stuff on the catwalk, you keep your nose clean. I don't care what they're shoving into your hand backstage or passing out at the parties and clubs. You do drugs, you're finished with me. Period. No second chances. I've seen too many lives destroyed by them, and I won't have that on my conscience. The same holds for alcohol. Even when the bubbly is flowing like the bloody Trevi Fountain, limit yourself to one glass. After that, switch to San Pellegrino with a slice of lemon. It's good for your skin."

As Damien Barnes ticked off his rules one by one, Margot felt an unexpected, extraordinary sense of liberation: he didn't care who she was or where she came from, only who she might *become.* Her past didn't matter to him. And he was offering a surefire way for her to prove to her father that she was more than a two-legged broodmare. This was her chance to show Travis, too, that she wasn't a spoiled princess, incapable of a hard day's work.

"And if the stress of all the baiting and backstabbing that goes on in this business starts to make you bonkers," he continued, "sign up for a gym membership. One of our models, Anika, swears by kickboxing. She's looking for a flatmate, by the way. Do you need a place to live?"

It had been two A.M. when Charlie and she rolled into the
city. She'd spent the remainder of the night curled up on the
leather sofa in his Chelsea studio. It wouldn't feel right to
stay there. Though Charlie was cool and a really good guy,
she didn't want to give him the wrong idea—especially when
she couldn't stop thinking of Travis. By now he'd have
learned about her leaving. Was he sorry? Was he already
missing her? Would he come find her here in New York and
bring her home?

The prospect lifted her heart. "Yeah, I guess I do."

He nodded. "I'll ring Anika, then. The two of you can
meet and see if you hit it off. Well, that's it. You abide by my
rules, you work your pretty bum off for me, and I'll do the
same for you. Do we have a deal?"

She stood and shook his outstretched hand. "Yes, Mr.
Barnes, we definitely have a deal."

"Damien, love," he corrected with a grin.

They'd both stuck to their deal.

Margot had worked her butt off learning how to pose
for photographers and she'd kept away from the drugs
and booze and other crap that messed up too many
others in the business. In return she found in Damien an
agent who was honest and who cared about the models he
represented.

For that alone she owed Charlie a huge debt. But Charlie
had done more than line her up with a great agent. He'd
quickly become more than the photographer who'd "discovered" her, too. He'd become one of her closest friends,
taking her to the best restaurants, clubs, and parties. And
though they both dated widely, they were spotted together
often enough to be considered an "item."

It occurred to her that perhaps Charlie had begun to
believe the ever-buzzing gossip. That would account for how
frequently he professed his love for her these days. But from
the very first, Charlie's declarations always struck Margot
as a bit too glib. And whenever she was on location or

modeling for a show, he lost no time finding a glamorous replacement to squire around.

While she knew he cared, she couldn't help feeling that she was just a shade *too* replaceable, and that if she were ever to leave town for good, Charlie wouldn't pine for long. So she'd resisted any steps toward a deeper commitment, saying that she wasn't ready to settle down yet and that she needed to focus on her career while it was going strong. This last explanation was a more than acceptable one, as anyone in the business knew that the day would soon come when some fourteen-year-old waif would be elbowing her off the catwalk and landing every booking in town.

But deep down, Margot had always recognized that the reasons she gave him were really just convenient excuses to mask the truth. While she adored Charlie, her heart didn't squeeze painfully at the mere mention of his name . . . the way it had when she'd heard Travis's last night.

It was insane for her still to be carrying a torch for Travis Maher. Walking through the barn last night, half-expecting to find him there, had shown her how deluded she'd been to believe she'd gotten over him. The news that he was gone from Rosewood, that in all likelihood she would never see him again, had left her with a terrible emptiness.

In the last twenty-four hours so many of her dreams had turned to dust. Perhaps it was time to accept the fact that Travis would never be more than a ghost from her past. She should move on with her life, instead of waiting for something that would never happen, yearning for someone who never had and never would love her.

It was funny; Margot had always heard people say they'd found their childhood homes or backyards to be shockingly small when they returned after a long absence. With her, the opposite was true. As she descended the wide, circular staircase, morning sunshine poured through the tall windows. Bathed in the pale golden light, the airy proportions of

Rosewood were even grander than her memories of them. It was she who felt tiny and insignificant.

She wandered through the double parlor overwhelmed by nostalgia. Everything, the mahogany furniture, the gilt-framed mirrors, the oil paintings of Rosewood's past studs, the broadloom rugs, even the knickknacks—the porcelain hunting dogs pointing at an unseen quarry, the silver-plated trophies transformed into table lamps—was in its place, just as she remembered. The dining room's oval table, which when fully extended could seat sixteen, gleamed from a recent polishing, its shiny surface reflecting the crystal teardrops of the chandelier.

Jordan was in the kitchen, seated at the granite-topped island. Her hands were cupped around a mug as she stared pensively out the window over the kitchen sink. A plate of toast sat untouched by her elbow.

"Hey, did you sleep okay?" she asked, giving her a quick hug.

"Pretty well, considering. How about you?"

Margot sat down on the stool beside her. "About the same. Is Jade awake?"

"No. I stuck my head in her room as I was coming down. She's fast asleep. The longer the better, in my opinion. We don't have to be at the funeral parlor until twelve. What can I get you? Coffee, tea, something to eat?" she asked, already getting to her feet.

"You don't have to make me anything."

"I'd like to, really. It makes me feel better. I'm totally adrift without the kids and Richard and the usual Stevens breakfast chaos."

"All right. Thanks. How about some coffee and toast?"

"Coming right up," Jordan said with a determined smile as she lifted the coffeemaker's carafe and filled it at the sink.

"When will Richard be here?"

"Any moment now. I've been jumping at every noise, hoping it's them. Even little Roy's impatient," she said, patting her tummy.

"Roy? Is that the name you and Richard have chosen for the baby?"

"No," Jordan said with a laugh. "I don't even know if it's a boy. But we've always picked silly nicknames for the kids throughout my pregnancies. This one," she said, splaying her fingers across the wool of her sage-green cardigan, "is Roy Rogers. During my first trimester I had such an insatiable craving for Roy Rogers hamburgers that Richard joked we should invest in the company."

Margot couldn't help feeling a pang of envy at the closeness Jordan shared with Richard and the family they'd made together. She wondered whether someday she'd be lucky enough to have that, too. If she was ever blessed with a little girl, she'd tell her that she could grow up to be anything she wanted to be.

"You're sure coffee and toast are all you can eat?" Jordan asked. "There's a lot of food in the refrigerator. We shouldn't let it go to waste." As soon as she'd uttered the words, she shook her head. "I can't believe I said that. It sounded so callous. I can't get my mind around the fact that Dad and Nicole are gone, not just on a trip but forever. What are we going to do, Margot?"

"Get through it step by step. What else can we do?"

Jordan nodded. "Right. First step, breakfast."

The kitchen was a direct contrast to the rest of the house, all efficient, twenty-first-century technology, Nicole having insisted on having it gutted and remodeled. Hence the gleaming, vaultlike Sub-Zero refrigerator, Viking range, and convection oven. The counters were granite, the cabinets were made of cherrywood, and the ceramic floor tiles came from Italy. Few restaurants had kitchens this fine or spacious. At the other end of the kitchen, near the back door and the mudroom/pantry, was a long pine table they'd used for lunch and casual suppers—not that Margot remembered meals with Nicole as ever being casual or relaxed.

As Margot watched Jordan fix her breakfast, it struck her how different they were. Her sister looked completely at ease in the space, while Margot hadn't a clue how half of the kitchen's gadgets worked, let alone what a convection oven actually did. Growing up, she'd preferred being outside, riding cross-country or hanging around the barns, grooming Suzy Q, Piper, and Killarney, and being near . . . No, she wasn't going to think about Travis anymore, and she slammed the door on yet another memory.

The toaster dinged. Jordan extracted the toast and, placing it on a china plate, walked over to the fridge. "Butter?"

"You must be joking."

"Come on, you're as thin as you were as a teen!"

Margot shrugged. "I have to be. The camera is unforgiving."

"Then, how about some honey or blackberry jam?"

"I'll take honey, please."

Jordan found a jar of honey in the door of the refrigerator. Turning back to Margot, she said, "Do you remember Edward Crandall, Dad and Nicole's lawyer?" as she placed the toast and honey before her and handed her a knife and spoon. "Coffee's coming right up."

"Thanks. Edward Crandall?" Margot said as she scooped half a teaspoon of honey and spread it on the toast. "No, I can't say I remember him."

"He's a big fox hunter. He's been the Warburg Hunt's field master for the past four years."

"Ahh," Margot intoned. "Enough said. And how many of Rosewood Farm's horses does he have?"

"Dad sold him at least three, maybe more. Anyway, I left a message on his answering machine last night, telling him about Dad and Nicole and asking him to notify the insurance agency about the crash. I imagine he'll be contacting us as soon as he arrives at his office." She paused to fetch Margot a ceramic mug from the cupboard and pour a dark, fragrant stream of freshly brewed coffee into it. Then, sitting down on the stool beside her, she picked up her own mug of herbal tea. "I can't help worrying about what will happen to Jade. I wonder who Dad and Nicole asked to be her guardian."

"Would they have named you?" Margot asked, taking the mug from her.

Jordan shook her head. "It wasn't as if Nicole was overly fond of me, either," she said ruefully. "And I'm sure they'd have told me if they wanted me to be Jade's guardian."

"I guess you'll find out when the wills are read. In the meantime, I'll help out in any way I can. Damien's not booking me for anything right now."

"Thanks. My head starts spinning every time I start to think about Dad and Nicole and what will happen to Jade, to the house." Her voice trailed off.

"Don't forget the horses. I saw Ned at the barn last night. With Dad gone, he'll be running the farm on his own. He's none too happy about that. I promised him I'd talk to you and try to figure out a solution."

"What about Travis?" she asked, frowning in bewilderment.

So Jordan hadn't known about Dad and Travis's falling out. "He's gone. According to Ned, Dad fired him."

"Dad fired Travis? No, he couldn't have." Jordan slumped in her stool. "This is terrible. I wish Rich—" She broke off at the sound of a car honking. "Oh, thank God, he's here!" And she rushed out of the kitchen to greet her family.

Margot was eager to see how much Kate and Max had grown, but she remained in the kitchen so Jordan could have a private moment with her husband and children. She poured a second cup of coffee and was munching a last bite of toast when Jade, dressed in baggy pajamas and slippers, shuffled into the kitchen. She looked like a wreck, her face puffy from tears, her eyes rimmed with red, her dark blond hair a matted mass of snarls. She may have slept, but the rest hadn't eased her suffering. Sympathy welled inside Margot.

"You're sitting in my mom's place." Jade glared at her, eyes hard and accusatory.

The half-swallowed piece of toast scratched the inside of Margot's suddenly constricted throat. *Don't react,* she told herself.

"I was just finishing my breakfast." Calmly she rose from the stool and cleared her coffee cup and plate.

While she loaded the dirty dishes into the dishwasher, Jade climbed onto the stool next to the one Margot had vacated. "Where's Jordan?"

"Outside." She decided to leave the coffee in the pot. Richard might want a cup. "Richard and the kids have just arrived," she added.

"Terrific." Her sarcastic tone had Margot glancing over in surprise.

"What?" Jade demanded, with the sneer Margot was beginning to recognize. "Those kids are brats. They never do anything but whine and cry."

"I like them a lot."

Jade stiffened in her chair.

"Do you want some breakfast?"

The sneer morphed into a glower. "I'm not hungry."

Margot suppressed a sigh. After drying her hands on the dish towel, she hung it on the oven door and then turned to face Jade. "Listen, I understand how you're feeling right now. I know you're hurting but you really need to eat, your body can't—"

"I already told you, *I'm not hungry.* And you don't know how I feel. You can't possibly know how I feel—you don't even *know* me. 'You really need to eat,'" she mimicked. "What a joke, you standing there and pretending to care about me. You don't care about anyone but yourself."

Margot recoiled as though she'd been slapped in the face. "Jade—"

"No, I don't want to hear anything you have to say. You're such a fake, you make me want to hurl!" She jumped down from the stool, sending it crashing to the floor as she ran from the kitchen, pounding up the back stairs.

Reeling from the open hostility, Margot gripped the counter. *Leave it to a teenager to find the chink in one's armor.* Her half-sister's weapon of choice was the cold, hard truth, and she'd driven it home ruthlessly. Although Margot tried to hide it, Jade must have sensed her lingering ambivalence and resentment toward her and Nicole.

The blistering accusation made Margot aware of another offense she'd committed: since picking her up at Malden she'd been looking for similarities between Jade and Nicole, mentally tallying up black marks against her young half-sister.

How pathetic. And Jade, as grief-stricken as she was, had seen right through her. Margot closed her eyes, sick and ashamed. She'd have to figure out how to apologize before she returned to New York, though a part of her doubted that anything she said could ever breach the gulf separating them.

The sound of footsteps ringing on the hardwood floors and of voices speaking all at once—Jordan, Richard, and the kids coming down the hall—had her thoughts shifting to what good families were all about: caring and sharing.

The family Jade had depended on had been destroyed. Margot had no idea who among her father's and Nicole's set had been named as Jade's guardian, but she hoped whoever it was possessed the patience and understanding required to help the grief-ridden teen.

THEY BURIED RJ and Nicole two days later in a private ceremony with only the family, Ned, the stable hands, and Ellie
and Patrick Banner, who oversaw the house and garden, in
attendance. Jordan had arranged for their Washington
babysitter to come to Rosewood to care for Kate and Max
during the ceremony after she and Richard had decided
that the double burial would be too traumatic for the
children.

The morning was overcast and cold enough that Margot's
breath came in little cloudlike puffs. She stood a few feet
from the twin gaping holes the backhoe had dug in the
earth. In the bottom of each lay a varnished walnut coffin.
The sweet clear notes of the flutist hired to perform floated
in the air. The piece, a Bach sonata, was beautiful and
solemn, yet Margot remained oddly untouched. She was
numb from the quiet, relentless horror of the events of the
recent days: selecting coffins and headstones with the funeral
director, rummaging through their father's and Nicole's
wardrobes for burial clothes, receiving endless calls from
neighbors and friends of RJ and Nicole as word of the
tragedy spread. Not even discussing the arrangements for
the burial with the minister had provided much solace, for
by then Margot had shut down emotionally.

They had all shut down, she thought, glancing at Jade's
drawn profile. She was as pale as a sheet but dry-eyed. On
the other side of Jade, Jordan clutched Richard's arm while
her lips moved silently in prayer.

The final notes of the sonata drifted away on the cool

breeze. Reverend Stuart Wilde stepped forward, his Bible
open in his hands. He read:

The Lord is my shepherd; I shall not want.
He maketh me to lie down in green pastures:
He leadeth me beside the still waters;
He restoreth my soul:
He leadeth me in the paths of righteousness for His name
    sake.
Yea, though I walk through the valley of the shadow of
    death,
I will fear no evil: For thou art with me;
Thy rod and thy staff, they comfort me.
Thou preparest a table before me in the presence of mine
    enemies;
Thou annointest my head with oil; My cup runneth over.
Surely goodness and mercy shall follow me all the days of
    my life,
and I will dwell in the House of the Lord forever.

"Amen," she whispered and the word echoed around her.
Silence descended as the reverend closed his Bible and
turned toward Jordan. He gestured toward the long-handled
shovel that was stuck into a pile of dirt at the foot of Nicole's
grave in readiness. Jordan nodded and stepped away from
Richard's side. She stopped first at Nicole's grave, scattering
a shovelful of earth over the coffin. In the hushed atmo-
sphere, the sound of the dirt hitting and bouncing off the
wood surface was amplified, an almost violent cascade.
Before their father's grave, Jordan paused, her auburn head
bowed. Margot could see her shoulders shaking beneath her
cashmere coat. Her head still lowered, she turned away from
the graves.

It was Margot's turn. She grasped the shovel, its shaft
smooth and cold against her palms as she sank the blade
into the earth. With a twist of her wrists, the dirt rained over

Nicole's casket. She thought of how young her stepmother had been. *May you rest in peace, Nicole,* she whispered in her head.

At her father's grave, emotions she thought had been blunted by shock rose inside her, as brutally sharp as ever. Tears clogged her throat. She found herself repeating the words she'd written to him so many times. *I'm sorry, Dad. I'm sorry for everything. . . . If only you would forgive me.*

She stepped back and held the shovel out to Jade. Her half-sister's face was set in harsh lines, a girl abruptly old before her time. Realizing she couldn't bear to watch Jade make her good-byes, she let her head fall back. She stared at the ugly gray sky, while salty tears stung her eyes.

When at last Margot lowered her gaze, it was no longer Jade who stood before the two graves, but Ned. He'd exchanged his favorite khakis for a dark suit. His shoes were polished to a high gloss. Standing in line behind Ned and, like him, dressed in their Sunday best were the stable hands. The sight of her father's employees, their hair neatly combed and slicked, solemnly waiting to pay their last respects made her want to rail against the injustice of fate. What would happen to these men now that her father was gone? What would happen to the horses they all loved?

After kissing both Jordan and Jade, Ned walked over to Margot. He cleared his throat, and then, with a frown of concentration, as if wanting to be certain his words came out right, he said, "Your father was never an easy man, Miss Margot. Near about everybody knew RJ was as hard-headed as they come, not the type to change his mind once it was made up. Couldn't and wouldn't." He sighed. "Some people are like that. Nothing can convince them to change their views or to see a situation from a different perspective. For them, it's almost like a point of honor, a code of conduct they pride themselves on. With RJ, that rigidity not only hurt others, it hurt him as well. I believe he came to regret the things he'd done but couldn't bring himself to undo.

Because at heart, your father was a good man," he finished stoutly.

She laid a hand on his arm. "Thank you, Ned. You're the person who knew Dad the best and the longest so it means a lot to hear that."

"I guess I was at that, though Travis and RJ were real close, too. These past couple years your father relied on him more and more. We all did. It's a real shame Travis wasn't here today. I called to tell him about the accident so he could come and pay his respects, but the gal at Hugh Hartmann's place said he was on a buying trip with some clients and wouldn't be back until the day after tomorrow, in time for the sales at Crestview."

That's right, Margot thought, it was the third week in October, which meant all the horsemen in the region would be descending on Crestview's Equestrian Center for the fall horse auction. Her father never missed it.

"Even with RJ's passing, I reckon on attending the sales," Ned continued. "I'll tell Travis the news when I see him there. It doesn't matter that he and RJ parted on bad terms: he'd want to know."

"Of course. And please tell Travis we're sorry that he couldn't be here," she returned evenly, despite the lurch of her heart. As soon as things were settled here, she'd be gone, she reminded herself. Hundreds of miles away. Perhaps after the Dior shoot she'd ask Damien to book her a location gig, in which case she could be anywhere . . . the Seychelles, Budapest, Paris.

The service was over. Her sisters and the others filed quietly out of the family plot, but Margot lingered to watch the men sent by the funeral home, who were bending to their task, scooping up shovelfuls of dirt and pouring them into the rectangular holes.

Fighting tears once again, she looked away, only to have her gaze land on an achingly familiar headstone. As a girl, she'd often stolen away here, to lie on the grass beside her mother's grave and pour out the secrets of her heart, telling her everything she couldn't say to the living. The grass in front of the marker was yellow and dry now, but she could summon the rich scent of clover and English tea roses, which her father asked Patrick Banner to plant a few feet from where her mother rested.

At that moment, Margot wanted nothing more than to fling herself upon the autumn grass and once again pour out all the loneliness and fear inside her. *Oh, Mama, I haven't grown up very much in all these years, have I?*

Her thoughts scattered when a hand touched her elbow. "May I accompany you back up to the house, Margot?" the reverend asked. "Or would you like some time by yourself?"

It was tempting to stay and try to find some kind of peace, but then Margot remembered that Jordan wanted to offer the minister a cup of tea before Edward Crandall, the lawyer and executor of the estate, arrived. "Thank you. I'd love your company."

He gallantly offered her the crook of his arm and together they wound their way past headstones carved with the names of Margot's ancestors, and then, near the worn fence, the line of smaller stones, on which were bronze plaques engraved with the names of Rosewood's finest studs.

The reverend paused at the gate so Margot could precede him. Shutting it behind him he said, "You were perhaps too young to remember, Margot, but I performed the burial service for your mother, too. As terrible as that day was and as heartbreaking as today is, I have always thought that this piece of land is one of Virginia's loveliest." He extended his arm in a broad sweep that encompassed the neatly fenced fields where the broodmares grazed, the wind lifting their tails and sending fallen leaves skittering between their sleek legs and barrel-shaped bellies, the barns in the distance, and the magnificent allée of chestnut trees leading to the house. "A body could do worse than live and die among these hills."

"Yes, a body could do a great deal worse."

"I'm glad you see that, too."

Though he'd smiled as he'd spoken there was something in his expression that made her ask, "Is anything the matter, Reverend Wilde?"

"Stuart, my dear," he corrected her kindly. "Let's not stand on formalities when we've known each other for so many years." He paused and his expression slipped back into a worried frown. "I hope you won't take what I say next for an old man's meddling, but I believe you should know that several unsavory rumors have been buzzing about town for a couple of months now." He gave a small smile. "I can see you're surprised. My dear, you'd be amazed at how much a man in my position is privy to. Now, I'm not going to repeat what I've heard—in all likelihood nothing more than petty gossip. But in case even a breath of it is true, may I give you some advice?" His steps and hers slowed to a halt.

"I'd very much like to hear it. My sisters and I need all the help we can get."

"My best advice to you is for you and your sisters to bear in mind the following. No matter how dark the coming days seem, remember that there have always been Radcliffes at Rosewood. You're a strong woman, Margot. Don't be afraid to stand up for what's in your heart. The easy solutions aren't always the right ones. Once something precious is let go, you risk living a life shadowed by regrets." Taking her chilled hands in his, he squeezed them encouragingly. "Don't let yourself make the same mistake your father did."

Margot helped Jordan with the tea, and then carried the tray laden with the service and a lemon pound cake baked by one of the neighbors into the double parlor. As news of RJ's and Nicole's deaths spread, people had started dropping by with offerings of food and words of sympathy, and now a mountain range of baked goods covered the kitchen counters. The refrigerator and freezer were crammed with foil-wrapped roasts and casseroles. There were stews and soups in Tupperware containers of every imaginable size.

Stuart Wilde was settled in a wingback chair by the crack-ling fire, which Ellie had lit to chase away the melancholy of the day. Jade had claimed the chaise longue in the corner and was broodingly watching Kate and Max, who were sprawled on the floor playing with a wooden farm and a bucket of plastic animals. Once the tea was poured and slices of cake offered around, Jordan sank down on the pale blue and gold damask sofa next to Richard and chatted politely with the reverend while he sipped his tea and made serious inroads on the cake.

Seated on the opposite side of the fireplace, Margot tried to follow the conversation, but her thoughts returned repeat-edly to what Stuart had hinted at earlier as they were leaving the family plot. What were these rumors circulating about her family? Were they the reason so many of the neighbors who'd dropped off their apple pies and meat loaves seemed set to burst with curiosity and why they'd made so many veiled remarks about the "terrible strain RJ had been under." What strain? Margot couldn't begin to imagine—unless it had to do with what Ned had divulged, about the woman who'd come between Dad and Travis.

Who was she, anyway? The question had been preying on Margot's mind more than she cared to admit. Had the woman left with Travis when he was fired or was she still here in Warburg? It occurred to Margot that she could be a local; she could be anyone, a friend, a neighbor—even one of the ladies who'd thrust an aluminum-wrapped offering into Margot's hands as she said how devastated she was for the family's loss. The notion made her want to run into the kitchen and toss every last coffee cake and frozen turkey Tetrazzini into the garbage.

Stuart was polishing off another slice of pound cake, pro-nouncing it "too delicious to resist," when the doorbell chimed.

Jordan glanced at the slim gold watch on her wrist. "That must be Mr. Crandall."

"I'll get it." Richard rose from the sofa with a look of undisguised relief and left the parlor like a prisoner making a jailbreak. Okay, so having tea with the local minister was admittedly not the most exciting activity for a high-octane Washington lobbyist, but this wasn't the first time Margot had noticed Richard's naked impatience. Over the past two days there had been times when Jordan was talking to him when that same expression had crossed his face. She found his attitude baffling and disturbing, because not only did Jordan really need his love and support right now but it also was clear to anyone with eyes that Richard and the children were Jordan's sun and moon.

But what with the funeral arrangements and the lines of grief marring Jordan's brow, Margot had refrained from asking her sister if she and Richard were having problems. And perhaps she was being hypersensitive. It was quite possible that Richard's irritability was caused by nothing more than the pressures of his career. If the amount of time he spent closeted in the study talking on his cell was anything to go by, he was swamped with work.

Stuart Wilde had risen from his chair despite Jordan's protests. "No, thank you, my dear, you've been extremely generous with your time and I've eaten far too many slices of that cake." He skirted his way around the grouping of chairs and the end table that held the tea tray to where Jade lounged. For a second she stared at him hostilely, but then, perhaps pricked by her conscience, she swung her feet off the chaise and stood.

"Jade, I've been meaning to give you this." He reached into his pocket and handed her a cream-colored card. "This has my telephone numbers—my office and the parish house. If you ever need someone to talk to, feel free to call me, day or night."

Jade's face could have been carved from marble. But at last she nodded and took the card.

Stuart Wilde beamed at her. Then, with a glance toward the far end of the parlor, he said, "Ahh, here's Edward now. Time for me to run off. I know you have much to discuss with him. No, Margot," he said as she made to accompany him. "Don't bother seeing me to the door. I can find my way." Then, clasping her hands and giving them one last encouraging squeeze, he whispered, "Remember what we talked about earlier. Good-bye and God bless you, my dear."

Surprisingly Margot recognized the ruddy-cheeked lawyer instantly, though he was significantly more portly than eight years ago. She recalled Jordan mentioning that Edward Crandall had bought some of Rosewood's hunters. Margot hoped her father had sold him big, solid crossbreeds out of their warm-blooded mares to carry him over the hunt field.

After Edward Crandall offered his condolences, he went on to exclaim how beautiful the three Radcliffe sisters were. "And all grown up—even little Jade. Why, it seems only yesterday none of you was much bigger than these two mites here," he said, smiling at Kate and Max, who had wrapped their arms about Jordan's legs and were shyly peering up at him.

"Kate, Max, please say hello to Mr. Crandall. He was a friend of Grandpa and Grandma's."

"Hello, Mr. Crandall," the children chimed politely.

"Absolute angels," the lawyer declared, gazing down at the matching pink bows at the ends of Kate's pigtails and the fire engine emblazoned on Max's knitted sweater. "To think these two adorable children will barely remember their grandparents." Fishing a snow-white handkerchief from the front pocket of his beige wide-wale corduroys, he vigorously blew his nose.

Fearing he might continue in this maudlin vein, Margot

said, "Why don't I take Kate and Max down to the barns? We can visit with the horses—"

"I'm afraid you'll have to postpone your trip to the barn, Margot." He lifted the leather briefcase that had been resting by his tasseled loafers, and patted it fondly. "You know how we lawyers are—sticklers for procedure, got to make sure all our *i*'s are dotted and *t*'s crossed. We'll be needing you for the reading of the wills."

Margot frowned. "I don't understand. Aren't only the people named in the will—the beneficiaries or whatever they're called—supposed to be at the reading?"

"Correct. Now, why don't we find a place where we can sit down and discuss the contents and terms?"

When Jordan suggested their father's study, Edward Crandall was more than agreeable. Margot imagined they'd spent many a pleasant hour drinking aged whiskey, smoking cigars, and discussing horses there. Waving away the offer of their father's desk, he lowered himself onto the cordovan leather sofa next to Jordan, and laid his briefcase across his lap. Unlocking its clasp, he withdrew a thick stack of documents.

"Before we begin, I want you to know you that I've contacted the insurance agency and given them what details I could about the crash. The agent I spoke with assured me they would begin investigating immediately. Because of the nature of the accident, however, it may take some time. I'll be sure to keep you abreast of any developments."

"Thank you, Mr. Crandall," Jordan said.

"You're welcome, my dear. Now, on to the sad business at hand. I have here triplicates of RJ's will and one copy of Nicole's will for Jade, as she is the sole beneficiary of her mother's estate." He passed them each a sheaf of papers. "I'll let you ladies read these. I have to warn you, though, there's a lot of legalese to wade through, so if you'd prefer I'll be happy to explain the contents and terms in each will."

"I'd much prefer having you explain the terms to us," Jordan said. She cast a quick glance at Jade, who nodded mutely.

"Margot? Is that okay with you?"

"What? Oh! Yes, that's fine," she managed, too preoccupied with getting over the shock that she'd apparently been included in her father's will to care how it was read. What would he have been willing to leave to her when he'd refused all contact for eight years? A sudden awful thought occurred to her: she'd heard of people composing bitter letters of denunciation for their relatives. She prayed her father wouldn't be so vengeful.

"If that's settled, I'll proceed." Crandall extracted a pair of wire-frame reading glasses from the breast pocket of his tweed jacket and settled them on his nose. "Let's begin with Nicole's last will and testament. Jade, according to the provisions of the will, with your father's passing you are the sole legatee of your mother's estate. This means that you will receive all of your mother's jewelry and clothing . . . oh, yes, and I have it noted here that one of the cars is in her name— the Porsche your father gave her as an anniversary present. Now, as regards money, you should know that your parents decided that any money you inherit will be held in trust until you reach the age of twenty-one. Once the estate is settled, I'll be able to tell you what that figure is. A more pressing matter will be to request that the court appoint a guardian for you until you've turned eighteen—"

"What? Why should the court have to appoint a guardian? Why would a court decide that? Aren't parents supposed to choose the person?" Jade's voice rose, ballooning with anxiety with each question.

Crandall raised his hand, halting the flow of words. A dull flush was spreading up from his shirt collar. "This is very difficult to admit, Jade, especially in light of the tragedy you've suffered, but you have no guardian—of course you *had* one originally," he added hurriedly. "Gigi Newhouse.

She was a sorority sister of your mother's from college. Unfortunately, Ms. Newhouse died last year."

"She died?" Jade said in disbelief. "My guardian is *dead*?"

Edward Crandall nodded sadly. "From complications following plastic surgery. After your mother and father learned of Ms. Newhouse's death, they had every intention of coming in and making the appropriate changes to the wills. We talked about setting up a date several times. But you know how days have a way of slipping by. . . ." He fell silent, putting an end to the pathetic excuse.

"But who'll be my guardian, then? Who's going to take care of me?"

The lawyer shifted uneasily on the sofa, the leather creaking audibly beneath his weight. "Well, in many cases, the court appoints a family member. As Jordan is married and has children already, perhaps she'd like to—"

Jordan started, obviously unprepared for this turn of events. "I—we—" she began in a strangled voice. But before she could continue, Jade leaped from her seat.

"Just forget it!" she cried. "Everybody's dead and you don't want me. Well, that's all right, because I don't want you, either!" With an anguished sob, she made for the door.

Margot was already on her feet. She grabbed Jade's arm, preventing her from racing out of the room. "I'll be Jade's guardian, Mr. Crandall," she said. Beneath her restraining hand Jade froze.

Jade wasn't the only one taken aback by the announcement. Jordan rose from the sofa and came toward them, her blue eyes wide in her stricken face. She opened her mouth to speak, but Margot gave a swift shake of her head, silencing her.

"You, Margot?" Edward Crandall said. "Well, this is certainly generous of you, stepping forward to assume responsibility for Jade. But perhaps you should consider the ramifications first. Your, uh, lifestyle is not exactly conducive to parenthood."

Margot bit back the instant retort that sprang to her lips. Edward Crandall knew absolutely nothing about her lifestyle. She'd be willing to bet it was darned near monastic compared to some of Warburg's citizens. Even as a kid she'd heard the stories of bed-hopping and infidelity. But because she didn't feel any more inclined to discuss her private life with him than she had with Thomas Selby, the head of Jade's school, she said instead, "I'm quite sure of what I'm doing, Mr. Crandall. Back at the hospital when I was holding Dad's hand, he said to me, 'Take care of her.' Now I understand what he was asking. I'm sure it was Jade that Dad was thinking of in those last moments."

At this, Jade turned to stare at her, but Margot kept her attention fixed on Crandall. "Our father was in too much pain to explain his wish fully, but I'm not about to ignore his last request." Refusing to dwell on how ill-suited she was to the task of caring for her sixteen-year-old half-sister, she repeated firmly, "I'll be Jade's guardian. You'll see to the necessary paperwork, Mr. Crandall?"

"Yes, yes, of course. I'll start the process immediately. Uh, I presume this solution is agreeable to you, Jade?" he asked, as they returned to their seats.

Jade dropped into her chair in a slumped sprawl. "Gee, it's not like I really have a choice, is it?" she said witheringly, before turning away to stare pointedly out the window.

Crandall opened his mouth, then wisely shut it. Clearing his throat, he began again. "Very well, if the question of Jade's guardianship is settled to everyone's satisfaction, we should move on to your father's will, as the rest of the estate is in his name."

"That's fine," Jordan said.

He took a minute to shuffle the papers before him. "Let's begin with the various bequests your father made. Just so you understand the procedure, as RJ's and Nicole's lawyer and executor for the estate, it's my responsibility to contact those who will be receiving smaller bequests. Once I've filed the will with the courts, I'll send letters informing each person of RJ's gift. Your father left instructions for three principal settlements. I'll read them in order. First, he has asked that Patrick and Ellie Banner receive the sum of fifty thousand dollars in gratitude for their many years of service. Second, Ned Connelly shall be allowed to live in his quarters at Thistle Cottage for as long as he so desires. In addition, he shall receive the sum of one hundred thousand dollars in gratitude for his work at Rosewood Farm. The last bequest is to Travis Maher. Your father also chose to leave him the sum of one hundred thousand dollars. And, in recognition of his work as Rosewood's trainer, your father stipulated that Travis Maher be given the pick of any living or future foal by a Rosewood stud and that he receive full breeding rights from said foal . . ."

A hundred thousand dollars. The sum represented a small fortune to someone of Travis's background. But of course, Margot reasoned, he'd been far more than just an employee to her father. In offering him one of Rosewood's foals, too, it was clear that her father had wanted to give Travis both the seed money and the founding stock with which to start a breeding farm of his own.

Crandall had paused to gaze at the three of them over the rim of his reading glasses. "As you girls have no doubt surmised, this will was written before certain 'events' unfolded. But as RJ made no attempt to effect any changes to it, I believe his stated wishes must be honored legally and morally."

"Yes, of course," Margot replied, as Jordan simultaneously said, "We have no objections to any of these bequests." Jordan looked over at Jade and said tentatively, "Are you all right with that?"

Jade regarded her coldly, then shrugged. "Yeah, sure. Travis is a good guy."

"Very well," Crandall said. "I'll inform them all of their bequests. Let's move on to the estate itself. Now, I'm going to be giving you an awful lot of information, so please feel free to interrupt with any questions. It's important that you fully grasp the situation and the options available to you." He gave what was doubtlessly intended to be a reassuring smile. Strangely, Margot felt anything but reassured.

"As regards your father's estate, with Nicole's tragic demise, you girls will inherit the remaining property and assets. This means that after the various bequests are disbursed and after the estate and inheritance taxes are paid, whatever monies and stock investments are left will be divided equally among the three of you—Jade's portion, as I mentioned before, to be placed in trust until she's twenty-one."

Margot stared at the lawyer, certain he'd made some mistake or misread the document. How was it that she, the banished daughter, was receiving an equal portion of her father's estate?

But before she could question him Jordan spoke. "And Rosewood? What about the house? What about the farm?"

"Ahh." Again the leather sofa creaked beneath him. "Let me preface this by saying that your father was extraordinarily proud of the fact that this house and the horse farm have been in the Radcliffe family for so many generations. His principal concern was that it should remain that way. In my opinion RJ may have been *too* concerned. Indeed, he and I exchanged words—heated ones—about his views and the restrictions he chose to impose. I felt and continue to feel that he placed an enormous and unnecessary burden on you."

"I'm afraid I'm completely mystified," Jordan confessed. "What are these burdens and restrictions you're alluding to? What exactly did our father decide should be done with Rosewood?"

Crandall adjusted his glasses so they sat farther down the length of his nose. He peered over the metal rims, scrutinizing Margot and her sisters closely. "Rosewood's property, which includes the house, the various outbuildings, the three hundred acres of land, the breeding farm, and all the horses—with the exception of the foal bequeathed to Travis Maher—has been left to the three of you jointly."

"This is impossible," Margot breathed. Why had her father repeatedly rebuffed her only then to decide to leave her an equal portion of Rosewood? *Why?* The question rang in her head. Then, conscious that Edward Crandall had begun outlining the terms of the inheritance, she struggled to focus.

"While RJ left Rosewood to the three of you, he did so with a number of stipulations. First, one-half of all the profits from the breeding operation—that is to say, the money generated from stud fees and sales of Rosewood Farm's stock—are to be reinvested in the farm with the other half to be distributed among the three of you. Second, no portion of the property is to be sold independently. This includes the house, the barns and outbuildings, and the land. Third and lastly, should one of you wish to sell your portion of Rosewood, you must offer it to your sisters to purchase at one-half the market value." At this he fell silent, sitting with his fingers steepled, resting against his pursed lips, allowing them to digest what their father had done.

"But why would Dad insist on having us sell our share of the property to each other at half the market value?" Jordan asked. "Wouldn't that mean that whichever one of us wanted to sell would lose an enormous amount of money?"

"I think Dad's idea was to make it really difficult for us to sell Rosewood—or buy it, for that matter. Just think how much even half the market value each of our shares would be worth," Margot pointed out.

"Margot is correct," Edward Crandall said. "When you consider the number of acres involved, the size and historical value of the house and outbuildings, and the equine facilities, the market price will be in the millions. Please believe that I did my best to explain what a difficult situation he was creating for you, but your father saw this as the best way to ensure Rosewood remained in the family." He shook his head, sighing heavily. "Unfortunately, when your father decided to impose these conditions he was a considerably wealthier man."

Even Jade turned to stare incredulously at the lawyer. The luxurious surroundings—the leather furniture, the marble fireplace, the framed hunting prints, the massive walnut desk—made a mockery of his words.

Crandall leaned forward, his face assuming an earnest expression. "You see, your father suffered a string of financial setbacks in recent years. Several real estate speculations he was involved in went quite badly, and then a slew of investments in some high-risk stocks resulted in some not insignificant losses. Combined they cut deeply into his capital. Needless to say, he saw the situation as only a temporary setback. He fully expected to recoup his losses over time."

Only Dad hadn't had time, Margot thought bleakly. What Crandall was telling them was so weird and disturbing. It was as though instead of sitting in their father's study, she and her sisters had been teleported to one of those carnival fun houses, where the halls were lined with mirrors that distorted everything out of recognition. The world had gone suddenly, horribly awry. And it appeared that they were still locked inside the fun house. She sensed more horrors lurking, waiting to jump out at them from darkened corners.

Thrusting the disturbing image aside, she said, "What exactly are you driving at, Mr. Crandall?"

Twin lines formed between his brows. "Unfortunately, because your father believed his financial situation would rebound, he made no significant adjustments to his and Nicole's rather lavish lifestyle. And he borrowed heavily, taking mortgages out against the property. I'm afraid I have to prepare you and your sisters for the very real possibility that after the bequests have been disbursed, the taxes and outstanding debts to the creditors and banks paid, there may not be much money left for the three of you to inherit."

"Are you saying we're poor?" Jade asked, cutting straight to the heart of the issue.

Crandall's frown deepened. "Well," he hemmed.

So that meant yes, Margot thought, slumping in her chair. Dear Lord. This certainly brought home the meaning of being "land rich, money poor."

Except that she wasn't exactly poor . . . though, admittedly, she could be a lot wealthier. She remembered when she'd started commanding higher fees, how Damien had called her into his office for one of his "life lectures," as Anika referred to them. Damien had told her that now was the time to begin investing so that when she retired from modeling she'd have a cushy nest egg. But while she generally followed Damien's advice, worrying about her retirement and setting up a 401(k) when she was in her twenties seemed downright weird. Then, too, many of her friends didn't earn the kind of money she did. There was always someone who needed bankrolling for a start-up business, another who'd fallen seriously ill and was without health insurance. And she contributed to charities, especially generously to those dedicated to cancer research, in the hopes that someone else's mother might be saved.

Of course not all the money she'd earned had gone to charity or to her friends; she was no saint. She spent a lot just having fun: renting villas and leasing yachts with a bunch of friends after a location shoot, or buying stuff simply because she could.

Even taking into account some of her more extravagant purchases, she didn't really regret the money she'd spent. And she did have some savings tucked away. But listening to Edward Crandall awkwardly reassure Jade that they weren't exactly *poor* made her realize that "having a little rainy-day money for when the castle roof is leaking buckets," one of

Damien's quaint Brit sayings, would have come in awfully handy right now.

Jordan's voice broke into Margot's thoughts. Her sister was speaking especially slowly and carefully. "Mr. Crandall, are you saying that although we've inherited the house and outbuildings, the breeding farm and all the acreage, there won't necessarily be enough money to maintain them?"

Crandall looked pained. "You can probably last a year at the outside if your horses fetch good prices." Bending forward, he reached out and gave Jordan's tightly clasped hands an avuncular pat. "I can't tell you how much I wish RJ had listened to me. But he insisted that you were Radcliffes through and through and that you'd understand his reasons. That was RJ for you—always convinced he knew better than anyone. It saddens me that he left you lovely girls with such a heavy burden to shoulder. Look at you, Jordan. You've got a family, a husband with a busy career, two young children, and a baby on the way. Margot here has her modeling and a whirlwind cosmopolitan life. She's not about to give that up now, is she?" He chuckled, shaking his head. His patronizing attitude had Margot stiffening with resentment. He didn't notice. "And Jade, why, she's just a child!"

"I'm sixteen, not two."

"And that's five years until you can touch your trust." Switching his attention back to Jordan, he said, "Fortunately, there is a way out of the present situation. If you'll recall, RJ's will stipulates that if any one of you wishes to sell your share of the property, you must offer it to the other two sisters at one-half the market value. But"—and he smiled— "there is nothing in the will that says the three of you can't *unanimously* decide to sell."

"Are you saying we should sell Rosewood?" Jade blurted out.

"But surely that's what our father most wanted to avoid, Mr. Crandall." Jordan frowned as if she, too, couldn't believe what he was suggesting.

"Of course it's what he wanted to avoid," Margot replied quickly, cutting Crandall off. "Dad believed there'd be enough money so the question of our being in a situation where we were forced to sell never entered his mind. Obviously he was counting on at least one of us wanting to keep the property and that we'd have the means to buy the others out if necessary."

"But the money's gone, my dear," Crandall quickly pointed out. "Selling Rosewood is really the only solution to your predicament, and the sooner you sell, the more likely the three of you might come out ahead financially. Bearing that in mind, it might interest you to know that I've already been approached by a party with a keen interest in the property. I'm quite optimistic that you'll receive a very satisfactory offer."

"No." The word was out of Margot's mouth before she even realized she'd thought it. "No," she repeated. "We're not interested in selling at this time, Mr. Crandall."

Her words had an immediate effect. Both Edward Crandall and Jordan looked shocked, Crandall unpleasantly so.

"My dear, you must be practical. Not only will you be assuming a huge financial burden, but by refusing to sell, you're hamstringing your sisters as well."

"Margot, are you sure about this?" Uncertainty laced Jordan's voice.

Jade was silent. But for the first time since picking her up at Malden, Margot detected a spark of life in her green eyes.

Like a captain sensing a possible mutiny and determined to crush it, Edward Crandall rose to his feet. When he spoke, his voice had a stern edge to it. "As your parents' lawyer and executor, as their friend, as *yours,* I must advise against—"

Margot stood, too. "If you'll excuse us for a moment, Mr. Crandall, my sisters and I would like a few minutes of privacy."

"I—I—" Stymied, he snapped his mouth shut and stalked

out of the study. The door shut behind him with an angry click.

"Boy, is he pissed," Jade said with relish. "Crandall must have thought he had this little side deal in the bag."

Jordan cast a worried glance at the door. "Yes, we've obviously upset him. But I'm sure Mr. Crandall wouldn't do anything that wasn't strictly aboveboard."

Jade gave a derisive snort.

"What could Dad have been thinking?" Jordan murmured abstractedly as she massaged her forehead with her fingertips. "The house is huge and requires constant maintenance. And the horses are equally expensive. What *can* we do but sell?"

Margot went over to the sofa where Jordan sat and dropped to her knees beside her. "Listen, I know keeping Rosewood sounds crazy. Totally irrational. But I have to try, Jordan. I can't simply let Rosewood go."

"But Margot—"

She took Jordan's hand and squeezed it. "Ever since we walked into this study with Crandall I've been racking my brain to figure out why Dad decided to leave me *anything,* let alone a portion of Rosewood. The only answer I can come up with is that maybe this was his way of giving me a chance—the chance he never let me have before. Ultimately, though, it doesn't matter what his reasons were. It doesn't even matter that right now there's a voice in my head screaming that I'm nuts to do this. Because the fact of the matter is that I could never live with myself if we just gave Crandall the go-ahead and walked away from all that Rosewood means."

"But—"

"Jordan, can you look me in the eye and honestly say you're willing to put Rosewood on the market and sell it to some stranger who won't have a clue who Francis and Georgiana were, let alone care? Don't you remember what you said to me the other night? About how Rosewood is more than just a big old house on a nice spread of land?

Rosewood is what binds us. It's all we have left of our family. . . ." Her voice dropped to an urgent whisper. *"Jordan, it's all Jade has left."*

Seconds ticked by. Then Jordan drew a shaky breath, and met Margot's and Jade's gazes. "How will we ever manage it?"

Margot pinned a smile to her face, hiding her own fear and uncertainty. "We'll find a way. Somehow."

Chapter %
NINE

"PLEASE TELL ME again why I'm doing this," Margot said as she and Ned walked up the long asphalt drive toward the Crestview Equestrian Center.

If Ned was annoyed that she'd already asked this particular question half a dozen times since he'd sprung the idea on her, he didn't show it. "Like I said before, convincing Travis to come back and work at Rosewood is gonna be a heck of a lot easier face-to-face than chatting him up on the telephone—especially since that boy's damned near impossible to reach on the phone," he added with a grunt of approval.

"You don't need me in order to talk to Travis. We both know he'd listen to you far sooner."

Ned let fly a stream of tobacco juice into the tall grass bordering the drive. "Ain't so," was his stout reply. "You're the boss lady now, Miss Margot. Your daddy left some mighty big shoes to fill. Might as well step into 'em."

"There's stepping and then there's falling flat on your face," she pointed out. Which was what she'd done last time she'd been with Travis. She'd idiotically thrown herself at him and landed flat on her face. The idea of having to ask Travis Maher for anything filled her with dread. Surreptitiously she wiped her damp palms against her alpaca sweater coat.

"It seems to me if you can walk in those heels you got on now," Ned said, eyeing her three-inch stiletto-heeled boots, "you ain't likely to fall flat on your pretty face. Stumble, maybe, but that's why I'm tagging along, to lend a helping hand. But it's your place to do the hiring. And the buying. You don't need me to tell you how important it is for people to see you at a sale like today's. There's some prime horseflesh that's going to be stepping into that auction ring. Like over there," and he nodded toward a chestnut that was being walked on a lead near the indoor arena where the auction would be held. Margot could see the energy radiating through the animal, from the forward prick of its ears to its tail flowing like a crimson banner. "Yup, there'll be some real beauties for the taking today," he continued in a voice that held the kind of fervent appreciation other men reserved for *Playboy* centerfolds. "Whether we buy one horse or three or none today doesn't matter. What's important is for everyone in the community to see that you're ready and willing to jump right into the action."

Her presence at the Crestview sale was about keeping up appearances. Margot supposed she knew as much about presenting an image as anyone. Realizing, too, that she could argue until she was blue in the face with Ned—who knew nothing of the financial mess RJ had left behind—she settled for warning him instead: "Just make sure I don't bid on anything with three legs."

What she desperately needed, too, was advice on how to calm nerves gone haywire at the prospect of seeing Travis again. Unfortunately she didn't think Ned's area of expertise extended that far.

Travis was in a fine mood. Nothing like walking into Crestview's fall sale with a client whose pockets were very, very deep. Lloyd Berenson was in the market for an experienced show hunter to ride in amateur owner classes. He was shopping for his daughter, too. Betsy was turning thirteen this month, so he was looking to buy her a new horse, one that could take her all the way to Harrisburg, Pennsylvania, and give her a shot at winning the Maclay, the national hunter championship for junior riders. A pretty nice birthday present.

Having Berenson by his side was like walking into a car dealership with a rich uncle and being told to skip the Hyundais and go straight for the Mercedeses. Hell, from what Lloyd had been hinting at, he might even be willing to splurge for the equine version of a Jaguar if the color was right.

Yeah, it was nice, very nice, Travis thought. Working at a large hunter/jumper barn like Hugh Hartmann's provided definite perks. And thanks to his job at the Double H, Travis was walking into the auction with money of his own to spend. He'd just come back from a road trip with some other big spenders, Michael Cutler and his wife, Josie, who'd recently moved to the Richmond area. First thing they'd done was to join the snootiest hunt club in the area. Second thing was to hire Travis to help them find mounts as fancy as their scarlet hunt coats. Since the Cutlers had more money than skill, Travis hadn't mentioned Rosewood Farm as a possible source for their dream hunters. Truth was, something in him balked at the idea of Michael Cutler sawing at the mouth of one of the horses he had helped bring into the world. Then, too, Travis was still too sore at RJ to be doing him any favors. Instead, he'd found Michael and Josie two mounts in North Carolina that were just expensive enough to make husband and wife preen with pride. Funny how being able to write a check with lots of zeros made a certain type of person practically giddy. But Travis wasn't about to gripe about such minor character flaws, especially when Cutler seemed equally happy to write a nice hefty check out to him, too. He'd been more than generously rewarded for his four days of tongue-biting patience. So, in addition to advising Lloyd Berenson, Travis was planning on doing a little bidding of his own.

He had his eye on a two-year-old Thoroughbred gelding. Riding for RJ and Rosewood Farm, Travis had competed in a gamut of classes, in everything from first-year green hunter to open jumper. And when he wasn't riding in horse shows, he was competing in hunter trials and hunter paces. While he enjoyed his career as a jack-of-all-trades and the challenge of riding all sorts of horses, what he loved most was working with a green horse and teaching it step-by-step. Nothing satisfied him as much as helping a young horse reach its potential—whether as a hunter galloping to the furious call of the hounds, a show hunter cantering in picture-perfect form around the ring, a jumper sailing over five-foot double oxers, an event horse scrambling down an embankment, or a kind and trustworthy pleasure horse that wouldn't so much as blink if a squirrel scampered across its path or a passing truck blared its horn. Each of these horses possessed particular talents that made it dear to its owner's heart.

So while Travis was still pissed as hell at RJ for believing that he'd stoop to cuckolding him with Nicole, he figured he nevertheless owed his former boss big-time for teaching him what this business was all about: the love of the horse. RJ might be a blind ass in some respects, but when it came to the horses he bred he ranked among the best.

He hadn't spotted RJ's Range Rover in the parking lot, but Travis figured he'd be running into him and Ned today. Before he'd been sacked, the three of them had talked about the upcoming sale as a chance to check out potential broodmares. Damn, seeing them sure was going to feel strange.

Margot and Ned spent the morning crisscrossing the grounds between the demonstration rings so that Margot could take a look at the five mares on Ned's "shopping list." The demonstration portion of today's sale was a lot like the horse shows she'd competed in as a kid: nonstop activity as far as the eye could see. The place teemed with horses of every size, shape, color, and ability imaginable. Because of the wide range in training, the auction's organizers had set up three separate rings for the sellers to show off their horses.

One ring was designated for barely broke to green horses, where the owners walked or trotted them in hand or exercised them on the longe line. The second was for horses working solely on the flat. In the third, a minicourse of schooling fences was set up, the heights of the jumps ranging from crossbars to a three-foot in-and-out. In each, a miked announcer called out brief descriptions of the horses as they took their turns in the ring.

What distinguished the morning's demonstration from any horse show Margot had ever competed in was that the spectators, standing three deep around the demo rings, necks craned, eyes intent, were the judges. And because many of the horses would be going for sums into the tens of thousands, it was crucial to judge carefully. Everyone wanted to avoid the dreaded case of buyer's remorse. Which was why Margot and Ned were looking just as carefully, and why they decided to eliminate one of the mares from Ned's list. The mare "winged" ever so slightly with her right hoof at the trot. "Corrective shoes might help, but she's not broodmare material," Ned said with a shake of his head. Taking his pen, he scratched a line through hip number 147.

After watching the other prospects, she and Ned went to the viewing barn to examine the mares more closely and gauge their barn manners and temperament, again searching for any flaws. As they progressed from stall to stall, Ned gave Margot a refresher course on conformation. His voice lowered, he pointed out what made each mare an attractive breeding prospect for Rosewood's studs: the set of the neck and slope of the shoulders; the proportion of the shoulders to the hindquarters; the fundamental importance of straight, well-defined legs; and, finally, the health of the hooves. Listening to Ned's running commentary, Margot realized that he was an even more exacting critic than the designers and fashion directors she worked for.

By the time they visited the last mare on their list, Margot had absorbed enough of Ned's lecture to know that this one rated a 10. An eight-year-old coppery chestnut Irish hunter, Mystique was an experienced field hunter and had performed well in the show ring, too. The owner was parting with her only because of a job transfer.

Of all the mares they'd looked at, Mystique was Margot's favorite. Not only had she sailed over the fences in the demonstration ring with picture-perfect form and lots of air between the top rail of the fence and her neatly folded knees, but there was something else, a certain spark in her large brown eyes that spoke of confidence.

"I like her," Margot said after the mare had been led back into her stall.

Ned grunted good-naturedly. "What's not to like? And if she's as good on the hunt field as she is in the schooling ring, you can show her off at the Warburg Hunt Cup. Perfect opportunity to spread the word that we're putting her to stud next season."

"Ned, what are you talking about? You don't expect me to ride in the Hunt Cup!"

"Sure, I do. It's a tradition. Your family founded the War-burg Hunt Cup. A Radcliffe has always competed in it. Don't worry. The Cup's not until the end of November. Plenty of time to get some muscle back on those bones."

"I have plenty of muscle, thank you very much. Look, this is utterly ridiculous. I can't—"

"Why not? I've been meaning to get you on a horse, only I know how busy you and Miss Jordan have been, taking care of Miss Jade and tending to your daddy's and Nicole's affairs. Riding would be the best thing for all three of you—though I suppose Miss Jordan will have to wait until after the baby comes. But Miss Jade, well, it would do that little girl a whole world of good to go out for a long gallop."

Margot opened her mouth to set him straight but Ned had started up again. "Listen, I need to use the facilities. Tommy Chisholm, today's auctioneer, runs a tight ship. There won't be time to duck out once the bidding starts. Why don't you meet me in the arena? I'll grab us a place up front, near as I can get to the auctioneer's box." And off he went before she could get a word in.

Ned must be out of his mind. She couldn't enter the Warburg Cup, a seven-mile hunt-pace event. She already had more than enough on her plate between figuring out what she was going to do with Jade and preventing Rosewood from being sold to some fat cat looking for a Virginia vacation home. And if that weren't enough, there was this little side gig she had going as a model. She thought of 101 pithy comebacks for Ned Connelly as she made her way through the barn's crowded aisles. But as she skirted past one seller who was talking up a palomino to a lady with a Jack Russell straining at its leash, she caught sight of a face that erased all else from her mind.

Travis Maher.

Margot had braced herself for the inevitable. Sooner or later today she was going to cross paths with Travis. She'd told herself that she was ready. Sure, it would be embarrassing and awkward, but she was no longer a foolish and impetuous eighteen-year-old in the throes of her first crush. She was successful and sophisticated. She could handle this.

But any smidgeon of confidence provided by her pep talk deserted her in the instant her brain registered who was standing by the cross ties ten feet away. Her heart betrayed her, too, its steady beat becoming a wild pounding that made her chest ache.

It wasn't that Margot had forgotten Travis was handsome. But perhaps she hadn't remembered *how* handsome.

Dressed in black jeans and leather boots, his overlong dark hair curling over the collar of his jacket, Travis looked like an outlaw. To Margot he couldn't have been more lethal if he'd had a gun strapped to his thigh.

When he bent down to run his hands down the leg of the horse standing at the ties, a lock of his hair fell forward, grazing his cheek. Margot's fingers tingled as she remembered its silky texture and the rough rasp of his beard-shadowed cheek.

Dear Lord, what was the matter with her? Her days and evenings were filled with beautiful people. She'd worked with lots of handsome men, every last one of them possessing all the right hunky attributes: bulging biceps, washboard abs, tight butts, and Adonis-like faces. The problem was, no GQ beefcake, no Calvin Klein boy toy, no Dolce & Gabbana studmuffin, had ever made Margot feel as if her heart might burst. Travis could without even trying. Like now, when he hadn't even noticed her.

His attention was riveted on the horse standing at the cross ties. Had Margot been in a joking mood, she'd have said that they were a perfect match, both superb animals. The horse was young, she could tell, by the narrow width of its chest and withers. Despite its immaturity, it stood quietly, raising its hoof without any fuss for Travis to examine. Setting the leg down, Travis continued his inspection, walking around it, stroking it. The intensity with which he assessed every aspect of the horse's build made Margot realize that his interest was more than professional.

Travis wanted that horse for himself.

Margot's gaze flew to the number affixed to its shiny black haunch: 156.

"Thanks for showing me Night Raider, Jim," she heard Travis say. He gave the horse a final pat and stepped back.

"Happy to oblige, Travis. Darlene and I are hoping this guy'll be the high seller of the day," replied the man standing by the young horse. He reached up and patted its neck fondly.

"You may get your wish. I got to tell you, though, I'm hoping I can sneak out of here with him."

"I'll be rooting for you. Night Raider has got heart."

Travis pushed back the sleeve of his jacket to glance at his wristwatch. "It's almost showtime. I'd better go find my client. Best of luck today, Jim."

"Thanks. See ya, Travis."

Margot maintained a safe distance behind Travis as she followed him outside, counting on the people milling about to shield her should he chance to turn around. If Ned could see her right now, he'd surely be spitting the words "cowardly," "skulking," and "pitiful" between well-aimed jets of yellow-brown tobacco juice. And she'd be guilty as charged. But she couldn't help it.

Confronting Travis was unthinkable. She was too shaken by her response to him. Those brief few minutes in the viewing barn left her painfully aware of just how vulnerable she still remained.

Pride demanded that when she asked him to return as Rosewood Farm's manager, she be strong and in control. And because so much was riding on him agreeing, she was going to make sure that she possessed something he really wanted: hip number 156.

Ned began speaking as soon as she slipped into the seat beside him. "Hey, did you see Travis? He's just across the aisle, next to the guy in the Barbour jacket. Did you talk—"

"No, I didn't talk to him," she whispered, cutting him off before his voice could carry to where Travis sat.

He opened his mouth, doubtless to demand why in hell not, so she added fiercely, "There were too many people about. And I'm not going over to him now, either, so don't start. Pass me your catalog, will you? Did you happen to notice 156? A black gelding with four white stockings, about sixteen hands?" she asked, quickly flipping through the dog-eared pages of the auction catalog.

"Number 156?" Ned paused in recollection. "Yeah, I think I remember seeing him. But we're not in the market for a geld—"

Margot had found the entry. "Here it is, 156," she read aloud under her breath. "Night Raider. Two-year-old black Thoroughbred gelding with papers. Elegant mover, one hundred percent sound. Sire is Dark Promise; Dam is Night Wing." Her breath caught as excitement gripped her. "Listen to this. It says Night Raider's dam is also for sale. Night Wing is hip number 145—was she ever on your list, Ned?"

"She would have been, 'cept she's already in foal. Look her up," he said, peering over her shoulder as she flipped the catalog pages to entry 145. "Yup, like I thought. They bred her to the same stallion, Dark Promise. Live foal guaranteed."

Margot's mind raced. A proven mare in foal. And the foal would share the same bloodlines as the gelding Travis wanted.

"I'm going to bid on that broodmare and the two-year-old."

Ned gave her a thoughtful look. "Hell if I'll argue with that. Jim and Darlene Cox run a darn good breeding program. They've produced a lot of talented horses over the years. 'Sides, it's your money."

Margot's stomach clenched. Ned had no idea how true those words were. Until all the bequests were made and the creditors paid off, any money she spent on Rosewood Farm would come out of her bank account. This gamble could rank as her most costly yet.

"Ned, where in the world are you going?" she exclaimed when he abruptly stood and edged past her.

"That's Dale Cozzens over there, the sale's vet," he said, pointing to the left of the auctioneer's box. Margot saw a man in a red-and-black-checked wool hunter's jacket talk-ing with one of the handlers. "I'm going to get the scoop on that dam Night Wing. Dale's bound to have examined her. I trust him to give me the straight story."

Ned edged his way toward the aisle, but his progress was hindered by the narrowness of the rows. People were forced to rise to let him pass. Ever courteous, he kept repeating, "Excuse me, sir. Beg your pardon, ma'am. Thanks. Thank you kindly."

Travis was idly shooting the breeze with Lloyd Berenson, waiting for Tommy Chisholm to step up to the auctioneer's box, when he heard Ned's familiar voice. He straightened in his chair and turned his head, a smile spreading across his face when he spotted him.

Damn, but he'd missed his old friend. "Ned," he called with a wave, his smile widening as Ned raised a hand in return.

"Hey there, Travis. Good to see you, son. Can't talk now, I gotta catch Dale before the sale starts."

"RJ running you ragged?" he joked.

"RJ's—" Travis was surprised by the shadow that crossed the older man's lined face. "RJ's not here, Travis. I came with Miss Margot," and he jerked his thumb over his shoul-der. "Damn, there goes Dale. Hey, Dale," he called. Then he was gone, his wiry frame hurrying up the aisle.

Travis didn't even notice. His world had narrowed to a single being: the blue-eyed, streaky-blond beauty who was staring straight back at him.

Margot. Her inexplicable presence stirred a welter of emo-tions inside him. He couldn't believe it. What was she doing here, at Crestview, of all places? Hadn't he seen her just the other day on TV, sauntering down the runway at some fash-ion show in Europe? She'd been three scraps of fabric away from breath-stealingly naked. Now all he could see was her face. And that was more than enough to send his system into overdrive.

She looked good, which was like saying that Secretariat had been an okay racehorse. He kept staring, wondering whether she would bother to walk across the aisle so she could spit in his face, as he richly deserved.

She didn't. Instead she simply turned her head, leaving him to gawk like a moonstruck fool.

Beside him, Berenson spoke. "Travis, do you realize who that is? That's Margot Radcliffe, the model."

"Yeah, I know."

"Glad to see she doesn't disappoint. She looks as good in person as in the photographs."

She looked better, Travis thought. A million times better. "Read a lot of fashion magazines, do you, Lloyd?"

"My wife and daughter do. Not that you have to read fashion magazines to get a first-rate peek at Ms. Radcliffe's charms. Did you see the billboard ad with her earlier this spring?"

Travis had. He'd nearly run off the road at the sight of Margot lying on rumpled sheets in a satin negligee that barely skimmed the tops of her thighs. With that image to torment him, he hadn't slept for nights.

Too busy ogling Margot, Lloyd Berenson didn't notice Travis's lack of reply. "Damned if I can remember what she was hawking in that ad, besides sex." He smiled and his voice dropped to a conspiratorial whisper. "You know, if the makers of Levitra had an ounce of marketing sense, they would put Margot Radcliffe's photo on the back of the instruction pamphlet, to provide a little 'inspiration' before heading off to the old conjugal sack."

Until now, Travis had never actually wanted to pummel a client. But before he could confirm his heritage as Red Maher's son and land himself in the slammer, Berenson spoke again. "What do you suppose she's doing here?"

"Must want a horse," he replied laconically.

"I hope she won't be bidding against me. These fashion models make scads of money—" He broke off as Tommy

Chisholm banged his gavel, signaling the start of the auction. "Ahh, the fun begins," he pronounced happily. "It'll be interesting to see how serious a player Margot Radcliffe is."

Oh, Margot could play with the best of them, all right. What Travis wanted to learn was precisely what sort of game she was playing here in RJ's stead.

Chapter ✣
TEN

WITH TOMMY CHISHOLM, a veteran of the auction circuit, behind the podium, the bidding progressed at a lightning pace. It was difficult not to get caught up in the excitement; Lloyd Berenson proved himself especially susceptible. He was squirming like a schoolboy by the time the Swedish Warmblood gelding he intended to bid on was led into the ring. No sooner had Tommy tossed out the opening bid of three thousand than Lloyd's hand was in the air. By the time the bidding came to an end, a mere two minutes later, Berenson's bank account was down by twenty thousand.

"I got him, by God," he exulted, high on the rush of winning and not yet having to face the harsh reality of writing that check in the sales office. But the horse was a good one, so Travis didn't think he'd be too unhappy later on, even though their agreed-upon strategy was for Lloyd to stop at fifteen thousand for the gelding.

"Congratulations."

"Whew! My heart is racing!"

"Take a deep breath, Lloyd. That blood bay Thoroughbred is coming up real soon. There are a lot of eager daddy-types in this crowd. Don't get into a pissing match with them, 'cause you can always try for that chestnut mare Mystique." Mystique was, in Travis's opinion, the superior horse, but the bay boasted Storm Cat in his bloodlines. In the horse world, that was pretty much like saying you were the queen of England's second cousin. Probably better.

Given Berenson's earlier behavior, Travis wasn't terribly surprised to see him act like a puppet on a string when hip number 144, the bay Thoroughbred, was led into the auction ring. Lloyd's arm jerked whenever Tommy so much as glanced in his direction. He didn't even stop when Travis elbowed him in the ribs, an unsubtle reminder that the bidding had climbed way higher than the agreed-upon limit of twenty thousand. He kept right on bidding until Tommy handed him the horse for thirty thousand dollars.

"Well, I did it," he said, looking as pleased as punch.

"Yup, you did it, Lloyd," Travis agreed drily. *And in the space of five minutes you blew about fifteen thousand dollars by overbidding on those two horses,* he added silently. But Travis knew the rules: the client was always right. If Berenson wanted to throw around that kind of money, that was his prerogative.

It occurred to him that he'd been feeling hostile toward Lloyd ever since he made those comments about Margot. Instinctively he craned his neck, sneaking a quick peek across the aisle, and was surprised to see Margot's hand in the air. Which horse was she bidding on?

He jerked his gaze back to the sale ring. Hip number 145 was being walked inside its small confines. Number 145 was the dam of Night Raider, the two-year-old he was planning to bid on. Why would Margot bid on a mare already in foal?

He watched as again and again Margot raised her hand. The rhythm of her bids had a deliberate air, markedly different from Lloyd's near-manic waving. Travis couldn't tell whether it was a conscious tactic on her part, an attempt to gauge the seriousness of the other bidders, or if she was simply less willing to part with her cash. Whatever the motive, her approach worked. When Tommy struck his gavel, Night Wing was Margot's. And seventeen thousand was a damned good price for a proven broodmare in foal.

Travis was still trying to figure out the answers to a dozen different questions, every one of them beginning and ending with Margot Radcliffe, when hip number 156, Night Raider, entered the auction ring.

The young gelding looked stellar. Night Raider could have been walking the red carpet on Oscar night. The strange setting, the noise emanating from the audience, the bright lights—none of them fazed him a bit. He carried his head proudly, his neck arched gracefully, his nostrils flared and ears pricked forward. Under the arena lights, his coat glistened bluish black. He was certainly a looker, but Travis was willing to bet that this young horse was more than merely flashy. Jim Cox had said his colt had "heart." Travis wanted to be the one to prove that it was made of solid gold.

Tommy Chisholm was nobody's fool. He opened the bidding for Night Raider at five thousand—a handsome price for a barely broke two-year-old. The auctioneer had obviously recognized that, young or not, green or made, this horse had promise.

Travis had attended enough auctions not to let himself be intimidated by how quickly the bidding escalated. Yet this was the first time the bidding meant something to him personally. Not only was he bidding with his own savings, but the more he saw of Night Raider, the more determined he became to own him.

He wasn't alone in this ambition. Bids were flying from all four corners of the packed arena, with Tommy Chisholm pointing and rattling off figures so fast, Travis could barely keep track. At fifteen thousand the pace changed, becoming slightly more deliberate, but there were still enough bidders for the price to reach eighteen and continue climbing.

At twenty-seven thousand, Travis had pretty much wiped out his savings account. *Well, there are always credit cards.* He raised his hand again.

At thirty thousand, he was picturing himself in a coat and tie, applying for a bank loan. Surely he had a credit history a loan officer would feel kindly toward.

At thirty-four thousand, he was silently cursing the other bidders. It didn't make a truckload of difference that their ranks had thinned considerably. All a bidding war required was a

single adversary. A blur of movement across the aisle caught
Travis's attention. His silent curse found voice *and* a name.

Damn it all to hell, Margot. Eyes narrowed, he watched
as, cool as a mint julep on a summer day, Margot raised her
index finger, bringing the price to thirty-five thousand.

"I have thirty-five thousand, do I hear thirty-five five?"
Tommy Chisholm was practically chortling with satisfaction.

Doggedly determined, Travis raised his hand. Margot
maddeningly followed suit.

And so it went. By thirty-eight thousand dollars, the arena
had gone quiet, the audience hushed as it followed the battle
of wills between the two bidders.

Then Tommy's amped voice rang out, "I have thirty-nine
thousand five. Do I hear forty thousand?"

It felt like someone had wrapped Travis's insides with
rusty barbed wire. Jesus, he didn't have that kind of money
and it infuriated him that the reason he wouldn't be walking over to the sales office and writing a check for Night
Raider was because Margot Radcliffe had decided to sashay
in here and throw some petty cash around.

"I have thirty-nine thousand five going once. Going—"

What the hell. His hand shot into the air defiantly.

Tommy Chisholm's teeth flashed white under the bright
lights. "I have forty thousand dollars for this fine two-year-
old Thoroughbred. Do I hear—"

"Forty-five thousand," Margot called out, as clear as a
crystal bell.

Staggered by the move, Travis could only hope he'd mis-
heard. But then Tommy was exultantly repeating, "Forty-
five! I have forty-five thousand dollars!"

Margot had won. Her power play, upping the bidding by
five thousand, had blown him straight out of the arena.
Tommy Chisholm was staring at him, waiting for him to
counter bid. Though it galled him, Travis gave a terse shake
of his head.

As he listened to Tommy call out, "Forty-five thousand going once, going twice . . ." he cursed silently. It would've been nice if he could have consoled himself with the thought that Margot had grossly overbid. But it'd be a lie. Had he the means, he'd have happily paid that sum for the gelding. He winced at the sound of the gavel. "Sold! Hip number 156 is sold to the lovely lady for forty-five thousand dollars!" Travis's wince became a scowl when he heard Tommy say, "Will the lady of what may very well be today's high seller please rise? Let's give her a round of applause, folks."

He saw Margot hesitate. But then Ned leaned close and whispered something. Up she rose, graceful and assured, as the princess she was. As the rest of the audience clapped, she smiled, seeming not the least unnerved by the fact that every eye in the place was fixed on her. She had on a long cream-colored coat that hid her body—thereby guaranteeing that the male half of the crowd would be fantasizing about being the one to peel it off and caress what lay beneath. A photographer's flash went off, capturing her incredible smile and those wide, unforgettable blue eyes. Excited murmurs began to sweep the arena as Margot was recognized. Discovering that there was a celebrity in their midst who'd spent a nice chunk of change in the most drawn-out bidding war of the day was a real treat. There'd be plenty to discuss over the dinner table that night.

For everyone except Travis. He wasn't likely to be regaling anyone with tales of how Margot Radcliffe had shown up at Crestview and beaten him out of a spectacular young horse. Nor was he about to talk about how damned lovely she was.

As if feeling the weight of his gaze, Margot turned her head. Seconds passed while their eyes met and dueled. Travis told himself that the frustration roiling inside him was from losing Night Raider, not from desiring something else with a ferocity that shook him to the core. He stared bleakly at her a few seconds longer before getting up and striding toward the exit.

Yeah, Margot was more beautiful than ever and just as unattainable.

Margot walked out of the sales office on legs that felt like putty. The afternoon had grown colder. Pulling her sweater coat tightly about her, she tried to ignore the ache at the back of her head. After years of modeling on the runway, she recognized her symptoms as the aftereffects of a serious adrenaline rush. Except that this queasy feeling in the pit of her stomach was far worse than any typical post–fashion show wipeout.

Maybe that was because instead of modeling a dozen or so outfits, she'd just blown close to eighty thousand dollars— she still couldn't believe she'd bought not only Night Wing and Night Raider but also the Irish hunter, Mystique. Thank God for Ned. After she'd won the mare Mystique, he'd plucked her sleeve and whispered, "Three and a half horses is a good day's work, Miss Margot. Let's get out of here."

Signing the checks to pay for her equine shopping spree had gone a long way toward deflating the bubble she'd been floating on. But it wasn't until Ned hustled her out of the cramped sales office with the stern directive that she go find Travis pronto that her stomach began to churn and her head to pound.

"Why don't you come with me, Ned?" She hadn't even cared that she was practically pleading.

"Can't, Miss Margot. I gotta call Felix to tell him and Andy to bring the van here to pick up the horses we bought."

"I can wait. Really."

"Not if you want to catch Travis. He left the auction earlier than we did, so he's probably all set to load up. Go on now."

Not if you want to catch Travis . . .

Ned was too kind to have purposely intended his comment as a reminder of her adolescent fixation, but there it was. And here she was, eight years later, still trying to figure out how to catch Travis Maher.

But she'd grown a little wiser than the hormone-addled eighteen-year-old she'd once been. She'd acquired sufficient sense to ask herself, as she set off for the parking lot reserved for horse vans, what in the world had induced her to enter into a bidding war with Travis over Night Raider?

What she'd initially considered a good tactic she now realized was a colossal blunder. Back in the arena, after she'd "won" the gelding, bitter disappointment had been etched in the proud lines of Travis's face and in the turbulent gray of his eyes. To make matters worse, the auctioneer had urged the audience to applaud Margot's success. The applause had highlighted the foolishness of her act: she'd won the gelding, but so what? It was Travis who possessed the skill to make the young horse into a champion. To Travis, the sound of everyone clapping must have stung like salt rubbed into an open wound.

Now she was going to have to confront the man her father had fired and whom she'd publicly bested and convince him to come back to his old job. Not an enviable situation. The worst of it was, no matter how clear-eyed she was in recognizing her chances of success, some tiny part of her former love-struck self was still spinning rose-tinted dreams of Travis. No amount of self-admonishment could temper those naïve dreams.

The parking lot had emptied, making it fairly easy to find the Double H Farm's silver horse van. She spotted Travis by the side door of the trailer. From the bits of hay he was brushing off the sleeve of his jacket, she realized he must have been filling the nets, tending to the final details before he loaded the horses into the trailer.

He'd be leaving shortly. The temptation to avoid Travis, to avert her gaze and hurry off in the opposite direction, was immense. She could simply tell Ned that she'd missed him. But her sisters and Ned and all her father's employees were counting on her to make sure Rosewood Farm was properly managed.

Perhaps talking to him wouldn't be so bad. Most likely Travis had forgotten that long ago night when she'd tried her sex kitten act on him. He probably had women stripping for him all the time—or offering him lap dances. All she had to do was pretend that she, too, had forgotten the hugely embarrassing spectacle she'd made of herself.

"Hello, Travis." She spoke loudly so that he couldn't help but hear. Forced to call his name a second time, she would doubtless have chickened out and dodged behind the adjacent horse van.

He turned at the sound of her voice and her breath caught, suspended. This close she could see the changes eight years had wrought: the fine lines fanning out from the corners of his deep-set eyes, the heavier beard stubble darkening his lean cheeks. His mouth was the same, stern yet sensuous. She found the contradiction as mesmerizing as ever. Remembering that mouth on hers, a heat spread through her that had nothing to do with her alpaca coat.

"Margot."

That was it, the extent of his greeting. Hysterical laughter bubbled inside her. No "Good to see you," or "Wow, I guess you really made something of yourself," or "Damn, if I'd had any idea of how beautiful you would become, I'd have . . ." What? Been a lot nicer to her? Maybe offered her a consoling pat on the head after she threw herself at him?

Yeah, right, she scoffed silently. For years she'd behaved like the worst kind of brat around him. Then she'd been idiotic enough to believe she could seduce him in a tack room. Now she'd gone and outbid him on a horse in front of several hundred people.

Could she have possibly done more to make Travis Maher dislike her? It was doubtful.

Yet having him stand with his arms folded across his chest while he waited for her to say her piece so that he could get on with his life was so at odds with the fantasies she'd spun that for a few agonizing seconds she lost track of what she needed to say. A distant neigh reminded her.

"I have to talk to you," she said.

"That's a shame. Much as I'd like to stroll down memory lane with you, I'm kind of pressed for time. I have two horses waiting for a ride to Richmond."

"I'd like to talk about having you come back to work at Rosewood. We'd like to offer you your old job as head trainer and manager."

He propped a shoulder against the side of the van. "Didn't RJ tell you? He fired me. I'm working at Hugh Hartmann's now. Hugh runs a great outfit. Why would I want to leave?"

Travis obviously hadn't heard about her dad and Nicole. How could she tell him the news? Simply blurt it out? Impossible. She wouldn't be able to tell him without breaking down. Stick to the horses, she told herself. They were what mattered.

"At Rosewood you'll be working with the horses you've raised and trained. Horses you know and love."

"I have good horses at the Double H."

"I wonder, though, if any of them compare to Night Raider. If you come back, he'll be yours to train."

"Oh, yeah." Inclining his head, he gave her a cool smile. "I forgot to offer my congratulations. Tell me, Margot, how high would you have gone in the bidding?"

"As high as necessary." It was true, she thought, remembering how at the height of the bidding she'd been seized by the ancient yet still terribly familiar impulse to challenge Travis by doing whatever it took to make him notice her—with the same disastrous results. Some things never changed, did they?

"I guess you can buy just about anything that tickles your fancy, huh?"

She ignored the biting comment. "I'm offering you carte blanche with Night Raider if you come back to work for us.

You'll have Night Wing's next foal to work with, too, from the day it stands on its four hooves. Who knows, that foal might prove an even finer horse."

"What are you up to now, Margot?" he asked, his eyes narrowing dangerously. "What's with buying Night Raider and then dangling him like a sugarplum in front of me? Did RJ put you up to this? He must be damn desperate if he was willing to call you. Was it that he was too embarrassed to face me himself? Or did he think having you bat your pretty blue eyes might sway me?"

He straightened and, taking a step toward her, raked her from head to toe with his angry gaze. "Sorry, Margot. I'm not tempted by anything you or your father has to offer. Do me a favor and pass the message on to RJ."

Margot flinched and felt the blood literally drain from her face. At that moment she hated Travis, hated the power he had to cut her to the quick and make her eyes fill with tears. She blinked rapidly, refusing to let a single teardrop fall.

"I wish I could tell Dad just how grateful you are for all he taught and did for you, but I can't. He's dead. He and Nicole flew to Hunterdon last week to see about hiring a new trainer. Their airplane crashed into the Chesapeake on the way home. Nicole died instantly. Daddy made it through surgery but then—" She swallowed forcibly. "We—Jordan, Jade, and I—were with him when he died."

Travis's face had gone blank with shock. "RJ's dead? That can't be. Jesus, Margot—" Remorse filled his voice. "I would never—"

Margot held up her hand, cutting him off. She really didn't want to hear anything he had to say. "It was Ned's idea that we ask you to come back. You know as well as anyone that no matter how fine a horseman Ned is, he's too old to be running Rosewood. He was sure you'd be willing to come back. He managed to convince me, too. But your loyalty is just one of many things I've been wrong about."

Abruptly aware that she was shivering, she shoved her hands deep into her coat pockets. She turned to leave, then paused. Refusing to look at Travis, she addressed the shiny metal siding of the trailer. "Oh, yes, I almost forgot. You should be receiving a letter from the executor of my father's estate. In his will, he left you a hundred thousand dollars and your pick of one of Rosewood's foals. With Ned as busy as he is, I'm sure he'd appreciate your having the courtesy to call ahead and schedule an appointment when you want to come and look over the stock." Without another word Margot walked away from the man who once again had shattered her fragile dreams.

"WHAT CAN I SAY, Ned?" Margot repeated wearily. "Travis turned me down." Again. She must be the world's biggest masochist, not to mention the world's biggest fool. Well, that was definitely the last time she'd give him the opportunity to reject her.

Staring out the passenger window as the car rolled past open countryside and through sleepy towns with clapboard houses and front yards with swing sets and piles of leaves and metal rakes lying abandoned on the ground, New York City and her life there seemed a million miles away. Except it wasn't. She needed to call Damien soon. Her modeling was more important than ever if she wanted to keep Rosewood afloat financially. That she'd just blown thousands on a failed gambit to get Travis to come back to Rosewood was too depressing for words.

Ned's voice dragged her thoughts away from one mess to another. "I'd like for someone to explain how I'm supposed to run Rosewood without him."

She couldn't bear to hear the bewildered hurt in the older man's voice. He'd been so certain of the man he considered his protégé. "You'll just have to find someone else who wants the job."

"And when am I supposed to find the time to do that?"

"Can't you buy an ad in *The Chronicle of the Horse,* or put the word out by making some telephone calls? For what it's worth, you have our total support in hiring whomever you choose."

Ned muttered something under his breath, his words too

low to decipher. Knowing she couldn't say the one thing he really wanted to hear—that Travis was coming back to work with him—she pulled the collar of her coat up for warmth and closed her eyes.

When her head bumped against the car window, she opened them to find the sky a somber gray. She blinked, astonished to find that they were already turning into Rosewood. The ruts in the gravel drive made the headlights bounce over the chestnut trees of the allée like a child playing with a flashlight on Halloween. "Sorry, Ned. I didn't mean to fall asleep."

"That's okay. It's been a long day. Not that it's over yet," he said as he parked the car. "Felix and Andy should be getting back with the horses from Crestview in about an hour. Tito's wife has been feeling poorly so I told him to go home early. That leaves me with three stalls to prepare. And Gulliver's leg still needs icing."

"I'll do the stalls, Ned. Just let me run inside and change."

"No, Miss Margot, you can't—"

"For Pete's sake, Ned. I bought the horses, I might as well help take care of them."

A pleased smile lit his lined face. "That's the spirit. Maybe you can get Miss Jade to lend you a hand."

"Uh, sure," she said, her conscience instantly pricking her. Since the reading of the will, she and Jade hadn't spent much time together. For one thing, Jade rarely bothered to emerge from her room. She spent hours holed up in there, lying on her bed, plugged into her iPod or staring glassy-eyed at her laptop screen. Whenever her half-sister did make an appearance, she left Margot in no doubt of her feelings. Those surly sneers spoke volumes.

For her part, Margot had yet to adjust to her new role as guardian, a role made all the more daunting in the face of Jade's grieving. She couldn't help but think that the best way for Jade to get past the pain would be for her to return to Malden. She'd be with her friends there. And wouldn't being immersed in the daily routines of the boarding school be beneficial, too?

She made a mental note to call Thomas Selby. Self-important though the man was, he was bound to have experience handling teens in the midst of emotional crises. In the meantime, she'd give Ned's idea a try. Perhaps getting Jade to lend a hand with the stalls would rouse her from her apathy.

Margot ran up the front-porch steps and opened the door, calling out, "Hello," as she tossed the Rover's keys onto the hall table.

"Hi, you're back." Jordan peeked around an enormous vase of chrysanthemums she was carrying. "Oh, hey, can you move those keys a bit? Thanks." Setting the vase down on the marble top, she stepped back and regarded it critically. "What do you think? Too much?"

"No, it's great." Jordan had arranged the mums so they arced in a shower of purple, gold, russet, and white. "I like how the bouquet's reflected in the glass," she said, nodding at the gilt-framed mirror.

"I know it's silly to be making flower arrangements with everything else going on, but I needed to bring some life and color into the house before the kids and I head back to Washington."

"When are you leaving?"

"Tomorrow. I'd like to get home in time to make dinner for Richard. He's been eating too much Chinese takeout in his office recently." Jordan gave a sudden start and her hand flew to her stomach. "Wow. I swear Roy Rogers here just did a backflip. This baby may only be the size of a cupcake but he's mighty energetic. Way more than his mama," she admitted, walking over to the circular staircase and sinking down onto the wide step. She patted the spot next to her, sliding over when Margot accepted the invitation.

"Tell me how things went at Crestview. Did you talk to

Travis at the auction? Is he willing to come back and manage the farm?"

"How did things go? All things considered, I'd say the day
was pretty much a bust," Margot conceded with a sigh. "I
spent a tidy bundle on three horses, two of which I basically
bought to use as bargaining chips with Travis. Unfortunately
my clever plan backfired completely. He made it crystal clear
he wasn't interested in coming back." And he couldn't have
made his contempt for her plainer.

"I simply can't understand it. Travis was so close to Dad.
Rosewood was like a home to him."

First Ned and now Jordan. God, she hated failing them.
But Margot refrained from telling Jordan what Ned had said
about the rift between Dad and Travis being caused by a
woman. Jordan had enough to worry about. And that foolish part of herself, which had let Travis's memory haunt her
for so many years, simply couldn't bear speculating about
the woman Travis might possibly love.

"I'm sorry, Jordan. We'll just have to hire someone else.
I've already spoken to Ned about putting an ad— Hey,
what's the matter?" Jordan had bent forward, covering her
face with her hands.

Jordan lifted her head, revealing a troubled expression.
"Maybe we're making a mistake in trying to keep Rosewood. Richard and I had a talk before he went back to D.C.
today. He's very upset about the terms of the will. He thinks
Edward Crandall's right, and that the only sensible thing for
us to do is sell. He said—never mind, it's not important."

"What did Richard say?"

Jordan fixed her gaze on the herringbone pattern of her
wool trousers. "He said that if you wanted to toss your
earnings into the house and the farm that was one thing, but
that it wasn't right to pressure us to do so as well."

Hurt stabbed her. "Is that what you think? That I'm pres-
suring you?"

"No." Jordan shook her head vehemently. "I understand

what coming back to Rosewood means to you, even with the successful life you lead now. Richard's under a terrible lot of pressure right now. There's this key bill his firm is lobbying for that's coming up for a senate vote in a few weeks. My being weepy and hormonal isn't exactly helping matters, and now there's the question of what we should do with Rosewood. It's no surprise he's so short-tempered." Her voice dropped to a whisper. "It's such a mess and I hate that we're fighting like this—we've never been at odds before." Overcome, she pressed her knuckles to her mouth.

"Oh, sweetie, I am sorry," Margot said, rubbing her bowed back.

Straightening, Jordan mustered a ghost of a smile. "I'm the one who should be apologizing. You don't need to hear about our silly marital spats. But the long and short of it is Richard believes that if we sell Rosewood, we can put our portion into a trust for the kids. If we keep it, however, we're running the risk of spending all our savings just to maintain the estate." Jordan laid her hand on Margot's knee. "Please understand it's not like him to act this way. Money's never been an issue between us."

Margot took Jordan's hand in hers. "The last thing I want is to come between you and Richard, or cause problems for you. But can't we give ourselves a trial period? How about if we make a go of it for a year? We can use my money to run the farm and pay for the house's upkeep. Then if we've lost more than I can afford, we'll discuss selling the place."

"But asking you to pay for everything isn't fair!" Jordan protested.

"What's fair about any of this? Nicole dying so young? Jade being left with no guardian? Dad's heart giving out before I could fix things between us? None of it is fair, and we can't change any of it. But I just can't sell Rosewood, Jordan. And don't forget Jade's feelings in all of this. We can't take the only home she's ever had away from her."

"You're right, of course," Jordan said, closing her fingers

around Margot's. "I couldn't live with myself. I feel so guilty already about letting Jade down."

"You mean because you didn't immediately say you'd be her guardian? Come on, stop being so hard on yourself. You're about to have your third child and Kate's only four."

"That's what I keep telling myself. And Richard's stressed enough by the arrival of the baby. The poor man might have a stroke if I told him Jade was coming to live with us. Not that we even have a spare bedroom for her in Georgetown. And somehow I can't see Jade happily bunking with Kate.

"Jade and Kate as roomies boggles the mind."

"Yes, it does," Jordan agreed with a sigh. "But even if I list a hundred more reasons as justification, it doesn't change the cold hard truth. I failed her." She slipped her hand out of Margot's to rub her face. "God, I hope she doesn't hate me."

"Don't be silly. She's not going to hate the sister who tirelessly bakes batch after batch of cookies and brownies for her."

The corners of Jordan's mouth lifted. "Maybe not. If I have to bake my way into her heart, I'll do so happily." Her smile turned rueful. "Lord, it's been ages since I could polish off a plate of brownies without having nightmares about my thighs."

Margot nodded. "Yeah, I've been struggling not to resent her for every last crumb of chocolate, butter, and flour she inhales. Or the jumbo bags of chips she scarfs down. Where is she, by the way?"

"Jade? Where else? Upstairs in her room. Why?"

"I thought I'd ask her to come and get the stalls ready for our three new horses."

"Good luck with that," Jordan said wryly. Standing up, she brushed off the legs of her trousers. "So we have three new horses?"

Margot rose, too. "Yeah. An Irish hunter mare, a two-year-old Thoroughbred gelding, and his dam, which is in foal. So technically we've got four new horses."

"I can't wait to see them, especially the broodmare. Did you ever notice how much wiser the mares seem once they've foaled?"

Hope rose within Margot. "So you're in, Jordan? You're willing to give running Rosewood a shot?"

Jordan smiled at her. "Of course I'm in. I'm not going to let my sisters down. Richard will come around once he understands how important keeping Rosewood is to me."

Margot wrapped her arms around her sister, hugging her fiercely. "Thanks. Thanks so much," she whispered.

After quickly changing into a pair of jeans and a charcoal-gray angora hoodie, Margot knocked on Jade's door, waiting until she heard a muffled "What?" to open it and step inside the bedroom.

Jade was sitting cross-legged in the middle of her bed, her laptop resting on her knees. "What is it?" she asked.

"We got three new horses today at Crestview. I'm going down to the barns to get their stalls ready. Can you come lend me a hand?" The flicker of interest in Jade's eyes at the mention of the new horses died as soon as she was asked to help.

"I'm busy doing something right now."

"Homework?"

"No," Jade snapped, "not homework."

"Well, I'd think your homework would be the only reason not to come and help out. Have you been doing it, by the way? I remember Mr. Selby saying it was important to keep up so you won't be behind in your classes when you return to school." That sounded parental and responsible, didn't it? Though Margot couldn't remember her father ever bothering to ask about schoolwork. And Nicole? Forget about it.

"I don't need to do homework. I'm not going back to Malden. I already told you and Selby that. There's no way I'm going back to that crappy school."

"Excuse me?" Margot stared at her.

Jade gave an exaggerated roll of her green eyes. "I said there's no way I'm going back to that crappy school."

"I sincerely doubt Malden's a crappy school. It looked pretty amazing to me."

"Oh, like you'd know." Sarcasm dripped from her voice. "Not that it matters what you think, 'cause there's no way I'm going back. I'm staying here."

Margot raised her eyebrows. "Oh, yeah? And who's going to take care of you?"

"You're my guardian, you're supposed to take care of me. Or have you forgotten what you said to Crandall?" she demanded accusingly.

"No, I haven't forgotten. But in case *you've* forgotten, I also happen to have a modeling career, which means that I have to be at fashion shoots. Who's going to take care of you when I'm in New York or on location?"

"Ellie can."

"No. She can't. Ellie and Patrick don't even *live* at Rosewood! And I don't think Ellie's going to give up her nights to babysit you."

"I'm not some baby who needs babysitting!"

Then stop acting like one, Margot was tempted to fire back. Instead she drew a breath and spoke through gritted teeth. "Listen, Jade, Malden is the school Dad and your mom chose for you, the school they wanted you to attend. As your guardian, I'm supposed to respect their wishes. And so should you. Now, if you can't be bothered to come and help in the barn, then you can pick up your room. It's a pigsty," she said, taking in the cans of Diet Coke, boxes of Cap'n Crunch, bags of chips, and clothes littering the floor. "And I'd get your homework started if I were you. I'm calling Mr. Selby tomorrow to let him know you'll be back at school next week." Without giving Jade a chance to reply, she turned on her heel and left the room, pulling the door shut behind her.

Her hand was still on the knob when the door's recessed panel shook as something heavy was hurled at it. Probably one of Jade's schoolbooks, Margot concluded grimly.

Lord, what should she do now? Go back into the room and get into a major catfight, or play deaf and dumb? And how had what should have been a basically straightforward conversation degenerated into such a nasty battle of wills?

She felt a sudden sympathy for Nicole, remembering how difficult she'd made things for her stepmother, fighting her to the last breath on every issue. The old saw "What goes around comes around" came to mind, mocking her.

With a sigh, Margot decided to let Jade be. The teen's attitude would doubtless improve once the pain of losing her parents lessened. And by now she knew Jade well enough to realize that nothing she said was going to get her down to the barns tonight. Arguing and pleading would only make Jade dig in her heels. She should save her energy for the stalls that needed prepping and her own conditioning workout, an hour of calisthenics and jumping rope. Then maybe, just maybe, she could go to sleep and put an end to this disaster of a day.

THE DASHBOARD CLOCK read ten P.M. as Travis drove through the sleepy town of Warburg and turned onto Piper's Road. It was several hours since Margot's revelation had hit him with the force of a megaton bomb. The idea that RJ was gone was incomprehensible.

One thing Travis did understand, however: he had a hell of a lot to answer for.

If only he had swallowed his pride when RJ began leveling those crazy accusations, RJ and Nicole would still be alive. Had he flat-out told RJ that he'd sooner chop off both his hands than touch Nicole, RJ might have calmed down enough to see reason. And if RJ hadn't fired him, then he wouldn't have been flying to New Jersey to find a new trainer.

If he'd told RJ the whole truth, there would have been no plane trip, no crash, and no tragic, senseless deaths. That RJ had apparently left him a huge sum of money and the pick of one of Rosewood's foals only increased Travis's guilt over the role he'd played.

But it wasn't simply his remorse over their deaths or the debt of gratitude he owed RJ that had made Travis, after unloading Lloyd Berenson's horses at the Double H, go directly to Hugh Hartmann's office and inform him that he was quitting his job there. Nor were they the reasons why he'd hastily tossed his stuff into the trunk of his Jeep and then made directly for Route 95, roaring down the dark highway like a modern-day knight on a quest to prove his valor.

No, what had him speeding recklessly back to Rosewood was Margot, the one woman he'd practically guaranteed would never perceive him as anything but a heartless bastard. How could she think otherwise when he was so thoroughly and repeatedly convincing in the role?

There was precious little hope in changing her opinion of him, not when he'd never reveal why RJ fired him. Hearing the sordid tale—that RJ believed he could have betrayed him by sleeping with Nicole—would only cause more hurt to Margot and her sisters. He'd have a hell of a time convincing Margot of his innocence; after the way he'd treated her, she probably thought he was exactly the sort of scumbag who'd screw his boss's wife.

And that wasn't the only thing he'd have a damnably hard time explaining to Margot.

How could he ever make her understand why he'd turned her away that summer night when she'd nearly destroyed him with her kiss and the sweet promise of her body?

How could Margot, who personified the word *privilege,* comprehend the choice he'd been forced to make: succumb to his desire for her, or keep his job at Rosewood, prove himself, and perhaps rise above the meanness of his background?

From his first day working at Rosewood Farm, Travis had understood that the Radcliffe girls were strictly off-limits to a kid whose clothes came from church handouts because his father drank every cent of his unemployment check as well as the money his mother earned waitressing. Steering clear of Jordan, who spent more time up at the house, had been easy enough, but Margot was a different matter. Horse crazy, Margot was always hanging around the barns. For some reason she quickly took to following him as he worked with the horses, becoming like a shadow he couldn't shake. While Ned might have harbored a soft spot for Margot because she rode like an angel, to Travis she was a spoiled little witch whose principal talent lay in ticking him off.

That was the story he told himself.

With hindsight, Travis realized the litany of grievances he recited to himself had been his way of dealing with the disturbing fact that Margot was growing up and getting sweet little curves in all the right places. By the time she was seventeen, the brush of her long-limbed body as she passed him was enough to make him grit his teeth against the raw lust exploding inside him. For all the myriad ways her body was developing she had no real clue of the sensual power she wielded.

If she'd only been older, if she'd only been anyone else, Travis would have been more than happy to show her just what she did to him. But she was Margot Radcliffe, RJ's teenage daughter. Enough said.

So he'd done his best to act like she didn't exist. He got really good at looking at anything or anywhere but her. When he couldn't manage that, he nursed his resentment by focusing on how much he detested Margot's "Princess of Rosewood" routine, a defense tactic that made it easier to ignore her spirit and tenacity, not to mention the way she looked in breeches and a tight T-shirt.

He'd been doing a damned heroic job of pretending she was no more than an irritating gnat until the night she waltzed into the tack room and nearly blew his mind with a single kiss. He'd barely recovered his wits when she undid the bow on her sexy little dress and let him glimpse heaven on earth.

God, how he wanted her.

He tortured himself with one long look at the body he'd dreamed about for months before forcing himself to drop his gaze and fixing his eyes on her sandals.

That's what saved him. The sight of those froufrou sandals opposite his own dusty, scuffed boots summed up the immense gulf between them. Margot was silk and satin, wealth and privilege. He was little better than the dirt coating his boots. Her sandals had probably cost more than he earned in an entire month while his own worn boots had been given to him by Ned, charity he'd happily accepted because it meant he could slip a little extra money to his mother, as the money she earned was invariably pocketed by his father and then transferred directly into the local bar's cash register.

Margot might have been too young to recognize the differences separating them, but Travis had never been that young or naïve in his life. She and her high-priced shoes wouldn't last two days in his world, and he and his hand-me-down boots would cause only embarrassment in hers.

The thought of making love to Margot, of moving deep inside her, had every muscle in him tightening in anticipation. But he couldn't allow himself to have what he craved most. He couldn't even risk a second kiss. Just a taste of those soft lips would send his hunger spiraling out of control. And then there'd be hell to pay. Once RJ discovered what he'd done, as he surely would, Travis would lose his job, and with it the chance to make something of himself.

Travis no longer remembered exactly what he'd said to Margot that night in the tack room, some load of crap about him not being into her; he knew only that he'd been a real son of a bitch. He'd had to be, because Margot had never been one to give up easily and there was no way he could have resisted her for much longer. To ensure the cut went deep he'd actually laughed as he told her to get lost. Christ, there was a ploy that should go down in the annals of prick history. But his pack of lies had worked.

Margot had eyes the color of the sky on the sunniest day of your life, and he'd made them cloud over with hurt. She'd run out of that tack room, her shoulders shaking with her suppressed sobs. He'd forced himself to stay behind, telling himself he would find some way to atone for hurting her later. But he never had the opportunity. The next morning he learned that she was gone, had driven off that very night with the party photographer, leaving RJ so enraged by this latest act of defiance that he refused to speak her name again. And leaving Travis with a vast wasteland of regret.

That was why his behavior toward her today at Crestview was doubly inexcusable. True, he'd been rocked by her unexpected appearance at the auction, and if he hadn't been staring at her like a starving man at a feast and then wallowing in bitter disappointment at losing Night Raider to her, it would have dawned on him that something must be seriously wrong. First, RJ would never have missed an auction like Crestview's. Second, he would never have been able to bring himself to deputize Margot. But instead of using his brains, Travis had let his frustrated desire and wounded pride do the talking. He'd sounded like such a callous bastard, he wasn't sure Margot would even accept his help now.

But she was going to get it anyway.

There were lights on in the upstairs windows when Travis pulled the Jeep up behind a minivan. At least he wasn't waking them up, he thought, as he ran up the steps and pressed hard on the doorbell. A minute passed with nothing but the distant hoot of a barn owl to keep him company.

The porch lantern came on and by the front door's side panel, the sheer curtain twitched. Another long minute crawled by and Travis stamped his booted foot impatiently. From the amount of time it was taking, he knew exactly who was standing in the entryway, debating whether to leave him shivering his butt off all night.

"Come on, Margot, open up," he whispered, his breath a cloud of white.

The door opened just wide enough for him to see her, but not so wide that he could kid himself into thinking she was going to invite him in.

She'd been exercising. Dressed in sweatpants and a cotton T-shirt, her feet were bare, her face was flushed, and her hair, pulled back in a thick, dark gold ponytail, was matted with perspiration. Even with the distance between them, Travis could feel the heat coming off her body. His own body temperature ratcheted up several degrees.

"Yes?"

He cleared his throat but his voice came out husky nonetheless. "First, I'd like to apologize for the way I behaved earlier this afternoon."

"Apology accepted." She made to close the door.

"Wait a second."

"What is it, Travis? Business hours are over. The barns are closed. Come back in the morning if you want to look over the stock."

He deserved that dig. "I'm not here for that and you know it."

"Really?" A perfect eyebrow rose to mock him. "Then what are you doing here?"

"For starters, I'm moving my things back into my apartment above the barn. I didn't want to frighten you when you saw the lights go on."

She crossed her arms and he tried not to notice how the gesture made the delicate mounds of her breasts shift beneath the thin cotton of her shirt. "And why would you be moving back?"

She wasn't going to give an inch and he admired her for that. "Because I'm assuming the job you offered me this afternoon is still available. I'm taking it. Your dad did a lot for me. I owe it to him and Ned to see that the horses at Rosewood are cared for and trained the way RJ would have wanted."

"How noble of you. And I suppose the same heartfelt intentions apply to Night Raider?"

"Knock it off, Margot. I just quit a sweetheart of a job at the Double H and a salary that was significantly higher than the one I had here."

She stiffened as straight as a poker. "We don't need your charity."

"You're not getting it," he replied in a tone as cool as hers. "I expect to be generously compensated for my work."

"Meaning?"

Travis thought of what he'd really like: a chance with her, a real chance. Instead he said, "Meaning I expect a raise."

"Of course," she drawled. "Anything else?"

"Yeah," he said with a nod. "I want a meeting with you and Ned tomorrow so we can get things running as smooth as ever around here."

"Fine. Now it's my turn. First of all, my sisters and I will have the final say in all decisions regarding Rosewood Farm. Not you, not Ned. You have a problem with women in charge?"

Travis shook his head. "Nope. Can't say I do."

She studied him closely, doubtless searching for a betraying smirk of insincerity. "Here's the second thing. I want to know why Dad fired you."

"There I'm afraid you're spit out of luck. What happened between RJ and me has nothing to do with my abilities as a trainer."

"Maybe that's for me to judge," she said.

"I don't agree. You want me to help you run Rosewood? I'll do it. But you take me as I am, no questions asked. By the way, RJ was totally involved in the day-to-day running of the farm, so you'd better be prepared to work your sweet little fanny off. This won't be a fashion show and you'd better know right now I won't stick around if you're not committed to your dad's vision of making this place the finest breeding farm in Virginia."

The look she gave him was about thirty degrees colder than the night air. She was something else, standing there so beautiful and proud. With her chin raised like that, she managed to look as regal as a queen—even in her sweat-dampened workout gear.

He thought about what it would be like to cup his hand under that pointy chin, adjusting the angle of her face so that his lips could cover hers. Would she taste the same?

Pretty sure that she'd fire him on the spot if he stole a kiss,

Travis folded his arms across his chest and returned her stare.

Seconds passed as they engaged in a silent battle of wills, the air between them snapping and sizzling with electricity.

Finally she gave a toss of her head, as if she were shaking off the intensity of the moment. "Is that all?" she asked with cool indifference.

Fuck no. Throwing caution to the winds, Travis stepped forward, closing the distance between. "No, that's not all. I wouldn't want to forget this." Wrapping a hand around her delicate wrist he pulled her flush against him. And his mouth descended, claiming hers.

He kissed Margot as he'd dreamed of doing. And the taste of her was better than any of his dreams—and even his memory. She tasted real; her lips carried a hint of salt with their sweetness. His tongue stole inside, seeking and then tangling with hers slowly and deliberately, each stroke fanning his desire. Needing more, he cupped the nape of her neck, his fingers caressing the damp silk of her skin, the fine tendrils of hair escaping her ponytail. His other hand traveled down the length of her back to her waist, urging her closer still. When she shuddered helplessly, her body arching into his, he felt the heady triumph of a conqueror. She wanted him.

Desire coursed through him. He longed to scoop her into his arms and carry her up the stairs to her bed. He'd spend the night kissing her, learning the subtle tastes and textures of her, and caressing her, exploring her every curve and hollow. He ached to discover what could make Margot shudder with pleasure, what could make her call out his name.

But his instincts warned him to slow down. Rushing things might ruin his chances with her. Stifling a groan, he raised his head, ending the kiss.

She stared up at him, her eyes wide with surprise, brilliant with passion. "What was that for?"

"I was just curious." Resisting the near-consuming need

to haul her right back into his arms, he said, "Remember our meeting tomorrow. Come to the office at seven o'clock, after the horses are fed and watered."

"That's too early. I can't—"

"Sure, you can. And seven's not too early with all the work we've got ahead of us. And don't try pulling a sleeping beauty act on me, either, Princess. I might be tempted to drag you down to the barn in your nightie."

He had only a second to admire the flash of fire in her eyes.

"My very own Prince Charming." And she slammed the door in his face.

Margot took a bracing sip of the coffee she'd fixed and broodingly watched the sun's rays bathe the back garden in pinkish gold. She'd been up before dawn, having hardly slept a wink. How could she, when she kept reliving Travis's kiss? The man was diabolical. He'd known exactly how to kiss her until she trembled with need, until all she knew was his taste and his touch.

And then he had stopped. Just like that, as if he'd flipped a switch. Why? She had the answer to that: undoubtedly because he'd satisfied his "curiosity." Basically the kiss they'd shared had been nothing more than a kind of test Travis had been conducting. And what exactly was he so curious to discover? Did he want to know if she was still so infatuated with him that he could make her respond in about two seconds flat? Or was he trying to determine whether she'd become enough of a "real" woman for him?

How infuriating.

Had he always been so arrogant?

How dare he tell her he wouldn't stay at Rosewood if she wasn't truly committed to her dad's goal of making it the best horse farm in the state. She was doing everything possible to keep Rosewood going, and until the estate's finances

were settled, it would be her money paying for it all—
including the raise he'd demanded.

Of course Travis didn't realize any of this, and the sigh she
gave chased the wisps of steam rising from her coffee. But
while explaining the predicament she and her sisters were in
might raise his opinion of her and her modeling career, Margot wasn't going to say a word. If Travis realized how bleak
their situation was and that Rosewood and the farm might
be sold if they couldn't keep afloat financially, what was to
keep him from returning to his job with Hugh Hartmann at
the Double H? He'd go where the best horses were, where
his career could grow.

She would simply have to suffer his obvious disdain for
her own profession. Because even if she wanted to quit
modeling—which she didn't—and devote herself exclusively
to running Rosewood, somebody had to bankroll the operation. From her talk with Jordan yesterday, it was clear that
Margot couldn't ask Richard and her for financial help. One
solution would be to sell some of the horses, but from the
gloomy picture Edward Crandall had painted, Margot realized it was more than likely that any profits would go
toward paying off the outstanding debts left by her father
and Nicole.

So no, she thought, taking another sip of her coffee, it
didn't look like she was going to be announcing her retirement from the fashion world anytime soon . . . and that was
surely for the best. Her career would force her to travel;
being away from Travis would allow her to maintain some
emotional distance, too. Perhaps then she could control the
riotous desire he aroused in her.

"Margot, whatever are you doing up so early?" Jordan
exclaimed as she entered the kitchen. Her sister was dressed
for the day in a pair of corduroys and a cowl-neck sweater,
her auburn hair pulled back into a simple chignon. The hair-
style accentuated the classic structure of her face but
revealed, too, the smudges of fatigue beneath her eyes.

"I must still be on Milan time," Margot said, seizing the handy excuse. Jordan might not remember her old infatuation with Travis. There was certainly no reason to reveal that the man still possessed the power to invade her dreams. "I had to get up anyway. I would have woken you, too—though not this early," she added with a frown of concern. "You should be getting more rest. Aren't you supposed to be sleeping for two?"

"That's eating. And don't worry, I'm doing plenty of that. I could hardly button the waistband of these trousers. In a few weeks I'll be wearing overalls and Richard's old shirts. Why would you need to get me up?" she asked, moving around the counter to stand in front of the stove.

"We had an unexpected visitor after you went to bed last night."

Jordan paused with her hand on the curved handle of the kettle. "An unexpected visitor? Who?"

"Travis Maher. It seems he's changed his mind and decided to come back to Rosewood. He wants us at the barn at seven o'clock for an organizational meeting with him and Ned."

"That's wonderful news! Having Travis run Rosewood won't solve all our problems, but still, he's such an incredible horseman."

"Let's hope he doesn't change his mind again and leave."

"Why would he do that?"

"Why wouldn't he?" she countered. "I'm sure he could get any training job he wants. Why would he stick around after learning we're teetering on the verge of bankruptcy?"

"Even after the money Dad left him? I can't imagine Travis doing that."

Margot shrugged. "Maybe, maybe not. I can't help but think Dad left Travis the money so he could buy some land and start his own business. He could easily find backers to help finance the venture. It'd be sheer stupidity for Travis not to consider other options once he realizes how iffy things are here. While Travis Maher may be many things, stupid is not one of them."

"No," Jordan said, smiling. "That's not a word I'd use to describe him."

"Right. So as far as Travis is concerned, the Radcliffe girls are flush and Rosewood Farm is in the black. Let's all avoid any mention of the financial mess Dad left us in. I'll make sure Jade knows to keep mum, too." She glanced at the kitchen clock. "I'll have to wake her up soon."

Jordan's brows lifted in surprise. "You do realize she hasn't been getting out of bed before noon?"

"Mhmm," she said, nodding. "I tried to tell Travis that seven o'clock was too early for Jade." But he'd been far too busy labeling her a lazy princess to let her explain. "Well, this'll be a blast and a half. I wonder what she'll throw at me this time."

"You're joking, right? She actually threw something at you?"

The corner of Margot's mouth lifted. "To be utterly fair, it was at the door—she tried to blast a hole through it with a blunt object. I think it was one of the textbooks I rashly suggested she study. She was a little ticked off to hear I actually expected her to return to school."

"Oh, dear." Jordan patted her arm consolingly. "Look, why don't I go wake her up after I've eaten breakfast? I have a better chance of escaping unscathed—Jade wouldn't assault a pregnant lady." In a more serious tone she said, "You can't take her moods personally, Margot. Jade's just lashing out from grief."

"I know that—at least I do when I'm not fighting tooth and claw with her," Margot conceded. "But last night's skirmish made me more certain than ever that it would be a lot healthier for Jade to act out on the hockey fields or whatever sport she plays at school. And wouldn't she be loads happier among her friends, Jordan?"

"Probably. And a place like Malden is bound to have a

psychologist on staff who can counsel her. That would help her, too." She set a bowl of yogurt topped with chunks of fresh fruit and almonds on the island's counter and sat down next to Margot.

"That's a good idea. I'll tell Mr. Selby we'd like Jade to talk with the school therapist." She took a sip of her coffee and straightened in her stool as a thought occurred to her. "God, I better get some sort of academic calendar from Selby, too, so I don't book any shoots while Jade's on vacation. There aren't any breaks until Thanksgiving, are there?"

"I don't think so, but private schools are a world unto themselves. Margot," she said more tentatively. "Are you going to be able to juggle the demands of modeling, running Rosewood, and taking care of Jade?"

She wasn't at all sure she could, but there was no point in making Jordan feel guilty about it.

"It'll be hectic." Her shrug made light of the admission. "Luckily I've reached a point in my career where the ad directors and fashion editors are actually requesting me for shoots, so I can kind of pick and choose. And in modeling, exclusivity sometimes boosts a reputation. That is, until the dreaded day comes when I start sagging everywhere or when the magazine people and designers find a new face to fall in love with. Then it won't matter how many go-sees I agree to or decline. I'll be yesterday's news."

"How cutthroat. I wouldn't survive five minutes in such an environment."

Margot shrugged. "You get used to it. And Damien's terrific at helping us keep a sense of perspective by reminding us that fashion is about the moment. We should take advantage of our success while we can, but always be thinking about the next step. That way when the moment's over, we're able to walk away without regrets. My friend Anika's already getting involved in designing clothes. She's got a great eye."

"And what about your next step? What is it you want,

Margot?" Jordan asked, scooping a spoonful of yogurt and fruit into her mouth.

Marriage, babies, a houseful of laughter, and a barnful of beautiful horses. How her father would laugh to hear that particular confession. But eight years had passed. And though she'd come to want those things, she wanted them on her terms. For that to happen, she had to find a man who thought she was everything. And despite her being a successful model and having men ooh and aah over her looks, their fawning admiration had zilch to do with love.

Resolutely she ignored her wayward heart whispering Travis's name and slid off her stool. "'Fraid I haven't quite figured that one out yet," she said lightly. "Which is why I better go do forty-five minutes of Pilates before we head down to the barn."

TRAVIS KNELT on the concrete floor beside Gulliver, his hands moving slowly down the gelding's cannon bone, gently probing for any signs of swelling or heat in the tendon. "The leg seems good, Ned. But just to play it safe, let's continue icing and wrapping it a few more days." He rocked back on his heels and stood, giving Gulliver's withers an affectionate pat.

"Should I tell Andy to longe him?" Ned asked.

"Yeah, but real lightly." Unsnapping the cross ties, Travis slid his hand beneath the leather halter and tugged. "Come on, big guy, it's back inside for you so you can finish your breakfast in peace." He led the gelding into the nearby box stall, his feet sinking into the fresh bedding. Unbuckling the halter, he pulled it off and braced himself, laughing softly when Gulliver lowered his large head and began rubbing it vigorously against Travis's torso.

"Darned horse thinks he's a cat," Ned observed affectionately by the stall door. "Gulliver's glad to have you back, Travis. We all are. I figured Miss Margot must have misunderstood you yesterday. Women get the strangest ideas sometimes."

Travis gave a carefully noncommittal grunt. Margot had always been a favorite of Ned's. Ned would chew him out if he discovered how Travis had behaved toward her at Crestview. The last thing he wanted was to explain why his mental faculties were shot straight to hell whenever she was around.

"So what time did you say this meeting was?"

"Seven o'clock." Travis shut the stall door and glanced at his watch. "We've got another fifteen minutes." Hanging the leather halter on the hook underneath Gulliver's brass name-plate, Travis wondered whether Margot would show or if she'd give him the excuse to drag her out of bed. Just thinking about wrapping his arms around a slumbering Margot was enough to make his heart thud heavily.

Jesus, he had it bad. He'd better pull himself together or his wise old friend would see right through him. "Have you checked on that new mare in foal yet?"

"Night Wing? She's doing fine. I was thinking we might turn her out with Colchester until she's been introduced to the other broodmares."

"Yeah, Colchester gets along with everyone. But have Tony put them in the near pasture where we can keep an eye on them. How about we take a look at that chestnut mare Margot bought—what's her name again?"

"Mystique."

"That's right, Mystique. Nice horse. I had her on my client's list but he went for a Thoroughbred out of Storm Cat and Cali Ali. Might be a good idea to hunt Mystique this fall, let folks see what she's got."

Ned nodded agreeably. "I said the very same thing to Miss Margot. Told her she should ride her in the Warburg Cup. With you astride Harvest Moon, the two of you should have a good shot at win—" He broke off at the sound of footsteps ringing on the concrete floor.

"Dang, time certainly does fly," Ned said quietly as he and Travis watched the Radcliffe sisters approach. "Seems like only yesterday Miss Jordan was sitting on her first pony, a cute little Shetland her mama bought just before she took sick. And look at her now. She's got two kids of her own and a third on the way." He whipped a handkerchief from his pocket and honked loudly into it before addressing the sisters warmly. "Morning, ladies."

The three of them returned Ned's greeting, but only Jordan

and Jade went on to wish Travis a good morning. All he got from Margot was a frosty look. Travis couldn't help wondering how quickly he might be able to warm her up if they were alone. What a fine way to start the day, kissing Margot until she smiled just for him.

"Hello, Jordan, Jade." He searched for the right words, frustrated to come up with nothing better than, "I'm real sorry about RJ and Nicole. Their deaths are a real loss, and we'll miss RJ every day here."

"Thank you, Travis," Jordan said. "I know I speak for Margot as well as Jade when I say how happy I am that you're back at Rosewood. Dad would have wanted it, too."

"Ned and I will do everything we can to make sure Rosewood remains the best horse farm in Virginia."

"And that's *definitely* what Dad would have wanted."

Travis returned her smile. He'd always liked Jordan, who in his mind was the perfect lady, all "please," and "thank you," and "I'm sorry to bother you with this." There was a gentleness about her that brought out the protective streak in a man. Then, too, Jordan was real easy on the eye, as beautiful in her own way as Margot. To Travis, though, it wasn't merely Margot's leggy blond looks that made her so alluring, but the fiery spirit shining from her vivid, sky-blue eyes. Jade was turning into a real beauty, too, though right now the kid looked like hell, her pallor that of someone who hadn't seen the sun shine in months.

"Hey, Jade," he said. "Doc Holliday will be mighty happy to see you." Doc was Jade's pony, a Thoroughbred Welsh mix. At 14.2 hands, Doc had carried her for years, but Jade had shot up significantly since the summer. She'd be needing a new mount soon. "You doing okay at that school of yours?"

"No, I hate it."

He frowned. "That's too bad. Why's that?" he asked, expecting a reply about the lousy food or some other such nonsense.

Jade looked uncomfortable, then gave a quick shrug. "It sucks, that's why."

Travis felt the others' collective recoil.

Then Margot spoke. "We're in a barn, not a gutter, Jade. That's no way to talk. Please watch your language."

Jade thrust her chin out defiantly. "Why? It's true. Malden *does* suck. I hate it and I'm not going back."

Way to go, Maher, Travis told himself. This is one hell of a big can of worms you've just opened.

Hoping to defuse the situation, he said, "A new school's often rough at the beginning, kiddo. I bet you'll be singing a different tune by Christmas." He smiled encouragingly at Jade, feeling like a total hypocrite. He remembered hating school. The only reason he'd stuck with it was that dropping out would have broken his mother's heart and been proof positive that he was no better than his lousy father. "Ned and I were just going to check on the new mare Mystique. Would you care to come along?"

Jordan shot him a grateful look. "Yes, please."

"How about it, Jade?" Travis asked.

"Fine, whatever."

"Well, come on, then," Ned said, ushering Jade forward with a sweep of his arm. "So what do you say to my saddling Doc for you? He'll be raring to go, and the ground is nice and firm."

Travis gave silent thanks to Ned, who continued his easy prattle while walking with Jade down the aisle. Jordan trailed a few steps behind them, murmuring to the horses and pausing to say hello to Felix, who was sweeping up the scattered bits of hay and grain that had fallen during feeding time.

Travis fell in beside Margot, who had yet to address a single syllable to him. "Sorry about that. I didn't realize school was such a touchy subject with Jade."

"Everything's a touchy subject with her. Of course, her attitude might have been a little less toxic if we hadn't had to wake her up so early," she said pointedly.

"Ahh. Then I'm doubly sorry."

She turned her head to look at him, gauging his sincerity, and her expression warmed a few degrees. "It's okay. Like I said, almost anything sets her off. Jordan thinks she's acting out her grief."

"Makes sense. In which case, Ned's probably got the right idea in suggesting she take Doc out for a long ride. Speaking of which, you should swing by Steadman's and pick up some breeches and boots. Can't exactly picture you riding your new mare in that outfit." He nodded at the cinnamon-hued pants and dark-purple V-neck sweater she wore with her high-heeled suede boots. The outfit was big-city chic, a forcible reminder of her other life.

"I'm not going to be riding—"

"Sure, you are. It'd be criminal to let a fine animal like Mystique laze about, and I've got my hands full working with the other horses."

"Gee, I hope that doesn't mean you'll be too busy to work with Night Raider."

He didn't bother to reply. They both knew he was going to work with the young gelding, even if it entailed putting in eighteen-hour days. "Steadman's opens at nine o'clock. You can go buy breeches and boots and be back here and ready to ride by ten." Then, seeing that Ned was leading the chestnut mare out of her stall, he smoothly switched topics. "Congratulations. You picked up a fine horse yesterday. Correction. You picked up three fine horses. With luck, four."

He was rewarded with his first smile of the day.

"Thanks," she said quietly.

He nodded, aware of how much he liked the new Margot he was coming to know. He wondered if she was comparing him as favorably. He'd flipped through enough of those glossy magazines at the grocery store's checkout line to know there'd been men aplenty in her life. Was she seeing someone now? Disliking the idea, he fixed his attention on the new mare Ned had hooked up to the cross ties.

Mystique looked calm and alert. As his gaze traveled over her, he happily noted the wood shavings stuck to her hindquarters, evidence that she had lain down in her stall during the night. A horse would lie down only if it felt comfortable in its environment.

"Seems nice and relaxed," Ned observed, echoing his thoughts. "And she's already finished her breakfast, so she's not off her feed."

"She's really lovely, Margot," Jordan said, stroking the mare's glossy neck. "Don't you think so, Jade?"

"Yeah, I guess. But looks don't mean everything. She could actually be a total witch." Her gaze slid to Margot, her message clear.

"That's absolutely right, Miss Jade," Ned agreed, seemingly oblivious to the undercurrents. "But your sister and I watched her in the demonstration ring. She's got a real fluid gait and is neat as can be over fences."

"Who's going to ride her?" Jade asked.

"Margot is," Travis answered.

Margot skewered him with a look and opened her mouth to reply, but Jade beat her out. "Why Margot? She hasn't ridden in, like, centuries."

"But it wouldn't take long for her to get her form back, would it, Travis?" Jordan asked. "You were such a good rider, Margot."

"No, it wouldn't take long," he said. "If Margot puts in the hours, she could even ride in the Warburg Cup."

"But you won't have the time, will you, Margot?" Jade interjected. "You have to go back to your *fabulous* modeling career in New York, and you'll be traveling, too, to shoots and stuff. Isn't that what you told me? Isn't that why you're making me go back to that dump of a school?"

So Margot intended to return to her glitzy world, and soon from the sound of it. The news hit Travis like a kick to the gut. How interesting that she hadn't mentioned anything of the sort last night. When had she been planning on sharing this nugget of information with him? A few minutes before she hopped in her car and drove off to the airport?

"Yes, I will be traveling too much for you to stay here," Margot said, a distinct edge to her voice. "But you know that's not the only reason you'll be returning to Malden."

"But if I were in school here, I could ride Mystique in the Warburg Cup. The mare looks like she might have some speed to her. I could win the Hunt Cup's junior division no problem on her. Right, Travis?"

Was this ever a lose-lose situation? Any answer he gave was destined to infuriate one sister or the other. Fortunately, he was saved from replying by Margot.

"Thanks for offering, Jade, but making sure you get the education Dad and Nicole planned for you is far more important. I'll ride Mystique in the Hunt Cup."

"I can't believe how unfair you are!"

Staring into her half-sister's narrowed green eyes, Margot was sorely tempted to retort, "Yeah, life really sucks," but she refrained. There'd been enough vulgar language for one morning. She couldn't believe how easily Jade managed to raise her hackles. Thanks to this latest skirmish, she'd rashly announced that she would be competing in the Hunt Cup, the last thing she wanted to do. Now, on top of everything else going on, she'd have to carve out time to get back into some kind of riding shape.

No, not just riding shape, she amended. The Hunt Cup was no afternoon hack. It was one of the Warburg Hunt Club's big events, attracting riders from all over the region to demonstrate the talent and versatility of their hunters. The timed cross-country course was seven miles long, over fields and through woods and streams, covering the terrain a foxhunter on a day's hunt might encounter. Horse and rider had to negotiate gates, ditches, logs, coops, and walls, and have the strength and stamina for hard gallops in between. Memories of her father grinning proudly, holding the Hunt Cup trophy aloft in his hands, were etched in Margot's mind. She recognized her own competitive streak well enough to know that if she entered the Hunt Cup, she'd be riding to win and have the Radcliffe name engraved on the accompanying plaque one more time.

Eight years ago, riding in a hunter pace event of this caliber would have been hard, but possible. After so many years out of the saddle, Margot was no longer sure she could stay in the saddle over a kiddie-sized jump. It looked as if she were going to have to find out.

She could of course renege. But backing out would create more problems with Jade, who already looked like she was gearing up for open rebellion. Keeping her own expression calm, she turned to Ned.

"Is there an extra saddle and bridle we can use on Mystique? I'll be riding her later this morning."

"We can use Indigo's tack. They're about the same size."

"Thanks. Since Jordan is driving back to D.C. today, why don't we all go to the office and start this meeting?"

Walking into the main barn's office was harder than Margot expected. The night she'd sat here with Ned, drinking whiskey-spiked coffee, the shock of her father's death had been so fresh it had driven all else from her mind. But as she took in the cluttered space, she realized that this office carried the strongest reminders of him. No wifely hand had ever dared redecorate or update it in anyway. His desk held the objects he'd used every day: a dusty Tally-Ho Tavern beer stein filled with pencils and pens; an oversized monthly planner, its squares covered with his bold script; a cut-glass ashtray that still held the dark-stubbed remains of his cigars. But it was his empty chair, as large and solid as a throne, that was the most difficult to behold. Set at an angle from the desk, it looked as if her father had merely stepped out of the room for a minute.

Remembering Jade's explosive reaction when she'd sat

on Nicole's stool, Margot said, "Ned, why don't you take Dad's chair?"

"No, thanks, Miss Margot. It wouldn't feel right. Travis, you go sit in RJ's place. Here, Miss Jordan," he said, pulling out a chair resting against the wall and swatting at a few stray tobacco leaves before letting her sit on it.

As Margot settled into another cracked-leather seat, her gaze was drawn to Travis. It didn't really surprise her that he looked so natural sitting in her father's place. He'd been as close as a favorite son. She didn't know why—perhaps it was the fatigue and stress—but she couldn't summon even an ounce of resentment for the man who'd won her father's affection when she, his daughter, had failed so utterly.

All she wished was that her father were still alive, ruling over Rosewood as he always had.

But the harsh reality was that Rosewood was now in his three daughters' woefully inexperienced hands. To make the horse farm a success, they were dependent upon the man sitting opposite them. It frightened Margot to realize that from the moment this meeting began, Travis, already so dangerously compelling, would become even more important to her. At least she understood one thing about Travis now: he wasn't the type to suffer fools, spoiled princesses, or women who were hopelessly attracted to him gladly. He'd eat her alive if he knew that she'd never quite gotten over her infatuation with him. Fortunately her years of modeling had taught her how to project an image of cool confidence; she was grateful for the skill now.

Deciding that it would be best to speak first and remind Travis who was at least nominally in charge, she said, "In his will, Dad left Rosewood to the three of us. To run the farm as best we can, we need to know what he envisioned for it, what his plans were. For instance, which horses were being brought along and which ones had Dad planned to sell?"

"Well, RJ always liked to say that for the right price, any horse at Rosewood was for sale," Ned said.

"Excepting Doc Holliday, of course," Travis interjected with a smile for Jade.

"That's right. Doc's too special to sell," Jordan seconded firmly. "So apart from Doc, how many horses do we have, Ned?"

Ned fished his tin of tobacco from his pocket. "Right now? Counting Doc and the three horses Miss Margot acquired yesterday, we've got twenty-four."

"Don't we have more stalls than that?" Margot asked.

"Sure do. The main barn alone has got eight empty stalls. Your dad sold a bunch of horses last spring, and six broodmares, too. One of his goals for this year was to replenish the breeding stock, so you took a step in the right direction bringing home that broodmare Night Wing and Mystique. You did real well yesterday."

A warmth spread through Margot at his kind words. "Thanks, Ned. I couldn't have done it without you."

"Don't know about that," he replied good-naturedly. "But back to the horses. Right now, our foundation stock consists of two stallions and eleven broodmares. Six of the broodmares—and that's including the new mare, Night Wing—are in foal. RJ planned to have Stoneleigh service Miss Molly, Allure, Hello Again, and Lena in the breeding shed next spring. He wanted Stoneleigh's last hurrah to be with his favorite mares."

"Stoneleigh's being retired?" Jordan asked.

"At Stoneleigh's last exam, the vet said that his, uh, sperm count had dropped way down." Ned's weathered cheeks turned an endearing shade of pink. "Ain't that right, Travis?"

Travis nodded. "Yeah. Stoneleigh will be twenty next year. He's had a terrific career as a hunter and stud. He deserves a break from getting hot and bothered in the breeding shed so he can devote his days to eating, dozing, and rolling in his pasture. Unfortunately, Faraday, our other stallion, has been having some back problems. Your dad, Ned, and I were keeping our fingers crossed that come spring he'll be able to perform in the breeding shed. So in addition to buying broodmares, your dad also planned to purchase a new stud. He had Ned scouring the auctions' sales lists. We also talked about driving to Kentucky for the Thoroughbred sales. There's one coming up in November, right, Ned?"

"That's right. Should be a good one."

Margot was glad she was sitting. Her whole body had gone jelly-weak with shock as she listened to Travis and Ned calmly discuss buying a stud at one of the Kentucky sales. What had her father been thinking? The opening bids alone would make the money she'd spent at Crestview seem like pennies.

Determined to avoid any further conversation about buying a wildly expensive stud with money they didn't have, she said as nonchalantly as possible, "And what about our other horses?"

"All real nice horses," Ned said with gruff pride. "Along with Night Raider, we have five other youngsters that we're training: Aspen, Indigo, Saxon, Sweet William, and Mistral. Then there are Colchester, Gulliver, Gypsy Queen, and Harvest Moon, horses RJ and Travis chose to bring along as show prospects or field hunters."

"Once we see how your new mare Mystique goes, we can decide whether to put her to stud next spring, or continue to show her. Then, too, if you and she do well in the Hunt Cup, we have to take into account that we might be on the receiving end of some very nice offers for her," Travis said.

Riding in the Hunt Cup. The topics Margot wanted to avoid were starting to pile up.

"And who's our top horse?" she asked quickly.

"That'd be Harvest Moon, right, Ned?" Jade answered, casting a superior glance at her.

"That's right, Miss Jade." Ned gave an approving nod, like a teacher pleased with an especially bright student. "He's been coming along nicely in the hunter classes."

"Have there been any interested buyers?" she asked.

"Yeah, there were some folks, but your father decided that he'd rather continue his training, let him get some more wins under his girth . . ."

Translated, that meant that her father had been holding out for a higher selling price. "And the others?"

"Well, there's Gulliver, the four-year-old I was icing the other night, Colchester, and Gypsy Queen. All solid goers."

"This is kind of a moot question since we have to wait until the estate is settled, and Mr. Crandall said that would take a few weeks, but should we be trying to sell any of our horses now, or is it better to hold on to them?" Jordan asked.

"Fall's always a good time to buy and sell," Travis replied. "The foxhunters are still in the market for extra mounts, and the hunter/jumper folks are gearing up for the indoor season and Florida circuit. I'll start putting together ads for *The Chronicle of the Horse* and *The Yankee Peddler*. And Ned can make some calls to let everyone know we're open for business. In the meantime, there are shows we can enter Harvest and the others in. Once Margot's back in riding shape, she can compete in some shows, too, so we enter that many more events. If Night Raider's training comes along this winter, we'll want to start showing him next spring. He could very well be our top horse in a couple of years."

No wonder her father had valued Travis so much, Margot thought. He'd been back at Rosewood less than twelve hours and already he'd formulated far-reaching plans. More than ever Margot knew that breaking the news to him and Ned that they might not *have* a couple of years to work with Night Raider, or any of Rosewood's horses if the farm went bankrupt, was to be avoided at all cost.

"Let's start getting prospective buyers over to Rosewood before we start talking about my return to the show ring— Oh, excuse me," she said as her cell pealed loudly.

Conscious that everyone in the room had fallen silent, she answered with an atypically breathless "Hello?"

"Hey, beautiful. Did I get lucky and catch you in bed?"

From Charlie Ayer's tone alone Margot could picture his accompanying lopsided grin and the teasing light in his blue eyes.

She ducked her head, her mouth curved in a small smile. "No, I've been up for hours."

"Damn. I was halfway into a really good fantasy."

"Stop," she commanded lightly. "What's up, Charlie?"

He gave an exaggerated sigh. "Work, that's what. I need that face of yours, babe. Damien and I have ironed out the details with the Dior people and they're practically peeing in their pants with excitement about the shoot. Can you be in New York the day after tomorrow?"

So soon. "Yes, I can make it. Will they need to meet me before the shoot?"

"Not necessary. Like everyone else in town, they've been playing the clips of you taking Milan by storm. The stills are pretty effing good, too."

"Don't, you'll make me blush. What time do you need me?"

"We're doing the shoot at my place, so let's say eight o'clock. I want you to get your beauty sleep."

"I'll be there."

"That's my girl."

"Later, Charlie."

"Love ya, babe," Charlie said. And perhaps that would have meant something to Margot if she hadn't heard him utter the very same thing to dozens of girls who stepped in front of his Nikon's lens. It might have meant something if she couldn't still feel the weight of Travis's lips moving over hers or the commanding touch of his hands on her body.

She flipped the phone closed and shoved it back in her pocket, careful not to meet Travis's gaze, which had been fixed on her the entire time she'd been talking to Charlie. She had a strange compulsion to apologize but stopped herself. There was no reason to feel guilty.

"So what was that about? What's happening?" Jade demanded.

Margot's stomach clenched. She didn't need a crystal ball to foresee that Jade wasn't going to like her answer. "I have to be in New York the day after tomorrow for a shoot," she said quietly. "I'll call Mr. Selby and let him know you'll be returning tomorrow afternoon."

Jade paled. "I hate you. I wish you were the one who had died," she whispered. Launching herself from the chair, she ran out of the office.

FOURTEEN

NED WAS THE FIRST to break the stunned silence.

"Holy Moses," he said in an awed voice. "What's gotten into Miss Jade?"

"She's a teenager. She's lost her mom and dad. And she hates me," Margot replied dully. "How else should she act?" She raked her hair back from her face and stood. "I'll go try to talk to her."

"Let me go, Margot," Jordan suggested. "Amazingly, Jade's not quite so hostile toward me."

"No, I should be—"

"Really, I want to. It's the least I can do when I'm abandoning you to return to my wonderful husband and my easy, teenagerless life in D.C." With a worried smile to Travis and Ned, she said, "If you'll excuse me, gentlemen, I'd better catch up with Jade and try to calm her down. Margot can fill me in on the rest of your discussion."

No sooner had Jordan left than Ned rose from his chair. "Time I got crackin', too. I got horses to tend. When are you riding Mystique, Miss Margot?"

She stifled a sigh. Better to get the humiliation over with. "I was thinking ten o'clock."

"She'll be tacked and ready." To Travis he said, "I'll find Tito and have him turn out Colchester and Night Wing in the near pasture. Want me to check on Night Raider afterward?"

"Let's do that together. I want to hear what you think of him. I'll meet you by his stall in a few minutes. Margot and I just need to clarify a few things first."

"Bye, Miss Margot," Ned said, as if this were perfectly natural, and made for the door while Margot tried to breathe. She wasn't sure if it was the subtle shift in Travis's tone when he'd said that he needed to clarify a few things with her or if it was the prospect of being alone with him that had her heart racing like the Indy 500, but every instinct screamed for her to beat a hasty retreat.

She stood. "Actually, I should be going—" Her sentence became a surprised gasp when his hand clamped about her wrist.

"Not so fast, Margot."

Though his grip was light Margot didn't fool herself that he was about to let her go. Could he feel the speeding of her pulse beneath his fingers?

"What is it? As Ned just said, we've got work to do."

"True, but I can't help wondering how much *work* you're planning on doing if you're skipping off to enjoy the bright lights of the big city. What's going on, Margot? What's this about leaving Rosewood the day after tomorrow?"

"As I told Jade, I have to be in New York for a shoot. Dior has a new cosmetics line. I'm the face."

"Congratulations. Now answer this. How in hell do you think you're going to run a horse farm when you're off globe-trotting, busy showing the world how beautiful you are?"

She yanked her arm free and glared at him. "Don't be condescending, Travis. The Dior contract happens to be a big deal, worth a lot of money."

"Since when has a Radcliffe needed more money?"

Deciding that she would rather have Travis believe her to be a greedy materialist than have him guess the truth, she stuck her nose in the air and affected a bored drawl. "No Radcliffe has ever sneezed at the chance to make money. Like they say, 'You can never be too thin or too rich.'"

"Well, I guess it's good you'll be earning such big bucks with this modeling job, since you're tossing buckets full of money out the window by not being around to do the work at Rosewood."

"Oh, excuse me!" Her voice dripped sarcasm. "I thought that's why we hired *you,* because you're one of the best trainers around. Or am I mistaken and we're just giving you a raise on account of your winning ways?"

"There's more to running Rosewood than simply training the horses. Countless decisions have to be made every day. As for my salary, you know perfectly well you'll be getting your precious money's worth, Margot," he growled, the sound as ominous as the threat of an approaching storm.

She smiled recklessly. "What a relief. As for any decisions, I'll leave you my cell phone number. Well, I'm glad we've cleared that up so you can go start earning your salary." She made to brush past him, but Travis simply grabbed her arm a second time. Resentful that his touch alone could make her feel as if a thousand butterflies had taken flight inside her, she demanded irritably, "What is it with you? Weren't you the one so keen to have me at Steadman's by nine o'clock?"

Travis ignored her remark just as he ignored her attempt to free her arm. "Who's Charlie, Margot?"

Surprised, she stilled. "What did you say?"

"The guy on the phone. His name's Charlie, right? Who is he?"

"And what possible business is this of yours?"

He gave a tight smile. "Humor me."

"Charlie Ayer's a world-renowned photographer and a friend. A good friend."

Travis moved closer, close enough for her to smell the fresh scent of soap and to feel the heat of his body. The fluttery sensation inside her redoubled. "How good, Margot? Good enough to perform a private strip show for him?"

It was so like Travis to bring up her past folly, she thought, embarrassed anger flooding her. She was suddenly glad he was so close. Her free hand whipped up to slap that too-handsome face. But her palm never connected. Lightning quick, he caught her wrist, imprisoning her. Then he had the gall to chide lightly, "Temper, temper, Margot," unholy amusement dancing in his gray eyes.

Schooling her features into a haughty mask, she said, "You know, I'm glad you brought up my youthful infatuation—my *blind* infatuation with you, Travis. It's lucky I left Rosewood when I did. Going away was immensely beneficial, an eye-opening experience." She cocked her head, studying him. Straightening, she gave him her sweetest smile. "Now that I'm back, I frankly can't figure out what I ever saw in you."

"Really? Maybe this will remind you." Slowly, inexorably, he drew her forward until their bodies met. Tension crackled between them.

"No, don't," she whispered, horrified that her voice had turned reed-thin with desire and that her body was already trembling from anticipation.

His eyes glittered diamond bright as his head lowered. "Can't help it," he murmured before sealing her lips with his.

His kiss was thrilling and dangerous. With brazen passion he plundered her mouth, his teeth tormenting the tender flesh of her lips, his tongue dueling with hers, demanding she respond in kind. A demand she could in no way resist.

With a moan, she arched into the heat and strength of him as she opened her mouth under his, offering herself. Her hands roamed over the sculpted muscles of his torso, the thunderous beat of his heart beneath her palms in sync with her own racing heart.

His hands were equally restive. Slipping beneath her sweater, his calloused fingers glided over her skin, testing and caressing. Then his hand was at her breast, covering it, squeezing gently. Her nipple grew taut. Aching, needing him so, she whimpered, pressing into his hand.

With a low rumble of approval, Travis deepened the kiss, his tongue mating feverishly with hers as he stroked and caressed, sending her senses in a dizzying upward spiral. His other hand swept down her back, bringing her tight against his erection. The feel of him hard and straining against her was unbearably arousing. Margot's head fell back, too heavy to support. His kisses moved southward, his mouth exploring the tender area of her neck, unerringly finding her every pleasure point. The heat of his open mouth and wicked tongue on her skin set off sparks, electric-bright inside her.

Then she felt his mouth close about the side of her throat, a stallion nipping his mare in the heat of mating, and the sparks exploded within her, bursting into flame.

She was so close.

Nearly desperate with arousal, she might have let him have everything, all of her, if not for her sudden awareness of something sharp and unyielding against her backside: the edge of her father's desk. Reality hit her like a bucket of ice water. The all-consuming fire Travis had so easily ignited sputtered and died. Hand in hand with the return of reason came mortification.

She was supposed to be proving her ability to run Rosewood Farm yet here she was, seconds away from having sex with Travis on her father's desk.

And sex was all it would have been: a torrid fuck in the office where she could still smell her father's cigars. She wasn't going to kid herself that Travis truly cared for her. And while her present feelings might be too entangled with past memories to sort out neatly, the intensity of her attraction scared her. She feared she might be falling for him all over again. And just because he was willing to "get down and dirty"—wasn't that the term he'd used before?—she couldn't bear the possibility of him rejecting her again.

Self-preservation spurred her. She gave Travis a hard shove, forcing him to release her. "No."

For endless seconds it seemed that all he could do was stare at her, his gray eyes glittering and intense, his chest heaving like a bellows. The sight of Travis aroused was more than enough to set her body trembling violently again; she gripped the edge of the desk hard.

Just when she thought she'd lose any semblance of composure, he shook his head as though to clear it.

"Did you say no?"

"I said no," she said, hating how weak her voice sounded. "It's not going to work, Travis. I already know about her."

His frown was fierce. "What are you talking about, Margot? Who is it you know?"

"The woman you and Dad fought over. Ned already told me about her."

At Margot's words, guilt as sharp as an arrow pierced Travis. Exactly what had Ned said to her? he wondered. Obviously not the entire ugly tale, that it was Nicole who was behind RJ's and his falling out, or Margot would have never asked him to come back to Rosewood, or let him kiss and caress her until he was ready to burst from the desire welling inside him. But she knew something, enough to make the situation even messier. Travis couldn't say that Ned didn't know what he was talking about without making his friend look like a gossipmonger. Besides, Margot would never believe Ned capable of idly spinning tales.

But there was no way in hell Travis was going to explain what had really happened and just who the supposed woman was. Neither Nicole nor RJ deserved that.

Dragging a hand roughly through his hair, he gave the only answer that might put an end to the topic. "She's out of the picture, Margot."

"Really? For some reason I find that difficult to believe."

"It's the truth." As best as he could tell it.

Her look seemed to see straight into his guilt-shadowed soul. "Right, whatever you say." She moved away from the desk, tugging her sweater into place, reminding him of what it had felt like to touch the soft curves hidden beneath the wool.

"I should go," she said.

"You think I'd kiss you if there was someone else in my life?"

"I don't know." She shrugged, averting her gaze. Her voice low, as if for her own ears, she said, "I still haven't figured out why you kissed me last night or today—"

"Haven't you?" He stepped forward and cupped her chin in his hand, turning her face to his. Her eyes were enormous, a storm-tossed ocean of blue. "I kissed you because I wanted to see if reality could ever compare to a memory. It doesn't. It's even better. And I want more, Margot."

"That's too bad," she replied. "I'm no longer the infatuated girl I once was, Travis. I'm your boss. You kiss me again and I swear—" She got no further.

"Careful, Margot," Travis said, pressing a finger to her lips. "You need me too much to let me go. And I want you too much not to touch you again." In a bold challenge, he traced the soft contours of her lips, then let his finger trail over her stubborn chin and down the satin smoothness of her throat, stopping at the reddened mark left by his teeth. With the sound of their breathing filling the room, he gently stroked the abraded skin, watching her pupils widen in involuntary response until only a sliver of piercing blue remained. Beneath his fingertip her pulse hammered, proof that no matter what she might claim, he affected her as powerfully as she did him.

At the moment the knowledge offered meager consolation. In too few hours Margot would leave for New York and go back to her high-flying, jet-setting, playboy-studded life. As he caressed the mark he'd left on her delicate skin, Travis found himself wishing it were permanent, so that all the Charlies in her world would know that Margot was his alone.

But she wasn't his, an inner voice mocked, and wishing wouldn't make it so.

Reluctantly Travis lowered his hand and his mouth tightened in a grim line when she hastily stepped away. To win

Margot he needed time with her, which meant he had to find a way to convince her that her life at Rosewood was as important as the one she'd made posing for the camera. The horses were the obvious answer. She'd always loved them. "Go buy some breeches and boots, and we'll see whether you can still sit a horse. The Warburg Cup is just weeks away."

Had she ever been good at this? Margot wondered as she rose up and down in a posting trot, acutely aware that if she were to try to sit to Mystique's trot, she would come perilously close to bouncing right out of the saddle and onto the neatly raked dirt of the exercise ring. Even posting was humbling. Her movements felt as stiff and jerky as that of a puppet on a string.

When she'd picked up her riding gear at Steadman's Saddle Shop, she should have swallowed her pride and bought some suede chaps—and a bucket of glue to smear along the inside of her legs. The narrow patches of chamois stitched on the inside of her breeches weren't sufficient to keep her legs locked tightly against the knee flaps of the saddle. Somewhere along the miles of fashion-show runways, she'd lost her inner-thigh muscles. What was that old joke her father, Ned, and Travis used to snicker over? How there was only one other activity that could keep a rider's muscles in shape? It was a shame her sex life wasn't nearly as active as the public believed; then she might not be in such misery. And she absolutely did not want to think about sex, because that would mean thinking about Travis and what he'd said to her in the office. Unbidden, his voice resounded in her head, "I want you too much not to touch you again." Oh, God, how those words thrilled and terrified her. They were exactly what she'd dreamed of hearing Travis say for so many years. But maybe her character had changed more than even she recognized, for now she couldn't help wondering whether Travis was moved by anything other than physical attraction. As great as the sex might be between them, could she handle it if all he wanted was a fling?

Her butt bumped gracelessly against the saddle as she missed a bounce in the trot and then another. She was flopping in the saddle like a sack of flour.

Concentrate, she commanded silently. Mystique was too lovely a horse to subject to such sloppy riding.

Fifteen more minutes passed as she and Mystique circled the ring. Her thigh muscles were screaming in protest, her lower back stiff and aching, bringing home the utter folly of having agreed to enter the Warburg Hunt Cup. How was she going to negotiate a seven-mile hunt course if she could barely handle a few minutes of trotting?

She was tempted to bring Mystique to a halt, dismount, beg the mare's pardon for abusing her back with all that bouncing and lurching, and then hobble away in disgrace.

But she couldn't. Travis and Ned had appeared and were leaning against the rail, observing her performance. Oh, please, God, no—was that Jade, Jordan, and the kids, too? Little Kate was probably a better rider than she. As she and Mystique rounded the ring, coming toward the group, she kept her gaze averted, certain her bleak assessment of her riding skills would be mirrored in their faces.

Doing her best to block out Travis and the others' presence, Margot focused on following the rhythm of Mystique's trot. She was a nice mover, alert and responsive. Margot had only to exert the slightest pressure with her inside rein and outside leg for Mystique to yield and cut across the middle of the exercise ring. In the center, Margot sat for a beat, switching diagonals, then guided the mare back onto the rail, trotting in the opposite direction.

When at last she slowed to a walk, she made sure she was far from her band of spectators. She had no desire to hear their comments; she already knew how badly she was doing and how terrific Mystique was. The mare even moved nicely at a walk—ears pricked forward, neck slightly arched, her gait a sprightly clip that was carrying Margot ever closer toward the others.

Okay, she thought. She could either pick up a canter or continue at a walk and slowly pass the careful blankness in Ned's, Travis's, and Jordan's expressions, and the certain, open gloating in Jade's. Drawing a fortifying breath, Margot gathered her reins and sat deeper in the saddle, dropping her heels to ensure that her legs were as long and strong as possible. Closing her fingers around the outside rein, she nudged her corresponding heel behind the girth and said a prayer.

Mystique obligingly picked up a canter. As Margot sank into the rocking cadence, she whispered a fervent "Thank you" to her, and reached forward to pat her shiny copper neck. She gave due thanks to the mare's previous owner for training her so beautifully. She would never have been able to pull off such a smooth transition from a walk to a canter with a less well-mannered horse. Her riding skills were far too rusty.

Indeed, it was a sign of how drastically lowered her expectations were that she experienced a spurt of satisfaction when she completed a lap of the ring; she hadn't fallen off and Mystique hadn't broken her canter. But the concentration and effort involved exacted a toll. Her wool sweater was stuck to her skin and now every muscle in her body was protesting. On the plus side, she'd passed the point of worrying about catching any stray comments from Travis, Ned, or Jade. Her head was pounding too hard from the effort of keeping Mystique moving forward in her rolling canter to hear anything.

She'd never felt so old or out of shape in her life.

When her leg muscles could no longer bear the strain of gripping the saddle, she brought Mystique to a walk. Leaning forward, she rubbed the mare's neck, ruefully noting that while she was drenched in perspiration, Mystique's glossy coat was only slightly warm. At least one of them was fit, she thought with a sigh, as she lifted off her hunt cap and wiped her sweat-dampened brow.

"So what do you think of her?" Ned called as she came toward the group.

She couldn't ignore Ned. Thanks to him, she'd bought this wonderful horse. But perhaps she could avoid looking at Travis and getting swept away by the memory of his kisses and the wild intensity of his caresses. She came to a halt before them. "Mystique's lovely. As smooth and easygoing as one could ask for."

"Sure seems it. When you get back from New York you'll want to take her out on a cross-country spin, do a bit of galloping, see how she likes the great outdoors."

She tamped down the hysterical laughter that welled inside at the idea of her galloping cross-country anytime soon.

"So are you going to jump her today?" Jade asked. From the mutinous line of her mouth and the defiant glint in her eyes, she could tell that Jade was not even close to forgiving her for making her go back to Malden.

There was probably nothing in the world that would put a smile on Jade's face faster than to see her go flying headlong into the dirt. But Margot wasn't sure her tired body would remember how to roll safely if she fell—another riding skill gone rusty from disuse. Besides, she'd sort of grown fond of Jade's trademark scowl—accustomed to it, at least. She shook her head. "No, I'm not ready to jump. Not today."

Jade's lip curled in contempt. "I guess I'd be afraid to jump, too, if my lower leg was as weak as yours."

"Lighten up there, Jade," Travis said. "Margot did okay."

Damned with faint praise, Margot thought, cringing inwardly. It was bad enough to have Jade remark on her metronome legs, but to be a Radcliffe and only do "okay" on a horse was a crushing blow. Well, she knew what she had to do. It was no different from when she'd started modeling. If she wanted to succeed, she'd have to work her butt off. Literally. Kicking her feet out of her stirrups, she lifted her leg forward and pulled the stirrup leather out of the keeper, then did the same with the other stirrup. Extending her arm, she dangled the stirrups over the rail.

"Here, Ned. Can you hold on to these?"

He took the stirrups with a grin.

"What, you're going to ride without stirrups?" Jade demanded incredulously.

"'Course she is," Ned replied. "Might as well go for broke, right, Travis?"

Margot half-expected Travis to say that she was a fool to consider finishing her workout without the aid of stirrups but he gave her only an enigmatic look before saying, "When you get back from the city and have put some more hours in the saddle, I'll snap on a longe line so that you can practice without reins, too."

Riding without either reins or stirrups: boot-camp training for learning—or, in her case, relearning—how to move fluidly on a horse. Without reins and stirrups, Margot would have to rely on her core and leg muscles and her sense of balance to stay in the saddle and control her horse.

Had anyone else suggested she forgo both of those aids, Margot would have told them they were insane. But as naturally talented as Travis was, he'd also always been one of the most hardworking riders she'd ever known. Instead of coddling her, he was assuming that she would be willing to work just as hard to regain her skills. Moreover, Travis would never put forward the idea of riding without reins and stirrups frivolously, which meant he must have seen that she was relying on them excessively. That was bad enough on the flat. She could get Mystique in serious trouble over the big, wide fences if she didn't address the problem.

Margot trusted Travis implicitly as a horseman. But could she trust him as a man, as a lover? She recalled the regret that had laced his voice when he'd spoken of the woman who'd come between him and her father. Perhaps it was as he claimed and he and this unknown woman were no longer involved. But if so, she didn't believe the breakup was Travis's decision.

She'd been a silly fool once before by throwing herself at Travis. No matter how much her body might crave his mesmerizing touch and yearn for the splendor of his mouth moving hungrily over hers, her heart would be unable to bear the pain of knowing he was using her only for sex, that he actually cared for someone else.

Her only solution, then, was to keep their relationship professional. She would simply have to ignore the fact that he still appealed to her as no other man ever had.

She gave him a brief nod. "As soon as I feel up to training without them, I'll let you know."

"The Hunt Cup's always the third weekend in November. No way will you be ready to compete by then," Jade predicted.

That this was one of the rare occasions where she wholeheartedly agreed with Jade was cold comfort. "All I can do is to try my best." And despite her own conviction that her best would fall far short of the mark, she nudged Mystique into a walk. Ignoring her protesting muscles, she bent her stirrupless legs into proper position, squeezed Mystique forward into a trot, and resumed her grueling workout.

Chapter
FIFTEEN

MARGOT WAS BACK in the New York apartment she shared with Anika, back in the world she'd come to think of as her own.

It was six-thirty and both Anika and she were dressed for work. In black jeans, biker boots, and a tight cropped turtleneck sweater, her cat-shaped eyes lined with pencil, Anika looked far too downtown chic to be doing something as prosaic as scrambling eggs—even if she was adding slivers of smoked salmon, crumbled feta cheese, and chopped chives as she stirred. She'd insisted on cooking their favorite breakfast dish before they went off for the day—she to a fitting at Zac Posen's and then later a go-see for Chanel. In anticipation of the day's shoot with Charlie Ayer, Margot had donned black leggings, a dark brown fisherman's sweater, and a pair of paddock boots she'd picked up at Steadman's and was breaking in. She liked to dress comfortably before a shoot. Soon enough the stylists and makeup artists would take over and refashion her.

While Anika scooped the eggs onto plates, Margot tore a peeled grapefruit in half and poured mineral water into two glasses, setting them on the small café table given to Anika by a smitten restaurateur. The apartment was filled with such love tokens.

"So did you manage to get ahold of your little sister last night?" Anika asked as they sat down.

Margot shook her head. "No, only Jade's voice mail. I tried her about six times."

"She must still be steamed over having to go back to

school. And it's not like you and she were real chatty before."

"Not exactly," Margot admitted. "Jordan said basically the same thing when I called her. I just keep remembering her expression when I said good-bye to her at her dorm. You'd have thought I was sending her to prison."

Anika took a bite of a Wasa cracker piled high with fluffy eggs. "It's harsh, being a kid and losing your parents. I can't imagine how I'd feel or act if mine died. How are you going to work it, sweetie, running that horse farm and modeling?"

Margot sipped her water. "To tell you the truth, I don't know if I *can* work it," she said, knowing she could tell Anika anything without it becoming tomorrow's talk of the catwalk.

Unlike many of the "friendships" that sprang up in this business, Anika's and hers wasn't tainted by professional envy. While it helped that they each possessed distinctive looks and were always in demand, they'd recognized from the first that their friendship was more important than obsessing about who raked in the higher modeling fee or who graced the cover of *W* that month. Other than Damien, Anika alone was privy to the details surrounding Margot's leaving Rosewood. In turn, Margot knew of Anika's childhood growing up in a cramped one-bedroom apartment in Chicago. Her parents, Rumanian immigrants, worked in a dry cleaner's shop, where her mother earned a few extra dollars as a seamstress. Although they'd been too poor to afford a car or health insurance, Anika had been given braces for her teeth, and ballet and art classes, her loving parents determined to provide what they could for their exotically lovely daughter. It paid off. A talent scout spotted her at a dance recital. These days Anika's father drove a Jaguar to his dry cleaner's—both car and business purchased by his daughter. Her mother owned her own shop, too: a couture dress shop that specialized in evening and wedding gowns. Wherever

Anika went she carried a sketchbook in her backpack. Between jobs she'd find a café, sit down, plug in her iPod, and sketch dresses, sending the finished designs to her mother.

"Did you see Damien yesterday?" she asked.

Margot nodded. "I went to the office right after my emergency session with Lars. I was so sore from riding our new mare, I had to have a solid hour of deep tissue massage. But at least when I left his studio, I could walk rather than crawl to Damien's office. Damien was a total love. I blurted it all out—Jade, the farm, the fact that we don't know how much money will be left once the estate is settled—the whole effing migraine. He was great. Just the way he listened helped calm me down. Then he took me out to Bar Boulud's for caviar and champagne. And get this, he let me have *two* glasses. He said this thing in Latin—"

"'*Nunc est bibendum;* now is the time to drink,'" Anika chimed in with a wide grin. "I just love it when Damien digs out that old Latin stuff. Reminds me of Father Thomas at Ignatius—not that he ever quoted anything remotely as fun. He taught me that one over dinner at Cipriani's back when I was worried sick about Dad's prostate." She broke off a corner of Wasa and popped it into her mouth. "Damien's a rock, all right. But don't forget, sweetie, it was your earnings that helped pay for that delicious dinner last night—as well as his villa in Capri."

Margot smiled and bit into a section of grapefruit. "I think he has your Versace contract to thank for the villa. Anyway, Damien's decided we should space out my gigs so I have more time at Rosewood. I gave him a copy of Jade's school vacations so that those dates are blocked out, too. The trick will be to keep landing jobs even when I'm not in the city. You know the saying 'Out of sight, out of mind.' And I'm hardly a fresh-faced kid anymore."

"With your bones you could keep modeling forever."

Margot shrugged. "Maybe, maybe not." Finishing the last

of her eggs, she put down her fork and said, "Anika, if I'm spending time at Rosewood, I may be gone for even longer periods than when I'm on location or doing runway shows. Will you still want me as a roomie?"

"*Of course.* This place is yours as much as mine."

"Thanks, I really appreciate it."

"Don't be silly. I couldn't imagine living here with another girlfriend. A guy maybe, when I'm ready." Without missing a beat she said, "Speaking of guys, I've been waiting super patiently. I want to hear everything. So you managed to get Travis to come back and work for you. Is he as you remember, the ultimate bad-boy loner? Is he just as hot?"

"No, kind of, yes." Margot's cheeks warmed in embarrassment at her confused response. She shook her head to clear it and began again. "What I mean is he's older—gosh, he must be thirty-two—and successful. I hadn't thought about it before, but he's really a self-made man. The job my dad gave him was as a groom. Then one day Ned let him get on a horse to see how he managed. Now Travis is one of the best trainers around, a fact Ned repeated about a million times on our way to the Crestview sales. In the horse business, the majority of successful riders and trainers start riding much younger. They have family who are involved with horses, too, and so are there to offer support. Often they're swimming in cash. Travis never had any of those advantages. So I guess if I were to describe him now I'd have to say that while he may still have some of the bad-boy rebel about him, what he really has is self-assurance." Cool and very attractive self-assurance.

"What about his ponytail?"

"He cut it—though his hair's still a little long." *And just as thick and silky,* she added silently. And his body was even more powerful, his muscles honed to sculpted perfection from countless hours of riding and working with horses. Her throat abruptly parched by the memory of those muscles beneath her palms, she drained her water glass.

"I guess the biggest difference is me. I'm not looking at him through this wildly distorted lens anymore. When I think about the overblown fantasies I concocted around him, I'm not even sure that having the ground swallow me whole would suffice to cover my embarrassment. At least now he's more like a real man to me."

"So the million-dollar question is whether the real Travis Maher can still be the man of your dreams?" Anika asked archly.

"You are such a romantic, Anika," she answered lightly. "I really haven't thought much about it."

Anika raised a disbelieving brow.

And despite Margot's resolve to think of Travis solely as the trainer who worked for her, she recalled the passion that had burned in his eyes when he'd held her close. Then she remembered the reassuring smile he'd given to Jade when she told him that Doc Holliday was far too special to be sold. If Travis were ever to smile at *her* with such protective tenderness, his molten gaze a shining reflection of the desire he felt, she would indeed have found her dream man.

"All right, yes," she admitted. "And to be perfectly honest, I'm scared that I may be as crazy about him as ever. But at least I have enough perspective now to see that nothing will ever come of it. Things are too complicated for it to work between us."

Anika gave a loud, inelegant snort. "When have you ever been interested in easy? Would you have left home to try to make it in this insane business if you wanted an easy life? No. You'd have been a good girl and done what your dad wanted and married some boring country squire. Easy is so dullsville. And besides, Tamara says things can't help but be complicated between you and Travis since you're both Cancers."

"Excuse me?" Margot said blankly.

"Didn't you tell me once that he was born at the end of June?"

"Yes. But Anika, how could you possibly remember that?"

"Oh, I remember all sorts of wild trivia. Latin quotes, birthdays, old telephone numbers, eighties song lyrics. I can rattle them off like that," she said with a snap. "But forget about asking me who the twenty-third president was or what the capital of South Dakota is. Anyway, at the Versace fitting yesterday, Tamara was doing Zodiac love charts. I had her do yours and I just happened to remember that the hot guy you just can't seem to forget is also a Cancer. And don't think I didn't notice how you avoided answering my question of whether Travis is still hot, so I'm assuming that's a big, big yes." She leaned across the small table, her eyes sparkling. "It might interest you to know that you had the best chart of all of us. Tamara was totally jazzed when she read it. She's certain you and Travis are a perfect match. That is, once you guys sort out all the junk keeping you apart. Aren't the stars just the coolest?" she asked happily, leaning back in her chair.

"Yeah." Margot smiled weakly. If only she believed in astrology.

"So when do you have to be at Charlie's?"

"Eight. Oh, my God, look at the time, I'd better get going." Margot stood and started clearing the dishes.

"There's no rain in the forecast. Want to hitch a ride on the bullet?" The bullet was Anika's pet term for her bright orange Vespa. She rode it whenever she could, claiming it was the only way to get about town. The Vespa eliminated all parking hassles as well as the unwanted attentions of taxi and limo drivers.

"I'd love a ride. I don't want to mess up the Dior shoot by being late."

Margot had long grown accustomed to the high drama of the fashion world. She'd worked at shows where the audience was kept sitting and waiting for hours because behind the curtain the designer was in the midst of a total meltdown, suddenly doubting the worth of his or her collection. Were the clothes truly sublime, or would every stitch and painstakingly chosen fabric get trashed in the next edition of *W*? The crisis of confidence could spread like a contagion until even the lowliest of assistants was running around, frantically adjusting hemlines and switching scarves and belts in a last-ditch effort to save the show.

Working on set or on location wasn't any easier. A shoot might drag on insanely because the photographer was dissatisfied; anything could be blamed for spoiling the shoot—the location, the models, the quality of the light. Then there were the stylists, the fashion editors, and other ordinarily sane people who walked onto the set and suddenly started acting like drama queens pumped full of amphetamines. Catastrophes and temper tantrums were the norm. It was no wonder why. Sequestering too many artistic, driven, and egotistical personalities together for a five- or six-hour period provided ample time for boredom, jealousy, and petty rivalry to ferment. Add some puffed-up VP or ad executive constantly shouting "*Come on*, people, time is money!" and things got ugly fast.

That was why Margot loved working with Charlie. Even behind the camera lens, Charlie was Charlie. Strangely enough, his relaxed, California surfer-dude charm could work magic on the most uptight of ad execs and fashion editors.

Thanks to Anika and the orange bullet, Margot arrived at his Chelsea studio a full fifteen minutes early. Even so, the enormous light-filled loft was already abuzz with activity.

Palin, Charlie's favorite stylist, spotted her first. Trotting over, he enfolded her in a hug. "Hello, doll. It's so good to see you."

"Hi, Palin. What's playing today?" An iTunes fiend, Palin loved compiling playlists and sharing them with friends. Margot's iPod held many of his "sound tracks to life."

"You're going to love it. It's got a little Diana, some Roxy Music, Bowie, Costello, The Cure, Seal."

"Can't wait to hear it. Is Kristin working on the shoot, too?"

"No. Charlie asked for her, but Dior's using their own makeup artist. His name's Deckert." His voice dropped to a whisper. "But all of us are calling him dickhead. He's already started bitching from *a* to *z*."

"Already? That's rich."

"He's quite the prima donna. Want to meet the big D?" Palin asked, wagging his brows over his rectangular-framed glasses. "He's over there, boring Evan and Keisha to death."

Margot glanced toward the other end of the studio. Evan and Keisha, Charlie's assistants, were doing a color check for the set they'd constructed, an opulent bedroom scene. A middle-aged guy, copycatting Karl Lagerfeld in a white T-shirt, leather pants, straggly ponytail, and dark glasses, was talking to them.

"Tempting, but no. I need to say hi to Charlie." She looked around the studio but didn't spot his shaggy blond head. "Where is he?"

"He's in the dressing room, going over the wardrobe picks with the ad director and the wardrobe consultant. Oh, and did I mention that you've got competition? Our pal Deckert's got a big hunk of burning love for Charlie." His grin was pure wickedness.

"Oh, great," Margot said with a roll of her eyes. "This is going to be really fun."

The dressing room in Charlie's studio was a former utility closet he'd had enlarged. Charlie, his back to her, was leaning against the door frame, shaking his streaky blond head at a lavender ruffled evening dress. "Nope. I still don't like this one, Sara. Unless you think Dior actually *wants* Margot to look like she's getting ready for a hot date with the queen of England."

The lavender dress shook as the wardrobe assistant holding it up for inspection giggled.

"Hey, Charlie," Margot said softly.

He spun around. "Margot!" Wrapping his arms around her, he twirled her in a tight circle. With a grin he set her down. "Damn, but I've missed you. How are you, babe? Has it been really rough?"

"Pretty rough," she conceded. "But we're coping as best we can."

"Good." He looked like he wanted to say more, but the woman to whom he'd been talking about the insipid dress stepped forward. Wearing a tailored pewter-gray power suit—Armani, without a doubt—the woman openly scrutinized her.

"Hi, I'm Margot," she said, stretching out her hand. She didn't have to be told that this woman was the ad executive in charge of the campaign.

"Yes." The woman gave a brief squeeze of her hand, her critical inspection continuing uninterrupted. "I've looked at your face so much these last few weeks I feel I could recognize you anywhere." Her gaze slid to Charlie. "I'm afraid you're right about the lavender. A pity."

"Margot, this is Sara Clarke. She's with Pace Morris. They've got the Dior account. And this is Erin, she's doing wardrobe. We've been culling a few of the outfits," he explained, gesturing at the two long metal racks laden with dresses and accessories. Dozens of pairs of shoes were lined regimentally against the wall.

"Pleased to meet you, Erin."

"Likewise. I just love your look."

Sara Clarke consulted her watch. "Now that Margot's here, Charlie, I'd like to get started."

"Sure thing, Sara. You ready, babe?"

"Of course. If I could just have a word with you first, Charlie?" She had to tell him about Travis. It wasn't fair to keep him in the dark.

"Erin, can you let Palin know Margot's just changing out of her street clothes and that she'll be ready in a couple of minutes? And tell Keisha I'd dearly love a cup of that joe he brewed."

Sara and Erin left the dressing room and Margot turned to Charlie. "Charlie—"

"God, it's good to see you, babe." He reached out, framing her face in his hands, and looked deep into her eyes. "I missed you a lot, sweetheart."

He leaned forward to kiss her. At the last second, Margot shifted, angling her head so that his mouth brushed the corner of hers. "Charlie, listen. I really do need to talk to you. It's about—"

"We'll have to save it for later, hon. As you might have figured out, Sara Clarke is a wee bit uptight. She has this thing about keeping to a schedule. But as I had Evan reserve a table for us at Per Se tonight, we can talk over candlelight later. How about it?"

Margot hesitated, considered insisting on talking to him now, but then discarded the idea. Dinner probably would be a better time to tell him about Travis.

She summoned a smile. "Dinner at Per Se? My mouth is watering already."

"Just don't drool during the shoot," he joked, giving her rear a playful swat. "So, have you met everyone on the set?"

"Everyone but Deckert. Palin told me he's quite the character."

"Jawohl, baby. But those angel eyes of yours are sure to win him over."

Unfortunately Deckert showed a distinct lack of interest in Margot's eyes, choosing to fixate on another part of her anatomy entirely. Margot had just sat down in his chair, freshly coiffed in an intricate updo by Palin, when Deckert let out a shriek that pierced Seal's "Crazy."

"Mein Gott!" he cried.

Before she could even ask what was going on, he spun on his boot heels and flew across the studio, arms flapping as he called for Charlie and Sara. He looked alarmingly like Chicken Little on speed.

Within seconds Margot was surrounded.

"Please explain. What am I to do about that!" Deckert exclaimed. Lifting Margot's chin he pointed a trembling finger to the side of her neck. Under the glare of the studio lights the mark left by Travis's teeth stood out like a red smudge on linen.

An awkward silence descended over the studio. In the mirror, Margot saw Sara Clarke's lips flatten in irritation. Fishing a razor-thin BlackBerry from the pocket of her jacket, she punched in a number and stalked off with rounded shoulders, delivering rapid-fire instructions to whomever was on the line, presumably some hapless assistant. Deckert had adopted an outraged pose: arms crossed over his puffed-out chest, his chin thrust out belligerently. Margot half-expected him to announce that there was no way he could possibly work with such a neck.

The situation was beyond ridiculous, but Margot had witnessed blowups over far greater trivialities at other shoots. She had always prided herself on her professionalism; starting out on a bad footing with Dior and the marketing people was the last-thing she wanted. What worried her the most, though, was Charlie's reaction. His expression, usually so open and carefree, was oddly blank.

Oh, God, she shouldn't have let him put off her telling him about Travis. But what to say? "Charlie, there's this guy I've never told you about who's been out of my life for the past eight years. And while I'm not sure how he really feels about me, I let him kiss me and, truth be told, I probably would have let him do a lot more if sanity hadn't prevailed." Yeah, that would have made him feel much better.

Her eyes sought his, pleading for understanding. After

what seemed like an eon, he said, "Aw, Deckert, man, from all that fuss I thought Margot must have gone and visited that tattoo parlor down on Tenth Street. That, or she'd gotten infected with a flesh-eating disease."

"That's right. Something—*nein, someone's* been eating her!"

"Watch it, Deckert," Charlie snapped. "Cover it up as best you can. I'll retouch any irregularities in her flesh tone afterward." He turned to the others and clapped his hands. "Okay, folks, drama's over. Let's get back to work. Erin, bring the ivory satin number over so Deckert can look at it. Margot's hair looks fantastic, Palin, but we may need to make minor adjustments once Margot's dressed. Deckert, you look like you're craving a cig real bad. Go take a smoke break. You can use the fire escape."

He waited until they were alone. "So, my rival has teeth."

Margot felt herself color. "Charlie, I am so sorry about this."

"Deckert's a flipping moron."

"No, I mean about not telling you earlier in the dressing room."

"Is it serious?"

She gave a tiny nod.

"Shit." Charlie drew a deep breath and rubbed his hand over his face. "Yeah, well, it's not like we ever promised each other exclusivity, is it?"

Feeling more wretched that he wasn't lashing out at her, Margot gave a minute shake of her head. "No, we didn't. But still—"

He sighed. "Margot, I'm not exactly lacking in perception. And remember, I was with you when you lit out. You weren't just rebelling against the 'rents. I always figured that there was someone back in Virginia, otherwise you'd have gotten that ring on my finger double-quick. You're the only girl who hasn't demanded I marry her. Usually I've got to fight you babes off with a stick," he said, a ghost of a smile playing over his lips.

"Don't think I haven't noticed."

"I just wanted to make sure you realize what you're losing. But listen, Margot," and Charlie's voice took on a rare note of seriousness. "You be careful, okay? I don't want to see you hurt."

Her throat tight with emotion, she swallowed painfully. "Thanks, Charlie. You're the best."

His crooked smile was so very dear. "Don't you forget it. Christ, here comes Deckert. I was kind of hoping he'd fall over the railing. Let's keep our fingers crossed that the nicotine's calmed him down. For our next Dior shoot, I swear I'm going to be the one throwing a hissy fit if I don't get Kristin for makeup. Christ, Sara Clarke is still jawing away on her BlackBerry. I'd better go distract her before she speed-dials legal at Dior."

Margot's butt had gone numb from sitting while Deckert pulled out pots, tubes, and creams, brandished an array of assorted brushes, sponges, and Q-tips, and worked on her like a painter tackling a three-dimensional canvas. But finally, after dusting powder over her upturned face, he stepped back. "*Et voilà*. She's ready for you, Erin. Be careful you don't ruin my work."

"I'll be careful, Deckert." Waiting until he was out of earshot, Erin said, "What a so-and-so he is! As if I'd let any makeup get on this satin. Have you heard what Palin calls him? Fits him to a *T*."

"Yeah, I suppose it does," Margot replied distractedly. "Hang on a sec, Erin." She flipped open her cell to check for messages, something she hadn't dared do while Deckert was daubing, outlining, and shading away on her. Nothing from Jade. It was pointless to try now. It was only ten o'clock; she'd be in the midst of classes. Tossing her cell back into her Marc Jacobs bag, she followed Erin into the dressing room.

Naked except for panties, Margot raised her arms. With practiced care Erin slipped a dress the color of pale champagne over her head, expertly holding the fabric so it settled without touching the makeup Deckert had applied. Adjusting the thin straps so they rested evenly on Margot's shoulders, Erin ran the zipper up Margot's back and then knelt, fiddling with the hemline.

The dress was a stunning riff on forties movie-star glamour, ultrafeminine with a pearl-encrusted bodice and tailored to emphasize her waist and the curve of hips. Stepping into the gold four-inch stiletto-heeled sandals that Erin and Charlie had selected, Margot held herself still while Erin made a few minute adjustments to the dress.

In the full-length mirror she saw Charlie's reflection and turned to face him.

"Very nice, don't you think, gang?" he said to Sara, Deckert, and Palin, who'd followed on his heels. "Palin, can you loosen her hair here and curl it, so it comes down across her throat? I want her to look real touchable. And Deckert, how about using a little more of that light pink blush high on her cheekbones and then misting her? I want her skin to glow like a woman who's just been made love to." To Margot he said, "Babe, lower your lids a fraction and give me a hint of a smile. Yeah, that's it. Perfect. Do you see what I mean, Deckert?"

"*Ja*, Charlie, I got it."

"What do you think, Sara?"

Sara tilted her head, considering. "Stunning. If you can get women to believe they're going to look like this, Charlie, they'll be flooding the stores for Dior's new line."

"Then let's go make Dior some megabucks."

On the bedroom set Margot and Charlie quickly fell into a routine that was part dance, part drama, with Charlie as choreographer and director cajoling poses and expressions from Margot as he circled her with his Nikon.

"Prop your elbows on the bed and lean back. Look at me, babe, and give me a smile to dream on. Yeah, that's it. Beautiful. Okay, now let your head fall back a tiny bit," he instructed as he approached with the surefootedness of a hunter stalking his prey, the camera's motor whirring smoothly.

Time was suspended as Margot struck pose after pose and ran through a gamut of expressions while Charlie sought the perfect angle, the perfect moment, in his camera's lens. She held still for close-ups. She shifted and twisted in and out of the countless provocative, come-hither attitudes that Charlie and she dreamed up, abandoning the sultry persona only when Charlie called for wardrobe changes or adjustments to her makeup and hair.

She was on her third wardrobe change, dressed in a gold lace affair that played peekaboo with her body. Her hair was down now, brushed so that it lay like a burnished fan across the dusky-pink satin-covered pillow. Charlie was standing above her, his jeaned legs straddling her, his camera pointed down as she rested her fingers over the shadowy hollow above her clavicle.

"Hold that pose. Think about your lover, babe. Imagine his hands, his touch. Let me see that in your eyes. Damn, yes, that's it, just like that. You're breathtaking, babe. Gorgeous. Now—" Whatever Charlie intended to say next was lost as a pealing note pierced the studio. "What the hell! Whose goddamn phone is that?"

Only one thing set Charlie off: being interrupted in the middle of a pose. He had a standing ban on cell phones during a shoot that even the company executives knew better than to flout. The ringing continued as everyone guiltily looked about or patted their pockets.

Then Erin spoke. "It must be Margot's, Charlie. It's coming from her bag."

The nightmarish memory of the last time she'd received a call in the middle of work still fresh in her mind, Margot jackknifed into a sitting position. Her heart in her throat, she rushed to her bag and grabbed the phone.

"Hello?"

"Margot, love, it's me."

Damien's clipped accent had her laughing with giddy, breathless relief. "Damien, you just scared several years off my life! I'm still at Charlie's. We're about halfway through the shoot," she said, in case he thought they'd worked extra fast and were already wrapping up. "I can't talk right now."

"I just had to tell you about this absolutely fascinating creature who's camped out in my office. The waif is rather scared but extremely defiant. She's got good bones and a mouth that's positively X-rated. I'm referring to the shape of her lips, of course. She hasn't uttered more than two words since walking in here. With looks like hers, though, she may not need words to communicate."

"Damien, what's going on?" she asked, her voice sharp with worry. "Did Bruno sprinkle something in your power shake this morning? Why in heavens are you calling me about some model hopeful?" She glanced up, horrified to find the others—Charlie, Sara, and the crew—openly staring, hanging on her every word.

"There's the rub, love. To my eternal embarrassment, it's not me she wants to see. It's you."

"Me?"

"Yes, love. Oh, did I forget to mention that this intriguing little urchin has the most enormous green eyes?"

Still in her makeup and the last of the outfits Charlie and Sara had selected for the shoot, Margot paced the length of the studio, her phone pressed to her ear, her formerly elegantly coiffed hair now a wild tangle from raking her fingers through it in frustration.

"Mr. Selby, how can Malden Academy be so inflexible in this matter? Wouldn't placing Jade on probation be a far more appropriate punishment?"

"Unfortunately, this is one rule our disciplinary committee is adamant about enforcing. The school handbook explicitly states that any student who leaves campus without permission will face immediate expulsion. This rule is also in the code of conduct that every student is required to sign. Students' safety and security are taken very seriously here, Ms. Radcliffe. Were the disciplinary committee to back down and let it be known that we allowed one student to flagrantly defy what we have repeatedly stressed as one of the most important school rules, this would send the worst possible message to the rest of the student body."

"But Mr. Selby, there are extenuating circumstances. Jade's distraught over her parents' death. She wouldn't have run away otherwise—"

"Let me remind you, Ms. Radcliffe, of your sister's recent travels. By her own admission she walked two and a half miles into town, then boarded a commuter rail into Boston, where she bought a train ticket to New York City. Once there, she rode the subway from Penn Station to Twenty-third Street and walked the rest of the way to your agent's address. At any point along her rash journey Jade might have been kidnapped, raped, even killed."

Margot shuddered, the blood in her veins turning to ice as she imagined what indeed could have happened to Jade. Needing reassurance, her gaze flew to the other side of the studio. Her truant sister was sitting on a leather-and-chrome stool by Palin's workstation. Damien, bless his heart, had gone to the trouble of escorting her to Charlie's personally. She looked fine—thank God—sipping a can of Diet Coke that someone must have brought her. With the shoot ongoing, Margot had not been able to do more than order her to call Selby so the school would know she was safe.

Perhaps feeling the weight of her stare, Jade lowered her soda and thrust out her chin in mulish teenage defiance.

Right then, seized by competing impulses, Margot honestly didn't know which she wanted to do more: storm across the loft and throttle Jade for her recklessness or hug her tightly in weak-kneed relief that she was unharmed.

She could do neither because Selby was still talking in her ear.

"We accept students to Malden with the expectation that they are mature enough to understand our rules and respect them. Jade's recent behavior falls far short of this standard. I'll make the necessary arrangements for her belongings to be packed."

"Mr. Selby, please—"

Ignoring her interruption, he continued. "The most convenient thing is for you to telephone FedEx and instruct them to pick up the boxes at Edwards Hall. If you should have any problems, please call my secretary. Good-bye, Ms. Radcliffe." There was a click and the telephone line went dead.

Slowly Margot lowered her cell, Selby's words echoing in her ears. "If you should have any problems . . ." It seemed like problems were all she did have. Now, topping a list that included wowing a major cosmetics company so that it wouldn't renege on a multimillion-dollar contract, Margot's principal means to paying off her father's debts and keeping Rosewood in the family, she had to figure out what to do with a runaway half-sister who'd just been given the boot from her fancy school. It wasn't lost on her that Jade must have known full well that getting kicked out of Malden was the perfect means to force Margot into enrolling her at Warburg High.

She crossed the studio to where Erin was watching Keisha and Charlie scroll through images of her on Charlie's desktop Mac, aware that Jade had jumped off her stool to trail after her.

Charlie looked up from the screen. "Hey, babe. The pics look real good. I think Sara and the people at Dior are going to be pleased."

"That's a relief. Hey, Charlie?"

"Yeah?"

"Thanks again for being so cool about . . . well, everything."

"Ahh," he said with a shrug. "As my crazy aunt Lulu liked to say, 'Shit happens, Charlie boy.' Let's show Margot the ones that have made the cut, Keisha."

Seated beside Charlie, Keisha clicked the mouse so that forty-odd photos appeared on the screen aligned in long rows, like on a proof sheet.

"You should use that one for the ad," Jade said.

Margot glanced at the picture Jade had pointed to and her cheeks warmed.

She remembered that shot.

Charlie had told her to think of her lover. Immediately she'd imagined Travis pleasuring her with his touch, setting her on fire with his kisses. Lord, was that really her, with those dreamy eyes and softly parted lips? She looked beautiful. She looked like a woman in love.

Charlie was studying the image intently. "Your kid sister's sharp. She picked out the best of the lot."

"Yes, Jade's clever. Terrifyingly so," Margot agreed, thinking of how flawlessly she'd executed her own expulsion from boarding school. "I'll go change now. Sorry to have kept you waiting, Erin."

"It's no problem. I'll come and help you with that zipper. It's a killer. Oh, and Damien asked you to call him and let him know how things worked out."

"How did it work out, babe?" Charlie asked, swiveling in his chair.

"As Damien would put it, bloody disastrously," she muttered.

"Aren't you even going to tell me what Selby said?"

She turned to her little sister and fought back the urge to scream, *Do you have any idea how stupid, how incredibly dangerous, that stunt was?* But what good would it do? Jade was a teen; she considered herself immortal. "That's Mr. Selby to you. And from the satisfied look on your face, you know perfectly well that you are no longer a student at Malden Academy. Congratulations, Jade. You've gotten your wish. I hope you enjoy Warburg High."

.

"PULL OVER at the stop sign. I'm getting out," Jade said, reaching down between her blue-jeaned legs for the padded straps of her backpack.

"Why? We're still three blocks away from the high school."

"I want to walk the rest of the way."

Before Margot could protest, she pushed open the Range Rover's door and jumped out, then slammed it without a word of thanks or even a simple good-bye.

Frustrated, Margot stared through the windshield as Jade, her shoulders hunched from the weight of her backpack, strode along the leaf-cluttered sidewalk. Then a flash of orange flapping just beneath the bottom of the bag caught her eye.

Damn it! That was her sweater. Jade had filched it without so much as a by-your-leave. But why should that surprise her?

It was two weeks since Jade had run away from Malden. She and Margot were now living at Rosewood—if that's what you could call it. Margot rather thought they were like two neighboring countries in the midst of an armed truce. Hostilities could erupt over the slightest provocation. Like now.

Stepping on the accelerator, she pulled up alongside Jade. With a press of a button the passenger window lowered.

"I'd appreciate it if you'd ask before you help yourself to my clothes. While you're at it, you might consider adding the words *thank you* and *good-bye* to your vocabulary."

"Good-bye," Jade sneered.

Like some cartoon character, Margot could feel the angry steam shooting out of her ears. "All right, that's it. Give me back my sweater."

"Why? You're not going to wear it. You only wear breeches and crummy tops."

"That's because I'm in a *barn* all day, and that happens to be an eight-hundred-dollar cashmere sweater. Hand it over," she demanded, sticking her arm across the passenger seat.

Jade glared hatefully. "Fine. Whatever." She jerked at the knot about her middle. "I'm supposed to wear something orange today to support the fall sports teams. It's called Spirit Day or some junk like that. Of course I had no one to drive me into town to buy anything and *you* won't let me get my driver's license—which means I'm the only kid in my grade that gets driven to school like some freakin' baby. I already have the Porsche Mom left me—not that you'd ever let me drive it. Here," she said, chucking the sweater through the open window. "Take it. Who cares if I'm the only one at this hick school who's not showing school spirit. *You* certainly don't." She spun around and stalked off, but not before Margot saw her arm move across her face, wiping away tears.

Overcome with remorse, Margot dropped her forehead onto the steering wheel. God, she was screwing this up royally. Hadn't she learned yet that arguing with Jade was like getting sucked into a giant whirlpool? It wasn't until after she'd kicked and fought her way free that she could think clearly and see how stupid she'd just been. How petty. How juvenile. The sweater thing was a perfect example. She'd have been okay with lending it to Jade—not thrilled, but okay. But Jade hadn't bothered to ask or explain why she wanted it. She'd simply taken it and then twisted the question of guilt around until everything was Margot's fault.

Their confrontations inevitably left Margot feeling guilty and despised. That was the worst part of it: being on the receiving end of such patent hatred. She wasn't used to being hated—at least not anymore, not since she'd lived under the same roof as Nicole. The last thing Margot wanted was to have the same poisonous relationship with Jade. But she couldn't figure out how to stop the cycle of viciousness.

She drove back to Rosewood and parked behind the main barn, pulling in between Ned's pickup truck and Travis's Jeep. As she stashed the keys in the glove compartment and climbed out of the Rover, thoughts of Jade consumed her. But spotting Travis leading Night Raider up the path that led from the exercise ring ushered in a whole new set of worries.

Oh, Lord, it was already happening; "it" being the helpless condition she succumbed to whenever Travis was anywhere near. The symptoms were humbling, relentlessly so: her heart fluttered, her palms went clammy, and her head spun until her brain felt like so much cotton candy.

Surely she should be desensitized by now. She was in Travis's company every day, working from morning till dusk. Often they shared the outdoor ring, circling around each other for a full hour as they put the horses through their paces. And not a minute slipped by without Margot's being achingly aware of him.

And when they weren't training or riding, Travis and Ned were providing her with a crash course in Rosewood's breeding program. Only now did she grasp how much work was involved in the fall and winter months. The pregnant mares required vigilant monitoring in addition to their scheduled veterinary checkups. Those mares not in foal had to be exercised so they'd be in prime condition when they were covered come spring. And the stallions, in and off season, demanded hours of hands-on care. Ned liked to boast that the excellence of Rosewood's foals was due not just to the quality of their bloodlines but also to their dams and sires being kept in prime condition.

Given the amount of time Margot spent in Travis's company, the devastating effect he had on her should have diminished. At the very least she should have built an immunity to make her resistant, rather than weak-kneed and delirious, her head filled with sappy romantic fantasies. After all, she'd been wined, dined, and pursued by handsome men before. And pretty much every single one of them had left her cold.

Travis could melt her with a single look.

But looking was all he seemed inclined to do. He hadn't tried to kiss her once since she'd come back from New York.

Was that it? Was it because he hadn't betrayed the slightest interest in kissing her again that she couldn't stop obsessing about the shape of his mouth? Was it because he hadn't once taken her into his arms that watching him brush Gulliver until the gelding's coat shone could make her tremble as if she were the one being stroked?

"Morning." Travis brought Night Raider to a halt in front of her.

There ought to be a law against such high-octane looks. The sunny weather they'd been enjoying had deepened his tan, making his gray eyes more mesmerizing than ever, enhancing the strong bone structure of his face. Dressed in a cable-knit sweater, breeches, and dusty field boots, he looked rugged and far too sexy for her peace of mind.

"Hey," she managed in return. Her eyes strayed to his mouth, and the need to feel it against hers made her want to cry.

"What's wrong? You look upset."

For a moment she wavered, tempted to blurt out the whole of it. *How's this for what's wrong: I'm scared silly by what I feel for you. It's not just the physical stuff—that I can't stop thinking about having you make love to me, that I dream of you holding me through the night. It's that I like you in a way I never did before. You're so knowledgeable and experienced and endlessly patient in explaining what I need to know about running this farm. I'm already*

completely dependent on you. But what am I to you? A
fashion model who's inherited a horse farm. If only I could
convince myself that you cared for me, then everything
would be different. . . .

But she didn't have the courage to tell him what was in her
heart, just as she didn't have the guts to tell him the truth
about Rosewood's precarious situation financially.

A situation that had yet to be resolved. Edward Crandall
was still settling the estate's finances. As a result, Jordan,
Jade, and she were basically left sitting in limbo.

A part of her kept hoping for a miracle, that Crandall
would stumble on some secret account Dad had left them
and they'd be set for life. However, with every day that
passed without a "I have such wonderful news" call from the
lawyer, Margot found her hope fading and her worry growing. What would Travis think of her once he learned that
she'd been lying to him?

Because lying was essentially what she was doing. By not
being forthright about Rosewood's shaky future, she was
preventing Travis from acting in his own best interest, and
from letting him choose either to return to Hugh Hartmann's Double H Farm or to use the money her father had
bequeathed to buy a place of his own.

Afraid he'd read the guilt in her face, she stepped in front
of the black gelding and began stroking his velvety muzzle.
"I'm worried about Jade," she said, at least being honest
about that. "We had another fight when I dropped her off
at school. According to her, I'm the cause of all that's rotten
in her life."

"The kid's hurting."

"I know. But somehow that doesn't stop me from saying
and doing everything wrong."

"Quit being so hard on yourself. Who's to say she
wouldn't be lashing out at anyone else just as often? Do you
think Jordan wouldn't have just as much trouble with her?"

"No, because Jordan's sweet and kind and understanding."

"And I'd lay odds on Jade turning Jordan into a screaming, rabid hyena within three days."

The idea of Jordan ever being anything but her calm and gentle self was so preposterous it made Margot smile. Her smile became a laugh when Night Raider lowered his head against her middle, snuffling delicately at the pocket of her vest as he searched for a treat.

"No, boy, I can't give you anything, not when you've got a bit in your mouth. I promise I'll give you a treat later. How was Raider today?" she asked. They'd discovered Night Raider was most aptly named. The young horse had a disconcerting talent for opening the latch on his stall door. Doing a final barn check the other evening, Travis had found him happily munching his way through a bin of dried carrot and apple treats, the safety catch on its lid no match for his clever muzzle and teeth. Luckily Travis put an end to Raider's late-night feast before he'd eaten much of the bin's contents. Otherwise he might well have ended up with a life-threatening case of colic.

"He was real good. Now that he's gotten used to his new home, he's settling down nicely. We're working on transitions. He listens well. Smart as anything."

The affection and pride in Travis's voice merely added to Margot's guilt. By all rights the gelding should be Travis's. The fair thing would be to let him choose Raider as part of her father's bequest, or prove that she was a serious businesswoman and sell him to Travis. Travis probably wouldn't even blink if she pinned a hundred-thousand-dollar price tag to the gelding. And the money would come in handy.

But Margot wasn't going to do either. Raider was a key bargaining chip in keeping Travis at Rosewood. She consoled herself with the thought that while Travis might not own him outright, he had a free rein in training the young horse.

"You still set on my longeing you on Mystique today?" Travis asked.

She nodded. She'd been riding the mare daily, as well as exercising other horses Travis asked her to help with. "I'm still relying too much on my reins and stirrups. I don't want to be grabbing Mystique's mouth when we take a wall. Landing in a ditch isn't the way to win the Hunt Cup—not that I expect to win," she added hurriedly. "But I don't think I could bear the smug look on Jade's face if I don't acquit myself respectably on Mystique." Since their return, Jade had embarked on a nonstop campaign to ride Mystique herself. Margot's refusal—she would have to be a total idiot to reward Jade for getting kicked out of school by giving her a new horse—was just one item in Jade's long list of grievances against her.

"Don't worry about Jade. Deep down she really wants to ride Doc in the Hunt Cup. That pony's a great campaigner and she's as competitive as they come. They'll be the junior team to beat. Given how much Jade's shot up in the last couple of months, this'll probably be the last event she can enter him in." He pushed back the sleeve of his sweater to consult his watch and Margot's insides fluttered at the sight of his sinewed forearm covered with a sprinkling of dark brown hair. "Tito should have Mystique ready for you now. You can take her down to the ring and warm up while I untack Raider. Andy should be finished in the stallion barn by then. He can hand walk Raider while I'm working with you and Mystique." He patted the colt's sleek neck. "I want this guy nice and relaxed for Jarvis."

Frank Jarvis was Rosewood's farrier. They'd used him ever since Margot could remember. The best blacksmith in the county, Frank was meticulous and careful in sizing shoes and fixing problem hooves. Endowed with a Zen-like aura of tranquillity, he could fit shoes to the most skittish of horses.

But Margot had spent enough hours observing how Travis

ran their barn to know that by the time Raider was hooked to the cross ties, a hoof propped against Jarvis's thick leather apron, Travis would have done everything to ensure the young horse was as relaxed and happy as a woman enjoying a French pedicure. One of Travis's many gifts as a horseman was his ability to anticipate what Rosewood's horses needed in any given situation. His method of training required both insight and endless patience. Careful and methodical, he refused to rush a horse. The results were worth the hours he devoted; Rosewood's horses were willing, confident, and brave.

"What time is Jarvis coming?" she asked as they began walking up to the barn, her stride matching his.

"Eleven o'clock. If we're not finished, I told Ned to have Frank skip Raider and shoe the other horses first."

Ten horses were due for new shoes. Margot tried not to think about the cost, one more bill in a never-ending slew that included vet bills, bedding, feed and supplement bills, and paychecks. All the expenses were necessary. But Margot personally considered the check she wrote in Travis's name the most vital of all. With the number of hours he put in each day, she should be writing a check twice as large . . . and she shouldn't be dragging him away from training to help her figure out how to ride better.

"That would complicate things for everyone. I'll go get Mystique and start warming up right away." Trying not stress out about the arduousness of the upcoming workout, she drew a steadying breath. "Do you want me to bring the longe line down to the ring?"

"No, I'll pick one up. Hey"—he angled his head, studying her—"you're not nervous, are you?"

Terrified was more like it. She shrugged. "I haven't ridden without reins and stirrups since I was a kid."

"We'll start out nice and easy on the flat. And you only have to jump if you're feeling up to it. Mystique's got a sweet jumping style."

It was nice of him to try to reassure her. She did her best to smile. "Okay. But if I do decide to jump, don't set the rail too high. I have another shoot coming up with Charlie. He'd never forgive me if I messed up my face."

It was impossible to miss the way Travis tensed at the mention of Charlie Ayer. Could he actually be jealous? Any such hope was quickly dashed.

"I'd kind of thought you were beginning to understand how much work there is to do here. You can't afford to keep dropping everything to go off and be this guy Charlie's glamour girl."

Was this really how he saw her, as some party-loving socialite who couldn't wait to hightail it off to the city? Couldn't he see any worth in what she did as a model? It cut her to the quick that after spending all this time in her company, he continued to be prejudiced against her career. But why should Travis care about her career when he didn't care about *her*? Obviously the only part of her life that he cared about was whether she was doing everything he considered necessary in making the farm successful.

Hurt sharpened her voice. "You may have an encyclopedia's worth of knowledge about horses, Travis, but you don't understand the first thing about my life as a model or how much I owe to friends like Charlie. I'll see you down at the ring."

Travis watched Margot walk away, stiff-backed with anger, and resisted the urge to go after her and apologize. What could he say without sounding like an idiot? That he didn't want her to go to New York or any other place Charlie Ayer might be? Sure. She would think he'd lost his mind, which he probably had.

These two weeks, he'd made himself back off, knowing that Margot had her hands full dealing with Jade. He'd been tying himself in knots, acting the perfect gentleman. And what had it accomplished? Squat, that's what.

How could his explanation of a pregnant mare's worming

schedule compete with Charlie Ayer's fancy, sophisticated world? How could the endless cycle of grooming, training, and feeding horses—backbreaking, dirty, exhausting labor—compare to the posh life she had in New York? How could he ever get a chance to spend time with her outside of the barn when, on the verge of suggesting that maybe she'd like to have dinner with him at the Coach House, that damned cell phone of hers would ring with Charlie Ayer on the line? If Travis continued to be all businesslike, how in hell was he supposed to let Margot in on the fact that he, like Ayer, might get a little upset if she were hurt riding Mystique? But his distress would have nothing to do with the earning potential of her beautiful face being jeopardized and everything to do with what happened to him when he looked at it.

It was a face Travis couldn't get enough of.

He loved how the autumn sun made her skin glow with health, how an hour's ride on Mystique or Colchester brought a flush to her cheeks. He loved how the soft light from the desk lamp in the office enhanced the drama of her high cheekbones and shadowed her eyes, making them deep and mysterious. When he made her smile, it was the stuff of dreams.

He could explain a hundred different things pertaining to her horses, but he hadn't a clue how to describe the feelings he had for her. Truth was, he didn't want to explain or talk at all. He wanted to take her in his arms, kiss her, and keep right on kissing her. That would show Margot what she meant to him, and to hell with the fact that she was his boss and that it was broad daylight and they were standing in the courtyard for any and all to witness.

He couldn't take it anymore. He was going stark raving mad from the need to taste Margot again, to plunge his fingers into her thick, silky hair and pull her close until their bodies were fused. He needed to hear her sweet moans of passion and know that he'd made Margot forget the rest of the world. That there was only him. Loving her.

And she thought Charlie Ayer was the only one who would care if she injured herself?

Travis would never forgive himself if she got hurt riding.

Luckily Margot's skills were returning quickly because while Rosewood Farm would certainly benefit from having her represent the family in the open division of the Hunt Cup, there was no way he would allow her to enter if she wasn't ready to tackle the course. He'd lock her in the main barn's grain room the morning of the Cup rather than risk her safety.

In the meantime, the best shot Travis had at keeping her safe in the saddle was to help her train as thoroughly and rigorously as possible.

Chapter ❧
SEVENTEEN

THE QUILTED NYLON VEST Margot had been wearing earlier was hanging on the standard of a brush jump when Travis climbed between the rails of the exercise ring. Carrying a coiled longe tape and a pair of side reins in his hands, he walked toward the center of the ring while Margot cantered on the rail. Thanks to the extensive riding she'd been doing, she'd improved 1,000 percent over the last two weeks. Her leg was more secure and she was sitting easily to Mystique's rolling canter. Still, a session of riding without stirrups and reins would help her achieve a rock-solid seat and a better sense of balance. In a hunt trial, with its timed pace, varied terrain, and tricky obstacles, she would need strength and balance in spades.

Margot rounded the corner. Sweet Jesus, he wished she'd kept that vest on, he thought, distracted by the soft bounce of her breasts beneath her sweater.

Bringing Mystique to a walk, she cut into the center and halted in front of him.

"You ready?" His question came out like the croak of a dying frog. *For God's sake, Maher, get a grip.*

"As ready as I'll ever be."

"Okay, then. Hop off so I can attach these side reins. They'll control her head carriage while you're working on the flat. I'll remove them when it comes time to jump."

"What should I do with the reins?" she asked, lifting the braided rein between her gloved fingers.

"Tie 'em in her mane. That way they won't slip up and

down her neck. If you think you're gonna fall, they'll be right there within grabbing reach."

"Good to know." Her dry tone had him grinning. She'd always had spunk. He liked that she hadn't lost it.

While Travis looped the side reins through Mystique's snaffle bit, Margot knotted her own reins in a thick chunk of Mystique's copper mane. Then, kicking her feet out of the stirrups, she swung her right leg over the saddle and dismounted, landing lightly beside him. Without further ado, she began removing the stirrups. As she tugged at the leathers, her elbow grazed his arm. His muscles twitched in response.

"Here, switch places with me. I've got to attach this end of the side rein around the girth," he said, stepping toward her. She moved simultaneously and when their bodies bumped, she gave a laugh. "Oh! Sorry!"

He hardly heard the apology, totally focused on the warm softness of her. She scooted around him while he blindly lifted the saddle flap and felt for the billets to unbuckle the girth. He breathed deeply—a mistake, he realized belatedly, as he inhaled the flowery scent she liked to wear. His head spun as the blood in his veins rushed straight to his groin. He groaned with need.

"Is it too stiff?"

He nearly jumped out of his skin. "What?"

"The girth," she answered. "I've been oiling it but the leather's still a bit stiff. It looked like it was giving you some trouble."

Jesus. She had no idea of the trouble he was in. And he'd be in a whole lot more if he didn't regain a modicum of control over his body.

She was staring, waiting for his response. He had only to pivot and she could be in his arms.

"Need help?" she asked.

Damn straight he did. "I've got it, thanks," he managed tersely, yanking the girth free and sliding the side rein over it before rebuckling it to the saddle. He let the saddle flap drop and stepped back, putting some sorely needed distance between them. "Let's get the other side done before Mystique thinks it's time for hay and a siesta."

After attaching the side reins and removing the stirrups, Travis threaded the longe line through Mystique's bit and double-checked the tightness of the girth, all the while careful not to stand too close to Margot. But that did little to cure his distraction or his body's anticipation at what was coming.

"Let me give you a leg up." Just thinking about wrapping his hand about her booted leg made his palms itch.

"No, no, that's all right. I'll go stand on the wall jump to mount."

"Not necessary. I'll lift you," he enunciated between gritted teeth.

"Well, you needn't act so ornery," she said, sounding mighty testy herself.

"I'm not ornery." *I'm horny.* "Give me your damned leg."

"Fine," she snapped. But she didn't move. And neither did he, lost in the clear blue sky of her eyes.

Her breath was like a warm current in the autumn air. He dipped his head to savor the petal softness of her lips, only to jerk backward.

Her blasted cell had started ringing from inside her vest pocket. He'd have given anything to grab the damned thing and hurl it across the exercise ring.

"Sorry." Margot ran over to the jump where she'd hung her vest, leaving him scowling after her. No need to guess who was calling. Travis wondered only how many times Charlie Ayer had already telephoned.

Her breathless hello was like a poison-tipped knife to the gut. Jealousy spread swiftly through his veins.

Biting back a curse, he gave a light tug on the longe line and Mystique fell into step beside him. Feeling mean and surly, he marched the mare around the ring, his eyes trained straight ahead, counting the minutes Margot stood by the jump, the phone pressed to her ear.

He should have kissed her. If he'd been kissing her, no way would she be talking to Charlie now. She'd still be in his arms.

There was an impatient yank to the back of his sweater. "For Pete's sake, Travis, will you hold up a second so I can mount?"

"Didn't want Mystique to tighten up while you chatted the morning away." He sounded like a jerk, but he wasn't about to let on that what really angered him wasn't so much the call as the caller's identity.

"Well, I'm finished. So perhaps you can see your way to giving me a leg up now." Margot's tone was haughty, the barn princess of old.

It should have been a damn sight easier to give her a leg up when he was good and pissed. He should have been able to ignore the sweet curve of her ass. He should have been able to breathe, damn it all. But this was Margot. Hadn't she always been able to turn him inside out? Turn him on without even trying?

He grabbed her shiny field boot midcalf and bit out, "One, two, three," tossing her into the saddle with enough force to send her to Mars.

She lunged for the pommel to keep from flying off the other side. "I thought the point was to put me in the saddle, not in the dirt."

"Just checking your reflexes, Princess."

It was a cheap shot to call her Princess, especially when she'd been working as hard as anyone at the barn. He saw her blink rapidly and felt like the worst sort of heel. Damn it all, now he'd gone and made her cry.

"Listen, Margot—"

But she ducked her head so the brim of her hunt cap shielded her face. When she straightened her expression was wintry.

"Shall we begin? I wouldn't want to keep you waiting." Her voice was as icy as her gaze.

His gut twisted with shame. "Yeah, let's," he said quietly.

She nudged Mystique into a walk while he played out the canvas webbing of the longe line. Nothing wrong with her posture, he thought. Her back was as straight as an arrow and the angled lines from her hip to her knee to the toe of her boot perfectly mimicked how her leg would look in the stirrup.

The question was how long she would be able to maintain that leg position at the trot, an even more challenging task than sitting to Mystique's smooth, rocking-chair canter.

As if she'd read his thoughts, Margot's inside leg moved back a fraction and her thighs closed about the saddle, urging the mare forward.

Travis let her grow accustomed to the sensation of trotting with nothing but the strength of her leg muscles and her sense of balance to keep her squarely in the saddle and Mystique moving forward. He watched as she made minute adjustments and corrections—pulling her shoulders back, lifting her stubborn chin, and using her seat to drive Mystique forward. Around and around the mare trotted smoothly, Margot's leg long and strong.

Time to up the ante, he decided. "You've got her moving nicely there. Take up a posting trot and see if you can maintain that pace." Then, succumbing to an admittedly sadistic impulse, he said, "And just to keep you from using your arms, stick 'em out to the side, like the wings of a jet plane."

There was the tiniest shift in the angle of her head as she shot him a look that consigned him to one of the nastier circles of hell. Then up went her arms until she was holding them perpendicularly as she posted.

The set of her jaw told Travis how fiercely she was concentrating on following the rhythm of Mystique's trot to help her rise out of the saddle. He could only imagine her thoughts. Probably picturing him being skewered and roasted alive, he decided. But she hadn't stopped posting and those arms were still out to the side.

Good for her. Though she might hate him for inflicting this particular brand of abuse, riding without stirrup and reins was the best training regimen he could devise. Another thing he planned to do was to get her out for a long gallop over Rosewood and the neighboring properties. Ring work and gymnastics were important, but so was remembering how to control the awesome power of a horse hurtling over open fields and fences.

As she continued trotting, Travis couldn't help but be impressed by how well she was holding up. She was all lean, taut muscle. A sudden, startlingly clear image of those long, strong legs wrapped about him, riding him, filled his mind, and it nearly felled him.

He coughed to clear his throat, which had gone desert-dry. Margot glanced over at him expectantly, awaiting instruction. And what was he doing instead of helping her? Standing around and weaving X-rated fantasies in his head.

"Okay. Lower your arms and pretend you're holding the reins as you return to a sitting trot. Your back's wobbling a bit. Use your core muscles to keep it nice and straight. Good. How're you feeling?" he asked.

She didn't so much as glance at him. "How do you think I'm feeling?"

"Like crap?"

"Such a mind reader."

Travis gave a bark of laughter. She was something else. And the fact that she could be sharp and funny and tough when he was putting her through such punishing exercises only fueled his hunger for her.

"Well, since you're already hurting, how about moving into a two-point position?"

"Arms out?"

"No, I'll make it easy on you." He grinned. "Put 'em behind your head. See how long you can hold it." Balancing in a two-point position so that her torso was angled over her mare's neck without the aid of stirrups required thigh muscles of steel. Placing her hands on her head increased the difficulty exponentially.

Margot's face was tight with effort as she circled in a two-point. Travis knew the muscles in her legs, abdomen, and back must be screaming in protest. Admiration welled inside him as seconds turned into minutes and still she held her form.

"Okay, that's enough. Bring her back to a walk." With a "Whoa," he applied pressure to the longe line.

Mystique obediently slowed to a relaxed walk. Margot straightened, dropping her rear into the saddle, and groaned in relief.

Travis fixed his gaze on the hoof-imprinted ground, hiding a smile. He didn't want Margot to leap to the wrong conclusion and think he was laughing at her. Not when he was so damned proud of the way she'd stuck with those grueling drills. Not when he liked her so damned much. "Shake out your arms and legs. When you've rested a bit, you can pick up a canter."

Margot took off her helmet and wiped her brow with her forearm. "How'd I do?"

Was she fishing for compliments? But then he caught the betraying hint of vulnerability in her face. "You're doing good. Real good. You think you'll be up to tackling a small jump?"

A minute earlier Margot would have hesitated. Her muscles were already taxed to the max by these few minutes of trotting without stirrups and reins. How could she possibly attempt a jump? But hearing Travis's husky voice say "You're doing good" made her feel as if this were the first sunny day after a long, hard winter.

"Sure, why not?" she replied as casually as possible. She'd jump a four-foot oxer if only to hear him tell her she was doing all right again.

Luckily for her, Travis didn't set up an oxer. After she'd cantered awhile he handed her the coiled longe line so she could walk Mystique around the ring while he set up a crossbar. The jump was barely two feet, a decidedly modest fence. Then he dragged over a third pole and placed it so it lay slanted against the jump's standard. This was so when she took the jump, the longe line would skim over the pole's angled length and not get entangled in the standard.

Satisfied that the guide rail was properly positioned, he came over and retrieved the longe line from her.

"This is what I want you to do, Margot. Pick up a nice canter. When you're ready, I'll shift closer to the jump so that Mystique's in line with the fence. You okay with that?"

"I guess so." Certain that she'd chicken out if she let herself think about jumping without stirrups or reins too much, she nudged Mystique into a canter.

Once she had the mare going at a good pace, she called out to Travis, "All right."

Out of the corner of her eye, she saw Travis position himself nearer the jump so that on the next lap Mystique would be cantering directly toward the large, striped wooden X of the jump.

Margot knew the instant the fence came into the mare's line of vision. Her canter quickened and Margot felt the coiled energy beneath her. Her own legs tightened, gripping the saddle in anticipation.

Just follow Mystique, she told herself as the mare, ears pricked forward, jumped daintily over the fence. Margot wasn't nearly as dainty. She started out okay, but on the landing she found herself listing alarmingly to the side. Instinctively she grabbed for the thick mane. Regaining her seat, she looked over at Travis. His carefully blank expression made her cheeks burn.

"Sorry."

"No need to apologize. You were doing fine until you let your eyes drop at the last minute. The rest of your body followed," he explained. "This time, keep your eyes up and fixed straight ahead."

Maybe it was because she'd tensed up or because she was trying too hard, but her next attempt at the jump was even worse than the first. As Mystique went up and over, Margot was left hanging, her torso jackknifing backward instead of folding neatly over the mare's neck. It was a good thing she hadn't been holding the reins, or she'd have yanked her horse's delicate mouth.

She couldn't bring herself to look at Travis. He in turn didn't bother to offer a critique of her last effort; they both knew it was too paltry for words. He merely waited while she regrouped.

Once she was cantering smoothly, he said, "Let's try it again. If you need to, hold on to her mane."

Although probably meant kindly, the suggestion made Margot feel like a total hack. She was only too aware that Travis could have taken a jump twice this size reinless, stirrupless, and probably blindfolded, too. Deflated, she barely mustered a smile when he added, "Come on, Margot, you can do it. Remember, the third time's the charm."

The third time wasn't so much the charm as the hex. She tumbled right off Mystique's back and landed ingloriously at his feet.

Thank God her body remembered the countless times Ned had made her practice falling off. The instant she lost contact with the saddle, those childhood lessons returned. She curled into a protective ball—a human hedgehog—and rolled safely out of harm's way.

If only her body could remember her old jumping lessons, too, she'd still be in the saddle, she thought, scrambling to her feet and swatting the dust off her rear.

Travis's concern only made her feel more foolish. "Are you okay?"

"Yes, yes, I'm *fine*," she replied, shaking off his hand to stomp over to where Mystique stood waiting, the very soul of patience for the pathetic human who was making such a hash of riding her.

Grabbing the pommel and cantle, Margot said, "Can you give me a leg up, please?"

"Look, you're tired. Maybe we should—"

He doesn't think I can do it. Margot turned to glare at him. "I'm not going to quit. I can't. If I do, I might as well give up any hope of competing in the Hunt Cup. Besides, you know what Dad always said. 'If you take a stupid-ass spill, get back on and ride smart.'"

He held up a hand. "Hey, I wasn't going to suggest you quit. But maybe we should put the stirrups and reins back on."

She shook her head. "No. I'll end up relying on them twice as much for balance and control. That won't help me or Mystique when we're jumping cross-country."

He regarded her silently for a moment. "You're right," he said finally. "But before I put you back on that saddle, I need to know if you're hurt."

She gave a short laugh. "Yes, my pride is definitely bruised."

"Like father, like daughter. RJ's pride bruised real easy, too," Travis said, his expression tightening.

Was he thinking about the woman he and Dad had fought over? Before she could summon the nerve to demand the identity of this woman so that at least she'd have a name to despise, Travis turned toward Mystique.

Patting the mare's withers, he said, "You bought a first-class horse, Margot. All you've got to do is trust Mystique and she'll take you over whatever fence you point her nose at. Trust her, Margot. It's as simple as that."

He lifted the saddle flap, checking the girth once more, while Margot stared at the back of his dark head, his words echoing in her mind.

Travis was right. It was a simple matter of trusting her horse. She'd half-recognized its importance when she told herself to follow Mystique. But fear and lack of confidence had sabotaged her good intentions. Because she hadn't believed in her equine partner, she'd tightened up—and screwed up. Her problem wasn't physical, it was mental. As Jade would put it, Margot needed a mega attitude adjustment if she wanted to jump well. Otherwise she'd risk injuring not only herself but also her mount.

After tightening the girth a notch, Travis lowered the saddle flap. "You want to give it another go?"

When she nodded, he bent forward and cupped his hand. As Margot placed her booted shin in Travis's palm, it occurred to her that the question of trust encompassed more than just her riding. Despite the intense attraction she felt for Travis, could she ever trust him with her heart?

Get over yourself, Margot. It's not as though he's shown the slightest interest in winning your heart, an inner voice mocked.

Wasn't that the sad truth? Shaking her head to clear it of any further distracting thoughts of Travis, she told herself to focus on the task at hand. Hauling herself into the saddle once more, she took a deep breath. "Right. Here we go. As Jordan says, practice makes perfect."

"What was that?" Travis asked.

"I was just repeating a favorite saying of Jordan's: practice makes perfect. That's what she told me on the phone just now when she heard I was riding Mystique without stirrups and reins."

"That was Jordan you were speaking to?"

"Yes. She called to say that she and Richard and the kids are coming to cheer us on at the Hunt Cup." Surprised to see Travis kneading his forehead with the heel of his hand, she asked, "What? What's the matter?"

"Nothing. I just didn't realize it was Jordan on the phone, that's all."

"Yeah. And as I clearly have a lot more practicing to do

before I'm close to perfect, I'd better get at it. Frank Jarvis has probably shod two horses by now."

Margot clucked, urging Mystique forward into a canter, while Travis stood there feeling like the biggest idiot in the world.

When, he wondered, was he ever going to get it right with Margot? Never, came the bleak answer. Not unless he was willing to put in a lot more practice, too.

Chapter ❧
EIGHTEEN

DAMIEN, ANIKA, and the other girls at the agency would laugh themselves silly if they could see her now. The grandfather clock in the parlor had just finished chiming eight o'clock and Margot could barely keep her eyes open. Eight o'clock, and she was more than ready to crawl into bed. Some sophisticate she was. But it was hard to summon an iota of energy or cosmopolitan worldliness when she felt older than the antiques and the large, too empty, too quiet house itself.

Ellie had left shortly after preparing a meal for them. They'd taken to eating in the kitchen, the dining room with its crystal chandelier and gleaming mahogany table too rife with memories of their father presiding at the head, Nicole facing him. Dinner had been a cheerless affair, with Jade picking at her shepherd's pie and moving the tossed green salad about her plate. Dessert, a baked apple, had been met with a similar lack of enthusiasm. She couldn't tell whether Jade's lack of appetite was due to the junk food she'd scarfed down before dinner or because of Margot's attempt to draw her into a conversation.

As Jade poked at the caramelized apple as if it were a science experiment, she answered Margot's questions about school with her usual stock of monosyllables: *Good, fine, no, yes,* and, finally, a terse *I. Don't. Know.*

Getting Jade to open up was like trying to break into Fort Knox, though Margot recognized the problem most likely lay in the fact that it was she asking the questions. Despite her doubt that Jade would listen, she was determined to say her piece—repeatedly, if necessary.

"Jade, I realize you're dealing with a lot of stuff right now. And I know you're angry with me and that I'm far from being your favorite person, but I really think it's important for you to have someone you're comfortable talking with about what's on your mind, what you're going through. I'd like to give Reverend Wilde a call. He might have the name of someone who—"

"No," she cut her off decisively. "I can handle my own problems. Just leave me alone. And stop butting in. I don't need your help or anyone else's. Can I be excused? I have an English paper to write."

Shoving her chair away, she bolted from the kitchen table as Margot listened to the furious pounding of her footsteps on the stairs and then the slamming of her bedroom door.

Strike one, Margot thought sadly, as the house fell silent around her. Well, she'd just have to try again. Stuart Wilde was a good man. She'd trust him to know how to best help a troubled teenager.

She put the dishes away, not exactly an onerous task, with only four plates and two water glasses. She turned off the kitchen faucet and the quiet felt almost oppressive.

Her memories of Rosewood were of a house filled to bursting with her father's and Nicole's outsized personalities. She ached for the ringing tones of her father's voice. She might even have welcomed a sparring match of old with Nicole.

She could hardly blame Jade for seeking the haven of her room. Her memories of what this house should be like were fresher for her, thus all the more painful. Thank goodness Jordan and Richard would be coming with the kids. Until then the evenings loomed silent, empty, and lonely.

They didn't have to, though, a voice reminded her. She didn't have to be sitting here like an old, dried-up prune. A handsome, too-sexy-for-words man was living on the premises. All she had to do was pick up the phone and invite him over for . . . what? Cookies and milk? Some leftover baked apples? A friendly game of Scrabble?

That she was even contemplating calling Travis scared her. If she were to invite him over, it wouldn't be to challenge him to a game of Scrabble. No, with Travis's devastating effect on her, she knew she'd be offering him a large helping of herself—Margot à la mode, with seconds on the house.

But she'd already offered herself up to him once and look what had happened. And what if this time Travis accepted? If he decided to go ahead and sample her like some tasty dish to enjoy and then casually shove aside, what then? She knew the answer to that, too. It would shatter her into so many little pieces.

The prospect was so real and terrifying, it managed what nothing else could. It chased away Margot's fatigue.

Work, she could do work. There were bills to pay, paychecks to sign, and tomorrow promised to be even more hectic than usual. After calling Crandall to make sure it was okay to sell some of the horses and being told it was fine as long as the money from any sale was put into escrow, she'd given Ned the go-ahead to spread the word that Rosewood Farm was once again open for business. Later this week a trainer named Dan Stokes was bringing a client who was in the market for a show horse. That meant Colchester, Gypsy Queen, Harvest Moon, and Gulliver would all get their ears and whiskers clipped. Then, on the day of the visit, their coats would be brushed to a high sheen and their hooves dressed. Her father had always insisted that the horses be impeccably turned out when prospective buyers came around.

She should go down to the barn and tackle the growing pile of bills. And while she was at it, she should go through the files in her father's desk and double-check that all the papers for the horses were in order.

Spurred by the lingering fear that if she stayed in the house

a minute longer she might opt instead to pick up the phone
and dial Travis's number, she hurried upstairs and rapped on
Jade's door. "Jade?"

"What?" The word came out a surprised squawk.

"Um, is everything okay?"

"Yes! Don't come in. I'm getting—dressed."

Margot shook her head. She'd overcome any shyness
about her body within a week of modeling. "Oh, okay," she
said, careful to suppress any trace of amusement from her
voice. "I just wanted to tell you I'm going over to the barn to
do some work. You can call my cell if you need me."

"Fine. Not that I'm gonna call. I'm tired. After I get done
writing this paper, I'm going to bed."

Margot stared at the door. *Wow*. Jade had uttered four
sentences with practically volumes of information included.
And she hadn't even sounded particularly hostile.

Tempted to go in and verify that it was truly her half-sister
in there and not some alien body snatcher, her hand reached
out to hover over the doorknob. But Jade would pitch a fit
at the intrusion. Why spoil their first decent and fairly peace-
able exchange in weeks?

"Well, then, good luck writing your paper and sleep tight.
I'll see you in the morning."

"See you."

The barn was nearly as quiet as the house. But the occasional sounds—the rustling of the shavings made by the
horses shifting in their stalls, the low whickering, the sleepy
equine snorts—comforted Margot as she sat at her father's
desk, filling out the payroll checks, the scratch of her pen
adding to the noises. She'd almost finished. Travis, as the
barn's manager, was the last on the list.

It was odd to be writing his name again. There'd been a
period when she'd written it constantly, right above her
own, before drawing a big, fat heart and an arrow, the trim-
mings of true love. Sometimes she would print his full name,

at others only his initials. She'd even practiced her signature, Margot Radcliffe Maher, loving the way the *M*'s framed *Radcliffe*.

Those starry-eyed days seemed a lifetime ago. She felt a pang of nostalgia for the girl who'd spun sugar-coated dreams in which Travis Maher fell in love with her and everyone lived happily ever after.

She filled in the dollar amount and signed her name with a grim flourish. How would Travis react if he knew that it was only thanks to her modeling that she was able to pay his, Ned's, and the stable hands' salaries? That the only reason Rosewood didn't have a big, fat FOR SALE sign posted at the foot of the drive was because of her shallow glamour-girl career?

Although she would have liked nothing better than to march right up to Travis and let him know where the money was coming from, so that at last he'd understand the depth of her commitment to Rosewood, she couldn't. Enlightening him would entail running the risk of him moving on to greener pastures. A spoiled, vain pleasure seeker she would remain. Oh, well, she was growing used to life's nasty little jokes.

With a sigh, she capped the pen. Tossing it aside, she ran her fingers through her hair, its ends still damp from the bath she'd taken earlier, while mentally she ticked off items from her to-do list. The vet, feed, and farrier bills were paid. The staff salaries, too. What else remained before she could call it quits for the night?

Oh, right, the papers. Dad had always kept the records for the horses in an oversized binder. Doubting that Bill Gates and a little old company called Microsoft could have caused her father to change his personal filing system, she began opening the drawers to the oak desk.

In the middle left-hand drawer she spotted the binder's worn corners and pulled the drawer out farther, lifting it out. As she did, she saw a slim leather-bound book lying underneath it. She slid it toward her.

It was a journal, she realized, its leather dyed an eye-popping fuchsia—definitely not Dad's usual conservative burgundy. Her curiosity piqued, Margot picked it up, the binder with the horses' papers momentarily forgotten.

For a second she simply held the journal, running her fingers over the buttery-soft leather. Turning it in her hands, she noted that the pages were gilt-edged. What was Dad doing with such a snazzy-looking thing? He couldn't actually have been writing in it, could he, her fingers already searching out the narrow satin ribbon tucked into its middle and opening it. Her eyes widened at the loopy cursive covering the pages inside. This wasn't Dad's handwriting but Nicole's.

"Margot?" The unexpectedness of Travis's voice made her jump.

"Gosh, you startled me!" she said, gasping. He'd obviously just showered, his wet hair nearly black. He'd changed into a pair of faded jeans and a black button-down shirt, its top two buttons open. As he approached the desk, she caught the clean, soapy scent of him.

"Sorry. I came downstairs to do a final check on the horses and saw the lights on in here. What's that you've got there?"

Belatedly she realized she was gripping the journal to her chest. She laid it on the desk. "I don't know. I found it in the drawer here when I was looking for the horses' papers. I think it must have belonged to Nicole. I should probably give it to Jade. She'd like—"

"No, don't." The harshness of his voice surprised her.

"What do you mean, 'don't'?"

"Don't give it to Jade. Don't even read it, for God's sake," Travis ground out. "The woman's dead. Let her have some privacy, let her rest in peace."

Perhaps Travis was right and she shouldn't necessarily hand over something that might have been private to Nicole to her teenage daughter. But something about his objection rang false. She looked up, suddenly noting the tensed wariness in his expression. Then their eyes met and what she saw in his turned her insides to ice.

Her fingers curled around the edges of the journal, blindly feeling for the satin ribbon. Slowly she opened the journal.

"Margot, don't." The guilt was there in his voice, too.

A terrible foreboding filled her. Ignoring Travis's plea, she lowered her gaze to the open page. But this time when her eyes scanned the loopy cursive covering it, they were drawn like magnets to the two initials, so masculine and angular. So familiar and so very damning: *TM*.

Pain, as jagged as glass, sliced her heart as she read the entire paragraph.

> *It's been a crazy week, but I managed to come up with an excuse to get out of the house to meet TM. These days I wonder what I would do without him. It's as if he's the only person I can be free with, absolutely myself, and know it's all right. I almost didn't want to leave afterward, but of course I had to. RJ might have become suspicious if I returned home too late.*

The pain in her heart radiated outward, so intense she thought she might be sick. Of course, why hadn't she figured it out earlier? Only one person on earth could have ever come between her father and Travis: Nicole.

She forced herself to look at the man who'd betrayed her father, the man her father had regarded as a friend, the man he'd treated almost as a son.

"You and Nicole were having an affair," she said flatly. "How could you do it? How could you do that to Dad?" Yes, she was going to be sick, she realized, the nausea rising thickly, chokingly. Frantic to escape the office and the man whom she'd thought was everything, she pushed back the chair.

He grabbed her arm as she passed, hauling her around to face him. And she slapped him hard, once and then twice, and he let her.

An ugly red mark bloomed on his cheek as he said quietly, "I deserve that and more but not for the reason you think. I never touched Nicole and I have no idea who she was seeing, but it wasn't me. I tried to tell RJ I wasn't the one she was writing about in that diary but he wouldn't listen. I'm telling the truth, Margot. I swear it."

Her mind was racing backward, memories flooding her mind. "Nicole used to flirt with you."

He laughed mirthlessly. "Sure, she did, when she got bored of reminding me that I wasn't good enough to lick the soles of her boots. But Nicole could have wrapped herself in a pretty velvet bow and I wouldn't have touched her. I would never have hurt RJ like that, not after all he did for me."

She cringed inwardly, his words a painful reminder of how she had offered herself to him and been summarily rejected.

Stop it, Margot, this isn't about you, she chided herself.

But imagining her father's rage and the devastation he must have felt when he read those words in Nicole's diary was equally distressing. "Dad didn't believe you."

Travis shook his head. "No. RJ was crazy with jealousy. I don't think I'll ever be able to forgive myself for not sticking around and making him see sense." His voice was heavy with self-reproach. "If I hadn't stormed out of here, pissed as hell, RJ wouldn't have needed to fly to New Jersey to find a new trainer. He'd still be alive—he and Nicole would *both* still be alive. But I was too sore and angry to admit the actual truth to him."

She frowned. "The actual truth?"

"Yeah. The actual, whole, unvarnished truth." Travis's mouth lifted in a bitter half-smile. "Of course, telling him would have had exactly the same result. RJ would have fired me the second he heard what I had to say."

Margot shook her head in confusion. "That can't be right. Dad would have forgiven you anything just to know that you hadn't betrayed him with Nicole."

"That so? You think RJ would have slapped me on the back and then offered me one of his fine Cubans when I explained exactly why I could never be interested in Nicole?"

"Of course. Nicole was everything to him."

"Come on, can't you think of anything that would enrage RJ as much as believing I was messing with Nicole? Nothing that would make him run straight for his shotgun?"

"A shotgun? You're exaggerating. What on earth could possibly anger him more than you sleeping with his wife?"

"How about my telling him that it was actually his daughter I wanted?"

"What?" Her heart quickened and began to race.

"You heard me," he said in a low voice as his hands moved to clasp her shoulders. She stared up at him mutely, transfixed by the intensity of his gaze. "There's only one Radcliffe woman I've ever wanted, and that's you, Margot." He paused, searching for something in her expression, and his mouth flattened in a grim line. "Jesus. You don't believe me, do you?"

"How *can* I believe you?" she cried, torn between memory and desire.

Frustration made his voice rough. "Margot, listen. I spent years working for your father, nearly half my life. I respected him and admired him as a horseman, and I think he respected me—for that very same ability. But that's a really far cry from his seeing me as someone who'd ever be good enough for his daughter. You're a Radcliffe, born and bred. I'll always be Red Maher's son." The bleakness in his voice made her want to weep. "So yeah, telling RJ that it was you I wanted would have pushed him right over the edge. But that doesn't change the fact that I should have told him the truth and to hell with the consequences." His broad shoulders rose and then fell in a heavy shrug. "You were right when you said back at Crestview that I owe your father an enormous amount. But even though he'll probably curse me from the grave, this time I'm not giving you up, Margot."

Doubt and desire warred in her. Could Travis be telling the truth? Had he really wanted her all this time? Uncertain, she hesitated.

"Right, I see you need something more than my words to convince you." He took her hand, lacing their fingers together. "Come on, we need to get out of here and go where you and I can be alone, with no ghosts from the past to come between us."

Chapter ✂
NINETEEN

MARGOT DIDN'T THINK to ask where Travis was taking her; she simply let him lead her from the office through the half-lit, slumberous barn, and then up the narrow stairs to his apartment in the converted hayloft.

She'd never been here before; the apartment had been Ned's before he'd moved into Thistle Cottage. The long, open space with its exposed beams and wide-planked floors suited Travis. Like him it was spare and utterly masculine. Her gaze swept the neat interior, taking in the functional kitchenette with its extra-wide counter and bar stools for eating. On the counter rested a compact stereo from which a smoky blues song was playing. A few steps away sat a sofa flanked by two comfortably worn upholstered chairs. On a wooden coffee table she spotted recent issues of *Practical Horseman, The Yankee Peddler,* and *Sports Illustrated.* A TV positioned between two windows completed the living area.

At the far end of the loft stood a dresser, and next to it, neatly made up with a charcoal-gray comforter, was a king-sized bed. Seized by sudden shyness, she quickly looked away, only to confront Travis's hooded gaze.

"What?" she asked breathlessly.

"I was trying to calculate the number of times I've thought of you when you were thousands of miles away. Now you're here, standing before me in the one place I never imagined you." He reached out and with the tips of his fingers traced a delicate path down the side of her face. The simple touch set her trembling. "You're so beautiful it makes me ache," he whispered. "I've wanted you for so long—"

Doubt goaded her. "Is this some kind of a line you're giving me, Travis? Do you really expect me to believe what you're saying? Okay, perhaps you're attracted to me *now*. But you've obviously forgotten what you said to me years ago in the tack room. You told me—"

He placed his finger on her lips, silencing her. "I lied to you. I lied through my teeth because I knew if I didn't get you out of that tack room and fast, I'd have ended up doing something we'd both regret. Christ, you were barely eighteen. You don't think RJ would have tried to flay me alive if I'd touched you the way I wanted to? And he'd have been right to. So yeah, I told you a bunch of bull about how you weren't my type. I was a jerk to say those things, but I didn't see any other way to convince you of my disinterest. Come on, Margot, haven't you ever lied before?"

She felt her cheeks color uncomfortably as her conscience ruthlessly reminded her that, yes, she had lied. And she was lying to him still. Travis, however, didn't catch her guilty blush. He was staring at the floor, shaking his head.

Straightening, he said, "Maybe this is the only way to convince you of how sorry I am." He drew a breath as if readying himself for some kind of challenge. "Okay. Here goes."

For a second she stared uncomprehendingly. If he was bent on seduction, what was he doing standing over there? Then his hands moved to the buttons of his shirt. Slowly, one by one, he slipped them free, his eyes never leaving hers.

Margot's heart tripped as understanding dawned. Travis was stripping. He was baring himself for her, offering himself as she had done so many years ago.

His shirttails hung loosely, exposing a tantalizing strip of naked skin. He shrugged the black cotton off and it drifted to the floor to land behind him, unnoticed.

In the muted light his chest was all sculpted planes, muscled ridges, and beguiling shadows. But what struck her most was that Travis had a farmer's tan, the lines marking the short-sleeved shirts he wore plainly visible. Margot had long grown accustomed to perfect tans, obtained over hours poolside at luxury resorts, or utterly artificial, poured out of plastic bottles, airbrushed on, or acquired in space-age tanning beds. She loved it that Travis would never bother with any of those things simply to enhance his looks. Then again, why should he worry when he was already perfect?

The muscles in his shoulders flexed as his hands came together below the seductive hollow of his navel. Breath bated, she waited as Travis unbuckled the black leather belt and then dragged the belt free, not even blinking when it clattered to the floor. A bomb could have exploded and Margot wouldn't have been able to tear her gaze from the sight of Travis working the zipper of his jeans down.

The zipper descended, revealing a V of black cotton. Then Travis was peeling his jeans down lean hips and sinewed legs and kicking off his leather moccasins. He stepped out of his pants to stand before her, clad only in black boxer briefs.

Her mouth went dry.

She could only imagine what would have happened had Calvin Klein discovered Travis for his underwear campaign. A brief-clad Travis plastered on the sides of metropolitan buses would have caused citywide traffic pileups.

She wondered vaguely if she was going to faint. She was having trouble breathing. She was years away from being that eighteen-year-old virgin and yet this had to be the most erotic moment she'd ever experienced. Dear Lord, was he really going to bare all?

She should have known better than to doubt. He didn't hesitate or rush. Slowly, deliberately, he eased the snug cotton briefs down his leanly muscled thighs. Stepping out of them, he approached with athletic grace, then stopped tantalizingly close. He was magnificent. A gloriously aroused male.

Her nerves leaped like live wires as her eyes drank him in and her heart thundered in her breast.

Travis spoke, and it seemed like ages had passed since

she'd heard the rough, thrilling timbre of his voice. "Look at me. Can you doubt that I've been wanting you these eight years and more? Here I am, Margot. If you want me, I'm yours."

Heat shimmered in his eyes, turning them molten silver. "Kiss me, Margot. Let me show you how much I want you."

His head dipped and her breath caught in anticipation of the dark, intoxicating taste of him. Yet his lips hovered over hers a mere whisper away.

Why didn't he kiss her? It took a moment to understand. Travis was waiting for her to decide, leaving it up to her to accept or reject what he was promising. Such restraint was awesome, intimidating even, so she could feel relief only when, like the Travis of old, he challenged her. "Come on, sweetheart, I dare you," he teased, his mouth curving gently.

His smile undid her. This was what she'd always longed for—being with Travis and having him smile while desire shone bright in his eyes. No one made her feel as he did, so intensely alive. If she turned away now, she knew she'd never have another chance with him. How could she do that when her life was filled with so many regrets? Turning away out of fear would be the greatest one of all.

Setting aside her doubts, she returned his smile and was surprised by the relief that lit his face. With a sense of shock she realized that some part of Travis had been expecting rejection. His uncertainty revealed not only his vulnerability but also how conscious he was of having hurt her. The glimpse of emotions he took such care to mask touched her, and allowed hope to unfurl inside her.

She reached out to run her palms over the warm expanse of his chest, reveling in the helpless shudder that seized him at her touch. Her hands moved upward, encircling his neck as her fingers plowed through the damp silk of his hair. Rising on tiptoe she leaned into him, brushing the solid shaft of his erection.

Dragging her lips slowly against his, she whispered, "Am I woman enough for you now, Travis?"

"I'm on fire for you." As if to prove his words, he wrapped his hands about her hips, urging her closer until her cleft was against his cock, the pulsing heat of him like a brand, easily penetrating the barrier of her jeans. Deep inside she quickened, melting for him. "You're all the woman I want," he whispered.

"Then maybe it's time you prove you're man enough for me. Think you're up for it?" Catching hold of his bottom lip, she bit down.

He groaned low in his throat. "I can prove I'm man enough real easily, sweetheart. How about I prove I'm the *only* man for you?"

The sensual promise in his roughly whispered words made her weak with need. "I might enjoy that."

"Me, too," he said with a wicked smile before capturing her mouth in a fierce kiss. His tongue swept inside, stroking hers, withdrawing only to return. Alternately demanding and then sweetly beguiling, each touch of his tongue stoked her desire until she trembled in his arms.

At last he tore his mouth from hers. "I want you naked. Now."

Catching the hem of her sweater, he pulled it over her head while she shrugged her arms free. His fingers made quick work of her bra, unclasping it and pushing it off her shoulders. Margot shuddered helplessly as his large hands covered her breasts, fondling them boldly, teasing her nipples into aching buds. She arched into his hands in a wordless plea for more. His teeth flashed white in his tanned face. He lowered his head.

A moan tore through her at the feel of his mouth closing around her areola, of his tongue circling as he suckled her nipple. Bright pleasure seared her like lightning flashing in a night sky. She clasped his head to her breast, urging him, begging for more.

His hands were at the waist of her jeans, freeing the top button, tugging the zipper down and then the denim, too, leaving her clad only in her panties. On his knees before her, she watched the progress of his hands slowly traveling up the length of her legs, moving ever closer to the violet lace covering her. Above him she trembled, her nipples beaded tight, aching for the sublime heat of his mouth.

His fingers plucked at the lacy material, rolled it down over her hips, then dragged the panties to her ankles.

He sank back on his heels, his gaze touching her everywhere. "You're the most beautiful woman I've ever seen, Margot." His tone was hushed, reverent.

She shook like a leaf in the wind as his fingers brushed her, parting her. She whimpered as he found her, then cried out as slowly he slid one then two fingers into her slick heat.

"You're wet for me." His words, the fierce approval in his voice, were as intensely erotic as the feel of him caressing her deep inside, and she felt her muscles clench about his long fingers.

Incapable of coherent speech, she stammered, "Travis, please—"

His smile stole her heart. "Believe me, I aim to please you, Margot. Again and again."

He leaned forward.

Margot watched his dark head close in, felt his hand wrap about her, anchoring her, as his other parted her slick folds. His warm breath fanned her and she moaned in helpless anticipation. Then his mouth was on her and it was too much. She moved against him, crying out as pleasure washed over her. Pleasure that radiated throughout her as his tongue swirled and slowly lapped at her clit, savoring her essence. With a magician's touch, he summoned a tempest within her. It raged ferocious, spinning her ever higher, until with a master stroke, she came in a thousand light-filled pieces.

And he held her, cradling her tenderly as she calmed. Then, lifting her into his arms, he carried her across the room and laid her on his bed. The flannel comforter against her sensitized skin reawakened her desire, her body clamoring for his possession. She shifted restlessly against the soft fabric.

Travis stilled. Did she have any idea how beautiful she was? he wondered, memorizing every detail of the picture she made: her blond hair spread in a silken fan against the dark of the bed, her eyes sapphire-blue sparkling with mysteries and secrets he yearned to uncover, her soft lips lush and swollen from his kisses.

He took in the delicate mounds of her breasts, remembering their softness, their incredible responsiveness to his caresses. Every atom of his being hungered to taste her again, to feel her sleek limbs wrapped about him. He ached with the need to part the triangle of dark gold hair covering the place he longed to be: deep inside her, loving her and hearing her cry his name as if he'd given her something no one else in the world could.

Though his body throbbed with urgency, ruthlessly he tamped down on his desire. Margot was incredible, a thoroughbred through and through, and the fact that she was here in his bed humbled him. He didn't deserve her or her forgiveness. He'd hurt her badly that night long ago—how deeply his words had cut he was only now acknowledging. Yet instead of damning him to hell she was rewarding him with stunning generosity, offering herself to him.

The way to heal the hurt he'd caused was to woo her body and soul with his loving. He'd told her that he intended to prove he was the only man for her. It was time to do some convincing.

He grabbed a condom from his nightstand drawer. In the soft light her eyes were huge, widening with awe as he slid the latex over his rigid length. Her reaction made him harder still, made him want to bury himself deep inside her right then and there. Then he recalled how exquisitely tight she'd been around his fingers; he'd never forgive himself if he hurt her.

He lowered himself over her. The feel of her body beneath his, the scent of her skin—a hint of flowers, a whisper of musk—and the salty-cinnamony-honeyed taste of her made his senses swim. His hands roamed, petting and caressing, worshipping every golden inch of her. When her hands answered him stroke for stroke, when her mouth began kissing him, sampling his body in quick nips and hot licks of her tongue, the blood roared within him. And when her lips called his name in a litany of desire, his heart exulted.

Now, now, need drove him. Lifting her legs so that they encircled his hips, he shifted, bringing the head of his straining cock against her slick heat. He pressed and felt her tremble and her thighs tighten reflexively. She was as nervous as a maiden mare.

"Shhh, we'll go easy," he murmured.

Eyes locked on hers, he flexed his hips, entering her slowly inch by inch, watching the emotions race across her face as he filled her. At last he was sheathed to the hilt. He held himself in check while his heart thundered her name.

She was quivering all around him. Tiny pulses caressed his cock. The sensation was exquisite, beyond description. He rocked, bringing himself that much closer to her womb. "Do you have any idea how you feel to me? Like an angel. Take me to heaven, Margot."

She gave a soft moan of pleasure, arching into him until their bodies fused. He ground into her softly, heightening her pleasure, before withdrawing slowly and deliberately, and their dance began.

Together they found their rhythm as over and over he thrust into her welcoming heat. She moved in perfect concert, her lithe body clasped to his. Her eyes shone vulnerable and wild, reflecting every sensation; she'd never looked more beautiful to him.

The cadence changed, quickened like the beat of their hearts, driving them ever and ever closer.

"Travis, Travis, please, please—" Then, with a cry, Margot was flying and, angel that she was, taking him with her.

Lead-limbed and sated, his heart pounding heavily from the force of his orgasm, Travis gradually collected himself. Dazed as he was, it wasn't easy to think, but he tried. What had just happened? Sex? No, he'd had that countless times. Sex was good, dirty fun, it got your rocks off. He liked it and was pretty good at making sure that whatever woman he was with enjoyed every minute of it.

What he'd experienced just now with Margot was altogether different. Special. Important. And unlike with the other women he'd fucked, he wasn't even calculating how soon he could politely say, "Thanks, that was great," careful to add nothing more in case it might be taken as a sign of commitment.

Instead he was fantasizing about what it would be like to spend the rest of his life with Margot. A part of him wanted to believe that all these fuzzy feelings flooding him were simply the result of having at long last indulged a decade-old desire for her. But the happiness wasn't superficial, it was bone-deep.

There was no crime in being happy, he told himself. Just go with it. No need to overanalyze what was happening inside him.

He lifted his head from the fragrant hollow of her neck and spied the tears sliding down her cheeks. The sight of them pierced him, moved him beyond words. With a soft murmur he brought his lips to her damp cheeks, kissing them as his thumbs brushed away the salty traces. He continued to plant lingering kisses until he'd coaxed a smile from her.

"You okay?" he asked.

"Mm-hmm," she nodded, but her trembling lips told a different story.

Rolling onto his back, he brought her with him and settled her across his chest. Silently he stroked the warm silk of her hair, while his other hand traveled slowly up and down the length of her back.

When her breathing finally evened, he slid out from under her, saying as he did, "It's all right. I'll be back in a second."

Margot watched as he padded into the adjacent bathroom. He was as perfect from the rear as from the front: slim-hipped and sculpted, his buttock muscles clenched and relaxed with each step. His dark hair, sexily mussed from her frantic fingers, grazed the base of his neck. Already she felt his absence, missed the warm comfort of his embrace, and into this emptiness worries crowded.

Oh, God, had she gone and ruined everything?

She'd cried in front of Travis. She'd cried, unable to pretend to sophistication, unable to act as if what they'd shared tonight had been anything less than earth-shattering. She'd expected the white-hot arousal and fierce need when he took her—they were both young and healthy, with fully operational parts and libidos. But it was the endless generosity, the selflessness in Travis's lovemaking, that had made her feel cherished. He'd made such exquisite love to her that she'd literally come undone.

Earlier, when she'd suggested Travis prove himself man enough for her, the challenge had been empty, meaningless; her feminine instincts had always known that Travis would be a potent lover. But then he'd made his counterproposal, offering to prove that he was the only man in the world for her. With her typical recklessness she'd accepted. When he'd entered her, embedding and holding himself deep inside her, she'd felt her heart go still. And when its pounding resumed, a radiant joy had flooded her. A feeling she had never had with anyone.

And never would.

It didn't matter how crazy it was; Travis was the only man for her. She knew it now—probably always had. He was her one love. What would she do if she were to lose him?

From the bathroom the sound of running water stopped.

Then Travis was crossing the room, washcloth in hand. She made to sit up but he was already by her side, gently dabbing her face with the warm, moistened towel. It felt divine. How could he know what she needed so expertly?

"Thanks," she said softly.

His mouth quirked in a crooked smile. "You'll like this even better." Scooting back, he placed the towel at the junction of her thighs. "Open for me, sweetheart."

After all the things they'd done it was silly for her to be overcome with shyness. Still. "Uhh, that's all right. You don't have to—"

"It's a question of want, Margot. You were really tight the last time. I don't want you to be sore when we make love again."

"Again?"

"Again and again and again," he whispered.

As before, Margot found herself captivated by Travis's sensual magic. And magic it was, as he transformed the bed where they lay wrapped in each other's arms into paradise itself.

TRAVIS AWAKENED to the sound of crunching gravel, of car wheels rolling slowly past the barns and continuing up toward the house. He shifted, propping himself on his elbow, his other arm wrapped possessively about a sleeping Margot. The windows were inky black, dawn still hours away. No one should be driving around Rosewood at this hour. Then he saw the pulsing blue and red lights splashing eerily onto the apartment's walls, a nightmare vision from his past. He sat up fully and swung his legs over the edge of the bed.

Cold air struck Margot's skin where once she'd been cocooned in the delicious heat of Travis's body curled about hers. She came awake instantly. "Travis?"

"I'm here, by the window. We'd better get dressed. The cops are up at your house."

"The police?" Panic had her scrambling out of the bed.

"Yeah." He turned from the window to find her already grabbing her panties and jeans off the floor and strode across the loft's roughly hewn planks to his own pile of clothes and began yanking them on. He shoved his feet in his shoes.

"You ready?" he said, extending his hand. Together they hurried toward the stairs. "Too bad it's still so dark outside. Otherwise I might have been able to see who was in the cruiser."

"You could have identified a police officer driving by?" Margot's tone was incredulous.

"I know just about everyone on the force."

"Why's that?"

"A legacy of my dad."

The patrol car was in front of the house, its flashing lights as well as its headlights illuminated, the driver's door left ajar. Margot saw a uniformed officer standing on the porch, his finger pressed to the doorbell.

"No, wait! I'm here. Please don't ring the bell," she called out, sprinting up the last stretch of the drive.

At the sound of her voice the officer turned and then waited for her and Travis to clamber up the steps.

"Thanks," she said, panting lightly. "I apologize for shouting like that, but I didn't want the doorbell to disturb my sister. She's got school tomorrow."

The police officer removed his cap and tucked it under his arm, revealing a shock of bluish-black hair and intense, electric-blue eyes set in a chiseled face. He was young—at least three or four years younger than she. But his bright gaze regarded her steadily before shifting over to Travis, doubtless sizing up the situation.

Margot could only imagine how she looked: flushed and heavy-lidded from the hours spent in Travis's arms, her lips swollen from his kisses. The tangles in her hair probably looked as wildly scary as Medusa's. Her chin rose.

"Are you Margot Radcliffe?"

"Yeah, this is Margot," Travis answered for her, stepping closer so his sleeve brushed hers, the tacit protectiveness of his gesture wondrous. "Margot, this is Officer Rob Cooper. Rob's dad is Warburg's chief of police. His uncle's on the force, too. They and my dad had what you might call a real hate-hate relationship. How are you, Rob?"

"Doing well, Travis. Thanks. And your mom?"

"She's fine. Moved to New Mexico after the funeral. She has some relatives there. What's up?"

"I'm here because of Ms. Radcliffe's sister Jade."

"Jade?" Margot echoed. "Excuse me, but what could you want with her at this hour? She's upstairs, asleep."

"No, ma'am. I'm afraid she's passed out in the back of my patrol car."

Margot swayed. Travis's strong arm circled her waist, supporting her.

"She was writing an English paper and going to bed," she said, feeling like the biggest fool on earth the second the words were out. Of course. Jade had pulled a first-rate con. "Okay, let me rephrase that. She was *supposed* to be writing her English paper and then going to bed. Wait!" Her voice rose in horror as Rob Cooper's words truly registered. "Did you say she's *passed* out? What happened—"

Travis squeezed her waist, checking her panic. "Let's get Jade inside and then we find out exactly what she's been up to," he suggested. "Rob, you mind if I carry her up to her room?"

"I'll give you a hand getting her out of the car. The back's a little messy."

"Ahh." Travis gave a knowing nod.

"She'll need a shower," he added.

"Right. Too bad about the car, though. Sorry."

Cooper shrugged. "At least she was sick."

Margot felt as if she'd fallen down Alice's rabbit hole. "Wait, why would Jade's being sick be a good thing?"

"Because given your sister's condition and the amount of alcohol and drugs we found at the Mayhews' house, I'd have had to call for an ambulance to take your sister to the hospital and get her stomach pumped."

"And once a person's admitted to the ER, things get official," Travis said.

She understood what "official" meant. Forms and reports and court appearances and juvenile records and social workers and maybe having Jade placed under someone else's guardianship. The prospect of having failed to do right by Jade was terrifying.

"Luckily your sister's body rejected the alcohol she ingested. She's also fortunate a neighbor heard the noise from the party and put in a call. We managed to break things up before anyone got hurt. Some of the kids we rounded up were already high as kites. We've had run-ins with a number of them before. They play rough."

Margot felt the blood drain from her face. "I'll go turn on the shower," she said faintly.

Travis came into the bathroom a few minutes later with a limp Jade in his arms. Her little sister looked so frail, her pallid face disturbingly slack, the deep violet smudges beneath her closed eyes stark. She looked impossibly young . . . and God, she stank, positively reeked of a noxious mix of alcohol, pot, sweat, and vomit. The vomit was splattered in drying clumps on her clothes—no, make that on *her* clothes, Margot amended, recognizing her Missoni knit tank, her favorite embroidered jeans, and her knee-high suede stiletto-heeled boots. Jade had obviously raided her closet before sneaking out.

The boots were certainly ruined, the knit top probably, too. But there was no point in crying over spilled vomit. The only thing that mattered was that Jade wasn't in the hospital or worse.

Travis lowered her onto the toilet and held her there. "She's beginning to respond a little. But if you need help getting her into the shower, I'll lend a hand."

"Thanks, I think I can manage."

He nodded. "Okay. And how about you? You all right?"

She shrugged. "I guess I should be used to Jade's special brand of self-destructive mischief by now. I feel like kicking myself all the way to California for not realizing something was up earlier this evening, but the fact is that she and I don't know each other very well. It's difficult to read her." She knelt on the tiled floor and tugged at one of the ruined boots, tossing it aside. "But this definitely isn't how I pictured spending the final hours before dawn. On the other hand, this entire evening's been pretty unusual," and she could have bit her tongue for letting this last remark slip out. She should be acting cool and nonchalant, as if she had earth-shattering love made to her on a nightly basis back in New York.

She grabbed hold of the other boot, yanking it for all she was worth.

"Margot—"

Consumed by the sudden fear that Travis was having second thoughts and more than half-convinced she'd embarrass herself by bursting into tears again if he tried to feed her some line about not being ready for a relationship, she began peeling the ruined knit top up Jade's hunched form. "I really better get these clothes off and clean her up. Would you mind going down to the kitchen and making a pot of coffee? I filled the coffeemaker earlier, so it's all set to go. And Ellie's cookies are in the jar by the fridge. Jordan would be horrified if I didn't give Officer Cooper something for all his troubles."

She felt his gaze bore into her, but refused to look up lest she betray herself.

"Yeah, I'll go down. We could all use some coffee. But as troubles go, I'm sure Cooper would be the first to tell you that vomit's better than blood any day."

After toweling off a dripping Jade and managing to shove her arms through the sleeves of an oversized T-shirt, Margot was sopping wet and exhausted—in addition to being angry, afraid, and sick at heart. But none of these feelings prevented her elation when Jade began whining feebly in protest at being made to walk down the hall to her room. She would never have believed the sound of Jade complaining would be music to her ears, but there it was.

Supporting her, Margot negotiated the minefield of Jade's room and got her seated on the bed. Immediately she flopped over on her side, her head landing with a thump on the pillows. Margot stared at her freshly scrubbed sleeping face. She looked impossibly young and innocent. Then she recalled how her sister looked awake: scared, angry, and defiant.

What could she do to reach her before she did something even more dangerous?

No answers came, only a muffled moan as Jade flopped over onto her stomach and began to snore. Margot shook her head and sighed. The kid was going to be one hurting puppy come tomorrow. Dragging the covers over her inert form, she switched off the bedside lamp.

She was going to have to figure out something before her rebellious sister got into the kind of trouble that might end up scarring her for life. But before she could do that she first had to find out what the Warburg police intended to do.

"She sleeping it off?" Travis asked as she came into the kitchen.

Margot answered with a tired nod.

"Here. This'll help." He passed her a mug of steaming black coffee.

"Thanks," she murmured, and raised the mug to her lips, drinking deeply, taking the opportunity to glance at Rob Cooper as she did. He was standing by the refrigerator. He, too, was cradling a mug.

"I'm afraid I didn't have the presence of mind to thank you earlier, Officer Cooper, for bringing Jade home instead of taking her to the station."

He had a nice smile. "Warburg's not a big town. We know your family's gone through a lot recently, Ms. Radcliffe. No point making things harder on you and your sisters."

"That's very kind of you. Our father's and Nicole's deaths have obviously been toughest on Jade. To say she's been having a rough time would be an understatement." Setting the cup on the counter, she pushed a lock of hair away from her face and forced herself to ask the question, the possible answers to which frightened her. "As I'm sure you know, Officer Cooper, my sister is underage. What will happen to her?"

"As I said before, your sister's pretty lucky. She didn't have a fake ID on her, and we've already ascertained that she didn't bring any of the pot, Ecstasy, or coke that was floating around the party tonight, so she won't be charged with fraud or possession."

"Well, that's good to hear," she whispered, gripping the counter behind her so she wouldn't slide to the floor on legs that had turned suddenly to jelly. Ecstasy? Cocaine? The high school parties she'd gone to had generally involved however many six-packs of Bud the most daring of the kids could smuggle out of their parents' house. Though pot had made an occasional appearance, nobody was doing cocaine or Ecstasy back then. And Jade was only sixteen.

"And unlike some of the kids we arrested tonight, this is your sister's first brush with the law. I have a kid sister, too, Ms. Radcliffe. Emma's a freshman. With three family members on the force, she's pretty much a straight arrow. But I'm not sure how she'd react if she had to deal with everything your sister's going through. So that's why this time I'm going to let her off with a hundred-dollar fine. Tonight's activities won't make it onto her record. But when you talk to your sister in the morning, you should let her know we keep a list of juvenile offenders at the station. She's made it onto that list now. If we cross paths with her again, it'll be bad news for her. Really bad news."

She nodded firmly. "I will tell Jade. And thank you for being so understanding."

"Again, your sister's lucky. My wife, Becky, and I had our first baby in August. Being a dad has made me see things a bit differently. I pray Hayley never gets mixed up in a bad crowd. But if she were to make some royally stupid teenage mistake, I hope the authorities wouldn't make it harder for her to straighten herself out."

Jade wasn't just doubly lucky, she was thrice so, for her run-in had been with Rob Cooper, clearly a good guy.

Margot smiled as relief washed over her. "If I may, Officer Cooper, I'd like to bring Jade by the station and have her clean the inside of your car."

He inclined his head. "That might be a learning lesson she won't soon forget." Raising the mug to his lips, he drained it. "I'd better be off. Thanks for the coffee. It was much appreciated."

Margot and Travis walked him to the door and then stood on the porch until the taillights of the patrol car disappeared into the dark of the allée. Absently rubbing her arms against the chill night air, she gazed out over the wide expanse of lawn and the outlying fields. Kissed by frost, they glistened pearl-white beneath the moon. It was a beautiful tableau, still and serene, quietly majestic.

Next to her Travis's shoulders lifted as he breathed deeply then exhaled in a long, puffy stream of white. "I should let you go so you can rest."

Her heart squeezed painfully. He was right. She should sleep—she would need her wits about her when she confronted Jade in the morning. But alone in her bed she wouldn't sleep, she'd only toss fitfully, consumed by a longing all the more powerful now that she'd lain in Travis's arms.

Pivoting, she faced him. He stood, hands balled deep in his pockets, his expression unreadable. She wished he'd kiss her. That's all it would take to seduce her; he knew it as well as she. Instead he was waiting, letting her make the decision. She should be grateful that he was showing such restraint, yet at the same time she would have loved to see some sign that it mattered to him—that she mattered.

She was so afraid of what the future held. Could she ever hope to hold on to him if they didn't succeed in keeping Rosewood Farm? A part of her wanted to explain the precariousness of the situation, but she couldn't take the risk that Travis might leave. She hated deceit. At least she could be honest about her desire for him.

Swallowing the lump in her throat, she said, "Don't go. Stay with me."

Thank God. Travis told himself it was because he hadn't touched her in a couple of hours that his hands shook as he lifted them, framing her face, drawing her near and then lowering his lips to drink deeply, savoring the fine taste of Margot.

And it was only natural to want to ease the fear shadowing her eyes. Seeing her kid sister passed out from a drinking binge had obviously terrified her. Tomorrow would be hectic, tons to do prepping the horses for Dan Stokes's visit. He could make her feel better tonight. Make them both feel better.

He let her lead him back inside. Hand in hand they climbed the grand staircase to her room. She left the lights off, but the moon was still high enough in the night sky to cast a pale silvery light.

She turned to him and wordlessly began to undress him. Her fingers grazed his bared skin like a heated whisper. Her mouth joined in, pressing kisses, running her tongue over skin stretched suddenly as tight as a drum. Every thud of his heart threatened to burst through. Enthralled, he let her continue.

Her hands glided over his buttocks and his muscles leaped in response. Her mouth had traveled over his chest and down, skimming over his abdomen and then moving lower still.

She was killing him. He was going to die from unholy feverish want. In exquisite agony, he groaned when her moist lips brushed the head of his straining cock.

God, she was so lovely, kneeling before him, her hair threaded with moonlight. She looked as ethereal as a fairy queen—no, a blessedly earthy, sensual queen who was giving him unspeakable pleasure. His need at a flash point, he reached for her, tangling his fingers in her hair.

"Margot"—her hoarsely whispered name a plea, a prayer—"I can't. It's too much—"

"Let me." Just two words and his desire broke free of all bonds. He felt her mouth close around him, drawing him deep into her dark, erotic heat, and he knew he was lost.

The gentle press of Travis's lips awakened Margot. "I didn't mean to wake you. Go back to sleep."

"What time is it?"

"Quarter of five. I've got to go."

She sat up and the bedcovers slipped to her waist. In the gloom she felt as much as saw his gaze travel south to rest on her breasts. The memory of how he'd lavishly adored them last night was like setting a match to kindling. Her nipples puckered tight.

Perhaps his vision was better than hers; perhaps he simply knew how effortlessly he aroused her. With a low rumble of hunger he dipped his head, bathing the peaked crests with his tongue. Pleasure unfurled banner-bright inside her and she wrapped her arms about him, wishing they could stay like this, with the rest of the world at bay.

But they both had obligations. So she tucked away in her heart the memory of Travis kissing her awake so deliciously, along with the others she'd hoarded while lying in his arms last night.

Lowering her head, she kissed the crown of his head, inhaling his warm scent. "I'll come down and make you coffee and breakfast."

"You should sleep."

"Not likely. Not when I have to figure out a way to help Jade before she ruins her life."

His hands traced slow circles over her back. "If you're bound and determined to get up, can I interest you in a hot shower? Then we can share the breakfast duties."

Her heart leaped at his suggestion, a chance to steal more time with him. And they'd be sharing a meal, sitting at a table. The idea made her absurdly happy. "A hot shower, huh?"

"A very hot shower, as hot and as long as you like."

His hushed promise alone was enough to melt her insides.

"Hmm," she said, pretending to consider. "That sounds pretty irresistible."

"Glad to hear it," he murmured, before kissing her with a thoroughness that made her toes curl. "Come on, then. No point in lying around in bed all morning."

Chapter ❧
TWENTY-ONE

SHE WOULD NEVER think of a hot shower in quite the same way or take for granted the glorious possibilities of thickly lathered soap.

Showering with Travis certainly was an energizing way to start the day. Even now, fully dressed in fawn-colored breeches and a black-ribbed turtleneck sweater, her body was still thrumming with the aftershocks of his loving.

She stood by the Viking range, ostensibly stirring a batch of scrambled eggs, all the while reliving the glorious sensation of Travis's slick body plastered against hers, her legs locked tight around his pumping hips as steaming water cascaded upon them. She felt the raw passion as he drove into her, then the blasting force of his climax as he poured himself into her. As she dissolved around him.

Swept away by sensation, she swayed on her feet.

Coffee saved her. She caught the potent whiff of java just inches away from her face and blinked to find Travis holding out a mug. "Here, this will clear away the cobwebs." He set the coffee on the counter. "Toast's done."

"Thanks," she mumbled gratefully, hoping he'd think the flush on her face was from the stove's heat. "Great. Can you grab the plates? The eggs are ready, too." She hastily glanced at the frying pan to make sure. As lost as she'd been in her erotic reverie, for all she knew they could have been burned to cinders.

They sat at the counter, Travis wolfing down the pile of eggs she'd heaped on his plate. No, she was not going to get all sentimental that he wasn't gagging at the first meal she'd cooked. But the man had obviously built up an appetite; she was glad she'd had the presence of mind to toss in a few extra eggs. She'd considered adding some other stuff, too, the way Jordan and Anika always did when they cooked, but then Travis truly might have gagged.

Truth be told, the finer aspects of cooking had never held much interest for her, and since in her line of work there were precious few dishes in which she *could* indulge, her natural indifference had always been something of a boon.

Was Travis looking for a woman who could cook?

Okay, time to stop being ridiculous. She had plenty more pressing concerns. But it was easier to obsess over her culinary abilities or lack thereof than wonder why, for instance, Travis hadn't bothered to ask about her previous lovers or boyfriends. She supposed she should feel grateful that he wasn't grilling her. It saved her the embarrassment of divulging how limited her experience was. And then she'd have to explain that while she'd had more than an ample share of offers, she had never been interested in sex for sex's sake.

Nonetheless Travis's lack of curiosity rankled. Why *didn't* he want to know about her past relationships? The obvious answer was that he didn't care because he wasn't thinking in terms of a long-lasting commitment.

She might as well have burned the eggs; they tasted like ashes. Setting her fork down, she took a sip of water. Travis had already devoured everything on his plate.

"Are there more?" he asked.

"Here, have mine," she said, switching plates. "I can't eat any more."

Travis swiveled in his stool to look at her. "You sure? You only took a couple of bites." He frowned. "You're going to starve."

She rolled her eyes. Of all the topics he could have broached, this was the one he picked? "I'm not anorexic. I don't have an eating disorder of any kind. I don't pop diet drugs or amphetamines or laxatives and I've never stuck my finger down my throat. I *do* have to be super careful about what and how much I eat, though. Most women do. But I've never really been into the idea of starving my body to death. But thanks for the concern."

His eyebrows had shot up at her diatribe. "Sorry. Didn't mean to rile you. I was just worried. You've been so physically, uh, *active,* and you've got a long day ahead of you."

She felt herself blush to the roots of her hair. Good one, Margot. Here Travis was being considerate and she'd almost snapped his head off.

"No, I'm sorry. It's hard not to get defensive about eating habits when you're a model." Then, choosing the one subject she felt she could address at a quarter of six in the morning without sounding unutterably pathetic, she said, "It's worrying about what I'm going to say to Jade that's making me lose my appetite."

"She's having a rough time of it."

"Isn't that the truth. First, she single-handedly stages her own expulsion from Malden, and now she's managed to land herself on the Warburg police's watch list for juvenile delinquents. Contemplating what she might do for an encore terrifies me. I'm supposed to be her guardian, but I don't have a clue what to say to her—other than that she's an idiot and is messing up her life royally, and that I don't appreciate having the clothes she filched from my closet ruined. And what else? Oh, yeah, that I'm tempted to ground her for the next two years." She drew a shaky breath. "Dear Lord. She's got me so freaked out, I'm babbling."

"That's all right. Babble on," he said with a crooked smile as he reached out and carefully tucked a lock of hair behind her ear.

Her heart lurched at the sweet simplicity of his gesture. The tenderness he showed her was as devastating as the passion of his lovemaking. "I only wish I knew how to get through to her. I've thought of contacting Reverend Wilde. Do you think that's a good idea?"

He took a sip of coffee and then nodded. "Yeah, I do actually. My mom used to go talk to him when things got ugly with my father. Something tells me Jade might open up to him in a way she wouldn't with a therapist or social worker."

"Or me," she added glumly.

"Don't be so hard on yourself. You're doing as fine a job as anyone could, Margot."

"I certainly don't *feel* like I am. I'm practically paralyzed with fear that I'm going to screw up with her." Broodingly, she ran her index finger along the rim of her cup. "But you know the worst part?" she continued quietly. "I'm not sure I even *like* Jade."

His laugh surprised her. Leaning back against the bar stool, he asked, "It hasn't occurred to you that maybe the reason you dislike Jade is because she's a hell of a lot like you?"

"She isn't!"

"Oh, yeah?" He cocked a dark brow questioningly. "Okay, maybe right now Jade's a little more toxic and out of control than you were at her age, but that's because both her parents are dead and she's scared out of her mind and grieving. But think back to what you were like at sixteen. You drove me nuts. Christ, there were times I wanted to wring your neck because of some stunt you pulled. That, or toss you, butt first, into the manure pile."

Her pique must have shown on her face, for he grinned with devilish enjoyment. "Yeah, I definitely see the similarities. Jade's more like you than anyone in your family."

"What about Nicole?"

He shook his head. "No comparison. Jade's smarter and more kindhearted than Nicole could have ever dreamed of being. And Jade's a damned better rider than Nicole, too—thank God. I have a hunch that deep down Jade probably idolizes you."

She opened her mouth. Unable to come up with a rebuttal, she shut it with an audible snap.

His eyes twinkling with amusement, he pushed her now empty plate aside and then reached out and cupped her chin. "Anyone ever tell you you're awfully cute when your feathers are ruffled?"

"No." People mostly blathered about how beautiful she was.

"Well, you are. Real cute."

Leaning forward he slowly brushed his lips against hers. He tasted wonderful, of eggs and buttered toast and coffee, and Margot's hunger for him returned with a vengeance. She opened her mouth, inviting the bold sweep of his tongue.

When at last they parted, Travis's breathing was gratifyingly ragged and his beard-stubbled cheeks sported red flags of arousal. Shaking his head as if to clear it, he said, "One kiss from you and I'm as randy as a buck in spring. I've got a couple dozen horses to tend to and all I want to do is get you naked on this nice, wide counter."

"We can't. Jade—"

"Yeah. I know." And letting his head fall back, he loosed a string of curses toward the recessed lights.

Margot bit back a smile. Okay, maybe it didn't matter that she couldn't cook. And just because she desperately needed to hear the words, she could hardly expect Travis to pledge his undying love for her after one night together. She had to give his feelings for her time to develop. Please God, let them have enough time for her to make him love her.

Finished venting his frustration, Travis sat up. "Okay, let's divide and conquer, boss. I'll go tackle the horses and you tackle your kid sister."

"Sure you don't want to trade jobs? Jade *likes* you."

The corner of his mouth lifted in a half-smile. "She wouldn't if I were ripping into her, which, after watching my father drink his job, marriage, family, and, finally, his life away, I might be real tempted to do. Besides, even though Jade likes me fine and I think she's a great kid, any talk will mean more if it comes from you."

"I suppose you're right," she said with a sigh.

"Want a piece of advice?"

"Please."

"Before you go upstairs, pour yourself some more coffee and mull over what it was you were missing at Jade's age."

She could answer that: she'd needed to feel she belonged to something. She'd needed to feel *needed,* that she had something worthwhile to contribute. She'd needed to be given an opportunity to appreciate the satisfaction that came from working hard and achieving goals. She wondered whether Nicole or her dad had ever challenged Jade that way. She would bet not. Nicole was too self-absorbed. And Dad had probably behaved as he always had: preferring that his pretty daughters grow up pampered and cosseted— decorative but essentially useless—while the men in their lives tackled the real work.

Her thoughts were interrupted by Travis's next words. "Of course, pinpointing what's lacking in her life isn't nearly as difficult as figuring out how to provide her with it. The real trick will be not letting her catch on that you're trying to help. Like you, she's got her share of the Radcliffe pride."

She glanced at the coffeemaker. It was three-quarters full, about three cups of seriously strong Colombian left. "I'm not sure there's enough coffee in the world for me to figure all that out."

Fueled by more caffeine than she usually consumed in a week, Margot marched into Jade's room and grabbed hold of the comforter and sheet and pulled them down to the foot of the bed.

"Up and at 'em," she said crisply. "Come on, Jade, time to wake up."

With a groan Jade flung out her arm, blindly searching for the covers. "G'way. I'm sick."

Margot caught hold of her outstretched arm and tugged, pulling her upright. "Wow, writing English papers really takes a toll, huh?" she said, panting. Lifting and hauling Jade's body was getting a mite tedious.

"Can't you see I don't feel well?" Jade mumbled in the direction of her navel. "Will you just leave me alone?"

"Sorry, it's a school day."

"Call the nurse's office." She made to lie back down but Margot caught her again.

"But it would be such a shame not to be able to turn in your English paper on time, especially after working on it so hard. I'm sure you'll be feeling loads better by the time you get to school."

Despite her best effort, Jade was gradually becoming more alert. Blinking groggily she peered out the window. "Why's it so dark? What time is it?"

"Six-thirty," Margot said cheerily.

"Are you nuts? School doesn't start till 8:45!"

"I know, but you and I have a couple of things to do beforehand. And I wouldn't want you to be late for school. Your teacher might think you hadn't finished writing that paper."

"I didn't have a paper to write," Jade muttered.

"Really? Then what could be making you feel so bad? Oh, wait! Could it be from all the alcohol you guzzled last night when you were out partying at the Mayhews' house instead of diligently writing a paper like you made me believe?"

"Will you stop?" Jade wailed before cradling her head with a moan. "Okay, already. So I went to a party at Ryan Mayhew's. Big friggin' deal."

"The big deal is you lied to me. You lied and then snuck out of the house and got trashed without my knowing where in the world you were. But you want to know what the really big deal is? I'm willing to bet Rosewood that you don't have the first clue how you got home last night."

Jade was silent. Finally she looked up. "I'm home, aren't I? Nothing major happened." A flicker of uncertainty betrayed her belligerent expression.

"So I'm right," she said quietly. "You have absolutely no idea. That scares the daylights out of me, Jade. And you're too smart to not be terrified, too." She drew a steadying breath that accomplished nothing. "How could you let yourself get so drunk that your memory is one big blank? You're a beautiful sixteen-year-old girl. Do you realize what *could* have happened to you at a party like that? Do you know how incredibly lucky you are to have puked your guts out so that this morning you only have a splitting head and a queasy stomach to moan about? Do you realize how damned fortunate you are to have come home in a police car—"

"Police car?" Jade croaked.

"You heard me right. A police car. It could just as easily have been an ambulance, and you'd have been driven to the hospital's emergency room. From what I've heard, getting your stomach pumped isn't exactly fun."

Jade dropped her gaze to stare at her bare feet.

Was she getting through at all? Margot wondered desperately. Determined, she tried again. "Do you have any inkling how terrifying it is to have a police officer show up at your door and tell you he has your little sister, unconscious and covered in vomit, in the backseat of his cruiser? Do you know how scary it is to watch you keep hurting yourself and to know that unless you stop it's just a matter of time before the damage is irreparable? I can't go on like this, Jade," she said bleakly. "I hate the way we fight tooth and nail, and I don't want to spend my days wondering if I can trust you. Most of all, I simply can't bear the thought of losing you. I need you to help me, Jade. Please." She pressed her fist to her mouth, trying to maintain some semblance of control. Until she'd uttered the words, she'd been able to keep her fear at bay. Now it threatened to overwhelm her. She turned to the window.

Jade's hoarse voice broke the tense silence. "I only went to the party to get back at Blair and her friends for spreading lies about Mom."

God, the poor kid. She turned back and came over to the bed to sit beside her. "Who's Blair? And what could this Blair and her friends possibly have to say about Nicole?" she asked, praying that Jade's answer would be different than the one she envisioned. A forgotten memory had flashed in her mind of the days following Dad's and Nicole's deaths. As word spread, all those women had dropped by the house, their arms laden with casseroles and cream pies, their eyes feral bright with curiosity. At the time, she'd been too preoccupied with her own worries to care, but of course Warburg's gossip mill must have been in full churn—and apparently still was. What twisted stories had reached Jade?

Jade shrugged. "Blair Hood, Courtney Joseph, and Amanda Coles. They're this super popular clique at school. They've been posting stuff on Facebook, about what an ugly loser I am and how no one should want to be my friend. At first I tried to ignore it. I figured they were just being bitches because Blair Hood has a major thing for Dean McCallister, and he's been coming over to sit at my table during lunch since I started at Warburg High."

"Dean McCallister? Is he Topher's little brother?"

"Yeah. He's a senior. He rides in the Warburg Hunt Club and Blair Hood's tongue hangs out of her mouth whenever he so much as looks at her, which is probably why he only uses her for blow jobs behind the back of the gym and then ditches her as fast as he can."

"Oh, dear," she said faintly.

"Blair's totally pathetic. It's freaking her out that Dean keeps hanging around me when I'm not doing anything to encourage him. He's not even my type. I was actually going to say something to him about how shitty he was being to Blair when she and her bitches started posting stuff about my mom."

"What'd they say?"

"That Mom was like this major ho and that she was cheating on Dad with any guy who'd do her. Then last weekend they wrote about how I'm exactly like her, and how I got expelled from Malden for gangbanging the football team." The words, issued tonelessly, merely underscored her pain and humiliation.

Margot's heart ached for her. "Oh, Jade, why didn't you tell me what was going on?"

She was silent, and only shrugged again.

Margot pushed her own hurt aside. She couldn't blame Jade for not wanting to reveal the vicious things being said about her. She wouldn't have admitted something so mortifying, either. "So you decided to retaliate."

"Yeah. When Dean asked me if I wanted to go to the party at Ryan Mayhew's house with him, I said yes, because I knew if Dean was going, Blair would get herself invited, too. He picked me up at the bottom of our drive and we got to Ryan's just as the party was starting. I made sure that the first thing Blair saw when she showed up was me with Dean's tongue halfway down my throat and his hands all over me. I'd have done a lot more with him to get back at Blair for what she wrote about Mom, but Dean was already pretty wasted from doing bong hits and Jägermeister shots. We fooled around some on the sofa and then he, like, fell asleep . . ."

Thank God for small favors. She didn't want to begin to think about the trouble Jade might have gotten into had Dean McCallister been in any state to take advantage of what she so foolishly offered. "And where was Blair during all this?"

"Blair? Oh, she'd already left. In tears," she added with cold satisfaction. "Then Ryan Mayhew asked me if I wanted to do some shots with him, and I said okay because there wasn't anything else to do and I was feeling kind of bummed. I can't really remember what happened after that."

Margot was silent, absorbing the contents of Jade's story. In retrospect, neither the explanation of last night's events nor the means of revenge surprised her. Of course the girls at Warburg would be jealous of Jade, a pretty newcomer, doubly so if they thought their turf was threatened. Their willingness to use the Internet to bully and hurt and slander with vicious rumors was, sadly, typical, too.

Nor was she surprised that Jade hadn't considered the consequences of her particular brand of vengeance or that she was in effect giving truth to the lies Blair and her friends had spread about her across cyberspace.

She wasn't shocked by anything her little sister had confessed to because Travis was right: she and Jade really were very much alike. Had she faced a similar problem at age sixteen, she would have reacted just as rashly and impetuously.

Jade's present predicament involved more than simple teenage angst and rebellion, though. How could she help her through it? This was one of those key moments in life, Margot realized, that called for looking inside oneself to offer some nugget of profound wisdom.

But what did she know? She was twenty-six years old, only a few measly steps ahead of Jade in terms of figuring out how *not* to screw up. If she appeared to have her act together it was because fortune had smiled on her, first gracing her with her mother's looks and her father's height, and then plunking her down in Charlie Ayer's path.

How could she be expected to be profound? She was a fashion model, for Pete's sake. And she was far from wise. Here she was on the precipice of falling terminally in love with Travis despite the fact that other than wanting her physically she had no idea how he truly felt about her.

Heartbreak loomed and still she yearned for him. Foolish.

So what could she say or do to help Jade deal with the questions surrounding Nicole?

That Nicole was foremost on Jade's mind was proven by her next words. "Those were lies about Mom, weren't they?" she asked.

Please let me say the right thing. "Don't let these girls' vicious stories tarnish your memories of her. Whatever happened or didn't happen is in the past."

"So you think it's true. You think she was cheating on Dad." How sad that Jade's voice wasn't even accusatory.

"No." Margot shook her head vehemently. "What I'm saying is that I really don't know. I doubt anyone knows the truth except for Nicole." Hell would freeze over before she mentioned the existence of Nicole's diary or the damning passage she'd read in it. "That's why you can't let toxic gossip destroy the truths you *do* know—that your mother loved you and that you loved her and that she made our father happy for many years. She did, Jade. Dad loved your mom. And they both adored you. If you lose hold of those truths, then girls like Blair and Courtney and Amanda will have won. You can't let them do that."

Jade said nothing as she stared at her clenched hands. Then, in a barely audible whisper, she said, "And what about the other thing they said, that I was just like Mom?"

"They only wish they could be as beautiful and exciting as you and Nicole," she replied fiercely.

"That's not what I meant. They called her a ho and said I'm just like her."

"That's a load of bull."

"But what about last night, with Dean?"

Though Margot couldn't help but wince at the misery in Jade's voice, sugarcoating her answer wouldn't be of any help. "Making out with Dean to get back at Blair definitely wasn't the smartest way to go about proving that you're not a—" She faltered.

"Slut," Jade provided.

"Yeah. And it was a lousy thing to do to Dean since he obviously likes you. You shouldn't lead a guy on if you don't care about him. I have a feeling you've already figured out that if Blair was jealous of you before, she's really going to hate you now. So, yeah, what you did was stupid and unkind—but that doesn't mean you're a whore. You acted badly, but you were also provoked." She rubbed her forehead. God, had any of that made sense? "Just remember, nobody's perfect—not you, me, Nicole, anybody. We all screw up."

"What about Jordan?"

Margot smiled. "Jordan's probably the exception to the rule. We, the rest of mankind, make mistakes. What matters is whether we face up to them and learn from them so we can do the right thing the next time around. What counts in life is what you make of the choices and of the chances you're given. That's what shapes you as a person."

Jade appeared less than convinced.

"You don't believe me? Look at Travis." She paused, startled that his name had slipped out. But why should she be, when he was always in her thoughts?

"Travis? What about him?"

"You know who Red Maher, his father, was?"

Jade nodded. "Yeah."

"Well, Travis didn't let the fact that everyone talked about his being the son of the town drunk stop him from making something of himself. He was given a chance to change his life and he took it. Now he's one of the most respected trainers in Virginia. Any job is his for the taking."

"You've got a thing for him, don't you?"

Trust Jade to go off topic. "What makes you say that?" she asked carefully.

"Your face. When you talk about him, it gets all soft and dreamy."

"I'm not sure what you mean."

"Remember the photo Charlie Ayer took of you for the

Dior shoot? Sometimes you get the same kind of dreamy look when you talk about him."

She felt her cheeks flame. Dear God, was she that obvious?

"Does he know?"

"Does who know?"

"Duh. Travis."

"Um, I guess so. Maybe." She fingered the blanket, wishing she could dive under it.

"He should. You should tell him how you feel."

There were times when Jade was too smart. "It's not that easy. It's complicated, actually. Really complicated." Restless, she rose to her feet and began pacing. "Speaking of complicated, I wasn't kidding when I said that you and I had a lot to do before school starts. I've got to drive you down to the police station."

Jade's green-tinged face turned a ghastly white. "Am I in really big trouble?"

"Not in nearly as much trouble as you could be. I have to pay a fine—which you're going to reimburse me for by mane *and* tail braiding whatever horses we enter in upcoming shows. You should also know that you've made it onto the police department's list of juvenile delinquents. Break the law again and no one will take pity, Jade. But this morning you're going to start your penance by going down to the station and thanking Officer Cooper for being so lenient. You're also going to wash the patrol car you puked in until it's as shiny and clean as the day it rolled off the assembly line. And, you should know, that I'm going to give Reverend Wilde a call. He's a kind man, not one to judge. I really think he'd be a good person to talk to."

That Jade didn't reject the idea out of hand Margot took as a good sign. Though she and Jade still had a long way to go in terms of establishing a strong relationship, maybe facing this crisis together would help them bond. She hoped so.

"Why don't you go take a quick shower while I fix some

toast? Jordan says it's the best thing for settling a queasy stomach. You can eat it on the way to the station."

"Do I really have to go to school?"

"Yeah. I'm afraid you do." But Jade wasn't going to be facing Blair and company's vindictiveness alone. Margot intended to have a talk with the school principal. He needed to be alerted to the Internet bullying being perpetrated by his students.

BALANCED ON A STEP STOOL, his chest pressed against Gulliver's long bony head, Travis switched on the electric clippers and then asked over their low buzz, "You ready, Tito?"

"I got him," he replied, standing on the opposite side of Gulliver, a sure hand wrapped about the gelding's leather halter.

Tito's presence was only precautionary. Some horses were frightened by the clippers' electronic hum and vibration, especially around the sensitive region of the ears. But Gulliver was a real sweetheart.

He stood placidly while Travis slowly raised the device, guiding its blades along the delicately curved contours of his ear. And when Travis had finished, he merely shook his head, sending bits of chestnut fuzz flying onto the concrete floor, hardly blinking when the men switched places and Travis went to work on his other ear.

The poll, situated just behind the ears where the bridle's crownpiece rested, came next in the order of clipping. Then Travis moved on to the muzzle and the underside of Gulliver's jaw. Then squatting with one knee propped on the concrete floor, he trimmed the shaggy growth around the fetlocks. The clip job complete, the aisle floor resembled a barber shop, chunks of coppery hair covering it.

Straightening, Travis gave the horse a hearty pat on the shoulder. "Good boy. Okay, Tito, he's all yours."

Tito led Gulliver away, outside to the pasture, so the horse would have a couple of hours to romp and roll before Travis rode him.

With well-orchestrated precision, Felix stepped up with Gypsy Queen on a lead shank, taking the spot Gulliver and Tito had just vacated. An all-black mare, she favored her sire Stoneleigh's rangy Thoroughbred build and hot-blooded temperament. Only four years old, she already possessed a huge natural jump. With the right training Travis knew she had the potential to be an outstanding three-day eventer or show jumper.

Gypsy Queen wasn't quite the mellow fellow Gulliver was. But Felix, who worked with her daily, had brought along a jar of peanut butter and a bag of carrots, her favorite treat. As she nibbled away, Travis switched on the clippers.

First he simply held them against the mare's shoulder, allowing her to grow accustomed to the foreign vibration. Then, slowly, while Felix talked to her and petted her, doling out peanut-butter-coated carrots, he moved the clippers slowly up her neck and then to the base of her ear. Though the mare swished her tail and struck the concrete floor with her rear hoof, she submitted docilely enough when Travis began trimming the fuzzy growth.

He'd finished Gypsy's fetlocks and was rechecking her velvety muzzle for any stray whiskers when a pair of work boots came into his line of vision. "Hey, Ned, what's up?"

"Wanted to see how you're making out. Gypsy's the last of the lot?"

"Yeah, we saved the best for last. Ain't that so, Travis?" Felix said, stroking the mare's forehead.

"That's right," Travis agreed equably, knowing Felix had a real soft spot for the mare he'd helped foal. Straightening from his half-crouch, he turned off the clippers. "Gypsy's getting better each time I clip her," he noted with satisfaction, adding, "Thanks, Felix," as Felix walked away with Gypsy.

"She's a smart one. Why kick up a fuss when she can chomp carrots and peanut butter and have Felix whisper sweet nothings in her ear. You seen Miss Margot yet this morning?" Ned asked.

Whispered sweet nothings. Margot. Hearing the words strung loosely together had Travis thinking of the sweet nothings he'd like to whisper in the delicate shell of her ear. Like how incredible it felt when he was inside her, how he loved the breathy little sounds she made when he rocked against her, how when he stroked the curves and hollows of her slender body and tasted the dewy fragrance of her skin he was filled with an unfamiliar kind of joy.

"Hey, Travis. You in there?" Ned asked, waving a hand in front of his face.

He started. "Sorry, what's that you were saying?"

The older man gave him a funny look. "I asked if you'd seen Miss Margot."

He pretended to check his watch. "No. I expect she's taking Jade to school. She should be here soon, though. Why?"

"You get your mail yesterday?"

"I didn't get the chance." He normally went through his mail at night after he'd done a final check on the horses. "I, uh, got caught up in something." He felt his skin warm beneath the collar of his wool sweater. Ned would probably tell him off but good if he learned just what Travis had been caught up in—Margot's delectable body.

"You might want to. I received a letter from Edward Crandall with a big fat check tucked inside it. My savings just tripled overnight," he said, and the awe was plain in his tone.

Travis had almost forgotten RJ's bequest. Guilt settled like lead in the pit of his stomach. Considering how he and RJ parted company, he shouldn't be getting a pile of money and the pick of one of Rosewood's foals. RJ certainly wouldn't have left him a nickel if he could have foreseen what Travis would be doing with his talented, glamorous daughter.

"I'll tell you something, Travis. I'm sorely tempted to tear the thing in half. Taking all that money don't sit right somehow."

"Yeah, I know what you mean." He walked over to the electrical outlet and unplugged the clippers. "But in your case, the money's well deserved. You've worked at Rosewood all your life. It's like a retire—"

"I ain't ever going to retire."

"Lord help us if you do. You're the heart and soul of this place," he said, laying a reassuring hand on Ned's checked-flannel-covered shoulder. "All I'm saying is that RJ included you in his will because you've worked at Rosewood longer and harder than anyone. You were his good friend."

The scowl on Ned's face cleared somewhat. "I guess that makes sense. At least RJ was rich as Croesus. That helps a bit. Speaking of money, have you talked to Margot about shopping for a new stud?"

"No, not yet." He began wrapping the bright yellow extension cord in loose loops.

Ned bent down to scoop up the can of WD-40 they used to keep the clippers running smoothly. "Here, let me take those," he said, holding out his hand for the clippers and electrical cord. "I'm headed to the tack room anyway to oil the new girth Miss Margot's been using on Mystique. You'll want to talk to her soon," he continued. "If Crandall sent us those checks, it must mean the estate's been settled. We should be going over auction catalogs and following up on any ads that catch our eye. We've got to find a stud that would make RJ proud."

"Yeah." Travis recognized and shared the older man's excitement at the prospect of introducing a new bloodline into Rosewood's stock. "I'll bring it up just as soon as I can, Ned," he promised.

He grabbed the broom that was propped against the wall and began sweeping up the multihued clouds of horse hair when a faint sound had him looking toward the barn doors at the other end of the aisle. He hadn't consciously realized he was listening for her, but of course he was. Damn, but he loved the way Margot's long legs ate up the ground. He'd seen her perform her model's strut on the runway, a superbly choreographed sashay that could transfix an audience. To him, her natural athletic gait was a million times sexier, and he itched to wrap his hands about those slim hips and tangle his legs in hers.

Tangled up in Margot, that's what he was. It seemed to him she was already a part of him, in his system, in his blood. It's why his heart thudded heavily in his chest as she approached, why everything in him tightened with urgent need. A sudden thought crossed his mind. There were empty stalls nearby, shadowed and smelling of fresh wood shavings and sweet hay . . .

"Morning, Miss Margot."

Ned's cheerful greeting quelled the mad impulse to steal Margot away to some hidden nook. But Travis couldn't help thinking how great it would be if Ned, Tito, Felix, and everyone else at Rosewood could magically disappear for a couple of hours, so he could drop the pretense that Margot was nothing more than his boss.

"Travis just finished trimming the horses. Once we've got them all groomed, 'dressed in their Sunday best,' as your dad used to say, they'll look so fine, Dan Stokes's client will be whipping out his checkbook. Stokes called, by the way," Ned told them. "His client had a business meeting that got canceled so Dan wanted to know if they could come by tomorrow. They're shooting for around eleven-thirty."

"A businessman, huh? I hope he's a successful one with really deep pockets. The farrier's bill was pretty scary," Margot said wryly.

Ned chuckled. "Jarvis's services don't come cheap."

Why did it seem like forever since he'd seen her? Travis wondered. And how was it that she appeared even more beautiful today? As if feeling the weight of his stare, she looked at him. At the flash of awareness in those sky-blue eyes, a warmth spread through him and he suddenly felt as happy as a kid. He smiled. Coloring, she gave him a quick, shy smile before returning her gaze to Ned.

"Ned, I'm glad I caught you and Travis together. There's something I wanted to discuss with you both. You know that dark bay with the two white stockings that you're just beginning to break to the saddle? What's he like?"

"You mean Aspen? The colt's a real treat. He's out of Faraday and Allure. He's got a nice balanced stride on the flat. Travis and I have sent him over a few jumps. Tucks his knees up for the takeoff neat as you please and he's got a good natural arc in the air. Personality-wise he's a fire-cracker. Always has a trick or two to try."

"So he's got spunk? That's interesting. What would you and Travis say to having Jade work with him? Is she good enough?"

Ned rubbed the side of his jaw as he considered the idea. "Well, she's got great hands. And she's pretty strong for a girl her age."

"And she's fearless in the saddle. That's key as Aspen will push her to the max," Travis added. He wondered whether Margot's question had something to do with helping Jade find another goal in life besides landing in scrapes. If so, it was a pretty darn good idea. Pairing her with Aspen might just fit the bill.

"She'll need supervision, though," Ned said.

"Absolutely," Margot agreed. "I wouldn't want to risk Aspen not being brought along properly."

"Of course not." He waved the notion away as absurd. "I can carve out time in the afternoons when Miss Jade gets out of school to give her a hand with him."

"Thanks, Ned."

"You know, though, that Aspen's still really green. Jade's actual time in the saddle won't amount to much at first. A lot of the work will be on the ground," Travis said.

Margot nodded. "I realize we don't want to overdo his training or we'll run the risk having him go sour, so that brings up the second thing I wanted to ask. I'd like Jade to start riding some of the other horses, too. We all know she's pretty much outgrown Doc. Working with a bunch of different mounts would be a good challenge."

"I have no problem with it," he said.

"It seems to me you're going to have to put that little girl on the payroll soon, Miss Margot. Sure you're not putting too much on her plate?"

"Yes, well, Jade's got an awful lot of excess energy these days."

Travis caught the underlying note of tension in Margot's voice, but he refrained from questioning her until Ned, saying he'd be willing to begin working with Jade and Aspen this very afternoon, went off to oil Mystique's girth.

Propping a shoulder against the wall of Indigo's stall, he said, "So how'd your talk with Jade go?"

Curious as to what the humans were up to outside her stall, Indigo, a splashy dark gray mare, abandoned her morning hay and stuck her head out to investigate.

Margot put her hand inside her vest pocket, withdrew a carrot treat, and offered it to her. Reaching up to scratch the underside of the gray's jaw, she said, "I honestly don't know. At first, I thought things were going pretty well. It seemed like we were actually talking, connecting. And I was certain I'd made her understand how narrowly she'd avoided getting into serious trouble with the police. And she opened up enough to tell me why she'd gone to the party in the first place. Some of the girls have been bullying her, posting vicious stuff on the Web about her—and Nicole. You can imagine what they said."

Travis grimaced. "Christ, that's the last thing she needs."

"I know. The reason Jade was at the party was to get back

at one of them, Blair Hood, by making out with a guy Blair's got a crush on. Typical catty girl stuff," she said with a tired sigh. Another carrot treat was offered up to a happy Indigo.

"Anyway, we talked and I tried to give her some advice and reassure her about Nicole as best I could. All things considered, I was feeling almost optimistic when we drove down to the police station. At the very least, I was sure she understood that getting back in the good graces of Warburg's finest would be a smart thing to do. . . ." Her voice trailed off.

The mare pushed her muzzle against Margot, obviously hoping for another handout. Abstractedly she stroked the dark gray head.

"But?" Travis prompted.

"What? Sorry. I'm still dazed from shock," she answered with a weary sigh. "It's only now dawning on me that Jade clearly thinks buttering up authority figures is strictly for losers. Instead of acting even remotely contrite, she went and deliberately secured herself top billing on Rob Cooper's personal list of teenage punks."

"What did she do?"

Before answering, Margot fished another treat from her pocket for Indigo to chomp. "It happened when she was scrubbing the patrol car. I'd left her with the bucket, sponge, soap, and the bottle of Nature's Miracle we'd brought with us to call and check in with Damien. When I hung up, she was still at it—I can only imagine how disgusting the interior was. So I decided to be efficient and go into the police station and pay her fine. It didn't take long, but when I walked out, she wasn't alone. Rob Cooper was there, decked out in full intimidation regalia."

Travis frowned. "Full what?"

"You know, the hat, mirrored sunglasses, bulky jacket, and holstered pistol. Scary police officer clothing. He'd obviously figured out who the kid in the baggy hoodie and jeans cleaning his car was, and decided that since she was fully conscious it would be a perfect time to read her the riot act. Even from a distance I could see by his posture that he was trying to scare her spitless."

"Bad idea with Jade."

"A monumentally bad idea."

He arched his brow at her dry tone. "So what happened?"

"I raced across the parking lot to catch Officer Cooper finishing his speech with a 'You got that, kid?' He was towering in front of her, arms crossed in front of his chest as if he intended to wait right there, boulderlike, until Jade looked up and gave him an apology just oozing sincerity."

"And Jade didn't opt for the apology route?"

"I'm afraid not," Margot said ruefully. "I saw her hood bob slightly as if she were looking him up and down, taking his measure. Then I heard her snarl quite distinctly, 'Move it, RoboCop,' and before Cooper could so much as react, she'd chucked the bucket, full of stale vomit and soapy water, so it landed all over RoboCop." She clapped a hand over her mouth. Lowering it, she exclaimed, "Oh, God, now I've started calling him that, too."

"RoboCop? It's pretty funny." A grin split his face.

"Well, Rob Cooper didn't think so. You should have seen him, Travis. He looked like he wanted to haul her off to jail right then and there. And, of course, as luck would have it, about five other police officers were milling on the parking lot—"

"Probably the start of their shift."

She nodded. "They were splitting their sides laughing at Cooper. And Jade, who I'm coming to believe would spit in the eye of the devil himself, was having a blast, apologizing outrageously as she slapped at his pant legs with her filthy sponge."

He chuckled. "I've always liked Rob, but, man, that's a priceless image. He can't have enjoyed being taken down a few pegs by a teenage girl. Jade is something else," he said, laughing now.

"I'm afraid she is." Margot, too, lost the battle to control her mirth. "Not that Robo—Officer Cooper found her remotely entertaining. It must really have gotten his goat that there was nothing he could do about it—though of course I promised him that Jade would pay his dry-cleaning bill. That kid's going to be braiding manes forever."

"I guess your new game plan is to keep Jade so busy she won't have time to get into any more trouble."

"It's pretty much all I could come up with. She needs to be given some adult responsibility. The only thing I could think of was to get her more deeply involved with the horses."

"It's a good idea, Margot. Really good. It'll be a great experience for her to work with Aspen. I'll draw up a list of the others I think she should start riding so we can work out a daily schedule."

A look that Travis couldn't fully decipher crossed her face. It seemed almost sad. Wistful perhaps described it best. But before he could ask what the matter was, she was patting her vest pocket. "Last treat of the morning, Indigo," she murmured to the horse. Then, with a start, she asked, "Oh, gosh, what time is it?"

"A little past nine o'clock. Why?"

"I have to be back at Warburg High at ten to meet with the principal. I don't want to be late."

He liked discovering this new side to Margot. She made him think of a mother hen, her feathers ruffled in concern for her wayward chick. The image was so incongruous and completely at odds with Margot's blue-blooded elegance that he couldn't help but grin.

He pushed away from the wall to stand in front of her, the tips of his field boots meeting hers. "I was wondering if you'd like to go out for a ride with me later this afternoon. We can see how Mystique likes the great outdoors." It wasn't dinner at the Coach House, but it was the closest thing to a date that Travis could manage, given the extra work they all had prepping the horses for Dan Stokes and his client tomorrow.

"I—I'd like that."

He watched her throat work as she swallowed. He badly wanted to kiss her, to press his mouth against the slender column and feel her pulse race with desire.

Succumbing to temptation, he lifted his hand to cup the back of her neck, only to pull away with a silent curse when her blasted cell began pealing. In his need to touch her he'd forgotten the rest of the world, the existence of Charlie Ayer and the countless others who demanded her attention.

She fished the phone from her inside pocket. "Hello? Oh, yes, hi. No, no, you're not interrupting but the reception in the barn is weak. Let me call you back once I'm outside. Thanks." Margot pressed the OFF button. "That was Edward Crandall. I, uh—" Her awkward pause had her coloring. "I have to talk to him about the estate."

She needed privacy. "Sure, I understand. Oh, yeah, that reminds me," he said as he began escorting her toward the double doors. "You and I need to talk about a couple of business matters, too, but I guess I can wait my turn." He grinned, feeling ridiculously cheerful for the simple reason that it hadn't been Charlie Ayer on the line, dangling visions of trendy clubs and restaurants and star-studded parties before her.

A quick scan of the aisle assured him that none of the guys were around. Slipping an arm about her waist he pulled her close and stole a kiss that was sweet as sin but all too brief.

"Travis—"

"Yeah?" In the barn's filtered light her eyes were shaded a dark, turbulent blue. "Hey, is anything wrong?"

"No." She shook her head quickly. "No, it's nothing. I, uh, better go call Crandall."

He could only imagine the headache of having to deal with an estate as big as RJ must have left.

"Okay. I'll see you later," he said, before kissing her again, this time pressing his lips to her brow to ease the furrowed lines that had appeared there. "Just don't let Crandall get started on how his hunters are going this season, or you'll never make your appointment with the principal."

Chapter
TWENTY-THREE

SINCE THE DAY of the funeral when Margot had listened to Edward Crandall weakly reassure Jade that, no, the Radcliffe sisters weren't poor, she'd braced herself for the worst.

She'd believed herself prepared, but actually hearing Crandall's doleful voice intone "The financial outlook is even bleaker than I originally feared, Margot. The estate doesn't have enough to cover your father's outstanding debts," and then having him quote the sum they owed, literally robbed her of speech.

She could empty her bank account to the last penny and still be unable to pay off her father's debts. Not even the money from the Dior account would cover such an amount.

"Margot? Are you there?"

"Yes, yes." She fought back her panic. "Yes, I'm here, Mr. Crandall. Are you sure it's so much?"

"I'm afraid so." There was a pause. "Perhaps you'd like to come to my office so we can discuss your options."

A chill settled over her as she stood in the courtyard that had nothing to do with the brisk breeze blowing this November morning. She already knew what Crandall was going to tell her, that there was only one viable option: to sell Rosewood.

"I'd like Jordan to be present at the meeting, too."

"When might she be able to come to Warburg?"

"She and her family will be here to watch the Hunt Cup. Surely that's soon enough, Mr. Crandall."

There was a pause. Margot assumed he was checking the calendar. "It would be preferable if she could come earlier."

"I doubt that will be possible," she said stubbornly.

"Well, I suppose we can delay until then. So, you all will be watching the Warburg Hunt Cup," he said, switching topics. "The event won't be the same without RJ. I don't think I can recall a year in which a Radcliffe didn't compete in the Cup."

She was really beginning to dislike Edward Crandall and his toadying.

"You misunderstood me, Mr. Crandall. As Jordan's pregnant, she'll of course only be spectating, but both Jade and I plan on competing. And Travis Maher, too. Rosewood Farm and our family will be well represented." Cool pride laced her voice. She was damned if she was going to let him see how devastated she was by the knowledge that this might be the last time the Radcliffes and their horses competed in the Warburg Cup.

"Well, it'll be a rare treat to see you ride again, Margot. Just be sure you don't fall off. It would make your insurance company very unhappy if you hurt yourself."

Her father's insurance policy—she'd completely forgotten about it. "And what about the insurance company that covered my father? Have you heard anything from them?"

"Not yet. As I said before, an investigation of this nature can take months. But I'd be remiss if I didn't warn you that they may very well refuse compensation."

"Why would they do that?"

"Insurance companies generally do their utmost to avoid paying out. That's why the Piper will be gone over with a fine-tooth comb by the investigators. If they don't uncover any obvious technical problems with the plane that could have caused the accident, however, they're going to dig elsewhere. And then they might well conclude that RJ intended the crash."

"*What* did you just say?"

"Naturally you realize that when they look into other aspects of RJ's and Nicole's lives, they'll discover the extent of RJ's financial difficulties. They'll no doubt learn that he was also having other, more personal problems."

She didn't dislike Crandall, she despised him. The man was lower than a snake's belly. Otherwise how could he stoop to hinting at such a thing as her father committing suicide and murder?

Though she spoke through gritted teeth, her fury came out crystal clear. "Well, I hope when they talk to you, you'll remember that my father was a fighter, competitive through and through. He would never have chosen suicide as a way out of his troubles. Nor, despite whatever odious rumors are circulating about his and Nicole's marriage, would he have done anything to harm Nicole. I would expect you, such a dear, *close* friend, to be the first to recognize this and defend him. Good-bye, Mr. Crandall." Trembling with outrage, she clicked the OFF button on her cell and shoved it deep into her pocket.

"You're still here?" Travis's voice had her spinning around. Distracted by her conversation with Crandall, she hadn't registered the sound of hooves striking concrete. Travis was leading Saxon out. The young gelding was tacked, high-stepping with a two-year-old's spirits. Travis brought him to a halt. "Crandall must have had a lot to say."

She nodded, unable to speak.

"Was he jawing about last weekend's hunt? It's a real test of patience when he goes on about how the hounds ran down the fox. Or didn't." He smiled.

Travis was looking at her exactly the way she'd always dreamed he might, his gray eyes lit with humor and warmth. She longed to confide in him, to give voice to all her troubles. He'd been so wonderful and helpful when she talked to him about Jade.

But this was different.

If she told him about the size of the debt her father had left behind, she'd lose him. How could she expect differently if every one of the horses he loved would have to be sold—including his beloved Raider—and that the plans he envisioned for Rosewood Farm would never come to pass unless she figured something out? With Rosewood already mortgaged, no bank in this economic climate would lend her more.

"Hey, you look pale. Is everything all right?" He reached out and stroked her cheek with the back of his hand.

She choked back tears. "I'm just a little tired." She was a liar—such a weak, selfish liar, she thought, filled with self-recrimination. She should have told Travis what was going on with Rosewood long ago. But in her heart there'd always been this kernel of hope that there'd be enough money to keep going. If she revealed to him now how abysmally low her family's fortunes had sunk, he'd think she'd been intentionally duping him all along. She couldn't bear the prospect of seeing the warm light of approval in his eyes turn icy cold.

Pinning a smile on her face to hide the fear eating away at her, she said, "I better run or I'll be late for my meeting with the principal."

On the way back into town, she speed-dialed Jordan and Damien, leaving messages to call when neither picked up. She had to call information for Stuart Wilde's number, but at least he answered.

"Reverend Wilde? This is Margot Radcliffe."

"Margot, how good to hear from you. How are things, my dear?"

"Pretty terrible, actually. I'm calling about Jade. She's been having a lot of problems since the funeral. She got expelled from her boarding school in Massachusetts—"

"Yes, I heard something to that effect. I'm sorry."

Stuart Wilde truly was privy to everything that went on in this town. "It wouldn't be so bad if things were going better here. But she's been having trouble with some of the girls at Warburg High. They've been saying things about her and

Nicole—I have a feeling you know exactly what sorts of things. It's made Jade miserable and more reckless than ever. The police brought her home last night. I was wondering if I could ask you to spend some time with her."

"I'd be happy to. How about bringing her by the parish early this evening, say, six o'clock?"

"Yes, that would be great."

Hanging up, she pulled the Range Rover into the parking space reserved for visitors at the high school. The dashboard clock read 10:02.

She ran up the steps of the school's main building, signed in with the receptionist at the front desk, then hurried down the corridor, stopping at the second door on the right.

The small vestibule outside the principal's office was empty except for a solitary figure huddled in the corner.

The kid must be in big trouble, was her immediate thought. She hadn't even glanced up when she'd entered the waiting room. Then something made Margot do a double take, and this time she noticed the curtain of dark blond hair hanging out the front of the hooded sweatshirt, spotted, too, the distinctive jade and silver bracelet peeking from beneath the sleeve.

"Jade?" she asked, astonished.

Her sister looked up. Her face was red and splotchy from tears. "What are you doing here?" Her voice was barely audible.

"I had an appointment with Mr. Farkas. The question is, what are *you* doing here?"

"I slapped Blair. I got sent here."

Margot's heart sank. "What happened?" she asked, hurrying over to where her sister sat.

Jade said nothing, her lips pressed in an unsteady line.

She placed a hand on her blue-jeaned knee. "Sweetie, don't clam up on me now. I can't help if you won't tell me what happened. Please."

She had to bend close to hear Jade. "I was online during

my free period. I went onto Facebook. They've taken a picture of me and Photoshopped it, sticking my face onto some naked woman's body. She's playing with herself." Clutching her middle, she began rocking against the chair. "They *hate* me. Everyone's going to see it. I feel so ugly."

Margot wanted to cry for her. She'd been afraid of this, that the girls would retaliate against Jade for making out with Dean at the party last night. She wrapped her arms about Jade, hugging her. "You think it was Blair? You should tell—"

Jade twisted free. "No! I'm not going to tell Mr. Farkas anything. If I rat on them, they'll only hate me more. And I don't want you talking to him about what they've posted about me on Facebook either. Don't you understand, Blair's *popular?*"

"Jade, what they're doing is wrong!"

"Like they care."

"They can be made to care," Margot replied grimly.

"Yeah, and that will only give them a reason to hate me even more."

"So what, you want me to remain silent about the malicious games they're playing on the Internet? The bullying's not going to stop. They'll come up with new ways to hurt you. And what if they decide to pick on someone else, Jade, someone who's not as strong as you? How would you feel knowing that you could have done something and instead let their viciousness continue unchecked? It's hard, but you've got to stand up against them."

"Yeah, me and Rosa Parks," she muttered.

"You prefer the alternative—being cowed by a clique of bitches?" Margot retorted.

Jade's jaw locked in a mutinous line.

"At least if you take the Rosa Parks route, you can look yourself in the eye when you stand before the mirror knowing you've done the right thing." More gently she said, "Staying silent won't win their friendship."

Jade's spiky lashes fluttered as she fought back tears. "I didn't fit in at Malden 'cause I didn't live on Park Avenue. Now I'll never have friends here, either."

"You will," she said fiercely. "It may take time, but believe me, they'll be much better friends than these girls could ever be." Desperate to give Jade something to cling to when life seemed like a giant whirlpool pulling her under, she said, "I don't know how much time you'll have for socializing, anyway."

Jade's head whipped around. "What? You're grounding me for last night?"

"No, I just need your help. There's a lot of work at the farm right now for Ned and Travis, and it looks like I'm going to have to take on a few more modeling gigs if we want to keep Rosewood." She kept her tone light. She wasn't going to tell either Jade or Jordan about Crandall's call until she talked to Damien. It was obvious that her modeling was the only solution, the only hope they had to pay off Rosewood's debts. Damien had said that her stock was running high. It was time to cash it in.

"What kind of stuff?" Suspicion laced Jade's voice.

"You know that dark bay, Aspen?"

"Yeah." She turned her head, swiping her eyes with the back of her hand. "He's the one that likes to play with a rubber ball in the pasture. Ned's been working with him."

Margot felt a spurt of hope. She nodded. "That's the one. I want you to help Ned train him. And I need you to give Travis a hand riding the other horses, too."

"You mean I'm going to be an assistant trainer, like Andy?"

"A part-time assistant trainer. Travis and you will have to draw up a schedule to figure out how many hours you can put in on weekday afternoons and weekends working with the horses he assigns you. But Ned wants you to start right away with Aspen—this very afternoon."

The door to the principal's office opened and Jade stiffened.

Squeezing her hand, Margot spoke in a hurried under-tone. "You're not alone in this, sweetie. You and I are going to go in there and let Mr. Farkas know what Blair and her friends have been up to. Those girls are going to rue the day they messed with a Radcliffe."

Travis scowled through the open doors of the barn at the rain that had begun falling in a steady sheet. For weeks they'd had clear skies, and on the day he planned to ride cross-country with Margot it had to rain.

Where was she anyway? he wondered as laid the saddle pad across Indigo's withers. Settling his saddle on top of the fleece, he slid them both down a notch along the mare's sloping back before ducking to catch the girth dangling beneath her belly. He'd ridden four horses since she'd left to meet with Jade's principal. With each trip back to the barn he'd had to feign a casual interest when he asked whether any of the guys had seen her.

It was driving him nuts how much he missed her.

Travis tightened the girth and Indigo did her habitual tail swish and deep-belly grunt.

Why was everything always so different with Margot? he asked himself as he grabbed the bridle from where it hung on the post. He wasn't the type of guy to fret and fuss about a woman. Yet here he was, nagged by worry because her face had been too pale, her expression strangely forced, when she'd gone off to her meeting.

The cross ties unsnapped, the halter off, Travis slipped the braided reins over Indigo's neck and pressed the steel bit to her mouth. The second the yellowed teeth parted, Travis slipped in the bit, lifted the bridle, and tucked the mare's ears inside the supple leather, pulling her graphite-colored forelock out so that it rested over the browband. His fingers dropped to the throat latch, fastened it, then did the same with the noseband.

But, then again, hadn't it always been like this? He'd

always been aware of Margot, even when she was a scrawny kid trailing after him from barn to barn. Back then, he spent most of his time trying to ditch her, redoubling his efforts when she began to develop in all the right places and blow his mind.

The weeks following her return to Rosewood had revealed her to be as lovely and spirited as ever, and forced him to acknowledge that he was as drawn to her as ever. But last night when they'd made love with a passion that shattered, when she'd come undone in his arms and he'd kissed away the salty tears from her cheeks, a seismic shift had occurred within him, changing him, perhaps irrevocably.

Reins in hand, Travis began walking down the aisle, the scrape of his leather heels and the metallic strike of Indigo's shoes echoing around him. Everything around him was familiar: the barn's sounds and scents; the passing, shadowed glimpses of the horses he loved; the fluid grace of the mare moving in step beside him. It was he who was different, unfamiliar, alien to himself. He'd fallen in love with Margot Radcliffe and he didn't know what the hell to do about it.

"Hey, Travis." Ned stuck his head out of the office. "Hugh Hartmann's on the phone, wants to speak to you. Here, I'll bring Indigo to the indoor ring and walk her while you talk to him," he offered, coming over.

"Thanks." He passed Ned the reins. "Wonder what he wants." Despite his abrupt departure, Hugh made it clear he bore Travis no ill will for his decision.

"Maybe he's looking for a horse and thinks you'll give him an insider's price."

Travis grinned. "Could be. Hugh's sharp."

"So what did Hugh have to say?" Ned asked when Travis entered the indoor ring a short time later. "You sell him a horse?"

"No. Turns out he's looking for a trainer for a new barn

he's bought in Sperryville. Sounds like a good-sized spread, over two hundred acres. Brand-new barns equipped with all the bells and whistles, stalls for thirty horses. He asked me if I knew anyone who might be interested." He checked the girth and pulled down the stirrups while Ned slipped the reins over Indigo's head.

Ned grunted. "Sounds like a sweet deal."

"Yeah." He put the toe of his boot into the stirrup and swung himself into the saddle. At the touch of his heels, Indigo moved into an easy walk.

"You give him any names?"

"No, I told Hugh I'd have to get back to him 'cause I had a horse waiting." Besides, his head had been too full of Margot to summon anyone else's name.

"Hugh will find someone, no problem. He was probably just fishing, hoping he could lure you away."

"A man can always hope." The time for chatting over, Travis guided Indigo over to the rail and moved her into a trot.

"I'm going upstairs to change into my breeches," Jade said as Margot unlocked the front door.

It was almost three. They'd left the high school shortly past twelve. Margot had spent the next two hours driving aimlessly around Loudon County's back roads, the windshield wipers slapping at the rain while Jade, who'd held up so bravely in explaining everything to Mr. Farkas and then directing him to the pages where Blair Hood and her friends had posted their vile trash, had cried her heart out.

"You sure you're up to working with Ned and Aspen today?"

"Yeah. And afterward I want to ride Doc."

Margot nodded. Riding would be the best distraction. "Okay. Are you hungry at all?"

"No."

She understood that, too. At one point they'd been driving

through some town and she'd spotted a pretty little café that looked blessedly empty. Margot had ordered tea and a plate of cookies for Jade, which she normally would have inhaled in a nanosecond. They remained untouched when they left twenty minutes later.

"I'll ask Ellie to make us something light, maybe a sandwich and soup that we can eat quickly. Stuart Wilde's expecting you at six."

Jade's shoulders slumped. "Do I have to go see him?"

Margot raised an eyebrow. "After a day like today I think he'd be the best person in the world to spend time with."

"I guess. So are you going to ride Mystique?"

"I thought I'd ask Andy to exercise her. I'm too tired to do a good job on her." Whatever energy she had left she had to reserve for getting Jade through the rest of her day and begging Damien to come up with a brilliant strategy to raise some major money fast.

That it was still raining was almost a relief. Otherwise she might have ignored her exhaustion for the chance to ride with Travis. The need to be with him was scary, it was so overwhelming. But even scarier was the worry that if he asked how things were going, everything bottled up inside her would pour out in an unstoppable flood.

"If you'll wait a sec, we can walk down to the barn together."

"Yeah, sure," Margot said, smiling. Jade's shy offer was a bright spot in their hellish day. At some point—perhaps during the conference with the principal, when Margot warned Mr. Farkas that if the school failed to take appropriate measures against the students who'd posted the comments about Nicole and Jade, and the Photoshopped nude picture, and see to it that the pages were dismantled immediately, she wouldn't hesitate to take the matter to the police—Jade had apparently concluded that she was no longer the enemy.

It moved her profoundly that her little sister had begun to

trust her. She couldn't destroy that belief by failing to keep Rosewood.

Margot had hoped to find Andy on his own when she asked him to exercise Mystique, but as luck would have it, Andy, Felix, and Ned were grouped in a loose circle around Travis and a freshly untacked Indigo. Travis was talking while he brushed the mare's dappled coat with a soft brush.

"After we've finished grooming the horses for Dan's client, Andy and Ned can exercise Night Wing, Tidbit, Sava, and Skylight. Tito, you can hand walk Plain Song and Ventura. If the rain's stopped, we'll put the other broodmares out to pasture. We'll worm all the horses in the afternoon. As for the stallions, I'll fit Stoneleigh into my morning schedule and then Faraday in the afternoon, once Stokes has—" He broke off and pivoted, brush in hand. His gaze locked on her. "Hi."

"Hi," she returned. "Sorry to interrupt."

"You weren't interrupting. We were just fine-tuning tomorrow's schedule. The normal routine's a little out of whack with Stokes coming tomorrow."

"It's a good thing Jade will be able to lend a hand exercising some of the horses."

"That's right. It's a big help. Your dad would be real proud of you." Travis gave Jade a quick smile.

"He sure would," Ned chimed in. "So you ready for your first day with Aspen?"

"Yeah."

"No sense wasting time, then."

Ned and Jade went off and Travis turned to Felix. "Can you get Mystique ready for Margot?"

Margot spoke hurriedly. "Um, actually, I'm not going to be able to ride today. I was wondering if I could ask Andy to hop on her for me. I'm sorry to ask so late, Andy. But she's a real treat to ride."

Though Andy Morris was only a few years younger than

she, he had a tendency to blush like a teenager whenever she spoke to him. "I'd be happy to."

"Thanks so much." She smiled and his blush deepened to the roots of his ginger hair. Mumbling something about fetching Mystique's tack, he ducked his head and hurried off.

"As Mystique's taken care of, do you mind tossing Indigo's blanket on her and putting her back in her stall for me, Felix?" Travis asked. "I need to go over some things with Margot before I ride Mistral."

"No problem, Travis."

"Thanks," he said, already taking Margot by the elbow and propelling her down the aisle to the office. Reaching the office, he crooked his boot around the door and kicked it closed as he pulled her close.

"Hi again," he whispered before settling his mouth over hers and kissing her slowly and deeply, as if it had been years rather than hours since he'd last tasted her.

They parted to stare mutely, their breath too ragged for speech. Travis managed to recover first. "So you can't ride Mystique?"

"No. I'm really too tired."

"You're not hurt, are you?" he asked quietly.

She frowned in confusion and then flushed in understanding. "No."

"Well, that's a relief." A smile tugged the corner of his mouth. "So I was wondering, since our cross-country ride is out, how about having dinner tonight?"

The conflicting desire to be with Travis and the need to make sure Jade was all right tore her apart.

She shook her head. "I'm sorry, I can't. I've got to take Jade to Reverend Wilde's at six. I don't know how long he'll keep her and I kind of want to be there for her when it's over. She's had a really rough day."

Travis did his best to hide his disappointment. But he could hardly begrudge her taking care of her kid sister.

"Hey, it's okay. We'll do it another night, maybe tomorrow. A celebration of your first horse sale," he suggested.

"That would be nice. By the way, did Ned draw up a price list for Harvest and the rest of the gang?"

"Yeah, they're on the desk."

He watched her go over to the desk, pick up the sheet of paper with Ned's scrawl on it, and begin scanning the figures intently. "Speaking of sales," he said, "I've been meaning to talk to you about the situation with our studs. It's time to get serious about finding a replacement for Stoneleigh. There's an auction coming up the week after next that we should attend."

"I'm not sure I can think that far ahead."

He frowned, not sure he'd heard right. She hadn't even looked up from Ned's price list. Indeed she was staring at it, biting her lip in concentration, as if she were memorizing the figures for a test. Still, he thought she must have been joking.

"Well, you'll just have to clear your calendar. Acquiring a premium stud is the key to Rosewood's future. You were a tough bidder at Crestview, so I know you'll enjoy the Thoroughbred sales. They're real high-end. We should be able to get a stallion without your having to mortgage Rosewood to the hilt."

TRAVIS RAN the soft brush over Raider's withers, back, and barrel with quick short strokes, erasing the slight mark left by the fleece saddle pad and making the gelding's black coat gleam. As he brushed, his eye traveled over the horse. The two-year-old was filling out nicely. Thanks to the training ring's sandy footing, he was already more muscled.

Their morning workout had gone well. Even though Raider had been feeling his oats, he'd settled down quickly enough. More important, as the workout progressed he'd continued to listen, responding to Travis's aids willingly; considering he was little more than a baby developmentally, it proved how smart and special a horse he was. Too bad he was gelded, Travis thought. With Raider's superb conformation and bloodlines, their search for a new stallion to stand at stud would be over.

Travis was no longer upset that Margot had outbid him at the Crestview auction. He was just happy she'd bought Raider. Despite having worked with him for only a few short weeks, he was convinced the gelding could develop into an equine star. He already had the next six months of training planned in his mind: the winter devoted to gymnastics in the indoor ring to improve flexion and balance. If all went well, by late spring Travis would start jumping him, crossbars mostly—nothing too intimidating that might shake the young horse's confidence or cause injury. Come June, he and Margot would have selected a few shows to compete him in. By then Gulliver and Gypsy Queen, if they hadn't already been sold, would be moving up in the hunter and preliminary jumper classes.

This is what he loved about his work, the challenge of bringing along a youngster from the ground up and continuing its training until, like Harvest Moon, it was ready to compete on the hunter or jumper circuit. Rosewood's horses presented such a wide range in terms of developing their abilities that each day and every ride offered something new for him as a trainer and rider.

Exchanging the soft brush for a towel, he glanced at his watch before he began wiping Raider down. It was almost eleven o'clock. Margot must be nearly finished riding Ventura. She'd volunteered to help Ned and Andy exercise the broodmares, just as she'd come to the barn directly after dropping Jade off at school to lend a hand with the grooming. She'd brushed Gulliver's bay coat until it shone like satin. Then she'd dressed his hooves and combed his tail and mane to picture-perfection.

Busy prepping the horses for Dan Stokes's visit, Travis hadn't been able to do more than offer Margot a cup of steaming coffee from the pot Ned had brewed and then press it into her hand with a quick smile before heading over to the stallion barn to tack Stoneleigh. He hoped the prospective buyer was a decent judge of horseflesh and had a good notion of what he or she was looking for. The sooner Dan Stokes and his client were gone—hopefully with a sales agreement signed—the sooner Travis could get Margot alone.

As physically beat as he'd been, he hadn't slept much last night, the loft and his bed filled with memories of Margot. But he'd had enough of memories. He wanted the real thing: Margot warm and generous, her silken body wrapped about him. He needed to hear her voice, breathy and awed, calling out his name as he filled her. He wanted that amazing sense of completeness he felt when Margot lay in his arms.

As he was running the towel over the crest of Raider's

neck, Ned's voice reached him. He looked down the aisle to
see him and Dan Stokes, along with another man, dressed
in breeches and field boots, making their way toward him.
From the pride ringing in Ned's voice it was clear he was giving them a tour of the barns.

Laying a hand on the gelding's shoulder, Travis greeted
them. "Good to see you, Dan."

"How are you doing, Travis? Glad to hear you're back at
Rosewood. Everyone's relieved to know that you and Ned
will be here to carry on for RJ."

"Thanks, Dan."

"Travis, I'd like you to meet Paul Ormond. Paul, this is
Travis Maher, Rosewood's trainer. One of the best in the
business."

Travis tucked the towel under his arm and stretched out
his hand. "Pleased to meet you, Paul." Paul Ormond was
about his age and about as well groomed as Raider. From
the suede jacket he sported to his oversized steel watch,
which Travis spotted on his wrist, he was clearly rich
enough to indulge his vanity.

"A nice-looking horse you've got here, Travis." Dan had
stepped up to Raider and was looking at him appraisingly.

"Yeah, this is Night Raider. Miss Margot, RJ's daughter,
whom you'll meet shortly, picked him up at the Crestview
sale. He's a two-year-old Thoroughbred, by Dark Promise
out of Night Wing. Miss Margot bought Night Wing, too.
She's in foal, again bred to Dark Promise," Ned told them.

"Raider and I are just getting to know each other," Travis
chimed in. "But I've got a really good feeling about him."

"He for sale?"

Travis tensed, wishing he'd bit his tongue instead of boast-
ing about how great Raider was.

"You'll have to ask Margot about that—" Abruptly he
turned his head. "Here she is now."

"Sorry I'm late," she said to him. "I stopped to ask Andy
and Tito to rake the outside ring."

"Thanks," he said. "I forgot to remind the guys. And Dan and Paul have only just arrived."

Turning to the men, she greeted them with an easy smile. "Hi, I'm Margot Radcliffe," she said, extending her hand.

While the pleasantries were exchanged, Travis tossed a Baker blanket over Raider, buckled it, and walked the gelding into his box stall, away from Dan Stokes's acquisitive gaze.

Closing the stall door he turned around and caught the dazzled expression on Dan's and Paul's faces. For Christ's sake, hadn't they ever seen a beautiful woman before?

He hung Raider's leather halter on the stall door's hook and wondered how this thing was going to play out. If the smitten look on Ormond's face was any kind of indicator, he'd clean forgotten he was there to shop for a horse.

A little prodding was in order. Travis wanted to get the show on the road so he could have some time alone with Margot. And he really wanted Ormond to stop drooling over her. "So Paul, we have a barnful of talented horses. What are you looking for in particular?"

Tearing his gaze away from Margot, he replied, "I've been showing in the hunter division for the past six years but I'm interested in branching out. I'm hoping to find a horse with enough scope to carry me in the jumper classes."

"Why don't we show Harvest Moon first, then?" Margot suggested. "Harvest is great, Paul." She began walking down the aisle with Dan and Paul Ormond on either side, Travis and Ned taking up the rear. "He's big. At seventeen hands, he can carry a tall man like you with ease. What are you, six foot one?" He nodded. "That's what I thought. Well, Harvest has been doing terrifically in the hunter division," she continued without skipping a beat. "The judges love him for his looks and because he jumps so neatly and is a beautiful mover over the flat. But he's also a great jumper. Brave, honest, with lots of scope . . ."

She was good, Travis thought, listening to her with pride.

He hadn't known exactly what tack Margot would take during her first foray as a horse seller. Had she opted to remain silent after shaking hands with the two men, he and Ned would have stepped in and provided them with a rundown of the most suitable horses. But Margot was doing just fine on her own. Her approach was different from RJ's—he'd always talked bloodlines and conformation and scores, which could intimidate the hell out of certain buyers. Margot's seemingly effortless chatter disarmed. Ormond was probably already imagining that champion ribbon fluttering against Harvest's cheekpiece and him clutching a shiny trophy.

Just as long as his fantasies stopped there.

What Travis didn't care for was the bright gleam in Ormond's eye when he looked at Margot or that his questions had moved away from horses to far more personal territory. He'd gotten her to admit that, yes, she was a professional model. And then Paul told her that he worked as a consultant for some big-name corporations in New York and had a penthouse in the city. His pied-à-terre. Travis marveled that a self-respecting man would actually use the word *pied-à-terre,* but his contempt morphed into seething antagonism as he heard Paul suggest that they should get together in town . . . and Margot neglect to tell him to take a hike.

Could she actually see something in this guy?

The thought that lurked at the edge of his mind uncoiled itself and struck. How many other men—in addition to her "good friend" Charlie Ayer—did she have following her around, tongues hanging to the ground? He hated that there were eight long years unaccounted for, during which scores of men had doubtless hit on her. Made love to her. Jealousy, sharp-toothed and poisonous, sank its fangs deep as he imagined his rivals. The poison spread and he wondered if Margot could truly care for him when she had countless others vying for her favor. Men with New York penthouse apartments and God knows what else to offer her. Margot wasn't a snob, but wouldn't she ultimately want to be with a man whose background and upbringing were as fancy as hers?

Was she just passing time with him until a better man came along?

"Is that all right with you, Travis?"

"No," he snarled, only to realize that he had no idea what Margot had just asked. "Sorry. I was thinking of something else. What was that you said?"

A frown line appeared between her brows. "Can you get on Harvest first so Paul and Dan can have a chance to see how nicely he moves?"

"Sure." It galled him that while he was on Harvest, Ormond would be standing next to her, feeding her more of his smooth lines. Travis consoled himself with the thought that once he'd put Harvest through his paces and taken him over a few jumps, Ormond would have to shut up and leave Margot's side.

But he couldn't help wondering about all the other guys Margot knew and whether any of them had a hold on her heart.

Margot loved watching Travis ride. Tito and Ned had tacked an impeccably groomed Harvest Moon and then Travis had led the big chestnut gelding to the outdoor ring. She was pleased the rain had stopped the night before. The pale blue sky was a perfect backdrop for the bold chestnut being so expertly ridden.

Travis on horseback made her think of a meticulous duet, his movements in perfect balance with his mount's. To the untrained eye it appeared as if Travis hardly had to use his aids to move Harvest through his gaits. The end result of such a disciplined riding style was what most dedicated equestrians strived for but few attained: a beautifully balanced horse that circled the ring with smooth, ground-skimming strides.

The pair was a grand sight to behold. She could tell Dan Stokes was impressed. And when they executed a seamless flying change in the middle of the ring, even Paul Ormond stopped his tiresome attempt to impress her by listing all the people he knew in New York City and watched Travis show off the gelding's talents.

She took advantage of his distraction to sidle up to Ned.

"Ned," she whispered. "On that price sheet you wrote up for me you listed a hundred thousand for Harvest, right?"

He gave a short nod. "That's what RJ was holding out for."

"Do you think I can go even higher?"

"With this guy? Sure, you can," Ned said with a snort. "He'll do anything for a date with you."

"I'm afraid that's highly unlikely. He'll have to content himself with one of our horses."

"And damned lucky Ormond will be to have a horse as fine as Harvest. Though Dan assured me he's a serious rider, willing to learn, he sure doesn't act like it. Never seen such silliness, the way he's been ogling you. I was worried Travis would toss him out of the barn. He takes placing our horses with responsible, dedicated owners real seriously."

Was that the reason for Travis's tight-lipped countenance? She'd been hoping his palpable irritation might stem from jealousy. But knowing Travis's professionalism, it was also possible he was simply annoyed that Paul wasn't acting like a serious horseman.

"I hope Ormond can ride." Ned didn't sound overly optimistic.

"I do, too." She couldn't afford for this deal to go south.

Paul Ormond came nowhere near Travis's caliber of riding, but at least he was smart enough to know he shouldn't fuss with Harvest. He left the gelding pretty much alone, simply urging him forward with his lower body and keeping his hands quiet. As willing as he was talented, Harvest performed just fine on the flat and, in keeping with his honest nature, went unhesitatingly over the bigger fences Travis set up for them.

Margot knew the deal was sealed when Harvest took a triple combination, adjusting for the distances practically on his own. A rider starting out in the jumper division would appreciate an equine partner this confident and brave. And with the right trainer coaching him, Paul could really grow as a rider.

Despite Travis's and Ned's disapproval, Margot kept up her casual small talk with Paul right up to the point where the five of them were in the office sipping freshly brewed coffee and negotiating a selling price. The other details, such as the veterinarian's exam and an agreed-upon trial period for Paul to try Harvest out in his own barn were all contingent upon reaching an acceptable price.

"It's great how well you and Harvest clicked, Paul. I think he's going to be a wonderful show horse for you. My father never rushed a sale of any of Rosewood's horses. He preferred to wait for the right buyer, one who would recognize the value of a great equine partner and treat him with the kind of care our horses receive every day at Rosewood. I'm glad Dan helped us find a match my father would have approved of."

"Harvest is certainly the nicest horse I've encountered since I started my search. Dan and I were talking about heading to Europe to look at prospects there when Dan got a call from Ned."

"Just think of the money you've saved. At one hundred fifty thousand, Harvest is a bargain. The taxes and transportation costs alone for bringing a horse back from Europe would come to half that. And with the dollar in the tank against the euro, why, you can buy Harvest, arrange for his board down in Florida this winter, and still come out ahead."

"One hundred fifty is a little higher than I expected to go."

Margot smiled, unfazed. She might have been more open

to bargaining if she didn't know exactly how much the monthly maintenance on a penthouse apartment on Manhattan's Upper East Side cost. Paul Ormond should have been more careful trying to impress her by flaunting his wealth if he'd wanted to negotiate the sale price.

"You get what you pay for, Paul. In Harvest's case, this means a sound, sane, impeccably mannered and trained horse that's consistently in the ribbons, a horse that's been carefully bred for conformation and performance. Ned started working at Rosewood when my grandpa was alive. He's been breeding our horses for longer than you and I have been alive. That's why practically every barn in Loudon County has at least one of our horses. I'd like to know that Harvest is with you, since my sisters and I intend to follow our father's tradition in selling to buyers who are a hundred percent committed to our horses. But we have Harvest entered in plenty of fall events where he'll get lots of exposure. Travis is planning on riding him in the Warburg Cup." She paused to lift her coffee cup and met Travis's gaze. *Your turn,* she telegraphed the message.

His lips curved in a half-smile. "That's right. As you'll find, Harvest has got a gallop that eats up cross-country courses. Last year, RJ—Margot's dad—won the Cup aboard Harvest's half-brother Southern Skies. Sold Sky the very same afternoon. Hap Donaldson will probably be riding Sky in the Cup this year, but I'm confident Harvest can take him." His meaning was clear. If Paul Ormond sat on his hands, someone else would quickly grab this talented horse.

Margot didn't care if it was her spiel or Travis's professional assurance that convinced Paul Ormond. What mattered was that minutes later they had a sales contract filled out and signed, and a deposit check for Harvest made out to Rosewood Farm. After that, the other arrangements—the vet exam, the shipping, the terms of the two-week trial period—fell quickly into place.

When Paul expressed an interest in taking a last look at

his new horse before he and Dan left, Ned walked him down the aisle, giving a verbal summary of Harvest's bloodlines in case he'd missed some of the names Margot had pointed to when she'd shown him his new horse's papers.

Travis, Dan, and she followed a few paces behind, chatting casually, when Dan said, "I've been meaning to ask you about that young gelding Night Raider. I have some contacts who would be very interested in taking a closer look at him."

Margot was tempted to tell Dan to get on the phone and call every contact he had. She knew how highly Travis thought of the two-year-old; other professionals would doubtless perceive his potential. She'd done well with Harvest Moon. With luck, she might finesse a seriously large sum for Raider—every single penny was desperately needed if they were to keep Rosewood in business.

But she'd made a promise to Travis that if he came back to work at Rosewood the colt would be his to train. And he plainly wanted the chance to train a horse he considered a champion in the making.

Again, it occurred to her that she should simply sell the horse to Travis. But not even the bequest her father had left to Travis could compare with the figure she might get from a truly wealthy buyer. Selling to Travis would mean forgoing the kind of profit that Rosewood required.

She'd never imagined that running Rosewood would be so complicated, or that the burden of setting to right the financial disaster that her father had bequeathed would be so heavy. The fact that she was about to turn down an opportunity to make a much-needed sale for Rosewood had her stomach clenching with anxiety. But she couldn't help remembering what she'd said to Jade. If she didn't do the right thing when she could, she wouldn't be able to look at herself in the mirror—a pretty serious problem for a fashion model, she thought bitterly. She already felt guilty enough for misleading Travis. The least she could do was to keep the promise she'd made.

Summoning a smile and what she hoped would pass for a carefree tone, she said, "Night Raider is Travis's special project, Dan. We're keeping him until Travis decides it's time for him to step into the spotlight."

"Well, please keep me in mind when you decide the time's come." Turning to Travis, he said, "You're a pretty lucky man, Travis, to have such an accommodating owner."

Travis's gaze met hers and she felt the magnetic pull of their gray depths.

"Yeah, I guess I am pretty lucky," he said, and her heart constricted. *Please let him truly believe that,* she whispered silently.

MARGOT, TRAVIS, AND NED WAITED as Dan Stokes put his Mercedes SUV in reverse. Seated on the passenger side, Paul Ormond lowered his window to call out, "I'll be in touch soon, Margot."

She gave a jaunty wave and shoved Paul's business card, on which he'd scribbled half a dozen ways to get in contact with him, deep into her vest pocket, burying it among crumbled horse treats and pocket lint.

Ned, who'd just filled his mouth with chaw, worked his bottom lip furiously, and spat. "That was a decent morning's work, Miss Margot, though in hindsight I'm thinking you probably could have gotten two hundred thousand out of him. That Ormond's brains are in his pants. At least Dan runs a first-rate barn. Harvest will be in good hands. I'll miss the big guy. He was one of your dad's favorites." He pulled a handkerchief out of his front pocket and blew his nose with a loud honk.

At Ned's gruff display of emotion, a lump formed in Margot's throat. She realized she would probably bawl like a baby when Harvest, his legs carefully wrapped for the trip, would clamber up the ramp into the horse van that would carry him to Dan Stokes's barn in Connecticut, and she'd known Harvest less than a month.

Travis laid a hand on his shoulder. "If Margot uses the money from Harvest toward buying a new stud, it'll be what RJ wanted, right?"

Ned blew his nose again. "I guess that's the only way to

look at it. We better get the finest horse we can," he said fiercely.

Margot lowered her gaze to the gravel, kicked a stone with the toe of her boot, and said nothing. There was no way the money from today's sale would be used toward a new stud. Her primary concern was trying to figure out a way to avoid selling *all* the horses in the barns. When she'd spoken on the phone to Damien last night, he hadn't sounded terribly surprised that her dad had left behind a multimillion dollar mountain of debt. But he'd promised to try to snag some plum contracts for her. Until then she was on tenterhooks.

"Well, I've got to ride Mistral. You want me to tack Mystique for you?"

"No, thanks, Ned. I can do it."

With a nod, Ned ambled off toward the main barn.

For several moments Travis said nothing, staring abstractedly at the distant line of trees, behind which Dan Stokes's car had disappeared. All morning long his mood had struck her as mercurial. Even now he caught her off guard by asking, "So how about that cross-country ride? The weather's perfect. The footing's good. And you need to practice for the Hunt Cup."

He wasn't the only one whose emotions were changeable. A giddy happiness welled inside her at the prospect of riding through the woods and over the fields with him. "It won't take too much time out of your day?"

"No, I'll take Colchester. I needed to ride him anyway. Do you want to?" And the quiet urgency in his voice made it sound as if he were thinking of an altogether different kind of ride.

She swallowed, telling herself to calm down, yet still her voice came out thready. "Yes. I'll just get Mystique ready."

"Meet me in the courtyard."

Did Travis feel it, too, the sexual tension crackling and dancing between them?

How could he not? The horses certainly did—from the minute Travis had given her a leg up on Mystique and then mounted Colchester, they'd been raring to go. Down the allée they tossed their necks and pranced like racehorses heading toward the starting gates, the gravel crunching loudly beneath their hooves. Margot was grateful for the weeks of intense training behind her. She was strong enough to hold Mystique to an extended trot as they warmed up on the narrow trail that wound through the woods.

The early afternoon sun cut through the trees in pale-gold bands and lit the russet carpet of oak and maple leaves that lay thickly on the ground. Around them was a riot of sounds: the cry of startled birds, the shriek of squirrels jumping overhead from branch to branch, the horses' restless snorts, and the crackle of leaves and the loud snap of twigs beneath their hooves.

For her part, Margot couldn't have spoken to save her life. Mystique, excited to be beyond the confines of the exercise ring, required her full attention—a challenge enough without the presence of Travis riding by her side to distract her. It would be the height of embarrassment to get dumped from her horse because she couldn't control her.

Beside her, Travis rode with the fabulous grace of a centaur. His face was a study in concentration, its planes and angles all chiseled strength, his beautiful mouth a flat line as he kept Colchester's high spirits in check. She wondered what he'd think if he knew that watching him control the powerful bay was as potent as any aphrodisiac. Then again, what about Travis didn't turn her on? He could make her wet simply by wrapping his long fingers around a coffee mug and raising the cup to his lips; she would watch and imagine his hands on her, his lips drinking her in.

Restlessly she shifted in her saddle and stole another peek at his profile, awed by his intense focus. But what did she expect? Travis could hardly leap off Colchester's back and carry her off to some leaf-lined bower and make passionate love to her while the horses cooled their hooves. *Yeah, right*, she thought, with a self-deprecating snort. This wasn't some Hollywood fantasy; they would never risk their horses' safety. Once again she fixed her gaze ahead, determined to match his concentration.

They were following well-worn trails, the routes familiar enough from her girlhood that Margot remembered the spots where they widened. Reaching one, she relaxed her fingers on the reins and Mystique shot forward like a loosed arrow, Colchester a split second behind and then cantering alongside her. The faster pace helped distract her from the fevered desire trapped inside her.

When she caught sight of the side trail that ran parallel to the main path and which had fences—logs, old gates, brush jumps—for jumping practice, she immediately guided Mystique over to it. Collecting the mare, they soared over a downed log that lay across it. With each jump she and the mare negotiated, her pleasure grew. Mystique was as able, brave, and sure-footed as Margot had hoped. She couldn't see Travis. Consummate horseman that he was, he was keeping Colchester several strides back, maintaining a safe jumping distance in case she and Mystique encountered difficulties.

Then they were out of the woods, flying over a stone wall that was centuries old and into a wide, rolling field. This time it was Travis who surged ahead, his torso angled over Colchester's neck, the gelding's long black tail streaming behind.

Mystique was not to be outdone. Neither was Margot. The mare strained at the bit and Margot let her have her head, eager to match Colchester's pounding speed. They came abreast of Travis, Colchester and Mystique's hooves thundering over the earth like a fast-approaching storm. Neck and neck they raced toward the weathered gray line of trees marking the beginning of Rosewood land.

Nearing the trees, Travis straightened, bringing Colchester back down to a canter and then to a trot. Margot followed suit. The circuit they'd covered was roughly four miles, a route that traveled over Rosewood and adjoining farms. The distance had posed no problems for the horses, who were tossing their heads, snorting energetically. While Mystique still had lots of go, Margot knew it would be the height of folly to tax her on their first day out together. To do so would be to court injury, and the date for the Hunt Cup was approaching.

"How are you feeling?"

Had Travis noticed that she was breathing harder than Mystique, her heart pounding from the adrenaline rush of the gallop? Adrenaline now liberally mixed with lust because he was looking at her with mesmerizing, diamond-chipped eyes.

Lord, she wanted him. The need bore down on her. She clamped her thighs around the saddle—as if that might stop the aching emptiness that only Travis could fill.

"Mystique was great. Just terrific."

"No, how are *you* feeling? Are you . . . sore?"

The unanticipated question thrilled like a stolen caress. In a flash, her desire burst into flames, the cool November air merely fanning the fiery licks of need.

"I—no." She swallowed and tried again. "I want you."

"Jesus," he said, and she saw the supreme control he'd displayed earlier crack to expose a hunger as deep and violent as her own.

The short trip back to the barns passed in a blur. By the time they reached the courtyard, she could no longer control her trembling.

The clattering of eight hooves over gravel was loud enough for Andy to come out of the barn and greet them. "How'd Colchester do, Travis?"

"Real good. You busy, Andy?"

"No, I just finished with Sweet William. I've got another

half hour before I need to bring the ladies in from the pasture and help Ned with the deworming."

"Do you mind taking Mystique and Colchester and cooling them down?" he asked as he dismounted swiftly. "I'm going to fix Margot something warm upstairs. She caught a chill on the ride."

Please God, let Andy accept that as a logical reason for her to be shaking as if wracked with dengue fever.

"No problem, Travis. And how was Mystique?"

She thought she managed a smile. "Great. Thanks for taking care of her, Andy."

"Sure thing. You go warm up now. I'll take Mystique into the barn. Here, let me help you down."

"I got her, Andy," Travis said.

He caught her by the waist as she slid down from the saddle. Margot bit down hard on her lip to stifle a moan at the feel of his strong hands gripping her hips. He didn't let go, steadying her, and she didn't know whether to laugh or cry at how his possessive grip and the brush of his muscled body against her back could make her weak-kneed with desire.

Andy left with Mystique and Colchester in tow. The second the horses' hindquarters were swallowed by the gloom of the barn's interior, Travis spoke, his voice low and urgent. "Come on."

She tried to shake her head. "We can't—"

"Now, Margot," he growled, already ushering her into the barn and up the narrow stairs to his apartment.

She'd barely crossed the threshold before he had her pinned against the wall. He swallowed her *"oof"* of surprise and then her moan of surrender as he ravished her mouth, his kiss plundering with a wild hunger. His hands were equally ruthless. In a frenzied race, he dropped to knees, yanking at her field boots, sending them sailing across the room. His fingers tore at her clothes, shoving down her breeches and panties in one fierce tug. The buttons on her shirt popped, bouncing on the wooden floor. Swept away by Travis's passion, she wouldn't have cared if he'd ripped the shirt to shreds.

She whimpered helplessly at the feel of his hands streaking over her naked skin, each rough stroke, each desperate kiss claiming her as his, and when he lifted her off the ground, she instinctively wrapped her legs tightly about his hips and gripped his shoulders, hanging on for dear life as he entered her with one powerful thrust. In the grip of some primal urge, he drove into her over and over, the rawness of his need so beautiful that she cried in near rapture as the pleasure built inside her. Then suddenly she was there, her orgasm washing over her, pulling her under, lifting her up. She clung to Travis, her only anchor. The force of her orgasm triggering his own, he gave a final, desperate lunge, then poured himself into her, shudders wracking his body.

As one they slid to the floor. Spent in a tangle of sweat-slicked limbs, they slumped against the wall.

Some semblance of sanity reasserted itself in Travis's brain and with it basic courtesy: he pulled Margot's limp body over his, cushioning her from the cold floorboards. He couldn't see her face. But the sight of her breeches still wrapped about one slender ankle made him wince.

Christ, he hadn't even taken the time to undress her. His own breeches were merely unzipped. He'd pushed them down just far enough to pull out his cock before nailing her against the wall. He could already see the imprint of his hands on her hips where he'd held her. He was damned lucky she'd been wet and ready when he'd slammed into her; otherwise he might have hurt her. Shamed, he closed his eyes.

Was it only two nights ago that he'd whispered a promise to show her he was the only man for her? Cocksure he'd be able to demonstrate what a great lover he could be. Well, he'd fucked that idea up royally. Did he think the Charlie Ayers and Paul Ormonds of her world handled her with such brute force?

He searched for the words to explain what had just happened. "Sorry, I guess I got a little carried away" just didn't cut it. How to make her understand the feral need to possess her, to make her his? The love he felt for Margot was too new for him to understand fully. But what was clear to him already was that his love wasn't neat and pretty. It was unruly and complicated and more powerful than anything he'd ever experienced.

She was so smart, so talented, and so unbelievably sexy. Every minute they were apart, she consumed his thoughts; every second he spent with her made him fall that much more deeply in love.

He wanted Margot completely. The lurking fear that he might lose her, that another man might win her heart, was enough to drive him out of his mind.

His arms tightened instinctively and she stirred, her head shifting against his chest. Warily he met her gaze, amazed to find no recrimination in her beautiful eyes.

"Hi," she said softly.

"Hi, yourself." He sneaked his hand along the curve of her waist to stroke the sensitive underside of her breast. With a shiver, she snuggled closer and he felt her lips press against his damp skin where the neck of his shirt opened in a V.

"Margot, are you okay? I didn't hurt you just now?"

Her head lifted away from his chest. "No, you didn't hurt me." The band of tension around his heart eased. "I was quite impressed by your display of passion."

The itchy heat of a blush stole over his cheeks. "Yeah, well, let's just say I like watching you ride," he muttered.

"Ahh, so I have a fan?" she teased.

He gazed at her and lost himself in the depths of her smiling eyes. He wasn't going to think about the legion of "fans" eager to adore Margot. He was the one who had her in his arms. And he was the one doing the adoring.

Lowering his lips to her mouth, he tasted her slowly, lingeringly. Her sigh of pleasure as she opened her mouth beneath his was the sweetest sound.

He needed to tell her. Needed to speak the words he'd never uttered to another woman before. But this was Margot, and here he was, sprawled on the floor, his breeches around his hips, his cock already rock-hard again with wanting. About as frigging lousy a moment to profess his love as he could imagine. He'd wait and tell her after he'd made love to her properly.

He raised his head a fraction to whisper, "Speaking of riding, Margot—"

"Hey, Travis, you in there?" Heavy footsteps sounded on the wooden stairs.

Shit, that was Felix's voice. Travis shot his leg out, shoving his booted foot against the door in case Felix tried to come in. Margot, too, had reacted with lightning-quick reflexes. She'd jumped to her feet and was already frantically yanking her panties on.

"Yeah, Felix, what's up?" he called.

"Telephone for you, man. And Ned wants you to come and take a look at Faraday."

"I'll be right there."

He waited until he heard Felix descend the stairs before moving his foot away from the door. Standing up, he hastily arranged himself and fastened his breeches, then went over to the coffee table and grabbed Margot's black field boots out from under it.

"Here you go," he said, holding them out to her.

"Thanks." She took them without meeting his eye.

"I'm sorry about this—I kind of forgot where we were." Christ, it was the middle of a *workday* and he'd been about to fuck Margot for the second time in the space of—he checked the clock on the wall—twenty minutes.

"Me, too."

He looked at her, hating the way her voice had gone tight with embarrassment. He didn't want her to regret what they'd just done, but there was no time to talk now. He had to go, or the next person marching up the stairs might be Ned, who wouldn't hesitate to come in and find out what was keeping him.

"Listen, I've got to go down," he said awkwardly. "Take as much time as you need."

When she only nodded, he stifled a curse and left.

Margot tugged at her field boots frantically, unable to spot Travis's boot hooks anywhere. Jumping to her feet she stomped, at last managing to shove her feet into place. Pulling on her shirt, she jammed its tails inside the waist of her breeches and thanked God she had a sweater to wear over it to hide the fact that her button-down shirt was now buttonless. Dressed, she hurried over to the rectangular mirror above Travis's dresser. Her reflection made her blanch.

Oh, God, they were going to take one look at her and know exactly what she and Travis had been doing.

What would Ned and the men think of her? She was supposed to be showing how competent she was, not how she couldn't keep her hands off Travis. She ran into the bathroom, turned the tap on full blast, and splashed cold water over face until it tingled. Dragging her fingers through her hair, she twisted it into a punishingly tight bun at the back of her head and wound an elastic around it. Spotting the telltale scrape on the side of her neck, she was filled with a terrible sense of déjà vu. As it was highly doubtful that Travis's medicine cabinet held anything like concealer, her only alternative was to zip her black vest up to her chin.

There, she looked positively hideous, like a dripping wet, crazed novitiate, not like a woman who'd just experienced the most passionate sex in her entire life and whose heart cried out for more.

"What took you so long?" Ned asked when Travis entered the stallion barn a short time later. He had Faraday hitched to the cross ties and was in the process of unbuckling the stallion's navy sheet. Travis went to the stallion's side and unfastened the straps crisscrossing beneath his belly, then pulled the sheet off Faraday's back.

"I had another phone call from Hugh Hartmann."

"What'd he want this time?"

"Seems you were right. Wants me to take the job as head trainer for his new barn. What's up with Faraday?" he asked, switching to the more important topic.

"I was taking him out of his stall to groom him for you because Andy said you'd gone to upstairs to fix something warm for Miss Margot—"

Then there she was, hurrying into the barn, and Travis's heart did that funny flip in his chest that only she could cause.

Recalling her earlier embarrassment, he figured she'd done her best to erase any vestiges of their lovemaking by pulling her hair back and zipping her vest all the way up, as if it were twenty instead of fifty degrees outside, but her efforts only accentuated the fact that her lips were still lush from his kisses and her wide blue eyes sparkled with an unmistakable radiance.

It occurred to him that with her hair pulled back like that, she must have decided to try to make herself look as ugly as possible. She'd failed on that score, too.

Didn't she realize her loveliness wasn't just her external packaging, gorgeous though it was? Her real beauty lay in her unflagging energy and luminous spirit, brightening any room she entered. Margot would be beautiful to him at 102.

He wasn't sure just what Ned would say once he'd cataloged the changes in Margot's appearance and put all the pieces together—the older man's principal focus was elsewhere right now. "Glad you're here, Miss Margot. You need to take a look at Faraday, too."

"What's wrong with him?" Margot asked. She was careful not to let her gaze stray to Travis lest she betray herself in front of Ned. Instead she focused on the stallion standing at the cross ties. He appeared fine, his sleek, muscular neck arched as he nibbled at the carrot treat Ned had pulled out of his pocket. He looked relaxed, even, his right hind ankle bent so that the toe of the hoof rested lightly on the concrete.

"Take a look and see whether you can spot the problem, Miss Margot." He nodded to Tito and Felix, who'd come in to see what was happening.

Oh, please, not a horsemanship test, thought Margot. Not now, not with Travis and Felix and Tito watching, judging.

Ned must not have heard Margot's silent plea. He grabbed a lead shank hanging on the wall and threaded it through the noseband of Faraday's halter. Unsnapping the cross ties, he asked Felix to walk the stallion out into the afternoon sun. Margot and the men followed.

It took only a few steps for Margot to see what the problem was. "He's lame," she said quietly, noting the shortening in his stride. The rear hoof that Faraday had been resting while he stood at the ties, which she'd first interpreted as indicative of a calm and relaxed animal, was actually a sign of pain. He'd been trying to ease his discomfort by shifting the weight off his leg.

"Good for you, Miss Margot."

She'd have been much happier if she hadn't passed Ned's test with flying colors.

Travis frowned as he watched the dark bay walk. "Hold him up, Felix. Tito, want to grab his halter on the other side in case he gets antsy with my poking around?"

Approaching Faraday, he ran his hand over the stallion's shoulder and barrel, his movements calm and unhurried. Reaching his haunch, Travis skimmed his hand down, bending as his fingers traveled down the hind leg, then lowering to a crouch as he carefully probed the delicate area from the cannon to the coronet. "No heat, no swelling," he said loudly enough for them to hear.

He continued his inspection, going back over the ankle and the pastern, testing for any sign of sensitivity. Then, raising Faraday's hoof, he took the hoof pick Ned silently passed him and scraped it clean. His thumbs pressed the frog and then the sole, checking for abscesses or bruises. Lowering it to the ground, he straightened and stepped back.

"The hoof looks fine," he said, handing the hoof pick back to Ned. "Walk him around some more for us, Felix, will you?"

In silence they watched Felix lead the stallion in a wide circle.

Then Travis spoke. "So what do you think is troubling him, Ned?"

"Could be his back is bothering him again."

"Damn it, I was sure we had that problem licked and that he was on the road to recovery."

Unwilling to interrupt, Margot listened carefully to the conversation. She'd understood the relief in Travis's voice when he said that Faraday's hoof looked healthy. One of the first lessons she'd learned from Ned as a little girl with her first pony, Suzy Q, was that a horse is only as sound as its hooves.

Ned crossed his arms in front of his chest. "I can't help but think that he must have been carrying his weight differently when his back was bothering him and that triggered whatever's ailing him now."

Travis's eyes had never left the bay. "Hold him up, Felix. Tito, I'm going to need you again." He went up to Faraday and patted his solid rump. "Okay, fella, you're not gonna like this, but it won't last too long. You got your watch, Margot?"

"Yes."

"I'm going to lift Faraday's leg. Once I get it into position, time me for two minutes."

"All right." She shoved the sleeve of her sweater back.

Travis slid his hand down to wrap his fingers around the pastern. With a soft cluck, he signaled to the stallion to raise his leg again. This time, however, instead of lifting the hoof toward the rear to inspect it, Travis drew the leg up and forward, flexing the stallion's hock.

"Okay, Margot, start now."

Margot looked at her watch. "What's Travis doing, Ned?" she asked quietly.

"A spavin test. He's trying to see if Faraday's got a problem in the hock joint."

The two minutes crawled by.

At last Margot said, "Time's up," and Travis gently lowered Faraday's hoof to the ground. "Jog him down the drive and circle back," he instructed.

Felix had to run alongside a trotting Faraday only a mere ten yards before Travis called out, "That's enough. Bring him back to a walk."

The Thoroughbred was hobbling as he came back toward them, the lameness in his hind leg far more obvious now.

Travis hung his head and cursed. Beside her Ned was silent, his expression doleful.

"So Faraday has spavin?" Margot asked.

Travis nodded tersely. "Looks like it. We'll need to have him X-rayed to confirm it. But first let's deal with Faraday's pain. Let's take him back to the barn. Ned, can you give him a local of bute to make him more comfortable? I'll go ring Bromley and try to get him over here to X-ray the leg. If we're lucky he might be able to swing by today." He rubbed the side of his face. "What time is it anyway?"

"It's almost three-thirty—oh, God, I'm late for Jade. I've gotta go. I'll be back as soon as I can."

The men watched her sprint up the drive to where the Range Rover was parked.

"Hell and damnation." Ned spat a jet of tobacco into the gravel. "If Faraday's got spavin and Stoneleigh's sperm count is still low, we'll only have the new stallion Miss Margot buys to stand at stud this spring. It'd better be a damned fine horse she gets to replace these two. You're going to need to talk to her, Travis, to make sure she understands the situation."

"Yeah, Ned. I'll talk to her."

Margot's cell phone rang as she pulled the Range Rover into the line of cars that were idling in front of the high school waiting to pick up students. She fished it out of her pocket while her eyes scanned the teenagers pouring out the school doors for a glimpse of Jade.

"Hello?"

"Margot, it's me."

"Jordan? Hi, sweetie. How are you?"

"I—I, Margot, I was wondering whether the kids and I could come to Rosewood."

"Well, of course," she said, frowning at the strange tension in Jordan's voice. "But you're already coming for the Hunt Cup, aren't you?"

"I was thinking we might come sooner. Tonight, actually."

"Tonight? But—Jordan, what's going on?" she asked sharply. "You sound really weird."

"I—I'm leaving Richard—"

"What!" Jordan was the last person Margot would ever imagine uttering those words. "Jordan, this is crazy. You love Richard! What's happened?"

Her sister's words came out in an anguished torrent. "I was emptying Richard's suit pockets to take them to the dry cleaner's. In the inside breast pocket of a jacket he'd worn earlier this week, there was a bunch of condoms."

"Oh, no—" Words failed her. Margot didn't even know where to begin. Awful seconds passed as she listened to Jordan's harsh breathing while she struggled for control.

"I confronted him with them. At first he tried feeding me the most outrageous, stupid lies. My God, we've been married eight and a half years, and we've never used a condom once. Finally he admitted that he's having an affair. Margot, he's been seeing her for *months*." She began sobbing.

"Jordan, Jordan." She lost track of how many times she whispered her sister's name, her heart breaking for her. At last the sobs subsided enough for Margot to speak. "Jordan, you've got to listen to me. Come down with Max and Kate as soon as you can—as soon as you want—but you've got to arrange for your babysitter to do the driving. Don't you dare make the trip on your own. If you can't get Susannah to do it, call me right back and I'll come get the three of you myself. You promise you'll do that?"

"Yes."

"Good. I love you, Jordan. We'll be waiting for you."

She hung up and sat staring blindly through the windshield, starting in surprise when the passenger door opened. Hastily she wiped her eyes.

Jade climbed into the seat next to her. Dumping her backpack between her feet, she looked over at Margot.

"What?" she exclaimed. "What have I done now?"

"Oh, my God, just get over yourself for once. Not everything in this world is about you!"

Jade recoiled as if slapped, her eyes wide with bewildered hurt.

Filled with instant remorse, Margot reached out and touched her sleeve. "I'm sorry, Jade. I didn't mean that. Really." Sad and weary to the bone, she dropped her head back against the seat.

"What's happened? Has someone died?" Jade's voice was small with fear.

"Jordan just called," she said quietly. "She just discovered that Richard's been cheating on her." There was no point hiding the truth from Jade. Her little sister would guess exactly what had happened the second Jordan walked through the front door. "She's devastated. She's driving down to Rosewood with the kids tonight."

"She's coming home?"

Margot nodded. "She said she's leaving Richard. I don't know whether that's what she'll do, but I'd like you to be as nice as you can be to Kate and Max. They're bound to be confused by all this."

"I can't believe he cheated on Jordan. What a rat bastard!" she spat. "How could he? She's pregnant with their baby! And she does *everything* for him. We're going to have to get her a really good divorce lawyer."

Dumbfounded, Margot turned to stare at Jade. "A divorce lawyer? Don't you think that's a bit premature?"

"No way. Half the kids at Malden had divorced parents. They were always talking about their parents fighting over alimony and custody and all that stuff. Victoria Forrester's dad was this hotshot lawyer and he screwed her mother royally. And Richard's a lobbyist, so he must know tons of lawyers, right?"

"You're right. You're terrifyingly right," Margot said, her thoughts racing. Richard had extensive connections in D.C. If he could stoop to cheating, who was to say he would act honorably if Jordan did decide to file for divorce? And Jordan was so innately kind, it wouldn't occur to her to protect herself. And what about Max and Kate; what if there was a custody battle? That would destroy Jordan and hurt the kids, as well.

She turned the key in the ignition. "We've got to get home so I can call Damien. He knows everyone in the world— including Washington. He'll know the name of a good lawyer for her."

She pulled out, then turned onto South Main Street, passing groups of kids walking toward the center of town. "So how was school?" she asked warily.

"Majorly crappy. Blair wasn't in school so I guess her parents weren't able to get her out of her suspension. She probably spent the day in her bedroom making a voodoo doll of me. Lunch sucked. I sat alone. I'm guessing it's because Jodie Thomas, a friend of Blair and her clique, cut through the lunch line to stand beside Dean. From the creeped-out look on his face I bet she was telling him I have some really gross

STD. I'm sure he hates me now. I hate school. I wish I could be homeschooled. Then I could ride most of the day."

"Don't even go there, Jade. Just forget it. I can't do math and my grammar's shaky at best. Besides, running away from your problems isn't the way to solve them."

"*You* ran away and you turned out fine. You're an incredible model. Your life is awesome."

Margot sighed. "I'm not going to deny that modeling hasn't been fun and exciting. But here at Rosewood, I feel like I'm doing something that's meaningful. I can almost sense all those ancestors of ours that Jordan knows so well."

Jade was silent for a stretch of the road, but then she said, "It's strange, isn't it? You had to convince Jordan we should try to keep Rosewood and now she may be the one who needs to know that it's still her home—maybe even more than you or me."

Her sister was unnervingly perceptive at times. "I hope for Jordan's sake that she and Richard can work their problems out. But whatever happens, she'll have us."

"You know, if she does come back home, I better get my driver's license. Then I can help out with all sorts of stuff."

Yes, she was perceptive and as stubbornly determined as they came. "That's a really neat and selfless idea, Jade, but I have some bad news on that front. There's no driving until you've worked off the fine I paid at the police station yesterday."

"But—"

Determined to switch topics before Jade began campaigning in earnest, she said, "So did I tell you we sold Harvest for a hundred fifty thousand?"

"Sweet."

"Yeah, I think Dad would be proud. Now, do you know anything about spavin? Faraday's come up lame. Travis was calling the vet when I left, but he and Ned are pretty sure that's what it is."

"Poor guy. I hope he can get better, especially since we

won't be able to book Stoneleigh for any live covers other than with our own mares on account of his low sperm count. This really sucks about Faraday."

Margot didn't even attempt to correct her language. "Yeah, it does," she agreed quietly. But with Jordan's news taking top billing on a growing list of things that really sucked, the status of Rosewood Farm's studs couldn't even break the top ten.

TWENTY-SIX

A DHL VAN was idling next to Travis's Jeep when Margot and Jade climbed out of the Rover. She saw Travis outside the main barn with a large, flat envelope tucked under his elbow. He was in the midst of signing the receipt on a clipboard. Glancing up at their approach, Travis handed the clipboard back to the uniformed man, who nodded his thanks before jogging back to his truck.

"This came for you, Margot," Travis said, holding out the envelope. "The DHL guy needed a signature release. No one was up at the house."

"Thanks. Ellie must have left for the day." She glanced at the return address. It was Charlie's. "Did you reach the vet?"

"Yeah. He should be here soon. Bromley's got a portable X-ray machine. We may have to give Faraday a mild sedative to get him to hold still. Margot, about Faraday—"

"Hey," Jade said, peering at the label affixed to the envelope, which Keisha, Charlie's assistant, had addressed in easy-to-read block capital letters. "Isn't that from Charlie Ayer? Aren't you going to open it? Maybe it's a photograph of you from the Dior shoot."

Margot was certain that was precisely what was inside the oversized envelope. Charlie always sent her prints to put in her portfolio. The last thing she wanted was to look at the photograph in front of Travis; she knew his attitude toward her modeling. And looking at a single, isolated image was a different experience, packing a far greater visual punch, than when one leafed through a glossy magazine chock full of such pictures. But Travis was watching her closely, noting her hesitation.

"Yeah, sure." She tore the cardboard flap open and pulled out the print. Her fingers clumsy from nerves, she bobbled it, and the cover sheet slid off, drifting to the ground.

Travis picked up the piece of paper, glanced at it as he straightened, then handed it to her with a stony look.

Charlie's careless scrawl ran across the paper: "I love you, babe. As always, you were incredible. Call me. We need to talk. Yours, Charlie."

"Wow. You look amazing," Jade breathed. She alone had bothered to look at the print balanced in Margot's hands.

Margot reluctantly eyed the picture.

Oh, no. Charlie had gone with the picture Jade had pronounced the best, the one where he'd urged her to think of her lover. And in the space of a heartbeat, Travis, with his bold, dark looks and thrilling, sensual magnetism, was before her.

Charlie had done an amazing job with the enlarged print. It was beautifully lit, with glorious, lush details. She tried to focus on everything in the photograph but herself and her dreamy, lost-in-love expression.

The truth was staring her in the face. Even before Travis made love to her, when all he'd done was kiss her with a passion like no other, she'd already been deeply, irrevocably in love with him.

"Don't you think she looks amazing, Travis?"

Jade's question to him was like having a hot poker thrust into an open wound.

Travis glared at the picture as jealousy burned through him. He recognized the expression on Margot's face that was captured in the photograph. It was a look that had made his heart leap and then soar with joy. It was the look she'd given him when he'd been deep inside her, their two bodies as one.

That Charlie Ayer, too, could summon that wondrous expression just by aiming a camera lens at her infuriated him. And how many other guys back in New York did she have proclaiming their love?

"Yeah, she looks amazing, all right."

Margot flinched at his caustic tone. Exhausted and overwhelmed by worry, she was suddenly fed up with Travis's disdainful attitude toward her modeling. She needed his love, not his censure.

"Thanks. Charlie and I do good work together. We always have. He's a wonderful man." She smiled with petty pleasure when his eyes narrowed.

"I think Ned's waiting in the barn, Jade. He wanted you to help him groom Aspen before you take him out to ride," Travis said, his steely gaze never leaving Margot.

"Oh, my God, why didn't you say so?" and she was off like a jackrabbit.

"We need to talk, Margot."

"I can't right now. I have to go make some calls." First to Damien, to see whether he'd performed the miraculous and landed a big-name contract for her and to ask him for the name of a top-notch divorce lawyer for Jordan, in case worse came to worst.

"And one of those calls will be to Charlie Ayer, won't it? He's more than just a 'good friend,' isn't he, Margot?"

Only an hour ago he'd made wild love to her and now he was interrogating her like a chief justice. "What do you want me to say, Travis? Okay, yes, Charlie was my boyfriend. I guess."

"You *guess*? What the hell is that supposed to mean?" he asked furiously.

There was no way she was going to explain that while she loved Charlie for many reasons, their relationship had never come close to what she'd felt for Travis all her life. He had

some nerve to be acting so outraged when he had yet to tell
her he cared for her.

"It means that I was on my own for eight years!" she fired
back. "What were *you* doing all that time, Travis? Did you
take a vow of celibacy and light candles around one of those
photos of me that you admire so much? Yeah, I bet you did.
And don't you dare try to feed me some hypocritical line
about how it's not the same thing."

A muscle jumped in his tightly clamped jaw. So he was
angry. Well, then, they were two of a kind, because her own
temper was dangerously close to boiling over.

"Bromley will be arriving any minute to X-ray Faraday,"
he ground out. "You should be there."

"Gosh, I think we've had this discussion before. This is
why we hired *you*. Now, if you'll excuse me, I'm going to go
be a frivolous model and call my agent so he can tell me how
beautiful I am. And then I'm going to call my photographer-
lover so he can tell me how incredible I am and how much
he loves me." Feeling the sting of tears, she spun around on
her boot heels and ran off to the house.

He grabbed her arm. "Damn it, Margot, hold on. You can't
walk away like that. We've got to talk about—"

Sure that Travis was going to tell her of yet another obli-
gation and responsibility when already she felt like a dam
about to burst, she wrenched free with a cry of "No! Whatever it is, I don't want to hear it," and she ran toward the
house.

Her cell rang before she'd even crossed the threshold. Seeing Damien's number on the screen, she pressed the green
button, sank down on the bottom step of the circular staircase, and dashed her tears away. "Damien?"

"The one and only," he replied. "Did you get Charlie's
photo? The Dior people are over the moon, love."

"I'm really glad to hear that," she replied, pressing the
heel of her hand against her forehead. "At least one thing's

going right in my life. Everything else is such a mess, I don't know what to do. Damien, my sister Jordan just called . . ."

Damien listened patiently as she poured out her troubles. "A real sodding bastard that brother-in–law of yours is. I'll be happy to make a few calls on Jordan's behalf."

"Thanks, Damien." She drew a steadying breath and tried to sound casual even though she was as nervous as she'd ever been. "How's it going on the contract front? Have you got any juicy gigs that might help me pay off some of these debts?"

"That's what I'm calling about. But first, I want to play the devil's advocate. Do you mind?"

"No—no, of course not."

"Brave girl," he replied approvingly. "Okay. You've had a nibble of what it's like to run your family's farm—the responsibility and the anxiety of knowing the hundred things that can and do go wrong, the endless expenses. Even if you succeed in getting Rosewood out of debt, none of those things are going to disappear. Your lovely horses are still going to get sick. Bills will still pile up on your desk. And you know the cold, hard truth: you won't have the earning power you have now for too many more years. So here's my question. Is this really the life you want for yourself? How about coming back to New York? You have friends who love you here. . . ."

She sniffed as tears filled her eyes again. "Thanks, Damien. I really needed to hear that. I'm so grateful for all you've done. But from the get-go you've always advised me to look to the future and figure out what I want from life after modeling. I know the answer now. I want to try to keep Rosewood, not only for myself but for my sisters."

He sighed. "This is my comeuppance for lecturing you girls so much. Well, I can't say I'm surprised by your answer. So here's a bit of delicious news."

"You have something?"

"Don't get too excited, love. This won't answer all your problems. It might, however, keep the wolves at bay until I can come up with something truly stellar."

"Whatever it is, I'll hop on a plane this week. Just let me make sure Jordan's okay first—"

"That won't be necessary."

"What?"

"Like the proverbial mountain, this gig's coming to you. There was a lovely fete last night with simply everyone in attendance. I ran into Charlie and we were raising our champagne coupes to you and the Dior campaign when Tracy Andrews from Ralph Lauren caught sight of Charlie—the poor chit has an absolutely transparent crush on him. Anyway, she hurried over and launched into this story about how everyone at RL was going mad, scrambling for a new location for an upcoming *Vogue* shoot. It seems the manse they'd originally green-lighted developed a slew of nightmarish problems—leaking pipes, dripping ceilings, and ruined wallpaper—turning it into something more properly resembling a set for a Tim Burton movie. Well, as I listened, I was struck by nothing less than divine inspiration. I told Tracy that not only did you have this wonderful old place down in Virginia, complete with lots of pretty horses, but that you were presently in residence. Good old Charlie chimed in, saying he'd seen Rosewood himself and that it was fantastic, the real deal. In short, we managed to convince her that your Rosewood would be the perfect backdrop for the blue-blood lifestyle that darling Ralph has been peddling ever since he left the Bronx. I said that if the company was interested, they should ring us."

"And?"

"I just got off the phone with Tracy. Ralph Lauren is indeed most interested."

"Oh, my God, Damien, this is so great!"

"It gets greater. *Vogue*'s jumped on board, too. They want to do a profile of you—a peek into supermodel Margot Radcliffe's life. Not your usual thing, I know, but what with *Project Runway's* success, this tell-all stuff sells lots of copies."

She didn't even hesitate. "I'll do it."

"That's my girl. Now, listen. Tracy, Natasha Mills, the ad director, and Simone Porter, *Vogue*'s fashion editor, want to fly down tomorrow. If they like what they see, we'll begin negotiations."

"Damien, thanks so much—"

"No need for thanks, darling. It'll be terrific fun seeing how much I can squeeze out of the interested parties for the privilege of photographing one of my top models, her home, *and* her horses. Now, let me ring off so I can flip through my Rolodex for someone with the name of a razor-sharp divorce lawyer."

Margot pressed the OFF button and had barely a minute to absorb what she'd just agreed to when her cell pealed again.

"Hey, babe, it's me. You get the photo?"

"Hi, Charlie. Yes, it's great. Jade oohed and aahed over it. Your target audience approves."

"I told you your sister's sharp."

"Yeah, she is." She paused. "So, I was just on the phone with Damien."

"Then you heard about the fun we had last night with Tracy. Sweet kid."

"Heard she's sweet on you, too."

"Looks like it," Charlie said happily. "Tracy ended up doing me a little favor in the bargain. She must have dropped my name to Simone Porter because *Vogue* called to ask if I'd be interested in photographing you for their profile. That wasn't bs when I told Tracy how amazing that old house of yours is. You and I could have a blast and create some really powerful, dramatic pictures. What do you say, babe?"

Having Charlie at Rosewood was about the worst thing that could happen for her relationship with Travis. But she wasn't about to reveal that his presence might make things difficult. Charlie was her friend. And if that weren't reason enough, she owed him for his constant professional help and support.

"I told Damien I'd do the profile but I wasn't too happy about it. Knowing you'll be behind the camera makes all the difference, Charlie."

"All right! Damn, this is going to be great. I'll call Tracy and sweet-talk her into flying Keisha and me down with her tomorrow. I miss your face, babe. See you."

"See you, Charlie."

Margot rose from her seat on the stairs and swayed. When had she last eaten? Not since breakfast. The memory of the meal she'd cooked with Travis made her recall everything else they'd shared. The incendiary passion when they'd made love, the sweet closeness when they'd talked.

All the same, she had failed to tell him the two most important things in her heart: that she loved him and Rosewood, and that she was desperately afraid of losing them both. Now, were she to reveal the critical financial situation her father had left them in, would he believe her when she told him she loved him? Or would he think she had been using him this entire time to keep him working at Rosewood and thus preserve its standing among the buyers in the horse world?

And when he heard that as early as tomorrow, the fashion world—Charlie Ayer included—which he so disdained and disliked, would be descending on Rosewood, what would he think of her then?

She should tell him everything and put her heart on the line.

But while she was afraid of losing Rosewood, the thought of Travis spurning her was even more terrifying. His rejection had devastated her once. As deeply in love with him as she was, she wasn't sure she could survive it a second time.

WITH THE COURTYARD'S exterior lights ablaze, it was easy for Margot to pick out Travis's tall form. He was by the open tailgate of a supersized SUV, talking with the vet, Joe Bromley.

"Here she is now, Joe," Travis said as she walked toward them. "Margot, you remember Joe Bromley? He's just finished X-raying Faraday." His tone was carefully neutral and Margot wondered whether he, too, regretted their earlier exchange. She certainly did.

She stuck out her hand. "Hi, Dr. Bromley, it's been a long time."

"Yes, it has. My condolences for your family's loss."

"Thank you. So, does the X-ray show anything about Faraday's hock?"

"I have the digital image right here on the computer. Travis and I were just looking at it."

"This is certainly high-tech," Margot said, peering at the illuminated computer screen set up in the back of the SUV.

"Yes, it's amazing what we can do on rounds now. Twenty years ago, when I was starting out in practice, the idea of being able to hook up a portable X-ray machine to a laptop in the back of my truck was as inconceivable as the idea of being able to watch a TV show on a cellular telephone while walking down a beach."

"And what has your space-age technology revealed about Faraday's hock?"

"Nothing good, unfortunately," Bromley said. "Here, come closer to the screen and take a look at the lower portion of the hock joint. This area is called the distal. It's where the spavin bone is located. Now, do you see how cloudy it appears, how the lines of the bones have been obscured?" His finger traced the area.

"Yes."

"That's the onset of arthritis."

Her hand tightened around the apple she'd plucked from the fruit bowl for Faraday. "What can we do for him?"

"First I'd like to get your farrier to take a look at him and see about fitting him with some corrective shoes. I'd also like to try a course of Adequan injections. Both might help. If Faraday's lameness persists, there are also various corticosteroids we can give him—I've seen good results using them—but I'd like to try the less invasive treatments first."

"Do you think we can cure his lameness?"

Bromley eyed the brightly lit computer screen again. "Faraday's nineteen. The problem with osteoarthritis in older horses is that these treatments I've mentioned may offer only temporary relief. Then, too, we have to be prepared for the possibility that Faraday's spavin may exacerbate his old back pain and cause a flare-up. If we don't find an effective solution to manage his condition over the next few months, it may be ill-advised to put Faraday through the physical stress of standing at stud." He paused, letting the prognosis penetrate.

Margot folded her arms tightly about her middle, trying to maintain her composure. Even though Travis and Ned had already given her much the same assessment, having it confirmed was a terrible blow.

"I realize I've painted a rather bleak picture for you, but I believe it's important for owners to be as fully informed as possible."

Lifting her head, she squared her shoulders. "Thank you, Dr. Bromley. I do appreciate knowing what Faraday's going through."

"If you'd like to start him on the Adequan, I can give him an injection now. You'll be able to continue with the bute for pain relief. There's no contraindication."

She looked at Travis. He gave a silent nod. "Yes, we'd like to start treatment immediately. We'll call Frank Jarvis first thing tomorrow and have him come and look at Faraday."

She turned to enter the stallion barn when she heard the crunching of gravel. Ned and Jade were walking up, with Aspen between him. "How was Aspen?" she asked Jade.

"Loads of fun. You have to go real slowly with him, make your signals really clear and direct so he doesn't get confused, but I got him to pick up the correct lead at the canter, and he backed up about five paces, smooth as you please. Ned says I'm a natural." Beneath the artificial lights, Jade's face glowed with excitement.

"It's true. Miss Jade's doing real well with him." Turning his attention to Joe Bromley, he said, "How's our boy Faraday, Doc?"

"It's spavin, Ned, just as you and Travis thought. We've decided to start him on Adequan."

"Arthritis ain't good."

"We'll have to see how he does," Joe Bromley replied. "There are all sorts of combinations of therapies we can try, beyond even those I mentioned to Margot and Travis."

"We know you'll try your best, Doc. We better get Aspen put away, Miss Jade. Thanks for coming by, Doc."

"See you, Ned."

With a heavy heart, Margot slipped into the stallion barn. From Bromley's carefully worded explanation, Travis's stoic reaction, and Ned's concern, Margot had been made to understand that while it was possible Faraday might recover sufficiently to perform in the breeding shed, it was unlikely. The three of them had been in the horse business too long not to know what Faraday was up against.

She walked over to Faraday's stall, clucking softly to gain his attention. He raised his head from the flakes of hay in the corner of his stall. Curious, he ambled over and stuck his muzzle between the metal bars.

"Hey, Faraday. This is for you, big guy," she said, holding the apple out for him. The stallion didn't have to be cajoled. He had the fruit between his teeth in a flash. She smiled sorrowfully as he backed up and began to chomp noisily. When he'd finished, he approached again and she fed him a carrot treat.

"He's going to be spoiled rotten if you keep this up," Travis said quietly.

She didn't turn around. "That's okay. He deserves it."

"Yeah, he does." The back of his hand brushed hers once, then twice, and she felt her heart expand. "Margot, I—"

"Okay, Travis," Joe Bromley called. "I'm ready for you to bring Faraday out."

Margot quickly stepped aside to give the men room to work with the stallion. Travis grabbed Faraday's halter and lead shank. Attaching them, he led the stallion out of the stall.

"I'm going to inject the hock directly, Travis."

"I'll hold him," Travis assured Bromley. Tightening the shank with one hand, he took hold of Faraday's lip with the other, pinching it to distract the stallion. "Okay, go ahead, Joe."

Without wasting a moment, Bromley moved his free hand down the back of the leg, found the spot on the hock joint he wanted, and inserted the syringe without fuss or hesitation.

At the sting of the needle Faraday tried to throw his head, but Travis held him fast. Then it was over and Bromley was backing away, capping the syringe.

"Thanks, Travis. I'll come by for another injection in three days' time."

"We'll be here."

"I'll be off, then. Good to see you, Margot."

"Good-bye and thanks."

Travis turned to Margot. "Can you hand me that Baker blanket?"

She nodded wordlessly, but her pale face spoke volumes. She was obviously shaken by the news Bromley had given them. Travis wanted nothing more than to walk over, pull her into his arms, and kiss her until her smile was no longer weighed down by sadness. Christ, his heart felt like an airplane executing a loop-the-loop. Forty-five minutes ago he'd been seething with jealousy over Charlie Ayer and whatever was between Margot and him. Now all he wanted was to figure out how to make things right with her.

Wordlessly she passed him the navy blanket. He shook it out and together they settled it over the stallion and buckled the straps. She waited silently while Travis walked him back into his box stall and shut the door.

The first step in making things right meant doing his job as Rosewood's manager, seeing to it that she understood what they were facing. "Margot, you realize we may be looking at a situation where we don't have a stud standing at Rosewood."

"We still have Stoneleigh."

"Maybe, maybe not. Stoneleigh's sperm count has gone down. Given his age, it could drop even lower, in which case he won't be making the trip to the breeding shed. We've got to be realistic about the likelihood that neither stallion will be able to perform. Ned's gone through the catalogs for the upcoming sales. There are some fine—"

"Did I hear my name?" Ned asked, entering the barn. "Has Bromley left?"

"Yeah," Travis said, nodding. "He finished up a few minutes ago. I was just telling Margot there are some stallions you've got your eye on. I think the three of us should sit down in the office and draw up a list so we can figure out what we want in terms of bloodlines and performance."

"That's a fine idea. The first sale is the week after the Hunt Cup."

The moment she'd been dreading had arrived, Margot thought bleakly. She was about to make Travis rue the day he'd given up his job at Hugh Hartmann's. They couldn't afford a stallion of the caliber Ned and he were considering. She wasn't going to be a spendthrift like her father and recklessly assume that everything would work out financially; she knew firsthand the consequences of that particular kind of folly.

"I'm not sure I want to replace Stoneleigh or Faraday just now."

"Excuse me?" Ned was staring at her as if she'd lost her mind. She couldn't bear to look at Travis's expression; Ned's was painful enough.

"I'm sorry if you're disappointed, Ned. We'll just have to keep our fingers crossed that Stoneleigh's sperm count remains stable and that Faraday recovers enough to return to the breeding shed."

"RJ would—"

"I'm not my father and I never will be," she retorted, unable to suppress the volatile mix of emotions that the mention of her father engendered. She so wanted to mourn him, but since his funeral she'd instead found herself resenting him for leaving them all—not just herself, Jordan, and Jade, but everyone who worked at Rosewood—in such impossible straits.

The knowledge that Travis and Ned were using her father as their yardstick and finding her sadly lacking caused her resentment to soar.

Well, there was nothing like the present to cement their negative opinions, she thought. "It's unlikely we'll be able to attend the upcoming sale anyway. Ralph Lauren and *Vogue* are thinking of doing a shoot here at Rosewood. The deal's still in the works, but if it goes through they'll doubtless want to use the horses in some of the shots. We'll need everyone on hand. I don't know how the schedule will unfold, but shoots like this can take several days—"

"Hold up there, Margot," Travis interrupted, his gray gaze boring into her. "Let me get this straight. You're canceling a trip to one of the best sales of the year because you want to be photographed in *Vogue*?"

"They don't have a lot of flexibility in their schedule." And she needed the money fast if she was to get the creditors off her back.

Her answer didn't appease either man.

"What are these fashion folks going to do with the horses, Miss Margot? Dress them up so they can prance in front of the camera?" Ned asked in an affronted tone.

"The horses will be treated with the greatest care. But that's why I need everyone here so we can ensure the horses are all right and the photo shoot goes smoothly." She paused and swallowed. "This shoot is very important to me."

"Yeah," Travis bit out. "I'm beginning to see that very clearly. One more question. You just arranged all this when you were on the phone with Charlie Ayer, didn't you?"

She lifted her chin. "Yes."

He turned to Ned. "I'll be in the main barn."

Without sparing her another glance, he walked out of the barn.

Deflated and miserable, she stared at the barn floor. She was losing him, she knew it. Despite the weeks spent working side by side, Travis still perceived her as little more than a spoiled, pleasure-seeking princess. And now one of her father's oldest friends was beginning to view her that way, too. Ned's continued presence simply meant that he wasn't through giving her a piece of his mind.

He didn't beat about the bush. "I don't know what's gotten into you, Miss Margot, but I'd think long and hard about that decision you're making."

"I have, Ned. Buying a new stud would be unwise—"

"Unwise?" he repeated incredulously. "This is a breeding farm. The stallions are Rosewood's *foundation*. Don't you realize that without them there's no future for the business your family started generations ago?"

"Sometimes things have to change."

"Not these things," he replied vehemently. "I would have thought you of all people would understand this, but I guess not. So I might as well tell you something else. You're not the only one who's been getting phone calls. Travis heard from Hugh Hartmann yesterday and again this afternoon."

A chill invaded her. "Hugh Hartmann? The man who hired him after he left Rosewood?"

"That's right. Hugh's opening a new barn in Sperryville and is looking for a head trainer. He called and asked Travis if he'd be interested in the position. I never imagined I'd be saying this, but I wouldn't blame Travis one bit if he called Hugh back and said yes. Think about that and maybe you'll change your mind about what's wise and what's damned foolish." As he stalked out, he passed Jade with a tight nod.

"What's going on?" she asked, walking up to her. "Ned looks really angry."

"I told him and Travis that I wasn't going to purchase a new stud for Rosewood," Margot replied dully. "And they're none too happy that I've agreed to a location shoot here at Rosewood. Ralph Lauren needs an old house and *Vogue* is interested in doing a profile of me. They've asked Charlie Ayer to do the pictures."

"And what was Ned saying about Travis leaving Rosewood?"

Margot turned away, ostensibly to check the latch on Faraday's stall door. Quickly she wiped the sudden moisture from her eyes. "Apparently Hugh Hartmann called Travis about this new barn he's bought. I wouldn't be surprised if he decided to leave. He gave me due warning that he'd only stay if he thought we were committed to the business."

"But we are committed!" Jade protested. "You're working your butt off. You should tell him we're broke."

"And what would that accomplish? This entire business

with the stallions underscores a basic fact. Farms like Rose-wood have to be bankrolled. And we've got *nothing* in the bank. Instead of buying we're going to have to sell as many horses as we can to make a profit this year. And instead of my chipping in with the day-to-day running of the farm, I'm going to have to accept as many high-paying modeling jobs as possible. That's not the kind of outfit Travis wants or deserves to be working for."

"But if he stays we'll have a better chance of making it."

"I know." She brought her fingers to her temple, massaging the pounding pressure points. "That was why I kept silent about the debts in the first place. But it was selfish of me."

"So tell him!"

"I can't!" Margot cried. "If I do, how will I be able to live with myself knowing he's stayed with us out of pity? Horses aren't just Travis's livelihood, they're his passion, his world. How could I keep him from accepting such a great opportunity like the one Hugh Hartmann's offered?"

"Oh, my God, you're, like, in love with him, aren't you?"

"Yes, I am," she replied with a quiet sadness. But that doesn't mean he loves me, she added silently. "Listen, it's getting late. We should go up to the house. Jordan should be here soon."

Overcome with weariness, she glanced through the open doorway. The moon had yet to rise, making the sky as somber as her spirits. It was cold, too, she thought, shivering. The night was cold and empty, just like her.

Grabbing hold of one of the double doors, she pulled it shut. Jade stepped forward, took hold of the other one, and they met in the middle.

"Should I hit the lights?"

"No, I'm sure Travis will be back to check on Faraday." Simply saying his name hurt.

"Do you really think he'll go?"

"Once he realizes I'm not going to purchase a new stud, I

can't see why he'd stay. Hugh Hartmann must have more money than God to be opening another barn. Travis deserves to be in a place like that."

"I'm starved," Jade announced in an abrupt change of topic. "I hope Ellie made something good. Hey, aren't you coming up to the house?"

"I'll be up shortly. There's something I have to do first."

Try as she might, she couldn't block from her mind Travis's scornful expression when he'd left the stallion barn. She had made such a mess of things. At least she could fix one thing.

TWENTY-EIGHT

IT WAS FEEDING TIME. Hay bales lay scattered along the center of the aisles. Margot found Travis at the far end, along with Tito and Felix. He and Felix were dividing the bales into three flake sections and depositing them in each stall while Tito poured scoops of grain into the feed buckets. Up and down the rows of box stalls, the horses snorted and whickered their anticipation, a few kicking the wooden walls in excitement.

Spotting Margot, Travis straightened, a section of hay bracketed between his hands. He looked at her impassively. He was still angry, she realized.

"I need to talk to you."

"The horses need to be fed."

"Then please come to the office when you're finished." Not giving him a chance to refuse, she left, walking back up the aisle to the center of the barn.

Entering the office, she sat down at her father's desk, pulled open the center drawer, and retrieved a stapled document she had stored there. In the middle side drawer she took out a bill-of-sale form and read it carefully before filling it out, transferring information.

Damn it to hell, Travis thought as he reached Sweet William's stall, the last on his side of the aisle. He didn't want to go anywhere near Margot right now. He was too furious, too hurt, too fucking miserable. He still couldn't believe what she'd told him and Ned back in the stallion barn.

What did she think she was doing?

He wanted to grab her and shake some sense into her. He wanted— God, he thought wretchedly, only this morning he'd caught himself fantasizing about a life spent waking up to a warm and sleepy Margot curled against him. These weeks had offered him a glimpse of what they might have together: horses, love . . . and lots more love.

He'd convinced himself that Margot shared the same dreams. But he was mistaken. Hers were as glossy and sumptuous as the Dior photograph he'd seen this afternoon. By announcing the imminent arrival of Charlie Ayer and the assorted entourage of fashion people, she'd made it plain that she had no intention of trading in her deluxe world for a guy like him.

It sure hadn't taken her long to conclude that life at Rosewood lacked the glamour she reveled in. Not even the fiery passion they'd discovered could compete. He'd spent most of the day tied up in knots trying to figure out how to tell her he loved her, while all the while she was probably rehearsing her "Sorry, Travis, but I just don't think it's going to work out" speech.

Although walking into that office was like walking into a torture chamber, Travis went anyway. He was her employee and, lovesick fool that he was, he couldn't stay away from her.

She was at the desk, reading some form. He leaned against the doorjamb waiting, watching her, feeling a perverse satisfaction at the embarrassed flush that crawled up the ivory column of her neck, and that when she laid the piece of paper down, her hands trembled. "You wanted to talk to me?"

"Yes, Ned told me Hugh Hartmann called."

"That's right. He needs a trainer for a barn he's opening in Sperryville."

"Ned seemed to think it was a good enough job to interest you. Is it?"

"What are you driving at, Margot? Do you want to know if I'm going to leave?"

"Yes. I remember what you said when you came back—"

Damn it all, Travis railed silently. How could she sound so calm and detached when he was bleeding inside? "That's interesting. I thought you'd clean forgotten my telling you I'd only stay on at Rosewood if you were serious about running the farm. Kind of begs the question of what *you're* going to do, Margot. Do you really plan to use Rosewood as some kind of fashion set so that you can smile your lover's smile for Charlie Ayer's camera?"

"If I do, will you leave?"

"What the hell do you want me to say to that?" he asked furiously.

"I'm going to continue modeling. You can't possibly know how important it is to me."

"Oh, I think I do. You've made it crystal clear what you really care about." No point in asking if her modeling was more important than them. There was no "them."

Christ, when had he gotten so stupid? All those years ago he'd recognized that the divide between Margot and him was too great.

"I guess this is it, then, the end of the line." He made himself speak the words evenly as if saying them were not killing him. Even as he turned around to leave, he prayed that she was going to come to her senses.

"Wait," she said, and hope soared within him. He turned back. "This is for you." She was holding the piece of paper in her shaking hand.

His hope crashed as quickly as it had taken flight. Grimly he took the paper, gave it a cursory glance, then looked again. "This is a bill of sale for Night Raider," he said in a sharp tone.

"Yes. He's yours now. He should have been all along. I want you to have him."

Jesus, this really was nothing more than a game to her.

That she could buy and then with equal casualness give away a high-priced horse was the final cut, slicing deeply. He would bear the scars from Margot forever.

"I'm real flattered, Margot. I only got two weeks' severance out of your dad when he gave me the boot. With you I get a forty-five-thousand-dollar horse." Summoning a cold smile, he struck back, in the hope that he would wound her just as deeply. "Or should I consider Raider a bonus for those extra services I rendered? Damn, maybe if I'd given you a few more orgasms I could have got a gold watch, too."

She cried in the shower, unable to block out the memories. Memories of Travis with her in the tiled stall, running his lathered hands over her until she was weak and trembling, lifting her against the slick wall, his strong arms holding her easily as he took her, his mouth fiercely gentle as he swallowed her cries, as she convulsed around his hard length. That memory, torturous enough, was eclipsed by another: of Travis's face in the office, his expression icy as he contemptuously degraded the love they'd made, deliberately turning it into something base and coarse.

She cried, hating him with all the power she possessed, knowing that even her fiercest hatred for him was no match for her love. After her hatred had faded away, her love, her aching, hopeless love for Travis, would remain, forever and always.

She probably would have stayed in the shower, letting her tears run like rain, if not for the loud banging on the bathroom door and Jade's shout of "Jordan's here!"

She pulled on clothes, grabbing anything that came to hand, doing so only because Jordan and the kids were here and needed her to be strong and not to dissolve in heartbroken misery herself.

She hurried down the hall and the stairs. Jade had already thrown open the front door. When Margot joined her on the bottom porch step, she looked over at Margot's face, frowned, and opened her mouth.

Margot silenced her with a quick shake of her head.

The minivan's front doors opened. Jordan slid out of the passenger side and Margot hurried around the van toward her, zeroing in on Jordan's red-rimmed eyes and too pale face.

Hugging her fiercely, she stepped back. "It's good to have you here, safe and sound."

"I just really needed to be with you, to be home— My God, Margot, you look terrible. What's happened?"

"It's nothing. It's just been a really long, bad day." Impulsively Margot hugged her again, this time noting the unmistakable mound of Jordan's stomach. Silently she damned Richard for his callous selfishness. What kind of a man cheated on his pregnant wife? "I'm so glad you're here."

"Margot, I feel so lost," Jordan admitted brokenly.

She closed her eyes. "I know. We'll talk inside."

Jordan spotted Jade, who'd been hovering a few feet away, and with a wobbly smile she went over to give her a hug.

Composing her features, Margot went over to help the babysitter with Kate and Max.

"Hi, Susannah. Thanks for driving Jordan and the kids. And you can stay the night?"

"Yes," Susannah replied.

"You're a lifesaver. Now, where are my favorite little rascals?" Sliding open the van's back door, she exclaimed, "Aha! I've found them. Kate, honey, how on earth do these child seats work? Oh, I see, thanks. Max, you look more than ready to be liberated. And *oof*," she grunted theatrically, lifting him out. "You've gotten really heavy! You must have grown in these past few weeks."

"Hey, Jade," she called over her shoulder. "Mind taking Max for me? I need both hands to free Kate from this contraption." She passed the toddler to Jade with a whisper of "Thanks."

"What's going on? Why have you been crying? Did you and Travis fight?" Jade demanded.

"Don't worry, I'll get over it," she lied.

Quickly shifting her attention to her niece, she released her from the child seat, then took her small hand in hers so Kate could clamber down.

A mountain of possessions were crammed in the back of the van. "Kate, hon, is there something here you can carry? Your teddy bear? That works for me. How about you take Max's puppy dog, too? You can lay them on your beds upstairs. They must need a nap after such a long car ride."

Max and Kate were worn out from the trip. After a quick supper of chicken, pasta, and peas, Jordan and Susannah ushered them upstairs for a bath and a story and then bedtime. Jordan came down to the kitchen a short time later.

"I told Susannah I'd bring her up a plate. She's exhausted, too. The Beltway was insane. What did Ellie leave for dinner?"

"Besides the grilled chicken? There's asparagus, and the makings for a salad." Ellie Banner had finally realized that the lumberjack meals she was fixing weren't the ideal menu for a model and a teenage girl. "Sit down, Jordan. Even I can get a meal like this together."

"No, I'll do it." Jordan was already opening the refrigerator. "It helps to have something to do. Otherwise I start to cry. And I would so like not to cry for a little bit."

Margot could understand that.

Jordan pulled out the platter with the chicken on it, found the asparagus and then the clear plastic bags filled with lettuce greens. Grabbing a cucumber from the bottom bin, she asked, "Where's Jade?"

"She's in the shower. Let's talk, Jordan. Tell me what happened." When her sister shuddered visibly, she hurriedly added, "But if you don't feel up to it—"

She shook her head. "No, I *should* talk about it. It was awful, Margot. The worst was having to listen to his lies destroy our marriage when the truth was literally in my outstretched palm. I've never felt so used, so betrayed."

"What are you going to do?"

"I don't know." Despair laced her voice. "What can I do? I have two young children who adore their father and I'm almost five months pregnant with his third child. I suppose we'll go to marriage counseling—though right now I don't see how therapy could help me get past the pain of what Richard's done and said. Do you know when he finally confessed to the affair, he said that he'd fallen in love with Cynthia—that's her name—because she *needed* him? He claimed that was what was wrong with our marriage. I was too 'capable and self-sufficient.' God, Margot, he made me out to be some kind of a Martha Stewart robot," she ended with an anguished sob.

Margot crossed the kitchen and wrapped her arms about her sister's heaving shoulders. "Don't you dare believe him. You're a great wife, a fabulous mother, and a wonderful, kind person. Richard's nothing but a rat bastard."

"What? What was that you called him?" Jordan asked, hiccuping.

"Rat bastard. Compliments of Jade."

"You told her?"

"I was picking her up at school when you called," she explained. "She knew something was up the second she saw my face. I'm only just beginning to realize how sensitive she is. Besides, she'd have figured it out the second you arrived with the kids. I guess I also told her because I wanted her to know she's not the only one having a rough time. I hope you're not upset I told, Jordan."

She shook her head. "No, I don't mind. Tell me what's been going on with her and you. I want to hear everything, really, I do. Maybe I need to know someone else is having a rough time, too," she said sadly.

Margot went over to the cutlery drawer. She could at least set the table while she recounted Jade's recent trials. She told Jordan everything: from Officer Cooper bringing a semi-conscious Jade home in his patrol car to Jade's car-washing fiasco with Rob Cooper, or RoboCop, as Margot now thought of him, and finally to their meeting with the school principal regarding the Internet bullying Jade was being subjected to.

Jordan had stopped slicing the cucumber to stare aghast. "Jade had all that to deal with? I'm surprised she didn't do something far more reckless and stupid. She must have been hurting so badly. God, I hate bitchy teenagers." With vicious strokes of her knife, she quickly finished cutting the cucumber and arranged the slices over the salad.

"But I don't get this stuff about Nicole," she said. "It's simply preposterous to think she'd cheat on Dad. That she would flirt with a handsome man to within an inch of her life, definitely. But not actually *cheat*."

Margot looked at her incredulously.

"No, I'm not being willfully naïve," Jordan said, placing the asparagus neatly on the plate she was preparing for Susannah. "It's not like I don't have firsthand experience that spouses cheat and then lie like rugs. But Nicole, from day one of her marriage, was obsessed with being Mrs. RJ Radcliffe. Dad was such a larger-than-life figure, I don't think any other man could compare."

"I found Nicole's diary in Dad's desk."

"Nicole kept a diary?" Jordan's astonishment was clear. "Did you read it? What did it say?"

"I only read a tiny portion, enough to understand why Dad fired Travis. He thought Travis was the one having an affair with her. I couldn't read more. I—was too upset by the idea."

Jordan shook her head. "There's another notion that's beyond absurd—of Nicole and Travis carrying on. Nicole was a snob. She'd never risk an affair with someone she considered beneath her socially, precisely because of how mortified she would be if it ever came out in the open. Besides, Travis wouldn't do something so repugnant, never mind that it was always *you* he watched."

"Did he?" How pathetic that she needed to hear that.

"Like a hawk. I think he's always wanted you."

Yes, that was the problem. Travis had wanted her. He'd liked her body, found her sexy and all that. But he hadn't loved her.

"Margot," Jordan said, interrupting her thoughts. "I'm not sure I'm up to it right now but I'd like to take a look at Nicole's diary. Perhaps I can piece together what was really going on."

"All right. But Jordan, Jade doesn't know about the diary."

"I understand." She was silent as she poured dressing on the salad and tossed it. "Do you suppose Dad died believing Nicole was unfaithful?"

"I know he died loving her. Remember how he asked about Nicole at the hospital? She was his first thought."

"But that doesn't mean he wasn't still tormented by thoughts of her infidelity."

"That's what Edward Crandall seems to think," Margot muttered, coming over and placing the chicken breasts on the plates.

"Edward Crandall? How does he know about any of this?"

"Warburg's gossip mill," Margot said by way of explanation. "He went so far as to say that if the insurance company found nothing wrong with the plane, they would assume Dad had intentionally crashed it."

"What a horrible thing to say. How dare he speak like that about our father!"

"My thoughts exactly. We have an appointment with him about the estate after the Hunt Cup."

"And boy, will he get an earful from me," Jordan promised grimly. "The nerve of that man, after all the horses

Dad sold him. Margot, I am so glad you didn't let him bull-doze us into selling Rosewood. It would have been too much to bear, knowing our home was gone along with everything else. . . ."

"Let's hope we can keep it."

"We will," Jordan said fiercely, as she scooped a large helping of salad onto Susannah's plate. "So tell me, how did Travis convince you he wasn't having an affair with Nicole?" Picking up the salad bowl to carry it to the table, she caught sight of Margot's face. "Ahh. Forget I said that. Well, that's been in the making for years. I'm happy for you, Margot. He's a good man and very, um, attractive." The nascent smile that was playing over her lips died. "What's wrong?"

Margot ducked her head to stare fixedly at the loaf of bread she'd been slicing.

"Margot, has something happened between you and Travis?"

She nodded once. More, and the tears that threatened would fall. "I'm in love with him," she whispered tightly.

"Oh, I knew that," her sister said, sounding relieved. "I think you've always been in love with him. Well, I better take this up to Susannah. I'll let Jade know dinner's ready."

Margot had brought everything to the table by the time Jordan and Jade came downstairs. No sooner had they taken their seats than Jordan spoke. "So what's this about Travis leaving Rosewood, Margot?"

She put down her fork and shot Jade a look. "Thanks. Don't you think Jordan has enough to worry about?"

"Rosewood was left to all three of us. Jordan should know what's going on. You can't be the only one dealing with all this junk."

"Yes," Jordan said. "I definitely want to know."

Margot sat mute with misery, which hardly mattered as Jade was already answering. "Travis and Ned are beyond pissed at Margot because she won't buy a new stud. Of course, they don't realize that the reason she's refusing is because we're broke. Margot would rather let them think she's an airheaded party girl who's more interested in having fashion people come to Rosewood than telling them that Dad left us without a penny. I bet she hasn't even told Travis she's in love with him."

"Thank you, Jade," Margot said. "And here I was, marveling at how nice and sensitive you were being since talking to Reverend Wilde."

Jade gave her a mulish look. "I'm just telling the truth. You're being a total idiot. Someone should tell you."

"I've really grown to dislike the feeling of being three steps behind everyone else. What's this about buying a new stud? And is there really no money? The estate's been settled?" Jordan asked.

Margot pushed her plate away. "Yes, Crandall called. There's no money, but we've got plenty of debts. I didn't mention any of this because I didn't want to add to your worries. I figured maybe you had enough on your plate just now."

"And today Faraday came up lame. He has spavin and may not be able to stand at stud. Margot didn't tell me about the estate either, Jordan. But it was easy to figure out since Margot's agreed to a profile and to let people swarm all over Rosewood for a shoot when she's never consented to an interview in her entire career." She dropped back against her chair and glared at Margot.

"And how would you know whether I've been interviewed or not?"

"Maybe because I have an album stuffed with pictures of you from magazines. If you'd ever had an interview, it would be in my scrapbook, too." She gave her salad a vicious stab.

A memory of a dog-eared album falling out of the tear in Jade's bag surfaced. "That scrapbook you wouldn't let me pick up in the airport?" she asked.

Jade nodded, staring fixedly at her plate.

Any previous annoyance evaporated. "You could have written. I'd have sent you any picture you wanted," Margot said gently.

"Yeah, that would have gone over well with Mom."

"Good point." Nicole would have been livid. "Jade, I'm really sorry she and I never managed to call a truce to our open hostilities. I'm especially sorry because it meant that you had to choose sides. And you're right, I should have told Jordan about Faraday and the shoot." She looked across the table at her older sister. "Do you mind, Jordan? Some execs from Ralph Lauren and *Vogue* are coming tomorrow. They want to check out the house to use for a possible location. And *Vogue* is talking about having Charlie Ayer photograph me for one of their profiles. Other than selling every single horse we own, it was the only way I could think of to raise a big chunk of cash."

"I don't mind. Rosewood is beautiful. It'll be great to see it photographed. And having people around will be a welcome distraction. But Margot," she said, reaching out and laying a hand on her arm. "None of that is nearly as important as Travis being mad enough to leave Rosewood. Or *you*," she added softly.

Margot's throat tightened convulsively, her tears choking her. "He'll definitely leave. I gave him Night Raider, hoping that would make him understand how much I care for him. Instead Travis turned it around, accused me of treating him like some gigolo I was paying off. There's nothing to keep him here now. I screwed up so badly. Sometimes it seems as if that's all I ever do—try to make the men in my life, first Dad, then Travis—love me. And no matter what, I fail. God, I love him so much," she whispered. The pain was too much. Unable to bear it any longer, she dropped her head to her forearms and wept.

Over her bowed head, Jordan and Jade exchanged looks.

Jordan laid her hand on Margot's back. "Come on upstairs. You're wiped out. You need to sleep."

As she helped a still-sobbing Margot out of her chair, she mouthed instructions to Jade.

Jade nodded. Silently she slipped from the room, out of the house, and into the night.

Ned hefted the coffeepot. "You want some more, Travis?"

"No."

"I might as well finish it," he said, refilling his mug. "It ain't like I'm gonna get a decent night's sleep anyhow."

Travis wouldn't, either. He didn't know how he'd go upstairs to his bed, its rumpled sheets still carrying the scent of Margot. He didn't know where to go. Logic told him he should pick up the phone and call Hugh, then go upstairs and start packing—again. But he just couldn't seem to be able to think of anything but Margot.

Ned carried the mug over and eased himself into the chair next to Travis's. "I saw Miss Jordan's van up at the house. What do you suppose she's doing here?"

Travis rubbed his bristled cheek tiredly. He needed to sleep but if he did he would dream of Margot. "No idea. Margot said she'd be here for the Hunt Cup." Damn, he'd been looking forward to riding with her in the hunter pace event, watching that competitive spark in her catch fire.

"Travis, I got to tell you, son, I just don't understand what Margot's—" His sentence stalled.

Travis, too, heard the sound of footsteps running toward the office, and was out of his seat like a shot, his heart pounding in expectation, her name on his lips.

"Thank God," Jade exclaimed, gasping for breath. "I ran to Ned's cottage first 'cause it's so late. I shoulda—"

"What's wrong?" Travis demanded, cutting her off. "Is it Margot?"

"Yeah, it's Margot, and you're a total frigging doofus not to have figured out what's going on," Jade said accusingly.

"Maybe you should tell us what's going on, Miss Jade,

'cause I'll tell you, Travis ain't the only one who can't figure out what's happening around here."

"For starters, there's no money."

Jade's bald pronouncement was met with stunned silence. Travis glanced at Ned. He was looking poleaxed. That was a relief; at least he wasn't the only one who had no fucking idea what Jade was talking about.

She must have drawn the same conclusion. With an impatient roll of her eyes, she repeated, "There's no money. Nothing in the coffer—zip, zilch. Crandall broke the bad news after Dad's and Mom's funerals. Dad apparently made some bad investments but kept on spending anyway. We Radcliffes have always lived large." Despite her exaggerated shrug, it was easy to see how much the admission hurt the sixteen-year-old.

"So you're saying . . ." Ned's words came out slowly as he sorted it all out. "But at Crestview, Miss Margot bought Raider. How could she—"

"She used her own money, didn't she?" Travis said. He bet she'd been paying for every last thing at Rosewood, down to the hoof pick Andy had lost last week. Recalling the asinine comments he'd made about her modeling, he felt sick.

"Duh." Jade clearly thought he had shit for brains. He was inclined to agree with her. "It wasn't like she had any choice. It was either that or let Crandall push us into selling Rosewood."

"That son of a bitch," spat Ned. "I beg your pardon, Miss Jade."

"Crandall's way worse than that. I doubt he lost a wink of sleep before he told Margot that after settling the estate, we still have a pile of debts."

"You girls are in debt?" Ned's expression mirrored his horrified tone.

"Yeah, so you can see why Margot couldn't possibly agree to buy a new stud when there are debts to pay off and Jordan may need money for a divorce—" The word hung in the air as she turned fiery red all the way to the roots of her hair. "Oh, shit."

"What's that about Jordan?" Travis asked.

"Jade was about to *not* tell you that Richard and I may be getting a divorce," Jordan said, entering the office.

Both Ned and he jumped to their feet.

"Please sit down," she said. "And it's okay, Jade. I'd rather Ned and Travis know everything. I'm not surprised to hear Margot was worrying about my being able to pay for a lawyer if—if things don't work out." She paused, struggling for composure, then continued. "What Margot's tried to do for Jade and me since Dad's and Nicole's deaths is pretty amazing. She's one of the bravest and strongest people I've ever met, and right now she's in her room crying her heart out over you, Travis." She pinned him with a hard stare. "So now that you've broken her heart, what are you going to do to fix it?"

Chapter ❧
TWENTY-NINE

TRAVIS WAS GONE. She'd expected it, predicted it, but the reality was worse than she could have imagined. He was gone, and yet not.

His spirit hovered, haunting her. She sensed him everywhere, her traitorous lover's ghost; saw him in the impeccably organized habits of Ned, Tito, Felix, and Andy, as they carried on, working with the horses as if Travis were still conducting the morning meetings, giving the day's instructions over steaming cups of coffee and fresh-from-the-oven bagels, which Felix picked up on his way to the farm.

He was with her when she rode Mystique and the other horses. She heard his voice offering her pointers, helping her to understand the animal beneath her, making her a better rider. And when she closed her eyes at the end of the day, he came to her and she felt the heat and glide of his hands, the weight of his leanly muscled body. And she would cry.

Thank God for Visine, cold cucumber slices, and carefully applied makeup. They allowed her to reconstruct the face that everyone expected to see, never mind that behind the façade lay a shattered ruin.

She managed to inject enough enthusiasm into her voice to fool Tracy Andrews and Simone Porter into believing she was thrilled at the prospect of having a horde of people descend on Rosewood. Charlie, of course, immediately detected that something was amiss; he'd studied her face for too many years. But she was able to prevent any painful probing on his part by revealing the additional reason for the shadows dimming her eyes: her concern for Jordan. She further diverted his attention by proposing that both Jordan and Jade be included in some of the *Vogue* profile shots.

"The Radcliffe sisters at Rosewood—modern beauties, Old South," he mused. "Yeah. We could have fun with that. Let me run it by Simone on the flight back." A minute later he turned to Keisha and began bouncing ideas off his assistant.

Tracy Andrews and Simone Porter spent their time waxing rhapsodic about how "awesome and real" Rosewood was. With the caffeine-fueled hyperenergy of so many in the business, they'd no sooner air-kissed Margot good-bye than they were whipping out their iPhones, speed-talking as they climbed into the rented Cadillac Escalade and roared down the drive.

Half an hour later, Margot got a call from Damien.

"Listening to Tracy's barrage of superlatives, one would be tempted to think she'd just visited Balmoral. This deal is becoming more delicious by the minute. As of now, the gigs will play as follows. Charlie, Keisha, Evan, and some lovely people from *Vogue* will be the opening act. The editors have decided they want Charlie to do a cover shot with you and the profile, pronto. They're delighted with the idea of including your sisters in the shoot, but they're balking at paying them. A shame, but c'est la fucking vie, love. And if Jade ever decides to model, you can bet I'll remember how stingy they were. Charlie's marshaling the troops as we speak. They'll be back at Rosewood just as soon as the wardrobe is selected. Ralph Lauren will be act two and lengthier— they'll want time to fuss over the rooms and drape paisley shawls over the settees and that sort of thing. I'll have Miranda express the *Vogue* contract to you as soon as I've gone over it. Coming to satisfactory terms with Ralph Lauren will take a little more time, but as you'll be busy with our darling Charlie . . ."

She should have been overjoyed; she'd taken a step toward securing Rosewood's future. But all she could think of was Travis. Where was he? Did he despise her? And God, why couldn't she despise *him*?

Because he wasn't solely to blame; this was her fault, too. She'd let fear prevent her from telling him how she felt.

No one mentioned Travis's name to her—not Ned and the guys, not Jade, not Jordan. They probably and perhaps rightly believed that by not uttering his name she was less likely to fall apart. Their concern showed in other countless ways, and despite her misery, Margot was deeply touched. It wasn't as if everyone didn't have worries of their own, Jordan's marital crisis topping them all.

Yet even though Jordan was an emotional wreck from protracted telephone conversations with Richard in which he alternated between being coldly accusatory and begging her to bring the kids home so they could patch things up, she had generously volunteered to help Ellie ready the house for the shoot and prepare the third-floor bedrooms for Charlie and the crew. Food was no problem as Jordan was baking up a storm with Kate and Max and they still had dozens of frozen casseroles packed away in the freezer.

And then there was Jade. She came home from school silent and drawn from the whispers trailing her from one classroom to the next, but she, too, was doing what she could: giving Kate and Max rides on Doc, and helping to exercise the horses Ned, Andy, and Margot hadn't been able to get to. Margot and her sisters' lives were in shambles, yet the three of them had never been more supportive of one another, or closer.

Belying his California laid-back demeanor, Charlie had moved at a lightning speed, organizing the shoot within forty-eight hours: booking Kristin for makeup, Palin for hair, and, in consultation with Simone Porter selecting a wardrobe that ranged from Badgley Mischka to YSL Rive Gauche, outfits not only in Margot's size but in Jordan's and Jade's as well.

Charlie and his crew were due to arrive within the hour.

If all went well, they'd be packing the gear back into the trucks on Friday.

Margot half-hoped some glitch would arise during the shoot that would force her to skip the Hunt Cup on Saturday. Had Travis been there to ride Colchester, to whisper "good luck" in her ear, and set her on fire with a kiss behind the van, she would never have entertained such a thought.

If the weather was any kind of predictor, however, the shoot would unfold with the meticulous precision of a Swiss watch. The sky was a flawless azure and the temperature had climbed back into the sixties. According to the forecast, the current warm front would linger into Sunday, which meant that if Charlie was seized by a notion to photograph her bikini-clad and cartwheeling across the lawn, she wouldn't have to be wrapped in thermal blankets between shots.

Jade had been let out of school early. She was beyond thrilled that Margot had arranged to let her miss school for the duration of the shoot. They were in the outdoor ring, Margot standing in its center, Jade astride Colchester. Margot had already finished riding Gulliver, her last horse of the day, and had showered and changed so as to be ready when Charlie arrived. He sometimes liked to jump straight into a shoot, with everyone scrambling to make it happen.

Perched on the wooden rollback, she watched Jade circle at a canter on Colchester. He was moving beautifully, his gait nicely collected, his ears swiveling back and forth as he listened to his young rider.

"You know, Jade, if you want to ride Colchester in the Hunt Cup, I'd be fine with that."

"Oh, no, that's all right. Tra—I mean, *Doc* would be really disappointed if I didn't take him. Doc's been so patient, taking Kate and Max around the ring these past couple of days, he deserves a fun morning's gallop."

Margot was proud of herself. She hadn't dissolved into a puddle at hearing the three first letters of Travis's name.

"Yeah, but we're trying to sell Colchester. Maybe I should ride him."

"No, you should stick with Mystique." Jade shifted in the saddle and closed her hands around the reins. As smooth as satin, Colchester went from a canter to an extended trot. "You two are great together, and if you want to breed her this spring, it'll be good for people to see her on the course."

"We may not have a stud to cover any of our mares this spring," Margot reminded her.

Jade opened her mouth and then shut it with a snap. A few strides later she said in a reproving tone, "You know, I really can't talk now. I have to concentrate on Colchester."

Such the budding professional. "Right. I'll leave the ring to you." In the distance, she heard the rumble of car engines and checked her watch. They must have floored it down Route 95, she thought. "Looks like it's showtime for me anyway," she said.

Taking a deep breath, she slid off the jump and prepared to go be Margot Radcliffe the glamorous supermodel, a role that might help save Rosewood but had cost her Travis.

The meeting of her two worlds was wild, to say the least, Margot thought, gazing at the double parlor. With Charlie's arrival, the space was utterly transformed. The rugs were rolled away to expose the lustrous parquet, the paintings removed to highlight the intricate moldings and Corinthian columns, the furniture cleared until only a few pieces remained: the chaise longue, a petit-point-covered bench, a marble-topped side table, and a silk-upholstered armchair. Towering klieg lights and reflectors were positioned to illuminate whatever areas captured Charlie's eye.

Keisha and Evan had spent the past hour and a half setting up the room with Charlie directing. When Jade and Jordan came in, he explained what he was aiming for in the shoot to them and Margot.

"Ralph Lauren will be coming into these rooms a couple

of weeks from now. I'm trying to create the absolute antithesis of Ralph's look. I want lots of mood and drama. Empty space filled with ghosts. I want to see the grand architecture of this place brought into high relief and the three of you decked out in these incredibly beautiful gowns. It'll be a modern take on a lost past when life was full of balls and soirees, a life the three of you are descended from. We'll start here in the parlor first. Then I want to move to the front hall so I can play with that incredible circular staircase. Tomorrow we can head outside onto the porch and the grounds. And we gotta do something with those chestnut trees, right, Keisha?"

"Absolutely, Charlie."

"Hey, guys," he called to Kristin and Palin, who were chatting on the chaise longue. "Let's get Margot gorgeous. And while I'm photographing her, you can start on Jade and Jordan. I want romantic, soft looks—updos that show off their killer bone structure. Palin, what do you think about leaving a few hanging strands for Jade?"

"Definitely," Palin said, nodding. "Mix in a little spice with the nice."

"You've got the idea. Kristin, I want big, dramatic eyes. You all know what you're doing? Okay, let's rock it."

Margot made to follow Palin to the station he'd set up next to Kristin, but paused when Jordan plucked her sleeve. "Margot, I'm not sure I can do this. I don't know how to pose or anything and I'm not beau—"

"Stop," she commanded softly. "You are beautiful and you're going to be amazed at how you look once Kristin's through with you. She's a magician. I've plunked myself down in her chair looking like something the cat dragged in. Forty-five minutes later, abracadabra. In the hands of a true artist, I can look pretty darn stunning. Have fun with this, Jordan. Remember when we were little and played with Mom's dresses? This is just like that, only the dresses fit."

"Not mine. Richard said I was getting hu—"

"Sweetie, I am not going to spoil the afternoon by telling you what I think of Richard." She took Jordan by the shoulders. "You *are* beautiful, and when Richard sees you looking absolutely stunning on the pages of *Vogue*, I hope he chokes on every small, crappy thing he's said to you."

"I love you, Margot. And thanks for asking Charlie to include us in the shoot."

"A profile of me here at Rosewood without you and Jade in it wouldn't have made any sense."

Jordan bit her lip as if debating what she was about to say. "Margot, I don't want you to be unhappy about—"

"I'm not." She shook her head. "I'm not even thinking of Travis." She said his name deliberately, as if that might exorcise him from her soul. "And maybe when he sees how beautiful Kristin, Palin, and Charlie are going to make me, he'll feel pretty rotten." Unlikely, though, as Travis was the last man on earth she could imagine buying a copy of *Vogue*. Even if he did, what would he see but what he'd always seen?

"Margot, he—"

"Can't talk anymore." She would cry if she did. She stepped back, pinning a saucy smile to her face, a smile that felt as heavy as her leaden heart. "Now let's go show Charlie what we Radcliffe girls are made of."

Margot had told Jordan the absolute truth. Palin and Kristin were gifted artists, and when they were finished, Jade, dressed in a gauzy, clingy, beaded chiffon dress by Alberta Ferretti, and Jordan, in a raspberry satin and tulle dress by Badgely Mischka, looked absolutely spectacular.

The shoot was intense, Charlie totally absorbed in capturing the images he was seeing in his mind's eye. Despite their inexperience, Jade and Jordan quickly got into the spirit of the thing, striking the poses and donning the expressions Charlie called for with far more ease than Margot herself did. No matter that Palin had the Fine Young Cannibals blasting out of his Bose speakers, Margot felt like *she* was the one being driven crazy. Perhaps it was Charlie's mention of Rosewood's ghosts. She certainly had her own phantom. Travis haunted as superbly as he did everything else. And her yearning and wanting was as sharp as a knife.

Charlie's decision to quit for the day was met with a unanimous sigh of relief. At dinner they gathered around the long dining room table, consuming a vast salad Ellie had prepared, assorted reheated casseroles, and piping-hot rolls. Jordan's killer brownies disappeared just as quickly, with only Margot abstaining, contenting herself with a cup of blackberry tea. By the time the dishes were cleared and put away, it was past midnight.

After kissing everyone good night, she crawled into a bed she hated because it lacked what she needed most: Travis's body curled about hers. She lay staring up at the ceiling, willing herself to sleep and praying that sometime during tomorrow's daylong shoot, when Charlie's camera would be focused exclusively on her, she would be able to summon a smile.

Charlie tossed the idea out over a breakfast of Jordan's mouth-watering blueberry pancakes—Margot's own breakfast consisting of oatmeal sprinkled with walnuts and chunks of apples. "How about using one of your horses for the shoot, babe?"

She toyed with her spoon. She didn't know how to explain her reluctance to bring the horses literally into the picture because by doing so Travis would be right there with them. She didn't want Charlie to know how badly she was hurting. "Sure, Charlie. I'll have to go down and talk to Ned to find out when the best time would be. He's kind of particular."

"Actually, babe, he already gave it the A-OK. I had Jade go ask him. I understand the horses come first here."

"Ned said it was all right?" It was true, Ned had been incredibly kind following Travis's departure, not uttering a single word of blame for her failure to keep him at

Rosewood. But she hadn't forgotten how offended he'd been by her decision to use Rosewood and its horses in a shoot. She'd hate for him to think she didn't care about his opinion. "Um, maybe I should just go down to the barn and make sure," she said.

"That's fine. Meanwhile, I'm going to charm your sister into whipping up another stack of pancakes. She's got real talent."

"Jordan's good at everything she does. But you should make your appreciation known, Charlie. She needs to hear something nice from a cute guy."

"Well, I am that."

"Yeah, you are," she agreed. "So use that charm for good, cute guy."

"Will do."

She couldn't understand Ned. She was sure he'd at least bring up how busy he and the guys were getting Mystique and Doc Holliday ready for the Hunt Cup tomorrow. With Travis gone and her time taken up with the shoot, they were down by two pairs of hands. "You're certain you can spare the time, Ned?"

"Sure, I am."

"And what horse do you think would work? I don't want to risk—"

"We'll use Stoneleigh. He's a beaut and seasoned—he won't spook at a bunch of bright lights and whatnot," Ned said, with his typical pride. Indeed, he struck her as almost enthusiastic about the photo shoot. But for all his gung-ho attitude, he wouldn't meet her gaze. This must be so hard for him, having to pretend he was all for Stoneleigh being photographed when it went against everything he believed in as a horseman. She wasn't going to make it harder for him by continuing to question him.

"That's a great idea, Stoneleigh will be perfect. I'll ask Jade to come down and help get him ready. When do you think you can have him ready?"

"Well, that's a bit of a problem. We should let Stoneleigh have his normal turnout time and maybe Andy should hop on him for a little to get him nice and relaxed. Then we've got to bathe him. Don't think he'll be ready until much, much later," he warned, with a fierce frown at his watch.

Here was the Ned she knew and loved: always putting the horse first. She wasn't going to push him to set an exact hour for all the money in the world. "That's all right. Charlie will have a lot of other shots to take first." Impulsively she kissed his cheek. "Thanks, Ned. I really appreciate your help in this. I realize it's not what you wanted."

Scarlet flags stained his weathered face. "You know we'd all do anything for you, Miss Margot," he returned thickly, before whipping out his handkerchief and blowing loudly. "You go on now. I'll bring the stallion out when I can."

Margot had lost track of the wardrobe changes and adjustments to her hair and makeup that Charlie had called for during the course of the day's shoot. She'd never known him to be this fussy. Then again, he seemed to be truly inspired by the visual opportunities Rosewood offered. Like a kid on Christmas morning, he wanted to try everything and have her pose everywhere: lounging on the porch in a body-hugging citrine evening dress by Zac Posen, nestling against the trunk of one of the old chestnut trees wrapped in a bloodred satin and velvet cape by Yves Saint Laurent, hanging from one of its bare limbs in a flirty chiffon cocktail dress by Balenciaga, twirling and leaping across the lawn and then dropping down to sit like Little Miss Muffet in a silver Nina Ricci. Charlie had gone through hundreds of frames. She was getting really tired of trying to be beautiful. And Ned had yet to bring Stoneleigh out.

It was past two o'clock and despite the balmy weather, the November sun was already at an angle. Yet Charlie had made no mention of the promised horse; this was an incredible display of patience, even for someone as mellow as he.

During one of the short breaks, while Charlie, Evan, and Keisha were doing a light-meter reading, Margot took the opportunity to speak to Jade. "Hey, Jade, where's Jordan?" Both her sisters had been watching the shoot from the sidelines, with Kate nestled on Jordan's lap and Max playing with his fire truck by her feet.

"She had to go upstairs and put Kate and Max down for their naps. Said to keep her seat warm. She can't wait to see what you're going to wear next."

Margot was happy to hear the shoot was providing a pleasant distraction for Jordan. "Listen, would you mind doing me a favor?"

"Sure."

"Would you go down to the barn and see what's keeping Ned?" She had told herself she wasn't going to rush him, but this was becoming absurd. Ned was surely finished grooming Stoneleigh by now.

"Nothing's *keeping* Ned. You know what he's like. He won't bring Stoneleigh out until he's show perfect."

"Could you do it anyway, maybe lend him a hand? I don't want to hold up the shoot."

Jade's brows drew together.

"Please?" she asked.

"Oh, all right," Jade said peevishly. "Not that it will make any difference. Ned's not going to bring him any faster just because I'm there."

Bemused, Margot shook her head as Jade stomped off. What was up with Jade? She knew full well that Ned positively doted on her and that she could get him to do anything. But then Charlie was calling out, "Okay, Margot, come on back. Kristin, can you give her foundation a touch-up?"

More poses, more wardrobe changes, more makeup and hair adjustments. Margot was growing numb with fatigue.

And then Jade was tearing over the lawn, a wide smile splitting her face. "He's coming. Just give him a few minutes and he'll be here. He looks fantastic. Totally awesome."

Margot's brows rose at Jade's enthusiasm. Then again, even at nearly twenty Stoneleigh was a beautiful horse. Maybe Ned had used a bluing shampoo in his tail to make it extra white and shiny. "Thanks, sweetie."

"Margot, why don't you change into that Vera Wang now?"

"You want me to change?" she asked in confusion. She'd only just been zipped into the Stella McCartney.

"Yeah," Charlie replied, fiddling with his camera. "The light's changed and the colors are all wrong. The lavender-blue of the Wang will work much better with the tans and golds of the landscape. Right, Evan?"

"Absolutely, Charlie."

"Okay, back in a few."

"Take your time, babe. And Kristin, give me a deeper red for her lips."

"Gotcha, Charlie."

And so Margot, Kristin, and Palin trudged back to the house for yet another wardrobe change and more fussing with her hair and skin.

Palin had used a curling iron to make her hair fall in soft waves about her shoulders. Kristin had retouched her makeup with a different blush, a red-wine-colored lipstick, and a hint of brown shadow around Margot's mascaraed eyes. When they slipped the silk-tulle Vera Wang on her, the blue-violet hue of the dress turned her eyes a deep, fathomless blue.

"Wow," Palin said. "We did some good work here."

"You guys always do good work," Margot replied, not bothering with a second glance in the mirror. Why would she possibly care how she looked? She just hoped Ned had

Stoneleigh so that they could get the shot done and call it a wrap.

Charlie had decided that he wanted to use the lawn by the front of the house for the last shot. With the fields behind the lawn mowed, the sweep of greenish brown continued uninterrupted all the way to the tree line.

Margot made her way over to him. He was talking to Jade about the shot and letting her look through the camera's viewfinder so she could see what he was trying to achieve with the setting.

Jade caught sight of Margot through the lens and lowered the camera. "Whoa. You look amazing."

"So where's Ned?" she asked.

"He, uh—he's—"

"Not to worry," Charlie chimed in. "I want to do some close-ups of you first. You look real good, babe."

"It's a nice dress. Where do you want me?"

"Over there."

She nodded. And the routine recommenced. It amazed her that even after so many hours she could practically feel the crackling excitement emanating from Charlie and the others. They were really something else, this bunch: die-hard fashion junkies.

Charlie rattled off instructions as his shutter drive whirred away. Margot followed them automatically, so focused she hardly registered Jade's voice eagerly announcing, "He's here, Charlie."

"And about fucking time, too," he replied with equal parts amusement and exasperation. "Okay, babe, look left for me and hold it. That's right. Just watch him coming toward you . . ."

Finally, Margot thought, as she caught sight of Stoneleigh coming up the drive. Then her gaze sharpened. Could it be a trick of the light that was making Stoneleigh's dapple gray look so much darker? Or maybe he'd brought out Faraday instead? No, there were no white socks. She looked again. She'd never seen this horse before and that wasn't Ned. That was . . . She froze.

"Hello, Margot," he said solemnly.

He was dressed in his outlaw black of dusty jeans and a black button-down shirt. His face was shadowed with stubble, his hair mussed as if he'd been raking his fingers through it. His gray eyes regarded her steadily.

Without a word, she turned and walked away.

Travis sighed. What had he expected after he'd hurt her so? That Margot would simply forget the callous things he'd said, throw her arms around him, and kiss him? With his gaze locked on her, he held out the lead.

"Boy, is she heated." Jade's voice was filled with awe.

"Yeah. Thanks for the news flash. Take him, will you?"

Margot had gone to stand at the edge of the field. Still as a statue, her arms were clasped about her middle. He approached her quietly, as he might an easily spooked filly.

Coming to a stop, he spoke to her stony profile. "I've been an ass, Margot. I only wish I could take back the things I said out of blind stupidity and jealousy. I said those things in the office the other day because I was being eaten alive by my doubts. I couldn't believe that you, so beautiful and talented, so special, might care for me—Red Maher's son. Because even while we were together and I was happier than I've ever been in my whole life, a part of me was waiting for you to toss me aside for what you really loved, your life in New York and Paris and Milan, and for a man who could be a part of that world. It's why I went crazy every time Charlie Ayer telephoned. I thought—"

"You thought that in addition to being a superficial, pleasure-loving twit, I was also willing to slum it and sleep with you until I could hook Charlie or some millionaire playboy?" Her lips had hardly moved but the words were precise, and as cutting as jagged glass.

He winced. "Like I said, I've been a blind idiot. But deep

down, I knew better. I saw how hard you were working on the farm, how determined you were to get through to Jade. I knew it when we made love and you cried in my arms. Making love to you was like nothing I've ever felt before." His voice turned ragged, rough with emotion. "Come on, Margot, where's that fiery spirit? Give me hell. Yell, scream, tear a piece off my hide for all the ways I've hurt you. I deserve it all. Only please love me. Forgive me."

"You left me."

Her bleak tone made him want to drop to his knees. "Yeah, I did. Leaving you was the most difficult thing I've ever done in my life, Margot. Once I learned the truth and finally understood what was going on, it was the only way I could see to helping you. Believe me, I haven't stopped thinking about you once since I left."

"What do you mean, 'the truth'?" For the first time her gaze wavered to glance obliquely at him.

"Your sisters came to the office and explained everything. Why didn't you tell me what you all were going through? Did you think I'd turn my back on you? Yeah, you did, and I can't blame you. I repeatedly made it impossible for you to trust me." He shook his head, filled with self-disgust.

She was still refusing to look at him, he thought sadly. "Listen, Margot, I've been on the road since I left you, first hauling Raider out to eastern Long Island. Dan would have delivered him himself, but I needed to see that Raider was settled and doing fine. Then I—"

"Why's Raider on Long Island?"

"I sold him."

"You sold Night Raider?" She turned to face him, her lovely eyes troubled, and he fell that much more in love with her for her obvious concern.

He stepped closer, his dusty boots grazing the hem of her gossamer evening dress. "Margot, if I'd had even an inkling of what you were going through, I'd have urged you to sell him to Dan the very day he inquired about him. Raider's a horse, a potentially great horse. It's you I love."

He reached out and touched her, his fingertips lightly skimming the side of her face. And when she turned her face to press closer into his palm, his heart expanded painfully, set to burst from happiness.

"I'm so sorry—" Margot's voice was choked with emotion. "I should have told you. It was so wrong of me—"

"Shh, you have nothing to apologize about," he whispered urgently. Withdrawing an envelope from the back pocket of his jeans, he handed it to her. "Here. This is for you. I got a really good price for Raider. No, don't cry, love. Raider will be in great hands with Steve Sheppard. There's a little extra in that envelope, too. Ned's check and mine from your father. And—"

"No, Travis! You can't give—"

"Yeah, we can. And Ned told me that if you try to return his check to him, he'll tear the damned thing up. Quote unquote. As for me, don't you understand? It's not money that's important. *It's you, Margot.* You're my love, my one love. You're my everything. If you'll let me, I'll spend every day of the rest of our lives proving it to you."

With a cry, Margot flung her arms about his neck. Joy flooded him, bursting out of him in a laugh of relief and happiness. He clasped her tightly, lifting her off her feet and twirling her in a circle as she, too, laughed, tears slipping down her cheeks while applause broke out around them.

His steps slowed as his mouth found hers. And when he kissed Margot he knew that he was truly and finally home.

Travis was still kissing Margot when a finger poked him squarely into his back. Reluctantly he released her to turn and stare blankly at Jade.

"Hate to interrupt, but Charlie would kind of like to get this last shot done and pack up the equipment. Travis, you forgot a kind of major thing here. Here you go, sis."

She grinned, passing Margot a lead rope . . . a lead rope attached to a beautiful horse.

Travis grinned. "Thanks, Jade. I had a few other things on my mind. Margot, I'd like you to meet Nocturne, your new stud, and, I hope, Rosewood's future."

Dazed, Margot looked at the dark gray stallion. She, too, had forgotten all about the horse Travis had been leading across the lawn. "Travis, he's incredible-looking," she breathed. "How, where—"

"He's a Thoroughbred from Kentucky. I got a tip from Steve Sheppard about him and hightailed it down there. I managed to negotiate a deal—I'll tell you all about it later," he promised. "Charlie Ayer needs that face of yours."

She searched his face, finding none of the former censure in it, seeing only love and pride in his eyes. She smiled tremulously. "Do you want to meet Charlie?"

"I guess it's past time I met the guy whose neck I've been wanting to wring."

"He really is a good friend. It's you I love."

"Damn, but I've wanted to hear you say that," he whispered, already drawing her back for another kiss.

Hand in hand, they led Nocturne over to Charlie.

"Travis, this is Charlie Ayer. Charlie, this is Travis Maher." She watched the two men size each other up, curious at the smile that spread over Travis's face.

"And Margot chose me."

Charlie cocked his brow. She held her breath, waiting to see how he'd respond.

"Man, you don't have to go and rub it in. Yeah, Margot chose you. Not that there was any real contest. If I had ever thought I stood a real chance, I'd have given it everything to win Margot." He sighed. "As it is, I'll have to console myself with all the other women who adore me."

"At least you'll be busy," Margot teased.

"You bet." Charlie smiled at her. "I hate to admit it, babe, but this guy brings out the best in you. I've never seen you look as beautiful. Mind if I borrow her?" he asked Travis.

Travis lifted Margot's hand, brushing his lips over her knuckles. "No, I don't mind." Angling his head, he spoke softly into her ear. "Go do your thing. I'll be waiting. I love you."

She leaned into him, brushing her lips against his cheek. "I love you, too," she said solemnly. "I always have. I always will."

He gazed deeply into her eyes, his hand warm and strong as it clasped hers. "Marry me, Margot. Be mine."

Her breath caught as her heart overflowed with happiness. "Yes," she replied, nodding tremulously.

"Say, Charlie," Travis said, his eyes never straying from her smiling face. "You do weddings, too?"

IN THE END, Charlie had photographed not just Margot but Travis and Nocturne as well, falling in love with the contrasting textures between the light-as-air tulle confection Margot wore, Travis's travel-creased, jet-black garb, and the slate-gray of Nocturne's shiny coat.

Charlie succeeded in coaxing Travis before the camera by telling him that the *Vogue* editors were going to flip once they learned they had exclusive pics of Margot Radcliffe's fiancé. Travis's agreement would earn Margot major brownie points with the editorial staff.

To see Travis submitting to Palin's and Kristin's ministrations—minimal compared to what they'd had to do to repair her tear-streaked face—served as added proof of the lengths Travis was willing to go to demonstrate his support, and Margot's heart swelled with love.

Her happiness was a physical thing: a golden, incandescent warmth that flowed through her. It must have shown, for after the series of shots on the lawn, Charlie whisked her inside, framing her against a light monotone backdrop Keisha and Evan had set up. Picking up his Nikon, he'd zoomed in for a close-up, giving her a single prompt: "Think Travis."

The shoot was finished, the equipment all packed away in the back of the rental truck. Margot, Jordan, and Jade walked Charlie to where he'd parked his rented SUV.

"Ladies, this has been a blast," Charlie said, stopping a few feet short of the car. "Jade, I'm going to express some proof sheets to you. I'll be waiting for your input. And kid, if you want to give modeling a whirl, I happen to know an agent who'd be real happy to sign you on."

Jade's eyes widened with astonishment, unable to believe what Charlie was saying. She glanced at Margot for confirmation.

The moment was bittersweet. Margot remembered the night Charlie had said those same words to her as if it were yesterday. Now her younger sister was being offered the chance to represent the next generation of faces. But Margot realized she would happily cede her place to Jade and do everything she could to help her in the business. She had her own future with Travis to look forward to.

"You'd be great at modeling, Jade, if it's what you want to do."

Jade was silent. Then, with a smile, she shook her head. "Thanks for the offer, Charlie. Right now my sisters need me. And this new horse I'm riding is going to need a lot of attention. Maybe I'll give modeling a shot later on."

Jordan and Margot exchanged looks, and Margot easily intuited her sister's thoughts, certain that they mirrored her own. What an amazing person Jade was turning out to be. Not many sixteen-year-old girls could resist such a lure.

Charlie didn't seem surprised by her decision. "Like I said before, you're one smart kid. Besides, there's no rush. Looks like yours will keep. But put me on speed-dial in case you change your mind." He glanced at his watch. "Time the gang and I hit the road. New York's gonna seem a pretty dull place compared to good old Warburg, VA."

Turning to Jordan, he gave her a hug. "Bye, beautiful. Thanks for the gracious hospitality. And make sure you remember what I said."

"I'll try. You're a kind man, Charlie Ayer. I hope I'll see you again very soon."

"After getting me to agree to shoot the wedding, I think Travis will make sure of that," he said with a laugh. Wrapping an arm about Margot, he pulled her close. "You better be prepared to have Damien ringing you nonstop with bookings. You're gonna be the hottest ticket in town once this *Vogue* cover hits the shelves."

No longer troubled by the competing demands of modeling and running the farm now that she was sure of Travis's love and secure in the knowledge that together they would work out a balance, she smiled. "Maybe I'll only take the jobs where a certain shaggy Californian is behind the viewfinder."

"Works for me, babe." He grinned, pressing a kiss to her forehead. Releasing her, he opened the car door and climbed inside. "So long. I'll call you tomorrow. I love you, babe."

The three of them watched the SUV and the equipment truck roll down the drive and disappear from sight.

Margot turned to her sisters. "So I guess I have you two to thank for going behind my back and saving me from throwing away my chance at love."

"Yeah, you do. And so does Travis. You owe us big-time," Jade said happily. Without missing a beat, she asked, "So do you think Travis'll teach me how to drive Mom's Porsche?"

Margot hid a smile. "Why don't you ask him?"

"I will. I gotta go over to the barn anyway to start braiding."

"I'd almost forgotten about the Hunt Cup," Margot confessed. "You don't have to braid if you're too tired, Jade."

"I'm not that tired. Besides, I want Doc to look extra special since this may be my last competition with him. And Mystique and Colchester have to look just as good when we get our picture taken with the Cup trophy." She went off at a jog toward the barns, leaving Jordan and Margot alone.

"What I wouldn't give for a thimbleful of Jade's confidence," Margot said.

"You and me both," Jordan agreed.

Margot enfolded her older sister in a hug.

"I've got to say it again. Thanks, sis, for being my

guardian angel and taking care of my heart. Especially when yours is close to breaking."

"It did it good to know you're happy," she said. More quietly she continued. "Seeing you with Travis made me realize that I have to go back to Richard and do whatever it takes to fix what's broken between us. If we're lucky we'll find our love again. I'm going to take the kids home to D.C. after we meet with Edward Crandall about the estate."

Margot squeezed her hand. "I think you're doing the right thing. You know we're always here for you, Jordan."

"I do know. I'm pretty darn lucky to have such amazing sisters. And such incredible friends." Jordan gave her a tremulous smile. "Speaking of friends, I want to go down to the barn and thank Ned and Travis for all they've done."

"Do you want to go now?"

"Definitely." Jordan threaded her arm through Margot's and together they started toward the barns. "I want to catch Jade at work on Travis, wheedling him into giving her Porsche-driving lessons. Want to hear something incredible, Margot?"

"I would."

"As wild as Jade is at times, if she gets her license, I'll trust her with Kate and Max in the backseat of that Porsche."

"Yeah. I certainly never thought I'd say this, but she's a pretty fantastic Radcliffe."

It was evening. Margot and Travis were alone on the porch, Jordan and Jade having shooed them out of the kitchen after dinner, insisting they would tackle the dishes. The springlike temperatures had disappeared with the setting sun. Margot sat on the step beneath Travis, her back nestled between his muscled thighs, her arms blanketed by his. The warmth of his body felt delicious, as did the kisses he was scattering in her hair, along the nape of her neck, in the sensitive hollow behind her ears.

The most wonderful thing of all, though, was the deep rumble of his voice as he talked to her, telling her about how he'd sold Raider to the Olympian rider Steve Sheppard and how generous Sheppard had been in offering him the tip about Nocturne, a stallion at his father's Thoroughbred farm down in Kentucky. "Nocturne's gorgeous. Perfect conformation. A real nice mover, too. He just doesn't have the speed to be a racehorse. Shepp's father had only decided on selling him last week. We really lucked out."

They had indeed. Margot had almost fainted at dinner when she'd finally opened the envelope Travis had given her. The three checks totaled $350,000. Combined with the money she'd get from the *Vogue* shoot and the Ralph Lauren contract, they'd be able to make serious inroads paying off the estate's outstanding debts.

"Travis, how did you afford Nocturne?"

She felt his shrug against her back. "I had some money set aside, earmarked for a horse. And Steve Sheppard Senior was real reasonable, though I did promise I'd offer Shepp first dibs on Nocturne's get. Only fair, since I sold Raider to him for one hundred fifty thousand."

"I would be proud to know that Steve Sheppard has one of Rosewood's horses. He did such an outstanding job at the Olympics last summer."

"I kind of thought you'd say that." He was silent for a moment. When he continued, his voice was husky. "Margot, I have enough money left over for an engagement ring. Did I rush you when I asked you to marry me? If you want to wait—"

She shifted on the step so that she could gaze up at him. "I'd marry you tomorrow if we didn't have a Hunt Cup to win."

"That right?" He laughed softly. "So, Hunt Cup first, marriage second?"

"That's right," she said, nodding. "I want to see the look on Edward Crandall's face when you, Jade, and I hold that trophy aloft."

He tilted her chin and brought his lips to hers, drinking in her smile. "Have I told you that I love you?"

"Only about five minutes ago." She rose on her knees to kiss him lingeringly in return, luxuriating in the sensual heat slowly building between them, knowing it would be theirs for a lifetime. "Tell me again," she whispered.

Acknowledgments

I owe a great debt of gratitude to my agent, Elaine Markson, and to Linda Marrow, Kate Collins, and Charlotte Herscher of Ballantine Books, who have worked with me these many years. Thank you for your infinite patience, wisdom, and humor. Without you I would not have been able to write this book.

And finally, thank you, Charles, for everything.

Read on for an excerpt from

BELIEVE IN ME,

by Laura Moore,

published by Ballantine Books.

"AND HOW DO YOU FEEL, Jordan? Do you believe Richard's been doing everything he can to prove his commitment to your marriage?" Abby Walsh asked in a voice modulated so that it conveyed just the right blend of sympathy, compassion, and reserve.

Indeed, everything about Dr. Abby Walsh, her smooth, lineless face, her sleek silver bob, her wardrobe of muted silk and jersey knits, was designed to soothe. As was the decor of her T Street office in Washington, D.C.: its light-sand-and-dove-gray palette, requisite black leather sofa with matching armchairs, Joan Mitchell–like paintings, Tang dynasty ceramics—reproductions, Jordan assumed, but maybe not, considering Abby's hourly rate for couple's therapy—and the dried arrangement of starflowers and corkscrew and pussy willow in a tall green raku vase positioned in the corner. Even the boxes of Kleenex were placed just so on the amoeba-shaped coffee table to mop up untidy tears.

Jordan and Richard had been coming once a week for the past ten months to this office to discuss with the perfectly coiffed Abby Walsh their feelings and their progress in rebuilding their marriage, ever since Jordan had discovered that Richard was cheating on her with an associate from his lobbying firm while she was four-and-a-half months pregnant with their third child, and she had come to despise this room as much as she now loathed being asked how something "made her feel."

As Jordan had discovered in the months following his betrayal, her feelings were pretty much like the floral arrangement in the raku vase sitting there in the corner: dry and brittle, and every time she was asked to bring them out into the open for Richard and Abby to poke at, they crumbled to dust.

"Jordan?" Abby prompted.

"Hmm? I'm sorry." She shifted on the couch and tucked a stray lock of hair behind her ear. "Olivia had a bad night. What was the question?"

"You see," Richard said, leaning forward, intent on Abby. "Every time *I* talk about us, she brings up the children. It's like she wants to remind me of what a failure I am."

"I'm not saying that you're a failure, Richard. I know you love the children and want to be a good father. I'm simply saying I'm tired because Olivia's colicky and didn't fall asleep until two this morning." And then five-year-old Kate and three-year-old Max were up at six, raring to go, and Richard had already left for the gym to get his workout in before a breakfast meeting.

"Right, sure," he huffed, crossing his arms. He was wearing one of his charcoal gray pinstriped suits.

Was it in this jacket's pocket that she'd discovered the condoms that had exposed his treachery? Try as she might, Jordan couldn't suppress the memory that flashed in her mind, of her in the bedroom of their townhouse, clutching the jacket she was taking to the dry cleaners, staring stupidly at the foil squares she'd found in the inner breast pocket. They'd practically glowed, sizzling hot with their alarm-red packaging. The shock of finding them was so great, she'd had to read and reread the word LOVE printed in big, bold letters across the packaging, underneath the promise of extra lubrication, before she actually understood what she was looking at. They'd been so absurd-looking. How funny that they'd managed to shatter a marriage of nine years.

"I get it," Richard continued. "You want to drive home the point that I didn't do my share last night and rock Olivia to sleep?" Richard said. "Well, I'm *sorry* that I have to work sixteen hours a day to provide for our family and pay the mortgage on our house. I'm *sorry* nothing I do satisfies you. Do you see what I have to deal with here, Abby? I'm constantly being judged and found lacking."

Jordan massaged her forehead. "That's not true. I don't blame you for your job or its hours. I know how demanding a firm like Hudson and White is. I've never complained about the long workdays you put in. It's that you chose to pad those hours sleeping with Cynthia Delaroux—"

"I can't believe it," Richard said, cutting her off. "I feel like I'm on a merry-go-round. How many times do I have to say it? Cynthia and I are over. I'm fully committed to you and the kids. I love you. What more do you want from me?"

He wasn't the only who was tired of uttering the same thing over and over again. "I want to be able to trust you again. I want to believe that when you kiss me it's because you really love me." Because these days, even Richard's most casual caress struck her as calculated.

"Why in hell would I kiss you or touch you if I didn't want to?"

"I don't know," she said for the millionth time since last November. It was true. Jordan felt as though she didn't know anything anymore. When Richard broke her heart and her sense of trust, her sense of everything else was destroyed, too. She doubted herself as much as she doubted him. She hated that. Even more she hated that these sessions had become a weekly competition between them, where she reminded him of the myriad ways he'd hurt her, and he accused her of being cold and unforgiving. She hated that every week she walked out of Abby Walsh's office half-convinced Richard was right. She hadn't always been like this. They hadn't been like this.

"I think what Jordan's saying, Richard, is that she wants the kind of relationship you two enjoyed before, and I can tell how hard you're trying to make that happen for her."

On his side of the sofa, Richard nodded his sandy blond head energetically, as if he were at a meeting with one of his clients.

"And while you two may not perceive it, I do feel real progress is being made here." Abby paused. "I know how hard it's been with Olivia and her feeding and erratic sleeping schedule, but getting away might do you good, give you a chance to break out of the rut of the daily routine. What are your plans for the coming weekend?" she asked.

"We *are* actually going away," Jordan said as Richard simultaneously answered loudly, as if hoping his comment would get into Abby's notes for the day, "Some break, going to Rosewood and being surrounded by your sisters and their constant disapproval."

Jordan stiffened. "The only reason they disapprove is because you hurt me. And they've been making every effort to forgive you. They're pleased you're coming." Okay, that was an exaggeration. Her sisters, Margot and Jade, were willing to tolerate Richard's presence for her and the children's sake. As for Travis, Margot's husband, Jordan still remembered how, after learning about Richard's infidelity, he'd taken her aside and offered to "fix" him for her. He'd been as fiercely protective as any brother, and she would always love him for that.

"How magnanimous of them." He drummed his fingers on the arm of the sofa. "I love that my morals are being judged by a fashion model, her redneck husband, and a surly, delinquent teenager."

"Richard, I don't think that's a productive attitude. Surely you can—"

Jordan cut off Abby's gentle admonition. "My sisters are pretty damned fantastic," she snapped. "Margot has almost single-handedly gotten my family's home and farm out of debt with her modeling, and Jade has had to deal with the tragedy of losing both her parents in a horrific accident. I would hope you'd understand how a scared and confused teenager can behave stupidly. And Travis is one of the most talented horsemen in Virginia."

"He acts like he'd enjoy castrating me," he said defensively. Though Richard would die before admitting it, Jordan knew her brother-in-law intimidated him.

But she wasn't going to let Richard attack her family after all they'd done for her. "You know, Richard, you might find your own family a bit judgmental if you ever bothered to tell them what you did with Cynthia. Instead you've kept them in the dark. You don't even want me to talk to our friends about what's going on, so how can you blame me that I turn to my sisters for support when I'm about to explode from all this stuff churning inside me? Or do you want me to have no one?"

"Easy there, settle down," he said, holding his hands up as if to halt her outburst before it reached the offices of Hudson & White, on K Street. "You know I like your sisters, babe. I'm just sick of dealing with their negativity. And the reason I haven't told my family about the stuff we've been going through is simple. I don't want to worry my folks when I know that you and I are going to work this thing out and that our marriage will be stronger than ever."

It was hard to stay angry when he sounded so reasonable. His hand, which only seconds ago had warded her off, dropped to the middle cushion of the sofa and slid across the black leather to cover her clenched one. "I was a stupid idiot last year. I don't want you hurt ever again. I love you." His warm hand squeezed hers lightly.

Jordan looked at him searchingly. But Richard's hazel gaze was level, and when he smiled, a teasing twinkle lit his eyes. In that moment Jordan thought she glimpsed the man whom she'd promised to love and cherish, for better or for worse. Hope flickered, caught, and flared to life. *God, please let us find a way back to loving each other.*

"Well, I think it's easy enough to understand Richard's point of view here," Abby said, warm approval in her voice. "I can't stress how important it is during this period of rebuilding your relationship that you be aware of each other's needs."

"Yes, I guess it is," Jordan agreed softly.

Richard's mouth twitched as if he were suppressing a grin. His expression invited her to share in his mirth. And for a moment it was as if they were newly wed again. She gave a small answering smile.

"Our time's nearly up for today. As I said before, I think you two are making some real progress. Now, let's go back to your weekend plans. It's great you're getting away."

Richard spoke. "Yes. Jordan and the kids are going this afternoon. I'll drive up tomorrow, hopefully in time for dinner. I wish I could take a Friday off, but I'm swamped with work."

"Well, you'll be there for the weekend," Abby said easily. "So here's what I'd like the two of you to concentrate on while you're at Rosewood. Jordan, as you'll be arriving first, it's going to be your job to lay the groundwork. I'd like you to take shameless advantage of your sisters and ask them to watch the kids so that you and Richard can steal away and spend some time together. Go out and take a walk, shop, have a candlelit dinner at a nice restaurant—whatever strikes your fancy. And when you're alone together, don't talk about the children or what you've been going through these past months. I want you instead to pretend that you're two people on a first date, just learning about each other." She smiled. "I think you're both going to be surprised at what you find. We'll talk about it next week."

Jordan loved Rosewood, her family home. In the spring, the stately Greek Revival mansion and its three-hundred-acre horse farm, set in the rolling hills of Loudon County, Virginia, were especially glorious. The fields were colored bright green, the towering chestnut trees of the allée that led up to the house were in full bloom, the heady scent of lilacs and viburnum sweetened the air. In the nearby pastures, the newborn foals, with their spindly legs, frolicked while their mothers nibbled on the tender grass.

With the birth of her own baby girl, Jordan had missed the foaling season, a magical time at the farm. On the drive to the farm, Kate and Max had been unable to contain their excitement at the prospect of seeing the new crop of Rosewood Farm's babies.

While Olivia napped in the Snugli Jordan had strapped on, Jordan and the kids spent the next morning watching the foals cavorting, racing over the fields on their tiny hooves and long, matchstick legs, bucking and squealing while their dams grazed. Now and then one of the mares would wander over to the fence to have her head and neck scratched, prompting her curious foal to come over, too. Kate and Max literally held their breath in delight to see it poke its nose through the wooden rails and sniff at their tummies.

Tearing the children away from their prime spot by the pasture was no easy feat. Only the reminder that they needed to eat a good lunch if they wanted another riding lesson aboard Jade's old pony, Doc Holliday, could get them to loosen their hold of the stained fence's bottom rail.

At the house, she nursed Olivia, changed her diaper, and then hustled the kids downstairs to help Ellie Banner, the housekeeper, prepare lunch. The kitchen was abuzz with activity when Margot, Travis, and Jade joined them. The children were putting napkins on the long kitchen table, Ellie was settling Olivia into her Kanga-Rocka-Roo baby seat, and Jordan was at the kitchen's granite island, chopping and dicing onions, chestnuts, and celery to make a stuffing for the turkey she was roasting for tonight's dinner.

"Hey, guys," Margot said. "That soup smells delicious. And you smell pretty great, too," she said to Olivia as she kneeled down to kiss her.

"Would you mind watching her, Margot? I just heard the timer go off. I need to go and put the wash in the dryer," Ellie said.

"Of course. Here, let's put Olivia up on the table so we can all enjoy her."

"She is kind of cute when she gets those legs and arms going," Jade said. "I'm starved. Wow, that's a major turkey," she added, eyeing the bird on the kitchen island. "You going to eat all that, Max?"

He shook his blond head. "No, it's for Daddy."

"Daddy loves turkey," Kate pronounced, saving the grown-ups from having to comment on Richard's arrival. "And Mommy's going to bake brownies and peanut butter cookies 'cause everybody likes them."

"We sure do, don't we, Travis?"

"Yeah, pretty much, though I really like Margot's frozen yogurt–granola desserts, too." He grinned at Jade's instant exclamation of disgust.

"Thank you, Travis," Margot said, smiling and giving him a light kiss.

It was great to see Margot and Travis's love for each other. Maybe the day would come when she and Richard would be that close again, too, Jordan thought, turning to wash her hands at the sink. The memory of the warm, teasing light in Richard's eyes when he'd held her hand during their session at Abby Walsh's office filled her with optimism. Maybe she and Richard *had* turned a corner. And while a part of her might never understand how Richard could have cheated, she loved him. Lord knew she was tired of being angry. She was ready to forgive him and put the past ten months behind them.

It was spring, the season of rebirth. Maybe being here in the beautiful house that had been in her family for generations would serve as the spark to rekindle their relationship.

"So where are you planning on going with Richard tomorrow night?" Margot asked as she filled the coffee cups and carried them to the table.

"I was thinking of the Coach House," Jordan replied.

"Mm-hmm, good choice. Travis took me there two weeks ago." She ladled soup into three mugs and then carried them over to the table. After setting down a plate of sandwiches for Jade and Travis, Margot went to the fridge and retrieved her salad.

Finished with chopping the chestnuts and vegetables, Jordan mixed them into a bowlful of bread crumbs, adding a small amount of boiling water and melted butter as she did. Setting the stuffing aside, she lifted the turkey onto the cutting board and patted it dry. "So you're sure you don't mind watching the kids tomorrow night?"

"Of course we don't," Margot answered.

From her workstation at the granite island, she listened to the chatter of her sisters and children. Jade, who was munching on her second ham and cheese sandwich with one hand, rocked Olivia in the Kanga-Rocka-Roo with the other, Olivia kicking and squirming with the contented serenity of a third child. It was wonderful to see them all gathered around the table, especially after the hellish year they'd endured.

This was good. And somehow she just knew the entire weekend would be good, too. With a smile, she looked down at the large turkey before her. Richard would be tired and hungry when he arrived tonight. She really had to get this sucker in the oven or it wouldn't be ready in time.

She pulled the bowl of stuffing closer to the turkey and gave the stuffing one last toss.

Carrying two mugs of coffee to the table, Margot said, "You should think of what you and Richard might like to do in addition to dinner over the weekend. We're completely—" She was interrupted by the ring of the telephone. "Travis, can you answer—"

"It's okay. I've got it." Jordan put down the spoon and crossed over to the other counter, where the telephone sat in the corner. "Hello?"

"Hey, babe, it's me. You weren't picking up on your cell."

"Richard, hi! Sorry, I must have left my phone upstairs when I was changing Olivia. It's Daddy," she said to the kids, then held out the receiver so that he could hear their happy cries of "Hi, Daddy!"

Putting the phone back to her ear, she said, "Kate and Max had a terrific morning. I'm stuffing a turkey for dinner to celebrate our first weekend away since Olivia's birth. When do you think you'll get here?"

"Oh, babe. Thing is, I can't make it to Rosewood for dinner tonight."

"Oh, Richard!" She couldn't hide her disappointment.

"I know, and I'm really sorry. But we're drafting this proposal for a new client—a huge account, babe—and the company just called and said they want to move our meeting forward to Monday, so the you-know-what's really hit the fan. I'm pretty sure if I work late, I can get this proposal in decent shape. I'll set out for Rosewood early tomorrow. That'll still give us time together, and I won't be preoccupied by office work hanging over me. I'll be able to focus on you, Jordan. On us."

She drew a deep breath. She wasn't going to make him feel worse by complaining. She knew how important his work was to him. "I understand. But make sure you get some sleep before you drive."

"I will. Maybe you and I can take a nap once I reach Rose-wood, too."

She felt her cheeks warm. Richard and she used to steal away for "naps" during the beginning of their marriage. Very little sleeping had been involved. "I thought we might go to dinner at the Coach House."

"Great idea. We haven't been there in years. Listen, babe, I gotta get back to this leviathan."

"Oh, sure."

"I'll see you tomorrow, babe. Bright and early, I promise."

Placing the receiver back in its cradle, she turned back to the turkey. Oh well, she thought with a small sigh, Richard liked cold turkey, too. She could always reheat the stuffing. She grabbed a drumstick to hold the turkey steady, scooped up a generous handful of stuffing, and inserted her hand into the turkey's cavity. At her elbow the phone rang again.

Damn it! "Hey, could one of you get that?" she asked, unwilling to pick up the receiver with raw turkey on her hands.

But her request went unheeded as chaos erupted around the kitchen table: Max knocked over his cup of milk; Olivia, deciding the baby seat was hell on earth, started wailing in outrage; and Kate suddenly needed to go pee-pee. The refrain of "Mommy, Mommy!" echoed around the kitchen.

The heck with it, she decided. The kitchen phone had an answering machine.

Hurrying to the sink to wash her hands, she called, "Just coming, sweeties!" but stopped as Richard's amplified voice came over the answering machine's speaker device. Why was he calling again? Had he forgotten to tell her something? "Shh, guys, be quiet for just a sec. It's Daddy. I need to hear what he's saying." She walked over to pick up the phone.

"There, all done. It looks like you and I have another night together, Cyn."

She froze, her hand mere inches away from the receiver. What was going on? Richard wasn't talking to her. Had he pressed the redial button on his phone by mistake?

"So she believed the story about your needing to work late?" The voice was a woman's. *Cyn . . . Cynthia.*

"Yeah. I only wish I could fix it so I could spend the entire weekend with you. I am literally counting the days till I can tell her it's over for good. Until then, I'm just going to have to make Jordan believe I'm shooting for Hudson and White's MVP award."

Richard's laugh, joined by a second, higher one, filled the kitchen. Then came his husky command of, "Come here, Cyn baby. I'm hungry for lunch. Yeah, that's it. Sit yourself right down. Oh God, baby, you have the finest tits." A muffled, suckling sound followed.

A new noise drowned out the ones coming over the answering machine. Jordan couldn't figure out where it was coming from. Everything was so strange all of a sudden, so difficult to process.

She saw the shock stamped on Margot's, Travis's, and Jade's faces, but it only vaguely registered. And she couldn't comprehend why they were suddenly springing into action, why Travis was scooping Max out of his booster chair and racing out of the kitchen with the toddler, or why Margot was bending over the baby seat, fighting with the straps to free Olivia. Cradling the baby, she grabbed hold of Kate's hand and rushed out, shouting something to Jade that Jordan couldn't make out. That awful noise, like an agonized keening, had grown intolerably loud. It ricocheted off the walls.

Then Jade was running over and wrapping her arms about her, holding her tight, which was just as well, as the bones in Jordan's legs seemed to have liquefied. Together they crumpled to the kitchen floor.

The kitchen was empty save for her and Jade. She wanted

to leave, too. The noise was unbearable. The high, rending wail rocked the walls, pummeled her brain.

Make it stop. Jordan rocked, clutching her ears to block out the sound. But it kept coming, on and on and on.

And even after her throat was raw, her vocal chords lacerated, the cry continued mercilessly inside her.